GARRICK JONES

the road
to
pienza

The Road to Montepulciano, Book 2

GRJ
press

 A catalogue record for this work is available from the National Library of Australia

https://www.nla.gov.au/collections

Title: The Road to Pienza

Author: Jones, Garrick (1948–)

ISBNs: 978-1-7643469-0-0 (paperback)
            978-1-7643469-1-7 (ebook – epub)

Subjects: FICTION: LGBTQ+ / Gay;
            Mystery & Detective / Historical;
            Thrillers / Crime.

This story is entirely a work of fiction. No character in this story is taken from real life. Any resemblance to any person or persons living or dead is accidental and unintentional. The author, their agents and publishers cannot be held responsible for any claim otherwise and take no responsibility for any such coincidence.

Cover design: Garrick Jones.
Cover images used under licence from iStock.

Editing by Linda McQueen: https://www.watchwordeditorial.co.uk

Proofreading by Nick Taylor: https://justwriteright.co.uk

GARRICK JONES

the road
to
pienza

The Road to Montepulciano, Book 2

GRJ
press

Contents

AUTHOR'S NOTES

"La Mensola" is a real house. It doesn't exist in the exact spot that I've placed it in the story, an area I know very well, having spent many summers holidaying and working in the region around Montepulciano. It's situated elsewhere in Tuscany and unless things have changed in recent years, it's still abandoned and in need of renovation.

The author wishes to stress that this book is historical fiction. Events, names, places, dates, and the activities of real people may have occasionally been tweaked to advance the narrative. The author also wishes to especially thank Laura Radiconcini, among the many Italian archivists, researchers and friends who helped with the background to this story. I'd need a few pages to list them all individually, but you know who you are and thank you!

This book is dedicated to the memory of my first close friends in Italy,
Peter Locke and Pierluigi Meneghetti,
both still deeply missed.

CHAPTER 1

Saturday 2 July, 1960

"Mr O'Reilly!"

"Over here, Carlo."

I'd found a nice, quiet spot where I could sunbake naked in privacy just near the prow of the ship. Of course, it was out of bounds to all passengers, but I had my ways. A complimentary blowjob—a term I'd picked up from my American pal in Florence, Randy—performed on Carlo, the attendant for the upper deck of first-class cabins, and I'd been shown where to go.

"I'm sorry to disturb you, sir, but I have a wireless transmission for you," he said in his accented English, smoothing back a strand of black hair that had fallen over his forehead. I snorted softly. He'd been staring at my dick.

I took off my sunglasses and sat up, tearing open the brown paper envelope emblazoned with the name of the ship and the passenger line company: MS *Neptunia*, Lloyd Triestino.

*HAVE TO GO TO VENICE TOMORROW. WILL
LEAVE INFORMATION ON YOUR DESK.
ALFONSO WILL PICK YOU UP IN GENOA. CAN YOU
USE SHIP-TO-SHORE.
GIANCARLO*

We'd sailed from Alexandria yesterday, in the evening. I wasn't sure whether I'd be able to place a ship-to-shore call to Italy this far out into the Mediterranean, so I asked Carlo. He told me that we were indeed too far from land but would be nearing the Italian coast in a few days and that would be the first opportunity to place a radio telephone call. So, when he asked if there was a reply to the cable, I asked to borrow his pencil and scribbled a quick message on the back of the telegram.

"Thank you, Carlo," I said, handing back the telegram. "I'm sorry, I can't give you a tip. As you see, I came here wearing just my shorts and with my towel."

He smiled and slowly began to unbutton his crisp white slacks, letting them fall to the tops of his shoes. I smiled, rose to my knees and watched while he pulled down his white French briefs. His cock sprang out.

"This is better than a tip," he said in Italian.

"You could always come to my cabin. My wallet's there …" I replied.

"Oh, Signor O'Reilly, *non mi prendere in giro così …*" he said with a broad grin, the head of his dick a few inches from my mouth.

I chuckled at his cheeky plea not to play games. His left leg was trembling.

"Will you return the favour?" I asked.

"*Ma certo …*"

My chuckle turned into a grin. We both knew his "of course I will" was a false promise. Anyway, I looked up into his eyes and then swallowed his cock down to the root as he let out a long sigh of pleasure.

*****

I was on my way home to Italy after a rather exhausting, over seven-week-long trip to Australia to promote my four books, the most recent of which had only been published a week before I'd flown out of Rome. The tour had been arranged in agreement with my London publisher and Travert Pty Ltd. Simon Travert, the wealthiest man in Australia, not only owned the largest publishing company in the country but also controlled a vast newspaper, magazine and radio empire that reached across the Pacific and Southeast Asia. I'd been engaged to spend five weeks on the road promoting my books, all expenses paid, but with an onerous non-stop itinerary that had started in Darwin and finished in Brisbane.

There was enormous interest in *Living with Monsters*, my third book, which dealt with two deranged serial killers, an investigation I'd become personally involved with, having, in all innocence, befriended both murderers when I'd first come to live in Tuscany. Everywhere I went, there were large audiences, and by the end of the tour, I was very pleased to learn that thousands of copies had been sold. My first book, *Living with Ghosts*, had appealed to ex-servicemen and relatives of those who'd lost their lives in the Pacific War. I'd given readings and talks at every Returned and Services League branch in every town and city along the way. I'd found it immensely draining and emotionally charged, having to relive my own wartime experiences in my mind while listening to stories of other men who'd gone through the same thing I had.

The Road to Montepulciano, the second of my four, was the most popular: the story of my life in Italy, arriving without a word of Italian after having lived in France for eighteen months, then buying a deserted farmhouse sight unseen. It dealt with the renovation of my house and becoming part of the community; however, the book was primarily focused on the daily lives of rural Italians, their food, culture and beliefs. Simon Travert had phoned me in Melbourne to tell me that they'd run out of copies and he'd obtained permission from my London publisher to print a few thousand more.

I couldn't have been more delighted to hear that news. Although I wouldn't see the royalties for half a year, there was still plenty of renovation needed at La Mensola and at our guest house, Il Fornaio, named because of its enormous outdoor bread oven. The new workshop and bathroom extension to my house hadn't quite been finished before I left and it had cost a fortune, even with some of the local men providing labour in exchange for my own carpentry skills. I'd refused to allow Giancarlo to pay for any of it; his donation towards the renovation had been the purchase of a small apartment in Trastevere in Rome in both our names for our visits there.

Finally, my recent fourth book, *Damson's Tuscan Kitchen*—which was full of local recipes accompanied by my own illustrations, along with episodes of daily life and Italian housekeeping tips—had fallen between the cracks. Nothing new to the Italians who lived in Australia but fascinating to Australian housewives, who'd been incredibly interested but had informed me that most of the recipes were impractical. Garlic? Where the hell did you find something like that? Not to mention *melanzane*, which were known neither by their French name, aubergine, nor by the common name in American English, eggplant. And don't get me started on *zucchini, mozzarella* or *peperoni* …

The one bonus of speaking at many Women's Institutes came in another form: the promise by Simon Travert of a feature article in *Housekeeper*, his monthly women's interest magazine, and a television documentary about my life in Italy. A film crew was due to arrive in Rome in August to cover the Olympic Games, after which they'd come to visit me in Tuscany and spend a few weeks following me around.

It was for that reason that Travert's son, Kendall, was sailing with me: to get a taste of the country, look at property investment in Italy and generally soak up the culture. He'd been waiting for me when I flew into Darwin and had acted as the tour manager. We spent every day in each other's company and most evenings.

Giancarlo had joined me in Sydney for the last two weeks of the trip, just as the tour ended. We went up north from Brisbane to spend another fortnight with my brother David, his wife and their four children. I hadn't seen him since 1939 when he left for war. Although we'd written over the years, I wasn't prepared for the change in the only man, other than Giancarlo, whom I loved deeply. Still smiling, strong and handsome as he was, his perpetual inner sadness had been on show, not hidden away for private moments with me as it had been when we'd grown up together. He told me there were still things he'd never even shared with his wife, though he loved her beyond measure. He'd never forgiven our parents for sending us off to the monastery when we were both so young, his pain exacerbated by the refusal of our mother, now living in Tasmania with another family of her own, to have any contact with either of us. He'd wanted his kids to know something about their grandparents and their Irish heritage.

The first night we arrived, David and I had grabbed a double sleeping bag and taken ourselves out into the fields to an empty cane-cutter's shack to spend the night catching up. We'd slept spooned up together, his arms around me, his head next to mine, the way we had done as children on stolen nights in the monastery. Although he was two years older than me, he felt more like a twin.

Of course, everyone had adored Giancarlo, my youngest niece asking naively over dinner one night whether he and I were going to get married. "If we could, we would," Giancarlo had replied, pulling her onto his lap and kissing her cheek noisily.

I wrote out a cheque for a thousand pounds on the day that I left and gave it to David. "Bring your family to Italy for a month or two. There's plenty of space for all of you and I want to share some time with my family in my new home." He broke down and cried. I knew he'd never come. Sharing my patch of earth with my brother and his family was *my* dream, not his.

He flew down to Sydney with Giancarlo and me to wave goodbye at Kingsford Smith Airport to my lover, who was returning to Italy three days before I boarded the *Neptunia* for my voyage home. I had another book in me and I wanted those five weeks at sea in which to gather my thoughts and to start to write. For the following three days, David and I spent every moment of every day together, filling each other in on details of our lives since we'd last seen each other, driven by the inevitable feeling that this might be the last time we'd ever see each other again. I wept miserably with him in my arms in my cabin aboard ship, then sobbed into my hands as I stood at the deck rail and watched his figure get smaller and smaller as the ship steamed away from the dock and sailed out into Sydney Harbour.

★★★★★

By eleven in the morning, the sun was becoming too hot, so I pulled on my shorts and grabbed my towel. The day I'd boarded the *Neptunia*, I'd booked second service in the dining room for both lunch and dinner for the entire voyage, so I intended to have a quick swim in the below-decks pool and see if I could get a massage before heading back to my cabin to write for half an hour before I got dressed for lunch at one.

Today, I'd been invited to the captain's table, so it was suit and tie. The captain only appeared at dinner, so today I'd be in the company of four other passengers and the staff captain, a pleasant dark-haired man with piercing blue eyes, who looked for all the world like the Italian movie heart-throb Marcello Mastroianni.

There was no one in the pool when I arrived and, although indoors, it was pleasant enough. Ever since I'd first boarded, there'd been one or two early morning stalwarts swimming laps, despite its being distinctly smaller than the lido pool on the upper deck. I dived under the water then breast-stroked for a while, until the attendant caught my attention and told me he was ready to give me my massage. He was a tall, energetic lad in his early twenties, muscular and very popular with the girls. His hands went everywhere, and I mean everywhere, when he massaged me, but nothing more than that. I was happy for the attention and he was a very good masseur. He made it very clear that there could be more—for a price—but I simply smiled and patted his arse, thanking him for his strong hands and excellent service. The crew was Italian, and since sailing from Sydney, I'd discovered that there were more than a few who were happy to indulge. The sexual fluidity of the Italian male still surprised me, even after having lived in the country for ten years.

I'd have preferred to travel by one of the British or American liners: P&O, for example, where first-class cabins were really spacious and very well appointed. However, Travert Senior had wanted his son to take advantage of the daily language lessons given on the Lloyd Triestino line to all passengers, many of whom were travelling to Italy to sightsee for a few months before the Olympic Games in Rome. I'd offered to teach Kendall myself, but his father had merely smiled and had said the immersion would be good for his son. As it was, all the crew spoke fluent English, and I'd had to force Kendall to speak even a few words of Italian.

Kendall was a very likeable man, thirty years old—six years my junior—and, despite his affluent upbringing, very down-to-earth and somewhat taciturn. I'd expected someone spoiled and vain before we first met. However, over the course of the weeks I'd spent with him nearly every day, I'd learned that he'd played first-grade rugby before joining the army for a ten-year stint, and that his rugged exterior was a front for a sensitive, rather shy man with an inquisitive, honed intellect and irreverent sense of humour. Physically, he reminded me of Father Justin, my old sports teacher at the monastery. He was more muscled, but had the same blond hair, craggy good looks and somewhat old-fashioned yet charming manners. I had to admit that I was smitten not ten days after first meeting him. He could also swear as robustly as I could in private, another thing that made me feel close to him, as if we had some sort of spoken bond forged by our time in the services.

He'd told me that he was bisexual, had never had, or wanted, a relationship, but was fascinated with men's bodies, especially those fortunate enough, like me, to be well endowed. He said he was basically attracted to older women, but that hadn't stopped him from knocking on my hotel door when he'd had too much to drink—or claimed he had—or barging in while I was in the shower, pulling out his dick and playing with it while he watched me soap up my body. He'd told me early on that he was essentially a voyeur, but then, when fully aroused, he was open to most things.

Of course I'd told him about Giancarlo and me and, in exchange for some of his stories about his infrequent mutual masturbations while in the army, I'd shared some of my own experiences, including parties at my friend Randy's South African pal's place in Florence, where everyone stripped off at the door and wore a black domino mask. He'd wanted to know more details and had become so aroused that it had become the first time that he let himself go and had fucked me.

I never asked, but he'd often share the details of what he did with the two married women passengers he was sleeping with, both of them in their fifties. He wasn't interested in young women at all. I didn't particularly care; I'd slept with married and engaged men aplenty in Italy. He attested that he just wanted to keep the record straight between us.

He was very closed about many personal things but freely admitted that he genuinely liked me and what we did. I knew that he hadn't had many experiences with other men before we'd started fooling around, and when I'd asked him why me, he'd simply replied that he was crazy over my cock. He loved to hold it, to squeeze it, fondle my balls, run his tongue over it and choke on it in an effort to get it all in his mouth. He'd take random opportunities to play with it through my trousers in all sorts of inappropriate situations, sometimes arriving at my cabin early in the morning just to suck on my dick while I was still half asleep then leave me with an ache in my balls, exasperated because when I tried to pull him into bed to finish the job he simply smiled and said he'd see me at breakfast.

Of course, during the course of the book tour, I'd begun to want more than the occasional tumble with him. He knew I was firmly attached to Giancarlo, who I'd explained had not minded when I'd told him that Kendall and I had been having sex. In fact, Giancarlo had lusted after him too, asking me to see if we three could arrange to spend an evening together. To Giancarlo's frustration—and I have to admit mine too—the evening in our suite at the Hotel Australia in Sydney had been supremely enjoyable on one hand, but disappointing on the other. Kendall had stripped off and sat in a chair playing with himself while watching Giancarlo and me fuck, teasing us both by occasionally wandering over to the bed, waving his long, plump cock inches from our mouths and running his hands through our hair and over our bodies, but pulling away if we tried to touch him. It was obvious that he was very aroused, but I enjoyed the teasing; it was extremely erotic. He eventually spurted over us both—I caught a great gob in my mouth—then allowed Giancarlo to suck out the last drops. As he'd so often done with me, he'd grinned, kneeled down and kissed us in turn, said thank you, got dressed and then left without another word, leaving us both laughing into each other's mouths as we began to finish what we'd started while he'd been watching.

There was a note from him under my door when I returned to my cabin after my massage. *Deck tennis after lunch?* I knocked on his cabin door. I heard a muffled, "Come in." He was in the shower.

"Where have you been?" he asked.

"Getting some sun on the foredeck, then I just had a swim and a massage."

"Did he finger you?" Kendall asked.

"Of course—doesn't he do the same to you?"

"Every time," he said with a laugh. "Did you blow?"

"Nope."

"Neither did I. I had one of my ladies in here this morning, but we'd only just got started when she suddenly said she had to leave." He turned around to face me, running his hands through his hair. He was hard.

"So, you were left high and dry … just like me," I said.

"Oh, you had an interrupted encounter too? Do tell."

"Well, it wasn't really uninterrupted, more like unreciprocated. A telegram from home came. Carlo brought it, and, as I didn't have any money on me to tip him …"

"Well, O'Reilly, get your arse in here with me. No use wasting all that juice in our balls; let's see what we can do about it."

Ten minutes later, on my back on his bed, I sighed with pleasure as he slammed me into the mattress, one of his hands behind my neck while his other kneaded my cock.

★★★★★

It was far too close to lunchtime to write a word. I was exhausted and amused … well, pleased with myself rather than amused. I'd turned Kendall on to his belly after he'd finished and had buried my dick deep in him. He'd always avowed that once he'd shot, he was uninterested in more sex. However, just half an hour ago he'd arched his back and pushed back against me, moaning softly into a pillow while I'd fucked him. I wondered what sort of monster I'd awoken.

I stretched out on my bed thinking that in five, or maybe six more days, I'd be rid of this "cosy" first-class cabin. It had a window at one end, underneath which was a bed, which Carlo converted to a settee while I was at breakfast most days, unless I requested it to stay turned down; sometimes, after getting to sleep in the early hours of the morning, I wanted to go back to bed for an hour or two. There was another bed hidden behind the wall panelling that folded down in order to turn the first-class cabin into second-class accommodation for two. In most cases, the return voyage of the Lloyd Triestino ships from Italy to Australia carried migrants, and the whole vessel was second and third class only.

Otherwise, there was a built-in wardrobe, a writing desk, an armchair and a compact bathroom with a shower stall, a washbasin and a toilet. A small folding table was stowed under the bed-settee on which to eat meals if I wanted to dine in my cabin. I also used it for writing and for filling in pencil sketches with watercolours that I'd made of life aboard the *Neptunia* or of things I'd drawn in the various ports of call since we'd left Sydney. I'd sold several of these to other passengers—one of the duties in return for my first-class travel was to give a lecture on each of my books during the course of the voyage. Pity that Simon Travert hadn't thought to send a few crates of books along with me; I could have sold them all. However, I did have business cards for my London publisher. On the back, I scribbled a short note, signing it, promising free postage to any address in Europe for those who wanted a copy of any of my titles. No doubt he'd be annoyed, but I'd sweet-talk him into honouring my promise; one book could easily be the start of the purchase of the rest of my titles … without the free postage, of course.

Giancarlo's telegram had confused me. Despite absolutely loving every minute of his time with me in Australia, he'd been anxious about a case. Since leaving the police force and finally finishing his law degree, he'd been extremely busy. His practice had grown at a phenomenal rate, a lot of it due to the publicity he'd had surrounding the serial killer case on which I'd based my book *Living with Monsters.*

While he kept an office in Florence, he'd also opened another smaller one in Pienza, close to where we spent the majority of our time. I know he'd have preferred me to move to Florence, but I had my business to run and I'd moved to the countryside specifically *not* to live in a town, no matter how beautiful Florence was. A young solicitor, Cosmo, worked in the Pienza office for him, and his secretary in Florence took care of most matters there while he was away.

The case that had preoccupied him had to do with someone who'd been receiving seemingly anonymous death threats from a member of

L'Ordine Nuovo, Giulio Evola's far-right, quasi-fascist party. Giancarlo's client had publicly denounced the man in a long letter to the press, accusing him of being the writer of the death threats. In turn, that man was suing Giancarlo's client. The police had refused to become involved, saying death threats were two-a-penny in post-war Italy, and wouldn't investigate whether there was any truth in Giancarlo's client's fear for his life, even dismissing suggestions that they should at least interview the man accused of writing the threatening letters.

"It all came about because my client spoke the truth in his letter to the newspaper," Giancarlo had told me. "He exposed the man as having been responsible for the murder, a few days after the Allies first arrived in Rome, of four nuns, members of a religious order who ran an orphanage and who'd been helping Allied soldiers."

I knew that the detective still lingered on in the man I loved. He couldn't help himself. He'd started to investigate and to put a case together, much of which would have been better left to the local cops, except that, as in many other parts of Italy, they were directed by a local chief of police who seemed uninterested in anything that wouldn't give him personal brownie points. Harsh, but true. These days, war-guilt and retribution had become sadly unfashionable. Older people wanted to forget, and those born during the war had no distinct memory of it, or taste for payback. I heard so many maxims about forgetting the past and starting over again that I had to force myself not to growl and raise my hackles.

So, Venice, he'd said in his telegram? I had no idea why he'd had to go there so urgently. However, I was used to him being as obsessed with his own projects as I was with mine. His mother, although married to a man from Umbria, had come from the same small town as Giancarlo's father's ancestors: Dolo, halfway between Venice and Padua. His mother had left him an apartment in Venice when she died. Giancarlo shared ownership of it with his sister, Carla, who disliked it almost as much as he did. However, it came in handy; we often gave the key to visitors from abroad to stay in very grand surroundings overlooking the Grand Canal and the Ponte dell'Accademia. We visited there infrequently ourselves: I loved the city, but Giancarlo was indifferent to it, finding it smelly—true—and the dialect bringing back bad memories of his frequent childhood visits from Aden. Plus, the apartment with its frescoed walls and immensely high vaulted ceilings was uncomfortable: airless in the summer, and impossible to heat in the winter. Once, I'd travelled to meet him there for a cousin's wedding and had found a note on the bed saying he'd decided to stay at the Cipriani, which had just then opened.

★★★★★

I'd hoped I'd be able to place a call from the ship as we sailed through the Straits of Messina, but the line was so unstable that every time a connection was made, it almost immediately fell out. However, as we sailed up the coast, it was announced that there'd been a medical emergency and that a passenger had to be unloaded at Naples. It was going to make us a day late arriving in Genoa and the ship wouldn't dock until very late tomorrow afternoon or early evening, instead of first thing in the morning. Giancarlo didn't answer the phone in Venice, so I called Cosmo, his assistant in Pienza, who told me that Giancarlo had now gone to Trieste, and promised me that as soon as his boss contacted him, he'd let him know that I'd called.

I next placed a call through to the residence of the Church of the Sacred Heart in Siena.

"*Mi dispiace, Signor O'Reilly. Credevo che Padre Ignazio alloggiasse a casa sua,*" the housekeeper told me.

Alfonso was living at La Mensola? I put a call through and he answered almost immediately.

"You're staying with us?" I said. "What's going on?"

"Damson? I thought you were arriving tomorrow. I'll leave around midnight and should arrive in Genoa in the morning."

"The ship's been delayed in Naples. I'll book a hotel for the night in Genoa and catch the train in the morning. Can you pick me up in Chiusi? I'll telephone to let you know what time I'm due to arrive."

"Of course. Are you sure you don't want me to come to Genoa anyway?"

"No, I appreciate the offer, but it's a seven-hour trip each way and you'd be too tired to drive back home straight away. But why are you living at La Mensola?"

"It's a long story. I'll tell you when I pick you up. Giancarlo said you wouldn't mind. He invited me."

"Have you done something wrong? I hope you haven't been booted out of the priesthood."

"Nothing like that," he said with a chuckle. "I'll see you the day after tomorrow."

*****

As it was, the *Neptunia* docked just a few hours late the following day, at seven in the evening; we were told that it was something to do with the availability of the pilot.

It threw Kendall's travel plans into disorder too. He'd booked to travel to Paris by train the day we docked and, because of the delay, he couldn't get another seat until the following morning at ten o'clock. So, I told him he could share the room I'd asked the ship's purser to book for me at the Grand Hotel Savoia.

"Well, blow me down," he said, gazing around the room as soon as the bellboy had closed the door behind us. "This isn't what I was expecting."

The hotel didn't have rooms as such, but suites. Even the most inexpensive accommodation had a sitting room, bedroom and bathroom, all of blue-ribbon standard.

"There's only one bed, Damson," he said with a wink, standing in the doorway between the two large, beautifully appointed rooms.

"Then I trust you'll keep your hands to yourself during the night," I replied with a soft smile.

He chortled a little under his breath, then stared at me for a while before lighting a cigarette.

"Have I got something on my face?"

"No. Just looking, that's all. I'll reimburse you for half the cost of the room. It's not fair that you should—"

"Don't bother. Your father's paying for it. I still have quite a lot left in the expense account he gave me. I'll add this to my expenditure and refund the rest to him."

"As you said yourself, don't bother. Use it to entertain me when I come to visit."

"Oh, you're coming to visit, are you?" I teased.

"You invited me."

"When were you thinking of coming?"

"I need a week in Paris with the local publishers, then a few days in Munich and a stopover in Milan. Perhaps after that … if I'm not in the way."

I started to quickly sort out rooms in my mind. I was sure Alfonso would be staying in the guest bedroom between Giancarlo's and my study. That left the large room that shared a common wall with my bedroom; it was the room in which a Nazi officer had been hanged, before being buried in my back garden. Kendall could sleep there.

"Of course you won't be in the way; you can stay here as long as you like."

He walked to the French doors and stood looking out over the city with his hands in his pockets.

"I've only ever been fucked three times in my life, Damson," he said in a rather matter-of-fact way and quite out of the blue, still facing away from me.

"I don't understand …?"

"I'm sure you've figured it out. All three times were you." I was about to say something when he turned abruptly. "I'm starving. Are we going to get changed and go downstairs to have something to eat?"

"Tuxedos, I'm afraid."

"I'd expect nothing less," he said, sitting on the edge of the bed while unlacing his shoes.

★★★★★

After dinner, while Kendall was in the bathroom, I tried to call Giancarlo again, this time using the number in Trieste that Cosmo had given me. No answer there either. I checked my watch—ten o'clock. He'd probably still be out. People went to bed very late in Italy; the afternoon siesta had a lot to answer for in that regard.

By the time I finished my turn in the bathroom, Kendall was naked, sitting up on top of the bed covers, so I perched on the edge of the mattress next to his knee and lit a cigarette.

"Come closer," he said. By now, I recognised that look in his eye.

He ran his hand over my thigh and cupped my balls. I leaned back and moved my knees apart while he gently massaged my chest and stomach, his hand finally coming to rest, encircling the base of my by-now hard cock. "I like this," he said, jiggling it a little.

"What about the rest of me?"

"Oh, yeah, that's all right, too." His accompanying cheeky wink made me grin.

"What you said earlier … I'm the only man who's ever fucked you?"

"Yep."

"Why me?"

"As I said, I like this." He squeezed harder, milking my erection, then leaned over and licked the shiny drop of fluid from the eye of my cock with the tip of his tongue. "I've always liked looking at big ones, but yours is the first I've ever wanted inside me."

"Kendall—"

He laughed, interrupting what I was going to say. "I'm not out to make trouble with you and Giancarlo. I really like him too. What we did in the hotel room in Sydney … I want more of that, and not just watching either."

"Where on earth does this come from? You've always seemed rather standoffish to me, especially when it comes to talking about sex."

"I dunno, Damson. Something just clicked between us that first night in Adelaide when I pretended to be drunk and asked you to suck me off."

"You returned the favour, as I remember."

"That's right, and yours was the first cock I ever had in my mouth, and the first time I'd ever swallowed or even tasted spunk."

"I'm confused."

"I'm aware that I always skirt around my history—my sexual history, that is. You know that I've always been into sex with older women. Not sure why—I don't remember my own mother, I was far too small when she died, so it can't be that. Fooled around a bit in my teens with lads my own age; that happens at an all-boys' boarding school. But then, when I joined up, I became fixated on what men had between their legs, especially the big ones, like yours. There was someone for a while, but all we did was swap tongues while we pulled each other off."

"You've never seemed to want to swap tongues with me," I said, by this time my legs wide apart and my erection almost purple because he'd been squeezing the base so tightly.

"Can we just be friends, Damson? I don't want anything more than you as a close mate in my life. Of course, I still want to do this with you—and Giancarlo if that's on the cards—but I'm not looking for a love affair. Is that all right with you?"

I closed my eyes for a moment. "That depends."

"Depends on what?"

I wrapped one hand around the back of his neck and pulled him towards me. I guessed the kissing part of what he'd done with his army mate was something he really liked, because before I knew it, I was almost choking on his tongue after he'd nearly sucked mine out of my head. I pushed him onto his back on the bed. The kissing became more languid, sensuous, exploring. He guided my hand down to his balls, then raised his hips. I massaged the rim of his arsehole with my fingers.

"Aw, fuck," he moaned into my mouth.

Damned if he wasn't one of the best kissers I'd ever met. He didn't even flinch a little bit as I eased my saliva-wetted dick into his body.

CHAPTER 2

I rang for breakfast to be sent up the next morning. Kendall was in the shower when it arrived, so after the young waiter had set the table, I told him that he didn't need to stay to serve the food. I tipped him; he thanked me and left just as Kendall appeared, towelling his hair dry.

The hotel was used to British guests so we were able to order a full English breakfast. Although I'd had one nearly every day while on my book tour in Australia, I still had flashbacks to the awful mess that was dumped on our plates in army canteens while I was serving in occupied Japan. Back then, powdered eggs had been used to make a loose omelette that had accompanied the bacon, sausages and fried tomato. Kendall polished his off and then, while I was still trying to eat, sat on my lap facing me.

"Care for more sausage, Damson?" he asked. Corny, I know, but in my heart of hearts, this man turned me on more than anyone I'd ever met, and that was saying something. Lust had nothing to do with what I felt for Giancarlo, even in our early days together when my attraction to him had been to do with the heart rather than my dick.

"How about I grease up your arse with bacon fat from my plate and fuck you on the table?"

He roared with laughter. I was only half joking.

We said farewell not long after I'd showered and got dressed. My train left at seven minutes to nine, due to arrive at Chiusi at three o'clock with two changes: the first with a thirty-minute stop in Pisa, the second with forty minutes in Florence. I'd rung Randy to see if he could arrange to meet me at the station and have a quick coffee while I waited for my connecting train, but he'd already left home. Arnie, his pal, answered the phone and said he'd love to see me instead.

Arnie had aged equally as well as Randy. They were both the same age, their joint fifty-second birthdays booked into our calendar for a belated celebration this coming Saturday. They'd had a party on the sixth of June for their other friends and family, which their wives had come up from Rome to attend. It had taken place while Giancarlo and I were both still in Australia.

Of course, with them being our closest friends, Giancarlo had told them both about Kendall, so Arnie teased me relentlessly, accusing me—and quite truthfully—of breaking my pattern. They both knew I was attracted to older men and yet here I was, infatuated with a thirty-year-old.

"Photos?" Arnie asked.

I rummaged through my travel bag and found a wallet of prints I'd had developed in Sydney the day before we'd sailed for Italy.

"*Non vedo l'ora di vederlo!* The man's a demigod," he said.

"You can't wait to meet him? How do you know he's coming here?"

"Giancarlo told us that he was planning to buy real estate in Italy. Why wouldn't he come to visit you?"

The train, surprisingly, not only left Florence on time but also pulled into Chiusi station not a minute later than scheduled. I remembered my early days in Italy of catching the same service to and from Florence every month when I picked up my war pension and royalty cheques at the Thomas Cook office. The train was rarely on time and used to stop frequently in the middle of the countryside for ages for no apparent reason. It was often the way I practised my Italian when I was first learning: chatting to the other passengers while wondering whether our carriages had been unhooked and the engine had taken off without us.

"Alfonso!" I called out. He was talking with the platform attendant and had his back to me.

"*Salve!*" he said, breaking away from the man and running into my arms. I hugged him, lifting him off the ground, slapping his back.

"I missed you," I said.

"And I missed you too, Damson, very much. Now, luggage?"

"Just my travel suitcase and one larger. I have a trunk and a crate, but they're being delivered by the shipping company."

We wandered down to the luggage van to find my suitcase already on the platform waiting for me to collect it, me asking him how everyone was, what was happening in Pienza, all the while trying to field questions from my friend about Australia and my journey aboard the *Neptunia*. He'd driven the Land Rover, saying that he'd washed the Maserati this morning in honour of my return. Giancarlo was famous for never cleaning cars; I'd often find the Jeep, the Land Rover and the sports car all caked with mud. However, there was no end of youngsters happy to wash all three cars in exchange for a donation to the local football team, even though I had to drive a relay to the sports field back and forth between each wash.

We'd been chatting about everything but the reason why he seemed to have moved into La Mensola, so, just as we were approaching Sant'Albino, in a rare pause when I could get a word in edgewise, I asked him.

He shook his head, then reached over and took my hand. "Can we talk about it when we get home, please? This is going to be harder to tell you than it was Giancarlo."

"You know I'm your friend and I won't judge, no matter what it is."

"Home, please. You must be excited to see the new extension now that the builders have finished."

"They've finished?"

"Yes, last week. It's wonderful. The Mori brothers have done an excellent job."

"Have you christened the new bathroom?"

"Yes. Giancarlo and I have both tried out the shower, and the new septic tank toilet is a miracle."

Back in early March, I'd helped Marco and Ennio Mori lay out the foundations to the extension I'd planned for the northern elevation of La Mensola. Sick and tired of driving into town to use the municipal baths to shower or soak in a tub—either that or visiting our guesthouse to use one of the two bathrooms there—I'd put aside enough to build a large new workshop at the northern end of the terrace outside the kitchen, and next to it a bathroom, accessed from the old workshop, and a guest room with its own terrace and small private garden. I intended to turn the room next to the kitchen, which had served as my workshop for ten years, into a breakfast room.

Now that we'd had electricity connected, a series of electric pumps had been planned in order to feed hot water to the kitchen and the new bathroom. Waste bath and shower water was to be collected in a large holding tank and used for the vegetable garden and the orchard. I was surprised that, according to Alfonso, not only had the construction of the extension been finished but also the infrastructure. Hot water on tap! I couldn't quite believe it.

As soon as we arrived, I jumped out of the Land Rover and opened the gate, walking down the driveway as I followed Alfonso down to the house. He parked the car next to the Jeep and my Maserati in the open-sided, roofed garage Giancarlo and I had built several years ago opposite the kitchen entrance to La Mensola.

"I'll take your bags upstairs while you have a look at the new extension," he said while we were standing in the kitchen.

I rekindled the stove and put on the moka pot—I needed coffee—then wandered through my former workshop, now empty, to see what had been done. The lads had followed the floor plan I'd left them and had done a wonderful job. Everything was in its place in the new workshop, which had large doors that opened onto the paved courtyard under the grape trellis. The new bathroom was wonderful: crisp white ceramic tiles with a dark green border at hip height around the room. A door opened off it into a short corridor, at the end of which was the toilet.

Another door led into the guest wing, which also had access to the main part of the house via the downstairs front room, the room in which one of the murder victims had been beaten up before being dragged into my sitting room and shot in the back of the head. Over the years, it had served as a "nothing" room. But now, with the new guest bedroom next door, I intended it to be a living area for anyone staying in the new extension. Carla, Giancarlo's sister, and her lover-slash-assistant, Roberto, often spent more than a few days with us.

I strolled into the bathroom, turned on the shower to test the hot water, then stripped off and got under the water, turning my face into the fine spray from the shower head.

"Coffee's ready," Alfonso said, standing in the doorway holding two cups.

"Give it here," I said, then gulped my shot quickly. "Get in with me," I added.

Over the decade that we'd been close friends, we'd showered together frequently at the municipal bath house near the deserted beach we often went to. Occasionally Giancarlo would come with us, but he considered it our boys' day out, and, as he didn't particularly like swimming in the ocean, his trips with us were infrequent and usually only when he had business in Grosseto.

I'd designed the shower stall to be large enough for two, with a tiled concrete bench at one side on which I could sit and scrub my toes, or to use while talking to Giancarlo while he showered.

"You're looking more muscled," I replied. "What have you been up to while I've been away?"

"More boxing, some training at the gymnasium in San Quirico d'Orcia …"

"Why there and not at the gym in Pienza?"

"It has to do with the reason I'm staying here."

"All right," I said, nudging him out of the way to get under the water for a moment. "I'm the least judgemental person in the world. It's best to tell me straight out. You said that Giancarlo already knows why?"

He nodded, then put his arms around me, leaning his head on my shoulder. Right at the start, when we'd first met, I'd found it very erotic, as I had the first day we'd been to the beach and had showered together. However, I shared something far more intimate with him these days, something that had nothing to do with sex. Besides, he was a celibate priest, and what I felt for him was more akin to love.

He sighed heavily then kissed my shoulder before moving away a little to look me in the eyes. "I've taken an *exclaustratio*, Damson."

"I don't know what that means."

"An exclaustration is a form of leave from the priesthood."

"Why on earth would you do that?"

"I've been struggling, Damson, more heavily over the past two years than at any time during my calling. The bishop suggested it."

"Go on …"

"An *exclaustratio* is an official release for any man who's taken a religious vow to have time away from priestly duties, to live for a limited time outside his institute while considering his future within the church."

"I'm stunned," I said.

"I haven't been entirely honest with the Church or with you, and it shames me to admit it."

"Unless you've killed someone, or stolen from the Church or … oh …"

"Yes, sins of the flesh, I'm afraid."

"You haven't …?"

He looked at me from under his lashes. I saw the truth in that glance. "For a year now."

"Why the hell didn't you tell me?"

"Because I love you; you and Giancarlo both. I didn't want to disappoint you or have to live with any feeling that you might disapprove."

"Disapprove? Us? For heaven's sake, Alfonso, you've known us for ten years. You lived through the period that Danny lived with us; I even told you what we got up to. You know every detail of our relationship and who we sleep with. We've never hidden the fact that, although we love each other, occasionally we sleep around, and I do remember one particular evening when we all got so drunk that you pretended to have passed out, and watched between your eyelashes while Giancarlo and I sucked each other off. We would never judge anyone for what you call 'sins of the flesh'."

"It wasn't just fear of your disapproval, Damson, although that was a major factor in not telling you what I've been up to. Guilt was the most pressing issue. I can't tell you the weight on my soul every time I …"

"With many people, or just one?"

"Just one."

I turned off the shower. "Let's have a smoke and another coffee and you can tell me all about it. And I mean everything, even the bits you haven't told your confessor."

"I've not told him anything, Damson, and that's the reason I've asked for an *exclaustratio*. Only God knows what I've done."

I pulled a towel off the rack and handed one to him, while drying myself with another. "I used to tell Renzo that God is not nearly as judgemental as the Church would like us to believe. Don't bother getting dressed," I said. "Join me in the kitchen. I'll put the pot back on the stove and you can tell me the naked truth."

"I can tell you meant that to be amusing. Perhaps it's a play on words in English that doesn't translate into Italian."

Indeed, the play on words didn't translate, even when I explained it. You'd think I'd have learned after all these years.

*****

Compared to my own life, what Alfonso had done was something that ordinarily would have been of no consequence. The majority of men spread their wings before settling down; it was just that Alfonso had not had the opportunity. I knew that he'd played around with other lads when he was a teenager but had stopped once he'd entered the seminary. Once ordained, he'd been tormented by thoughts, confessing to me over the years that when he could bear it no longer he would put a sock in his mouth and masturbate the ache away, then go to confession.

However, while visiting his family in Rome twelve months ago, his motor scooter—I'd loaned him the money to buy it at auction when the local dealership had gone into liquidation—had broken down on the way to catch the train. A recently arrived immigrant driving a three-wheeled Piaggio VespaCar—also known as an *Ape*, which means bee in Italian—had stopped to help him, loaded the scooter onto the tray and driven him to Chiusi in time for his train. The man was a few years older than us, recently arrived from Toulon and spoke very little Italian. His name was Gaspard and, like me, had taken advantage of the Italian agrarian land reform—which still continued ten years after I'd bought La Mensola—to invest in real estate. He'd purchased a ruined farmhouse with, like my purchase, five hectares and a condition in the contract that he had to put two under cultivation.

Once Alfonso had arrived in Rome, he'd phoned me with the story of his motor scooter and told me at which garage he'd left it, so I'd driven to Chiusi later that day to pick it up and had fixed it while he was away. He'd left out the part about Gaspard. Of course, he'd found out where the Frenchman lived and, after returning from Rome, had visited to thank him for helping out.

There'd been an obvious attraction, and Alfonso told me that before he knew it, they were kissing … and the rest. After some cajoling, I got the full story, my friend's admission that, because Gaspard didn't really know who he was or what he did, Alfonso's penis, as so many other men's did, had taken over and before he knew it, they were in bed.

He'd resisted for a month, trying not to think about what had happened, but then had returned, more and more gripped by the ache in his loins and the promise of what his friend had to offer.

"Why are you smiling at me, Damson?"

"Because what you've told me only makes me care about you even more than I already do. Putting the religious conflict aside for the moment and according to Damson's Law of Human Behaviour, you've just acted like any other normal man. Besides, it's the sin that's in your heart that counts—"

"But I've broken a vow."

"And you're neither the first, nor will you be the last," I said, sipping what was now my third cup of coffee.

"You and Renzo, when you first got together, I know how hard it was for you to communicate."

"Yes, you were our intermediary for such a long time … how much Italian does your friend speak?"

"I think he finds the language very difficult. He can say simple things; he often talks to me at length in French and I've no idea what he's saying."

"Well, if you ever need an interpreter, I'd be only too happy to be the go-between," I said. "I owe you that at least."

"Damson, I'm feeling very embarrassed … I feel I've let you down."

"Let me down? You could never do that. You've merely demonstrated that you're human. And, if you want to keep your Frenchman private and if there's something you want to ask him, I'd be only too happy to write it down for you."

"I—"

We were interrupted by the phone ringing. I'd had two handsets installed, one upstairs in my study, the other in the former workshop, which was now to become our breakfast room. The phone seldom rang at home, so I excused myself and went to answer it. It was a familiar voice.

"Giancarlo! Finally! Where have you been?"

"Hello, sweetheart, I've missed you," he said.

Alfonso knew who was on the phone, so he lit a cigarette and wandered out onto the terrace, standing naked under the grapevine.

★★★★★

It was getting on for seven o'clock by the time I returned home that evening. After speaking with Giancarlo, I'd walked across the field to Il Fornaio to say hello to Stefano, his wife and their children, checking to see whether there'd been any problems while I'd been away and promising to spend the following morning with them to go through bookings for the rest of the summer.

During the season, we'd decided to have guests for only once a month for ten days each time, mainly because it had become a chore and exhausting for all concerned to look after a dozen enthusiastic visitors every fortnight, as we'd done for the past six years, and Stefano not only had his growing family to care for, but was also helping me with the running of the combined acreage of both properties under cultivation. When Giancarlo and I had accepted the offer to sell from the former owner of the land that adjoined mine, we'd inherited a large olive grove and a hectare and a half that had been put under potatoes and cabbages. That field abutted my two acres of sunflowers, so we'd amalgamated them, getting rid of the potatoes and cabbages—which were very labour-intensive—and growing rapeseed on one hectare and durum wheat on the rest. It gave us a lot to do.

Giancarlo and I had discussed it at the end of last year and had decided that, between the farm income and my book royalties, the combined businesses were enough to keep me more than financially solvent, to pay Stefano a decent wage and to put money aside. As Stefano had grown up in the area, he knew everyone, so we employed locals at harvest time, something that made them very happy; no one begrudged a few weeks of hard work for the above-average hourly rate that we paid for labour.

I'd only spent less than an hour at Il Fornaio because it was dinner-time for Stefano's children; I'd forgotten how early they fed their kids. Afterwards, needing some time alone, somewhere quiet to think about what both Alfonso and Giancarlo had told me, I skirted the sunflower field and sat on the edge of the rock that overhung our private pool.

I was very concerned for Alfonso. He'd gradually unburdened himself of the secrets he'd kept to himself, those he'd never confessed and for which he'd not received absolution—another torment that had almost crippled him with guilt for most of his adult life. Years of voyeurism, visiting many of the spas that abounded in Tuscany, taking advantage of changing rooms and men's areas in the health spas to glance at naked bodies, and then taking those fantasies home and masturbating over them. Once or twice, men had made passes, and he'd briefly fondled them back, but had always shaken his head and extricated himself from the situation.

Guilt was a heavy burden for most Catholics, magnified a hundred-fold for members of religious orders. As part of the terms of his *exclaustratio*, he was forbidden to officiate at mass or partake in any official capacity. He could also not hear confession or bless anyone. But the thing that wounded him the most? He was no longer able to be called Father Ignazio. He'd been using my Jeep to drive to distant towns to attend mass, but, because of the huge burden of unconfessed transgressions, hadn't been taking the sacrament. I knew that was immensely painful for him and I'd sat with him on the sofa, my arms around him while he sobbed his heart out, saying that he felt that he'd been cut off from God.

His pain was my pain; it was something that true friends felt for each other. I'd been loath to leave him when I went to visit Stefano, but he'd insisted that he was all right, saying that unburdening himself on me was as close to confession that he could get and that he loved me for it.

Sitting by the pool, watching the swallows dart over its surface and listening to the tiny song birds chattering in the trees surrounding it, made me smile, thanking God that life was not quite as complicated for me as it was for some others.

Alfonso's problems aside for the moment, the content of Giancarlo's phone call had left me feeling unsettled. After ten years together, I knew him like the back of my hand. Lovable, forty-one years old, sexy, intelligent, but living with a self-belief of invincibility, the man who I counted the most cautious and wise when handing out advice to others was, on the other hand, the most infuriating. When it came to himself and his own problems, he couldn't always accept good advice, no matter how judiciously and carefully it was handed to him, or by whom. We rarely argued, except on those occasions. Invariably, now almost fully Italianised in behaviour, I'd throw up my hands in the air and walk out of the room in frustration, something that always made him laugh, relent, search me out and fold me in his arms.

In his very soul, despite being one of the best lawyers in Florence, he was still a detective at heart. More than once, I'd expected him to tell me he was giving up law and going back to the police force.

He'd apologised profusely for not picking me up at the wharf in Genoa, in only the way Italians could do, pleading for forgiveness and promising it wouldn't happen again, just as if this were the first time that something like this had happened. For one of the most contained, quiet men, who loved nothing more than to spend time curled up with me while reading a book, he could be incredibly passionate about some things; his current case was one of them.

We had talked for about ten minutes—me mindful that Alfonso was pacing on the terrace, chain-smoking, continually running his hands through his hair and in a very emotional and fragile state. I told Giancarlo that I'd been brought up to date and assured him that I didn't mind Alfonso staying with us for as long as he needed to sort things out.

As for my lover, the moment I knew that this case had taken over his life was when he said that I should come up to Venice for the weekend and asked whether I could call in at his/our flat in Florence and search out a few legal reference books from his library and bring them with me.

"Have you forgotten Randy and Arnie's birthday party on Saturday?" I'd said.

"Oh, dear God. Yes, I had … completely. Do you think that they would—"

"You cancel on them and you can pick up your own books, Giancarlo."

I rarely used his name when speaking to him directly, and only when I was cross with him; he'd backed down very quickly and said he'd meet me in Florence on Friday night.

★★★★★

Alfonso was cooking something when I eventually extricated myself from the tranquillity of the pool and wandered back home; it smelled delicious. Although it was me who'd written and illustrated a cookbook, I wasn't really a cook. I could follow recipes and throw things together, meals that often turned out far better than I'd expected. However, some people had a natural instinct for it. He was one of those.

Surprisingly, between them both, Alfonso and Giancarlo had kept my sourdough starter alive while I'd been away. I didn't know when he'd done it, but he'd made a focaccia base and had left it to rise in the refrigerator. Once it was smothered with my home-made passata and strewn with prosciutto, marinated artichoke hearts and black olives, he asked me to put it in the bread oven, which he'd lit as soon as I'd left to visit Stefano. Smaller than the stone monster at Il Fornaio, the bread/pizza oven was another addition to the outside terrace. I didn't always use it to bake bread, but often enough that it was worth the trouble it had been to build it. With a tossed green salad and a bottle of Chianti, the focaccia was to be our dinner.

He didn't ask why I'd been away so long, nor had he asked about my telephone call from Giancarlo earlier in the afternoon. The meal was absolutely delicious, made more so because my time away in Australia had given me fresh eyes to notice things in my house that I'd taken for granted over the past ten years.

"How are you feeling?" I asked him, dinner finished, reaching over the table and taking his hand.

"Worse than before," he replied.

"How so?"

"Pouring out my heart to you was harder than I thought, and it's brought everything bubbling up to the surface that I've spent so many years fighting to keep under control."

"How can I help? Is there anything I can do?"

He shook his head and smiled at me. "No, not really. Just being with you is balm in itself."

"Do you want me to drive you to your Frenchman so you can stay overnight with him?"

He laughed. He'd caught the glint in my eye and knew I was jesting. "Sex isn't a universal panacea for everything that ails a man, Damson."

"I know that, but sometimes it helps to lie on your belly and let a handsome man fuck the miseries out of you for an hour or two."

He roared with laughter. "Does that work for you?" he said, wiping the tears from his eyes.

"Sometimes. But a cuddle from a good pal is far better medicine; at least, that's what I've found."

We cleaned up in silence, Alfonso washing the dishes while I cleared the table. I put the leftover focaccia in the fridge to be crisped up in the oven tomorrow for a mid-morning snack and the remaining salad would go to the hens or the geese, whichever got there first when I opened their pens at first light.

"I've been thinking," I said.

"About?"

"About you. We have a guest coming to stay for an as-yet-unknown period of time and—"

"I'm only here temporarily, Damson. I can find somewhere else to stay while your friend is here."

"No, no. You should be here, with friends, and you'll find him wonderful company. What I was going to say is that you should move into the new guest area. The bathroom's right next door, and you can use the attached sitting room next door whenever you'd prefer to be alone."

"No, I can't do that. Why not put your guest up in the new extension? I'm happy with the room upstairs. It's small, I know, but I'm not used to—"

"I'm trying to spare you."

"Spare me from what?" he asked.

"Noises."

"What sort of noises? Oh …"

"The friend who'll be staying will probably be sleeping with either Giancarlo or me, or both of us together. And, as I've learned over the years, the upstairs isn't nearly as soundproof as I'd originally thought. I just don't want you to be confronted with sounds you'd rather avoid while you're struggling with your sexuality."

"That's very thoughtful of you, but you misunderstood me. I'm not struggling with my sexuality. I've known what I wanted ever since I can remember. What I'm struggling with is my guilt and shame at not being able to control my desires."

I put my arms around him. "You know, I think the English church has got it right. Priests can marry. I don't think it's for everyone to sublimate their basic desires in service to God. You probably know the scriptures far better than me. Timothy goes on endlessly about the possibility of the clergy having wives."

"Yes, but there are other admonitions, from Paul, for example. Besides, they were thinking about normal men, not—"

I put a finger to his mouth, stopping his words. "Please, never use the word 'normal' to describe heterosexuals, Alfonso. That's merely demeaning the love and the passion between two members of the same sex and making it sound somehow abnormal. I see myself as no less blessed than Stefano, or Signor Marino, or any other married man. You, my friend, need to learn to love yourself first; once you do, I think your problems will fall into perspective."

I removed my finger.

"But I—"

I stopped him by kissing him gently on the lips. "Enough for tonight. We're not going to solve everything the first night I'm home. We have all the time in the world to talk. Just know that we love you, and that we'll support you through this crisis in your faith, no matter the outcome."

★★★★★

Before going to bed, I leafed through the documents on Giancarlo's desk. It was mostly research into the Ordine Nuovo and the man behind it, Giulio Evola, a right-wing, fascist philosopher who, according to Giancarlo's margin annotations, described himself as *an aristocratic, monarchist, masculine, traditionalist, heroic and defiant reactionary*. A heady combination at this time in Italy's history.

There was a small book and several pages of Giancarlo's notes, which I took to bed with me to read. If this case had him so caught up, I felt it was my duty to know what I was going to be dealing with over the coming weeks or months.

Surprisingly, while reading, I discovered that Evola was an atheist; something that didn't seem to fit with being a traditionalist and monarchist. He had strong views on the metaphysics of sex and war—I made a note in the pad I kept next to the bed to read his published article on the subject; it interested me—and there were rumours that he'd worked for the Sicherheitsdienst, the Nazi intelligence service, during the war. In Vienna in 1945, a piece of shrapnel had paralysed him from the waist down.

What a powder-keg of a man, I thought, while I began to leaf through the book about L'Ordine Nuovo, which meant "The New Order". The more I read, the more disturbed I became. Should Giancarlo be getting caught up in an organisation whose leader was not only strongly misogynistic but also a vehement antisemite? A man who I judged by reading between the lines seemed to be a supreme iconoclast? He sounded vile; I couldn't help wonder about the sorts of followers someone like him would attract.

The New Order had originally been the name of a radical left-wing newspaper before the war, but it had been hijacked by the extremist right-wing faction during the fascist regime. It was founded by Pino Rauti, who'd stated that the movement had no political aims—I found that extremely unlikely, if not a downright lie—and purposed itself to espouse parts of Evola's philosophies: a denouncement of modern, materialistic ways from a rather pompous-sounding aristocratic vantage. Elitism was alive and well in a society that had voted, in a referendum after the war, to abolish the monarchy.

It was at the bottom of the last page of notes that I found the name of the man who was suing Giancarlo's client: Giovanni Scavola. Written in Giancarlo's hand was an address, a telephone number and a few personal details: the man's date of birth, *vedovo*—widower, written in caps and underlined—then, in Arabic script, a word which I read to be *khara*, meaning a turd, something unpleasant.

Over the time we'd been together, he'd taught me Arabic and I'd taught him French and a little Latin. I could have an everyday conversation in Arabic and could, with a bit of a struggle, read newspaper articles. For him to write something in Arabic really stood out. For him not to write it in Italian or English was a danger signal. I hoped he knew what he was getting himself into.

"What are you reading?"

I looked up. Alfonso was standing in the doorway, looking miserable. I threw back the covers. "Get in," I said.

"Are you sure?"

"Shut up and get into bed, but take off those ridiculous pyjamas. Who wears pyjamas these days anyway, unless they're in hospital?"

He smiled and peeled them off, then sat on the edge of the bed, took my packet of cigarettes and lit two, handing me one.

I ran a hand over his shoulder, so he fell back onto the bed, the back of his head against my chest.

"You promised me a cuddle," he said. *Mi avevi promesso una coccola.* It sounded so sweet in Italian, cute even, as if it were something a kid would say to their parents.

"When you've finished your smoke, you can have a cuddle all night long."

He turned to look at me, smiling wanly. I could see the pain and confusion in his eyes, but with it, gratitude. I kissed him; he smooched me back in response.

"Thank you, Damson," he whispered, then settled down on the bed next to me.

I didn't know how long we lay there, my arms around him, stroking his shoulder with the hand of the arm that I'd threaded behind his neck. At some stage he must have woken, got out of bed and turned off the light, for when I woke the next morning at the crowing of our two roosters I was lying on my side, the covers over us both, him spooned up behind me snoring so very softly that he sounded like Milli, our house cat, who always purred with pleasure at the slightest touch.

CHAPTER 3

In 1950, when I first arrived in Italy, there were very few private cars on the streets of large cities; Milan, Rome and Naples being the major exceptions. People didn't travel the way they did now, ten years later, so finding a parking spot outside our apartment in Florence was always a trial.

I often used the spare parking space in Randy's garage, but whenever Arnie was staying, I had to find street parking, something not easily done, because the streets weren't designed for motor vehicles. I ended up paying to use the parking space in Via Maffia; at least there the attendant looked out for my car for however long I was staying. He looked rather disappointed when I drove into the lot in the Land Rover; he rather liked the prestige and clout among his peers while he stood endlessly shining the Maserati, even allowed to turn over the engine and move it around the lot, though forbidden to take it out onto the street. I always tipped well, and he flirted with me in the way that heterosexual men of his age often did, with no expectation that anything would come of it.

"*Buongiorno, signora,*" I said to the caretaker, handing her a basket of fruit freshly picked from my garden and a few jars of apricot jam. It paid to have her on our good side; she was the eyes and ears of the four apartments that occupied our building.

"*Buongiorno, dottore,*" she said, then tilted her head towards the ceiling and rolled her eyes. "*Gli inglesi sono lassù.*"

"Thanks for the warning," I said, kissing her cheek. She was old enough to be my grandmother, if not great-grandmother, but loved her "boys", as she called Giancarlo and me.

Informing me that our upstairs neighbours had arrived from England was a way of telling me that she disapproved of them, especially their son James, a young man who couldn't seem to keep out of trouble. The former owners of the floor above ours were elderly and had passed away three years ago. We'd tried to buy the apartment with Carla for her to live in, but were unsuccessful, outbid by the aristocratic English family who only visited for a few months during the summer. It suited us well, though, because they didn't impinge on our lives, except when they entertained on their balcony with a lot of very noisy local expatriates, most of whom had returned to Florence after fleeing during the war.

Giancarlo wasn't home when I called out. I'd brought a stack of documents for him, given to me by Cosmo at the office. Mail had also arrived at La Mensola: a letter from his father, another from his aunt and a third from our mutual friend, ex-inspector Salvatore Venturi, who'd been in charge of the serial killer case ten years ago. I knew there'd be a page or two in the letter for me written in French—his mother was French and he'd obtained a degree at the Sorbonne. He'd left the police force about the same time as Giancarlo; his father, a duke, had died and he'd inherited his title and the responsibility of running the family estate. He spent his time between a rather grand apartment in Rome over-looking the Campo de' Fiori—where we were often invited to stay—and a sprawling villa on a large estate in the Frascati hills.

I poured myself a gin and tonic, stripped off and went out to the terrace, noticing that Giancarlo had forgotten to water the potted shrubs again. I stretched out in a chair and started to wonder what we'd have for dinner when I heard him call out my name.

"Hello," I yelled back. "How did you know I was here?"

"*La carceriera* told me that you'd arrived. Can I have one of those?" he asked, leaning over my shoulder and kissing my cheek while trying to wrestle my drink from my hand.

"Don't let her hear you calling her a jailor," I said, laughing, "she'll tan your hide—and the gin is on the drinks table, the tonic and the ice are in the fridge. Go make your own."

"Aw, don't you love me anymore?" he said, kissing my shoulder.

I shushed him then warned him that our English neighbours had arrived and, if they were out on their terrace, would probably have heard every word.

"*Me ne frega un cazzo*," he said loudly, aiming his words at the terrace above us, knowing that none of the family spoke a word of Italian. *I don't give a fuck* was what he'd said, although in Italian it didn't have the same pithiness as the English version. He ruffled my hair and then disappeared back inside. When I didn't hear any noises for a few minutes, I wondered what he was up to, so wandered into the apartment to look for him. I heard the shower, so climbed in behind him, running my arms around his waist.

"Hello, you," he said in Arabic, turning his head for a kiss.

"Giancarlo! What the hell!" He had a black eye and a bruise over his cheek. "Where did you get this?"

"Stupid really. Some idiot tried to rob me in Trieste as I was returning to the hotel late at night."

"Let me look at it," I said.

He batted my hand out of the way. "Don't fuss, Damson. I'm all right. I had a doctor check me over. There's nothing broken."

I knew I'd get nowhere if I persisted, so shrugged and sighed. "This never would have happened had you—"

"Allowed you to give me self-defence lessons. I know, for the thirtieth time. You do go on about it. The war is over, Damson. I'm not a cop anymore; there's no reason for me to learn how to disarm thugs in any more ways than those I was already trained in."

"I've told you a thousand times that what you were taught was rudimentary and basically ineffective against anyone who knows what they're doing," I said. It was an argument I could never win, so I picked up the flannel and ran it over his back. For a moment, I had a very quick flashback of soaping up Renzo's back in his apartment in Pienza not long after I'd first arrived in Italy. But then, when Giancarlo turned into my arms and kissed me properly, I smiled into his mouth.

"What's that for?" he asked, grinning back.

"You look like such a thug. All I need to do is knock out one of your front teeth and you'll scare the wits out of all your clients."

He laughed then kissed me again. "Where's my gin and tonic?" he whispered into my ear.

"Finish your shower, go lie on the bed and I'll bring it to you," I said, my index finger sliding down between his buttocks.

"No, no, Damson, I want to fuck you today," he said, his hand having found my dick. "After all, it's almost six weeks since we—"

"Sounds good to me. Hurry up, then," I said, slapping his arse, then got out of the shower to towel myself dry.

Although we'd been together for ten years, I still found him immensely sexually attractive. We didn't indulge as much as we had when we'd first got together—we had differing arousal cycles, but neither of us seemed to mind if one was needy when the other one wasn't particularly in the mood. I loved everything about him. My focus was on his pleasure and less on mine. I tended only to put my own sensual feelings foremost when I slept with other people without him present—and that was in fact quite rare. Before Kendall, there'd been no one for a few years.

In quiet moments of reflection, I often thought that someone had designed Giancarlo just for me. I blessed the day that he came into my life and, despite the diversions I'd had over the years with other men, he was still the only one I dreamed of when we weren't together, and I thanked God that He'd looked down on me with such grace.

*****

Giancarlo's black eye raised more than a few questions when we arrived at Randy's flat the following evening for what we'd thought would be a party. In fact, Randy informed us that it would just be us four, and that he'd arranged for the dinner to be catered by our favourite local restaurant.

"We've known you two for such a long time, and we wanted to hear all about your time in Australia without a dozen other people around," Randy said, once we'd taken off our jackets and he'd poured us a drink.

I'd brought presents for them, a pair of black opal cufflinks for Randy and a silver cigarette case inlaid with polished petrified wood for Arnie. I'd never seen the like of it when I spied it in the window of a jewellery shop in Adelaide, so was pretty sure he wouldn't have either.

I passed around photos I'd taken during the trip, both of our friends marvelling at how different the Australian countryside was from what they'd imagined it to be: endless red desert and scrub. The photos of the Blue Mountains and the Jamison Valley took their breath away, especially when I explained that after the Grand Canyon, and only seventy miles west of Sydney, the valley complex was the largest in the world.

Of course, every time a photo was passed around with Kendall in it, it got a lot of attention and a lot a teasing.

"So how's the new book coming along?" Arnie asked over our starter, a magnificent scampi risotto, cooked in Randy's kitchen by one of the restaurant chefs while we'd been having drinks.

"I've come up with a title," I said. "Seems to fit the other books. I'm going to call it *Living with the Enemy*."

"Wow! That's great, Damson, especially for a book about the lives of people who lived through the war."

"Civilians who lived through the war in occupied territories," I clarified. "Despite the punishing schedule, I interviewed dozens of immigrants in Australia, many of whom were traumatised by their experiences but desperate to get the word out. Can you believe that already there are people who think what happened all over Europe was somehow fantasised, blown out of all proportion?"

"Those interviews you did with Randy and me—will they be used?" Arnie asked.

"Of course. It wouldn't be a balanced account if I didn't have some corroborating evidence from combatants who'd seen what happened to those people. I spoke to a few pals who introduced me to men and women who'd been in Japanese, German and Italian prisoner-of-war camps too."

"That sounds like a mammoth undertaking," Randy said. "How long do you reckon it will take you to write?"

"I've a lot more research to do yet, mostly here in Italy, but I should say three to five years."

The waiter cleared our plates and readied the table for the fish course—*orata*, or sea bream, roasted in the oven on a bed of tomato and olives. Since 1957, we'd been able to get fresh ocean fish a day after it had been caught in coastal towns. Before that, we'd been able to buy those same fish, but no one knew when they'd been caught; new laws and refrigerated railway cars had all sorts of seafood delivered to the markets in Florence and even in Pienza and Montepulciano.

"That's not all he's doing," Giancarlo added. "He and Stefano are writing a children's book that Damson's illustrating."

"It's the story of an Italian field mouse who builds a home in the wall of a Tuscan kitchen, and what he gets up to while he watches the owners of the house go about their business. Of course, they're renovating it, which will provide for some charming scenes and stories. Stefano and his three children have wonderful imaginations. We've stolen a lot of their stories to use. We rather hope it will appeal to teenagers as well."

"And adults," Arnie said. "Will your illustrations be line drawings?"

"I'm hoping my publisher will give in to blackmail and accept watercolours. I did give him a subtle reminder that other publishing houses, like Kendall's father's, are chomping at the bit to get me to sign a contract."

"I love your paintings. The book sounds charming; I'd buy a copy for myself."

I couldn't help but notice the look that passed between him and Randy. Friends from childhood, who as teenagers had discovered sex together, separated and then reunited in an extraordinary encounter during the war; they'd both married, but had maintained their relationship over the years. Randy's marriage was one of convenience, something that suited his wife, whose sister Arnie had married. I never pried; it was none of my business, but it was obvious to Blind Freddy how much they cared for each other.

"How's your case going, Giancarlo?" Randy asked.

"Slowly. You know the Italian Right; despite being at each other's throats most of the time, all the various factions have something in common—hiding their past transgressions—so I keep running into roadblocks."

"There was an article about your friend Giovanni Scavola in this morning's paper. Did you see it?"

"He's no friend of mine, but no. Which paper?"

"The *Corriere della Sera*. He's running for mayor."

"Where?"

"In Venice. Hang on, I'll get you my copy; it's in the den."

"Can we wait until after dinner?" I said, a rather little too forcefully than I intended. "You know what he's like. He'll bury his head in the newspaper and then rattle on about the case all night."

Giancarlo lowered his head, grumbling at me, but in a very playful manner. "I wonder he's got time to run for mayor," he said. "He's the head of a major industrial conglomerate across the northeast of the country, and I don't know how he thinks he'll profit from such a position if he does win."

"From what I've read, he's far from being public-spirited or socially aware. He refuses to have unions on the factory floor," I explained to Randy and Arnie. "Although he's obsessed, Giancarlo's business is my business. I did my research too."

Most of the rest of dinner was taken up by Giancarlo's account of his two weeks in Australia, how much he'd fallen in love with the country and wanted to relocate. A few of Arnie's friends had served in the Pacific theatre of war and had spent leave in Sydney and Brisbane. He avowed they had said much the same thing.

The main course was *porchetta*: suckling pig stuffed with herbs and oven-roasted. The waiter later told us the owner of the restaurant had cooked it in their bread oven and the chef who was looking after tonight's dinner had finished it off in Randy's kitchen. Crisp pork skin, golden roasted potatoes and a side dish of *arugula* and green beans sautéed in butter—it was delicious, and I had a second helping.

The conversation moved on to news of their wives' excavation.

Both sisters were archaeologists and had been working on a buried villa, discovered over ten years ago in a farmer's field while he was ploughing. I'd been to visit it myself, fascinated by the vast mosaic floor that was painstakingly uncovered at the rate of about a square metre every ten days. I liked both women very much and they'd warmed to both Giancarlo and me; I had absolutely no idea whether they knew what went on from time to time between their husbands and us. I never asked Randy or Arnie; we were close enough that I knew they'd tell either of us if there was a problem. I suspected that Randy's wife, Helen, had a lover—he'd hinted as much—but I'd never seen evidence of it in the times I'd been with her in Rome, or when she'd visited Florence or come to stay with us at La Mensola.

Randy had bought a few new pieces from an antiques shop in Rome that I hadn't seen, so between the main course and dessert, he took me to his library to show me a pair of black-painted Athenian terracotta vases.

"Oh," I said, staring at one. It had a band of men in various sexual poses painted around the circumference. "I had no idea ..."

"The Greeks didn't mind erotic scenes painted on their vessels. A lot seem to show that what we do is nothing new."

I smiled at him and he kissed me. "Will you two stay tonight?"

"Perhaps not tonight, but soon, Randy. I haven't seen Giancarlo except for two weeks in nearly three months. Perhaps in a day or two?"

"I can wait."

"Thank you. Has Giancarlo seen these?"

"Of course. We even tried some of the positions with him while you were away."

I laughed. "I guess I've got a lot of catching up to do."

Randy had been my first real sexual partner in Italy. He'd had a voracious sexual appetite when we first met, and possessed the largest cock I've ever seen. He'd fucked me a lot in those early days, but had progressed to discovering the pleasure of being the passive partner. We still slept together from time to time—not as often as he'd have liked. In private, he freely admitted that he still carried a torch for me, but respected my relationship with Giancarlo, so didn't press the issue.

Dessert turned out to be a favourite of mine: *zucotto*, a Florentine speciality. Comprised of layers of cake, flavoured ricotta and ice cream, it derived its name from *zucca*, the Italian word for pumpkin, because of its shape.

We moved out to the terrace after dinner while the dining room was cleared and the chef and waiter cleaned up and washed the dishes. Just before they left, Randy tipped them both an extravagant amount.

"It's us who should have paid for dinner," Giancarlo said. "It's your birthday party after all."

"No, really—how many times have you cooked for us at La Mensola or taken us out to dinner in Montepulciano and Pienza? Forget it; it was a wonderful evening and we're just happy to have you both here."

"I'll drink to that," Giancarlo said.

So, with a bottle of champagne, that was just what we did.

★★★★★

"You didn't want to stay?" Giancarlo said to me, an hour after we got home and were lying in bed chatting. "I wouldn't have minded."

"Another time," I said. "I haven't seen much of you for ages. I wanted to spend the night with you."

"You have a soft side, Damson O'Reilly. I love that in you."

"And also, I know something's on your mind. I've sensed it ever since I arrived yesterday. If you tell me it's this case, I'll—"

"Of course it is. I'm really worried for the safety of my client. I've been to the local police to share my concern and they seem keen to do anything but take me seriously."

"Scavola is running for mayor …"

"Yes, and it drives me crazy that we haven't progressed as a society. It might as well still be 1935, when the only way you could get anything done was by knowing someone or greasing the palm of the local chief of police."

"Your former status doesn't help?"

He snorted. "They consider me a has-been, a traitor who turned from law enforcement to the type of person they generally have to face in court as a defence lawyer."

"But your reputation is of being tough but fair—"

"Only in Tuscany and mentioning something like that is like waving a red rag to a bull anywhere else in the country. Despite my family coming from the Veneto and being fluent in the local dialect, it's given me no leverage. I couldn't even get Scavola's business records without almost emptying out my wallet."

"We've spoken about this before—"

"My client reimbursed me. Yes, you've told me endlessly not to fork out my own money, unlike you, who gives away your paintings at the drop of a hat, even when they're selling so well at high prices in Carla's gallery."

This was an argument that came up time after time. I did give away sketches and paintings, sometimes to complete strangers. I loved to draw; that was my only explanation. Oddly enough, I never gave away anything I'd turned on the lathe, or furniture I'd built; for that, I charged a reasonable price compared to other hand-crafted kitchenware I saw at the markets. I also never fixed people's cars or motorbikes for nothing—unless they were very close friends, and still they nearly always insisted on paying me something. I'd been so dirt-poor most of my life that the gift of giving usually gave me more pleasure than it did the recipient.

"What have you got planned for the morning?" I asked, as a way of moving on.

"Nothing much. I have some documents to go through."

"How about I give you a hand?"

"Why would you want to do that?"

"Because I know you only too well. This case is eating you up, and I know I'll be living it with you for the next however long you're up to your eyes in it."

"Damson … I have something to tell you."

"Is it a man or has it to do with work?"

He slapped my shoulder playfully. "No, it's not a man. My black eye—it wasn't an attempted robbery. I told you that so you wouldn't be angry."

"Go on …"

"There were two men, not one. One held my arms behind my back; the other slugged me."

"Jesus, Giancarlo—"

"The guy throwing the punches said '*Sta attento, Manetti*,' then they pushed me to the ground and walked away.

"*Be careful?* For fuck's sake, be careful of what?"

"I don't know."

"Of course you know. This was a fucking warning from that arsehole Scavola."

"You're jumping to conclusions, Damson."

"From what I've read about him and his associations with Giulio Evola, I wouldn't put it past him. That was a warning to drop your client."

"But why? Scavola is already suing him; it's a case in which I'll struggle to save my client from either a huge fine or time in jail. I've no proof that the death threats against him came from Scavola; it's all conjecture. And I sincerely believe that what my client wrote in his letter about Scavola's involvement with the murders of the nuns during the war was true. However, his letter to the newspaper could be interpreted as meaning that it was Scavola himself who pulled the trigger."

"If that was true, it could be a reason to threaten to kill your client. Can you find proof?"

"It happened in Vatican City, Damson."

"Oh. So I suppose that whatever happened has been locked away with the misdemeanours of Pius XII …"

Giancarlo crossed himself. "I didn't shed a tear when that Nazi sympathiser kicked the bucket two years ago, did you?"

I shook my head. "You need someone on the inside who can dig a little deeper."

"I know who you're suggesting, but he's retired: busy planting vines, creating vintages and putting down cheeses."

"You know very well he's doing nothing of the sort; his estate workers are doing that. Last I heard was that he was bored shitless with a wife twenty years younger than him who spends money like water and rarely lets him sleep with her."

"How the hell do you know all that?"

"You never read those pages in French that he sends me with his letters to you?"

"Salvatore never mentions anything like that in letters to me; why you?"

"Sometimes it's easier to be more intimate in one language than in another."

"You are joking, surely—"

"Ah, Signor Manetti, what you say to me in Arabic when I push those last few inches into you bears no comparison to what you normally say in English."

"And what's that?"

"It's usually 'shove it all the way in' or 'fuck me like you hate me'."

He laughed very loudly. "Guilty, as charged, your honour."

"Give ex-inspector Venturi a call. Invite him and his wife to Florence for a weekend. If he doesn't jump at the chance to do a bit of Vatican City investigation, I'll eat my hat."

"Perhaps you're right—"

"In the meantime, starting tomorrow morning, I'm going to start to teach you some proper self-defence exercises; nothing like that rubbish you Italian police were taught during the war."

★★★★★

I kept calling it "our" apartment—it was Giancarlo's actually, but common usage between us also called La Mensola "ours" and his flat in Venice the same. The building in which our apartment took up one floor had been built in the mid-1400s but renovated—if you could call it that—in the late 1800s by an Italian aristocrat who had unsuccessfully tried to give a beautiful Renaissance building a Palladian uplift by restructuring the entire front elevation and losing much of what had been, according to engravings I'd seen, made at the time, a very large, manicured garden.

That was how we, and the floor above us, had inherited a wide terrace. With an easterly elevation, sunlight flooded onto it, making it perfect for late, lazy breakfasts and for sunbathing up until almost midday. That was where we were this morning, our large outdoor table strewn with documents, the remains of a cooked breakfast on uncleared plates, and me showing Giancarlo how to extricate himself from the precise hold that had led to his black eye.

The first manoeuvre was to move back abruptly into the person holding you, butting their face with the back of your head, then swivelling to give them a chop to the side of the neck. It worked best if your assailant was of slighter build than you and about the same height. We'd practised several times in the sun, our dressing gowns discarded, until Giancarlo started to get the feel of it.

"It's all in the feet," I kept saying. "Make sure you have complete control of your balance, otherwise you might fall over yourself."

The second, and most effective strategy, especially if the attacker was behind you holding your wrists in his arms, was to lean forward, move your weight onto your less dominant leg, then half-swivel and mule-kick behind, right into the balls with your strongest leg. It sounded very complicated when I explained it, but he soon got the hang of it, nearly connecting once or twice.

"Jesus, don't you two ever wear clothes?"

"Don't you ever knock, James?"

"Why should I? You gave me a key."

Giancarlo laughed and then started to clear the table. "Coffee?" he asked.

"Yes please," our upstairs neighbours' son said, plonking himself heavily onto one of the wooden sun-lounges I'd made especially for the terrace.

"Don't tell me you're just getting home?" I asked, smiling as he peeled off his suit jacket and pulled off his tie.

"What were you two homos doing? Was it something I need to add to my list of bedroom activities?" He had a very wry sense of humour; I loved it, Giancarlo less so.

"You, you pervert?" I replied with a chuckle. "What could there possibly be in the repertoire of sexual tricks that you didn't already master at Eton?"

"Ah, boarding school prepared me for more than a first in Greats at Oxford with a *summa cum laude* in Latin, Damson. You have me there."

"I was teaching Giancarlo some self-defence moves."

"His black eye?"

"You don't want to know," I said. "Have you eaten?"

"Last night. Dinner with a very boring Swedish couple at Luigi's." He reached into his pocket and slammed a wad of lire on the table, then stood, peeled off the rest of his clothes and stretched out naked in the sun.

"You are such a tart. Your parents are incredibly wealthy. Why do you sleep with people for money?"

"One, because I like it, and two, because Mummy and Daddy have cut off my allowance … again!"

"What have you done this time?"

"The daughter of some friend of Pater's from his golf club says I got her up the duff."

"And did you?"

"Not unless my semen miraculously travelled from her back passage into her womb. I only fucked her because I wanted to get a feel of what it might be like to be buried up to the hilt in her twin brother."

Giancarlo arrived with a tray, bearing cups of coffee for each of us and some pastries we hadn't eaten at breakfast. He arrived in time to hear James's last words, frowning at my laughter. I knew what he'd said probably wasn't true, but he amused me.

"How long are you staying this time?"

James glanced upwards. "They're only here for a week or two. I've been banished from home until after the Olympics. I have tickets, do you?"

"Yes," Giancarlo answered. "We bought them last year. Damson was keen to make sure we saw all the Australians."

"Swimming and athletics, Damson?"

"Yes. Giancarlo will be at some of the gymnastics while I'm at the pool, but yes, I met quite a few of the athletes on my tour. I'm looking forward to it."

"Do either of you have sunglasses I could borrow?"

"In the bedroom," I said. "On the bench in the dressing room."

As James headed off to get them, Giancarlo switched to Italian, knowing James still didn't speak a word, even though his Latin was astoundingly good, as one would expect with someone with a *summa cum laude* in the language from one of the best universities in the world.

"Dear God, that boy is a problem."

"He's only, what, twenty-three? He'll grow out of it. You were probably the same when you were his age."

"When I was twenty-three, we were at war and I was a policeman. I had no time to fuck everything that moved."

"You would have if you could have," I said, smiling and taking his hand. "It was during your years of denial, my love."

"Before you came along and corrupted me."

"Me, corrupt you? Who was it who—?"

"Do you poofs have any friends who aren't queer?" James asked, returning from inside.

"Why, do you?" Giancarlo asked.

The look James gave him over the top of his sunglasses made me chuckle.

"Well, perhaps none of the girls is," he said. "But I want to meet your friend Randy McCall."

"Why?" I asked. "He doesn't pay for sex."

"Honestly, Damson, sometimes you are such a cunt."

I roared with laughter. Giancarlo's upbringing made him frown at the use of the word, but as it was a very versatile one for Australian men, especially those who'd served; it had a myriad of meanings, even used to describe a mate you were particularly fond of.

"Why do you want to meet Randall?" Giancarlo asked, rolling his eyes at my juvenile behaviour.

"Well, it's not really him I want to meet, but Helen, his wife. She has a PhD in Roman funerary inscriptions."

"And?" I asked, wiping the tears from my eyes.

"I'm thinking of starting my own doctoral research, and before you ask, Giancarlo, it's not about cock-sucking or fucking for money. I know she and her sister are excavating a villa south of Rome and I wanted to pick her brain. I'm very curious about *tabellae defixionis*, there's a PhD in there for sure."

"A *tabella defixionis* is a curse tablet," I translated for Giancarlo.

"The Romans were very fond of writing curses about their enemies on pottery shards or strips of tin or lead to ask the gods to visit calamities on them," James explained.

"I've always thought there might be some hidden in the mud at the bottom of our pond at La Mensola," I said. "There was a Roman settlement not far away. The whole area is riddled with thermal springs—"

"Just the sorts of places they loved to throw their bundles of hate," he said. "You must invite me sometime."

"Well, I'm sure we can provide an introduction to Dr McCall. You don't need to go through Randy."

"I'd be really grateful, Damson. Honestly, I'd rather spend the next few years far away from the clutches of my odious father, who wants nothing more than to whack me into a suit and tie, put a briefcase in one hand, a brolly in the other and a bowler hat on my head and send me off to work in some stuffy office with a room full of chinless wonders to see out my days."

This time, Giancarlo laughed with me.

"Helen is great fun," I said. "It's too early to phone her now; she sleeps in on Sundays. I'll give her a call this afternoon, then put you in touch with each other. Now, if you'll excuse us, I'm only too happy for you to laze here in the sun as long as you like, but we've got work to do and we'll be speaking in Italian … I promise you it won't be about you."

"You are far too lenient with him," Giancarlo said, a short while later while we were washing the breakfast dishes and tidying up the kitchen.

"We're not his parents, even though you behave like his father most of the time. He's a nice kid with an intellect twice the size of yours and mine put together. Just let him stretch his wings. You've met his parents; imagine what sort of upbringing the poor bastard has had. And to be perfectly honest, I think much of what he says about sleeping with people for money is bullshit. He says it to impress us."

"Why would he want to do that?"

"You've seen how his father treats him, like some idiot-savant. His intellect dwarfs that of his father a thousandfold; he loathes everything to do with the British aristocracy and won't play their games, something that puts *Pater*'s nose out of joint. You've seen it yourself, the way he gets slapped down every time he opens his mouth. James feels comfortable around us. I bet that kid's been a loner all his life and he's finally met two people who treat him like an adult—at least I do. Let him find his feet, Giancarlo; get to know him a bit better and don't be so judgemental."

"I suppose you're right … I just wish he didn't try so hard."

"I'm going home on Tuesday. How long will you be here?"

"I have two cases tomorrow, then I'm defending a third in Arezzo on Tuesday, and back here for a magistrate's hearing on Wednesday."

"Why don't you take him out to dinner one night, get to know him?"

"People will think he's my gigolo."

"So what if they do? Fuck 'em."

"That's your reply to everything, Damson."

"And it works most of the time, wouldn't you agree?"

CHAPTER 4

Giancarlo telephoned me at La Mensola on Wednesday morning to tell me that he'd had a very pleasant evening with James at Da Stefano, one of the leading Florentine restaurants, just a few kilometres out of town on the road to Bottai. It was situated in the huge barn of a country farmhouse, owned by two friends of Randy's, and very hard to get into. It served a variety of cuisines that seemed to rotate month by month, so when you arrived, you never knew what you were going to find on the menu.

"James was actually very shy in company," he said.

"So you got on well?"

"Surprisingly well. I asked him about his sense of humour and he said that he likes to shock. I believe he thinks I'm a bit of a prig."

I knew when not to say anything. "Do you know if anything came of the phone call to Helen?"

"He was very grateful to you, and yes, she'll be in Florence this coming weekend, so has promised to meet up with him to discuss the ideas for his project."

"I've been reading about your friend Scavola," I said.

"He's definitely *not* my friend, Damson."

"It's Australian reverse-speak; surely you recognise that after all these years? Friend in that context was a euphemism for someone you don't like."

"What have you learned?"

"Well, on Monday morning, while you were in court, I went to the library and borrowed what I could on Evola. I think to understand Scavola you have to first get a grip on the man he seems to idolise, or at least follow as part of the Ordine Nuovo group."

"Do you think you could make some notes for me as you go along? I'm up to my ears—"

"Why do you think I'm doing this? It's to help you because I love you."

"Aww, I promise I'll learn how to turn wood on your lathe to help you."

I chuckled. "Spare yourself the trouble. When will I see you next?"

"On the weekend. I need to spend some serious time with Cosmo on Saturday morning to catch up on the civil cases, deeds of authority and the normal things a *rappresentante legale* has to do: mostly petty squabbles that will never reach court. I don't have any more court appearances until next Wednesday in Siena so should be home for more than a few days."

"And what will you do about the Scavola case in the meantime?"

"Why do you insist on calling it the Scavola case?"

"Because, for some unfathomable reason, you've never told me the name of your client."

"Haven't I? I didn't mean to avoid it. His name is Mario Celestino."

"Mario Celestino, the film actor?"

"Yes, that's him. Perhaps now you understand what a high-profile case this is going to be."

For the rest of the morning, while reading through articles about both Scavola and Evola, I couldn't get images of Mario Celestino out of my mind. He'd been a first-class footballer and was spotted by a talent scout just before the war, only making three movies before Italy sided with Hitler. I remembered reading somewhere that he'd gone to Switzerland, only returning in late 1943 to fight against the Germans when Italy had sided with the Allies. He wasn't a coward—he was an anti-fascist, unable to support Mussolini's alliance with the Nazis.

He was incredibly good-looking, often mentioned in the press as seeing some new starlet from Cinecittà every few months. It made for good sales in the fan magazines; however, to me, without any insider knowledge, it sounded like a front for something else, or was that my fervent imagination going wild? I'd seen one of his movies in Japan, dubbed of course for the American audience at the PX, in which he'd wrestled with the villain wearing nothing but a very skimpy, revealing briefs. I'd gone home and masturbated twice over the fantasy in my mind … I was sure I was only one of millions of men and women who'd done the same thing.

About eleven o'clock, it was getting very hot; the rhythmic chirping of cicadas meant that the heat of the day was almost upon us. So, I grabbed a towel and headed down to our rock pool with a book and my sketch pad. I left a basket at the edge of the orchard on my way; the apricots and nectarines were ready to pick and my two cherry trees laden with fruit. Last night, I'd asked Alfonso to help. On Wednesdays, he told me, he drove to Castelmuzio to attend mass; he was still too timid to show his face in Pienza, people puzzled that he no longer seemed to be one of their familiar local priests, and he unwilling to lie to them about his reason for taking an *exclaustratio.*

I'd no sooner got out of the water, lit a cigarette and settled down with my book when he appeared, stripped off and dived into the pool.

"Hello," I said when he eventually joined me.

"*Fa un caldo pazzesco!*" he said, then shook his head, his hair flinging drops of water all over me, then grinning at my pretended annoyance.

"Yes, it is bloody hot!" I said, in English, then laughed as he tried to pronounce it, mimicking my broad Australian accent.

"There was a phone call for you this morning when you went into Pienza."

"Oh, yes? Usually you leave a note for me. Who was it?"

"I have no idea. A man who spoke in English and a bit of broken Italian."

The only English-speaking person I knew who had broken Italian other than James's father—and I had absolutely no idea why he'd be calling me—was Kendall. It wasn't quite ten days since we'd parted in Genoa and he'd said he was spending a week in Paris, then a few days in Munich. He knew about my afternoon siestas—a time I told him I was invariably at home—so guessed that if it was him and if it was important, he'd call back.

"How was Castelmuzio?" I asked.

"Beautiful, serene, a lovely mass, but so few people … you've never been there, have you?"

"Once, in my early days here, not long after I bought the Jeep. I drove everywhere. But, to be perfectly honest, I saw so many Tuscan hilltop towns that they all seemed to blend into each other."

*****

The phone rang shortly after two o'clock.

"Hey, it's me!"

"Hello, Kendall. I suppose it was you who phoned earlier."

"Yes. Who was that who answered the phone?"

"A friend who's staying for a while."

"Oh … does that mean that I can't—?"

"Not at all; the house is well big enough for both of you. We're putting you in the large bedroom next to ours. Where are you?"

"Right now? Um … let me see. I'm on platform two at Basel."

"In Switzerland?"

"Yes. I have a meeting in Milan tomorrow morning and after that I thought I'd head down your way."

"One sec," I said, running to the study to find my copy of Thomas Cook's European railway timetables. "Here we are," I continued, leafing through the pages. "There's a train at twelve minutes to two in the afternoon, which will get you to Chiusi just before seven. I can pick you up at the station."

"Don't bother, I'll catch a cab."

"This is rural Italy, Kendall: we'll have to wait another thirty years before we have cabs in this part of the world, if then. It's no problem; it's a half-hour drive and I do it all the time."

"My meeting is due to finish at half past ten. Isn't there an earlier train? I'd like to see some of the countryside as we drive to your house."

"There are a few, but most of them require at least one, if not two, changes and with them being local services and you not speaking Italian, you'd never know which platform to go to. Besides, it will still be light at seven in the evening and I'll drive past Montepulciano; you'll see it in the dusk when it's at its most beautiful."

"Are you sure I won't be in the way?"

"I hope you'll only be in the way in the nicest possible positions," I said.

He laughed. "All right, the twelve minutes to two it is."

"When you get to your hotel in Milan, ask the concierge to book you a seat; they'll also drop you at the station. I'm looking forward to seeing you; I can't wait to show you around."

"See you tomorrow evening, then."

*****

I woke early the following morning and wandered down the corridor to the shelf—after which my house was named—where I lit a cigarette and leaned on the balustrade that I'd built around it nearly ten years ago. The window boxes were ablaze with bright red geraniums. I'd been given dozens of cuttings when I'd first asked whether anyone had any spare. For weeks I'd find rooted plantlets in small terracotta pots outside the trellised gate I'd built at one end of my outdoor terrace. I hadn't wanted to build it, but I needed privacy; there were still many visitors to the shrine in the old stables, and many of the locals used to poke their heads in the kitchen to say hello. It was common in rural Italy when visiting a friend to arrive unannounced, but more often than not, especially in the summer, I didn't bother wearing anything, on the odd occasion just underpants and sandals when preparing food or fiddling with something in the workshop.

The folding chairs that Giancarlo had bought at the army surplus store at Pontassieve when he first moved in with me were no longer used outside. I'd built more suitable outdoor furniture for the shelf over the years. It was now a great place to sit, perhaps have a beer and watch the sun go down over the olive grove at the front of the house and the hills towards Montefollonico.

Milli, our house cat, was a lazy bugger. She occasionally caught mice—the reason I'd adopted her in the first place—but was indifferent to birds, and for that reason, the pine tree just in front of the shelf was a haven and favourite nesting place for many species. The Italians loved to shoot birds; come September, the air would reverberate with gunshots. I'd never really come to grips with the fact that even songbirds in their thousands were slaughtered both for sport and for food. I still couldn't get used to *uccelli*, tiny birds plucked then threaded whole on skewers then eaten in a mouthful, beaks, bones and all. The Italians loved to eat them and, unlike people from English-speaking countries, saw nothing wrong with it. When they were served, there was usually a lot of banter and sexual innuendo in the conversation: *uccelli* was one of the less vulgar slang terms for penises. I'd go as far as pigeon—which I loved to cook—or pheasants and other game birds, but munching on those tiny creatures whose calls gave me so much pleasure at dawn and at dusk was still something I wouldn't do. I often got curious looks from friends when *uccelli* were served up at table around Christmas time. *Paese che vai, usanze che trovi*, I'd quote, using an Italian proverb, which meant something like customs and tastes differ from country to country, and we shouldn't judge what other cultures do based on what we were brought up with.

I'd planned out my day last night when I got into bed. The Palazzo Piccolomini in Pienza had an extensive library in one wing. Originally built as a summer retreat for Pope Pius II, it was a jewel of Renaissance architecture, and I'd sketched and painted all of its elevations several times. The collection had up-to-date books on Italian politics. I wanted to research Giulio Evola, see if there were any references to Giovanni Scavola, then go to the high school to talk with my friend Andrea Gagliardi, the geography and French language master, to ask him to accompany me to the school library. The librarian there was a rather fussy, tight-lipped man, who didn't like me much because he thought I'd drawn the wrong sort of attention to Pienza, his hometown, in my book *Living with Monsters*.

The great thing about the current Italian education system was the concentration on contemporary culture. If I couldn't find a lot of material about Giancarlo's movie star client in the high school library, I'd be very surprised.

Alfonso and I ate breakfast together, then I watered the vegetable garden while he showered. We'd picked a full basket of cherries yesterday and I knew that Signora Marino adored them. I hadn't seen the Marinos since I got home, so intended to have lunch at the restaurant I used to work at and to give her the cherries at the same time. Stefano told me that a new man had taken my place. Gino was his name; he was another cousin of my long-dead friend Lorenzo, and had inherited his apartment, where he now lived. Alfonso told me to be prepared; the family resemblance was very strong.

I told Alfonso to take the Jeep for the day; no one was staying at Il Fornaio for another two weeks so it wouldn't be needed until then. I had an income-earner driving guests around the Tuscan countryside to show them the sights, and, as the Jeep had not only become famous in *The Road to Montepulciano* but was also mentioned in *Living with Monsters*, it was photographed almost as many times by visitors as I was.

Before I left, I threw him the textbook that Signor Gagliardi had given me when I'd first arrived here. It was a French primer for Italian high school students. If he was having an affair with a Frenchman who couldn't speak Italian, I thought it might come in handy to learn a few phrases.

"I'm not going to see him, in case that's what you're thinking."

"I wasn't thinking anything, and besides, what you do is none of my business. I'm merely the friend who loves you and whose shoulder is always available … as are my hugs."

He smiled and moved into my arms. I squeezed him, then slapped his bum. Laughing, he told me he'd see me for dinner, asking if he needed to prepare anything. I told him I'd fire up the bread oven before I left to pick up Kendall at Chiusi, but that I had all afternoon to prepare dinner.

I was able to find plenty in the Piccolomini archive about Evola, but very little about Scavola. Most of the references were in either newspaper articles or magazines and about his huge industrial business;

there was absolutely nothing about the man himself. I borrowed five books—I'd obtained a special research reader's card when I was working on my book about the serial killers and had kept it renewed—then walked to Giancarlo's Pienza office.

Cosmo Bertini, the young lawyer who worked for Giancarlo, was a well-mannered, good-humoured young man with a bright smile, twenty-eight years old, with a cultured, very beautiful wife and three small children. They lived in an apartment directly behind the office. His wife had been hit by a car that hadn't stopped after the accident and was confined to a wheelchair. For that reason, the office was on the ground floor, not very far from the Piazza Pio II, where my favourite café, the Bar Azzurro, was situated.

Cosmo was a very bright young man who had a passion for research. He'd first worked as Giancarlo's legal assistant-apprentice while he was still studying law, and had shown a particular skill for finding facts. He seemed quite busy but then, when I explained that I'd called by to use the telephone—the office had discounted billing for long-distance calls—he offered to do some investigating for me on the private life of Giovanni Scavola. I left my books with him, then walked to the high school.

Andrea was in his office; it was the official summer school break and he was catching up on the new syllabus, which had just landed on his desk.

"Have a look at this," he said, throwing the document over the desk to me.

"Conditional, pluperfect and subjunctive, all in the first semester of the first year?" I said. "Who wrote this nonsense?"

"Someone who thinks that Italian grammar that's taught to Italian students should be exactly the same for both French and Latin. The Latin teacher is even more annoyed than I am."

"Let me think about it. I'm happy to pitch in—that is if I'm allowed to, of course—we could concoct some sort of game; a conversation in which we gradually introduce those forms using contemporary language. If the principal agrees, I could pop in once a week to help you out."

"That's a wonderful idea and you're right, it would work very well. Perhaps you could mention it to the Latin teacher?"

I shrugged. The *Magister Linguae Latinae*, as he liked to call himself, was another local who did not like me. He'd never learned to converse in Latin but had studied it at university as an academic subject. He'd often replied in Italian when, in the early days, Alfonso and I had met him in the street. I decided that rather than talk to him I'd send him a note—in Latin, of course—rather than suffer his thinly veiled pretence at bonhomie whenever we had occasion to speak.

Of course, there was plenty in the school library on Mario Celestino. He was a big star, idolised by the boys because of his early football career and then later as a tough outdoors man in Italian Westerns, and by the girls for his smouldering good looks and his constant changes of girlfriend—something that Andrea explained to me gave all of them hope that he might some day cast his piercing blue eyes and thick, dark lashes in their direction.

With another pile of reference material, I headed back to Giancarlo's office. Cosmo was on the phone and held a finger up when I opened the door. He seemed to be listening intently, nodding his head and saying "*Si, si ... capisco,*" every so often. I sat and waited. Eventually he hung up the phone and tore several sheets from his notepad, telling me he'd written in shorthand and would type up what he'd learned about Scavola and that he'd have it ready in about half an hour.

I told him not to worry; I was going off to the trattoria to have lunch and I'd call past at about half past one to pick up my pile of books before he closed the office for siesta.

There were less than a dozen people in the trattoria, most of them locals. It took me an age to get to the kitchen after stopping to talk to everyone. I got the biggest hug from Signora Marino and copious tears when I handed her the present I'd brought back from Australia for her: a necklace of rock crystal beads, each interspersed with small, polished aquamarines, all threaded along a silver chain. The was also an opal tie pin for her husband, who was having a day off.

The biggest surprise was Gino. In fact, I felt the blood drain from my face when I first saw him serving at one of the tables. He was an almost dead ringer for Renzo. Skinnier, for sure, and not nearly as handsome, but his features were almost the same, as was the way he combed his hair. He obviously knew who I was, because he embraced me when Signora Marino introduced us, then shook my hand over and over, thanking me effusively for tending Renzo's grave.

I took the outside table, the one at which Signora Marino and I had always had our morning coffee break with pastries purchased that morning from the baker. I was famished, not even having glanced at the chalkboard to see what was on the menu. When food arrived without my even ordering, I turned and looked; no menu of the day for Damson O'Reilly, Gino said, telling me that Signora Marino had cooked my favourite pasta dish: her version of *pici all'Etrusca*. Hand-rolled pasta, parboiled asparagus and tiny cherry tomatoes with basil, parsley, mint, garlic and heaps of grated pecorino. Where the hell did she get asparagus at this time of year? I wondered as I wolfed it down.

She came to join me for the *secondo*: an enormous *bistecca alla Fiorentina*, which we shared with a green salad and a half bottle of *Vino Nobile di Montepulciano*. We chatted about my trip, her grandchildren and how much she'd missed me … and I her, I assured her. I stayed behind to help clear up, laughing and joking with Gino, who had Renzo's same smile but a far livelier sense of humour. He told me he was engaged to one of the local girls, Rosa, something that reminded me of how long I'd been part of the community. She'd been a child when I first arrived, a shy little thing with plaits and rose-red shiny cheeks, always clutching a toy monkey. And now they were to be married in October! He wanted to know if we could hold the reception in the garden of Il Fornaio after the marriage ceremony in the cathedral. I told him it would be our honour and that I'd liaise with Stefano; that he should give us a call, and we'd work out the exact arrangements. We never had guests that late in the year, so I knew that in saying yes I wouldn't be somehow double-booking.

*****

Giancarlo phoned at four that afternoon.

I'd woken from my afternoon nap and had wandered down to the kitchen, stoked the stove and put the moka pot on. I didn't often drink coffee that late in the afternoon, but I'd brought home half a *torta sbrisolona* that Signora Marino had baked and which hadn't sold during the ten o'clock *Kaffeeklatsch*—a German word that was doing the rounds, meaning a get-together over coffee to have a natter and to gossip. Despite its being one of my favourite indulgences, the only reason it hadn't sold well was because she'd also baked her renowned *torta di mele*—apple cake—and that was so popular that it almost always flew out the door the moment she pulled it out of the oven. However, I coveted the *sbrisolona*; it was a Milanese treat that I baked quite often myself using her secret recipe. More like a biscuit than a cake, made with semolina flour, it resembled a shortbread topped with a streusel-like mixture, and was melt-in-the-mouth delicious.

Just after breakfast this morning, I'd asked Alfonso to help me move one of the tables I'd rescued from a house that I'd helped demolish ten years ago, not long after I'd moved in here, and put it in the new breakfast room—my former workshop. Much of the furniture from that house was still stored in the large shed at the bottom of my orchard, along with some farm equipment. It was nice sitting in the new breakfast room in the heat of the afternoon, sheltered from the direct sun, the doors flung open on to the terrace, some of the reference books I'd gathered this morning in front of me, and I was slowly working my way through two slices of the *torta* and with a cup of coffee and a cigarette when the phone rang.

"Where are you?" I asked Giancarlo.

"What are you eating?"

We often had these sorts of conversations, consisting of a string of unanswered questions. My question was rhetorical; I'd heard the distinctive bells of the Basilica di Santa Trinità, the closest church across the Arno from our apartment in Florence.

"I just got back from court to find James asleep in our bed … stark naked," Giancarlo said.

"Did you fuck him?" I asked, almost choking on a few crumbs from my last mouthful of biscuit.

"He's a child, Damson."

"I know, just teasing. But he's got one of those cocks you really like: fat, with a big head and long overhanging foreskin."

"Shut up," he said, laughing. "How's Alfonso?"

"Coping," I said. "He took the Jeep today and headed off to God knows where."

"You left a message saying that Kendall was arriving this evening."

"He'll still be here tomorrow night when you get here. I've moved Alfonso into the new downstairs area so Kendall can be next door to us."

"Well played."

"I've been at the library and Cosmo did some digging for me. I have some information about Scavola."

"Do tell?"

"I'll let you know when you get here; I'm still collating information about him and his association with the Ordine Nuovo, as well as some background on your client."

"Celestino? Why him?"

"Again, I'll tell you when you're here. I spent quite a bit of time thinking about the men who thumped you and their possible connection to Scavola. I think Mario Celestino might need to watch where he goes."

"You don't really believe that Scavola might—"

"I'm only reading between the lines, and I need to do a lot more work before I'm ready to share what I really think. However, I'm starting to find things that suggest that he may have been a *squadristo* as early as 1930, years before the war." The *squadristi* were a fascist militia that operated outside the law, known for their extreme right-wing views and their unbridled violence.

"He'd have to have been very young."

"He'd have been fifteen. But, just like the Nazis at the end of the war, they had kids in their squads, some as young as twelve. Many of those youngsters got caught up with the fascists and became Blackshirts."

"Can you prove it?"

"Not yet, but the literature seems to imply that Scavola was an active member of Mussolini's black-shirted thugs."

"Hm … all right. I'll give Mario a call and tell him to lie low."

"Where is he now?"

"Filming on location at Ostia."

"Filming? Maybe suggest he hires a bodyguard, Giancarlo. I have a funny feeling about all of this."

Hanging up the phone, I went back to my notes. Scavola was born in 1915 and had just turned forty-five. He'd been married twice; his first wife died during the war in an Allied bombing raid in Rome, the second, a fabulously wealthy heiress, in a snorkelling accident at Portofino, a short way south of Genoa. Just after the war, his father had died, leaving him a fortune and an impressive industrial portfolio, which included manufacturing plants, construction businesses and a substantial retail chain specialising in tobacco and alcohol. There were Scavola kiosks all over the country selling booze and cigarettes; one had even opened at the bus station in Montepulciano.

He'd served in the army, but without access to military records, I couldn't find out exactly what he'd done. All Cosmo had been able to discover was that, when the Blackshirts were dissolved in 1943 after the Armistice of Cassabile between Italy and America and Britain, all members of the group had been mobilised into the Italian army and forced to fight the Germans who still remained in the country. According to Giancarlo's notes, the massacre of the nuns had taken place on the ninth of June 1944, four days after the Americans had occupied Rome, in a railway carriage of a train waiting to leave the Vatican railway station.

There seemed to be no official records of the massacre … none, anyway, that Giancarlo or Cosmo had discovered. Maybe when Giancarlo got in touch with our friend, former Inspector Venturi, and if he decided he was interested, we might learn more.

As for Giancarlo's film star client, there were heaps of references. He made Spaghetti Westerns for the American market under the name of Gary Firth, and Italian movies as Mario Celestino, which, unusually for Italian film actors, was his real name. Born in 1922, he was two years older than me. Much of his history I already knew: his soccer career, going to Switzerland at the outbreak of war, then returning once Mussolini had been deposed to fight the Nazis. He was a war hero: six commendations and a medal from the king. Never married but linked to an endless succession of pretty young hopefuls from Cinecittà, whose stars shone brightly, but briefly, in the cinema firmament. He liked fast cars—who didn't?—and had a villa on the Amalfi coast but lived in what looked, according to the magazine photos, like a magnificent apartment on the Fondamenta delle Zattere in Venice, not far from our own. There were loads of photos of him in his swimsuit and not a few poignant ones of him with his arm around his fraternal twin brother, Emilio, who had remained in Italy while Mario was in Switzerland and who'd been killed in a street brawl one night during the war.

Again, reading between the lines, I couldn't help thinking that perhaps the handsome, still-unmarried film star might be one of us. One day I rather hoped that we'd have a larger presence on the world stage, and not suffer persecution if our sexual preferences were discovered.

I checked my watch. Five o'clock. I had two hours before I had to pick up Kendall at Chiusi and I'd done nothing about dinner. I had too many ducks. Two males, both about eight weeks old, were already causing trouble with the alpha drake. If I got a move on, both could be slow-cooked in the oven of the kitchen stove: duck and cherries; the thought made my mouth water. I'd get some bread rolls made, ready to throw into the outdoor bread oven along with some vegetables to roast. We'd eat outside, by lamplight, a perfect welcome on a perfect Tuscan evening to greet our Australian house guest.

★★★★★

I smiled when he alighted the train. He was dressed casually, wearing pale fawn slacks, a white polo shirt, aviator sunglasses and a large tan bag under one arm on a strap slung over his shoulder. He looked, as Giancarlo would say, like a million dollars.

I'd arrived about five minutes before the train, which, wonder of all wonders, had pulled into the station right on time.

"Hello!" he said, giving me a quick hug.

"How was the trip?"

"Very comfortable. The concierge at the hotel packed me a very decent food pack to keep me going, but I didn't eat much of it because I guessed you've planned something for dinner. I'll go down to the baggage van and grab my suitcase. Where did you park the Land Rover?"

"I didn't bring it, sorry."

"Then the famous La Mensola Jeep?"

"Nope—this beauty over near the fence," I said, pointing at my Maserati. Showing off? Who, me?

He whistled softly. "That's not in any of your books, Damson. Is it new?"

"No, it's about four years old. *Living with Monsters* paid for it, and then some."

It was a beautiful evening and I drove slowly; the way the wind whipped around the windscreen sometimes made it very hard to hear what the other person in the front seat was saying. He took off his sunglasses and slid them into his trouser pocket, then ran a hand over the back of the tan leather bench seat, rubbing the back of my neck.

"Pull over for a sec, I need to piss."

We were not far from Montallese and there was a narrow lane ahead on our left. I knew it well. Lined with wild hazelnuts and almonds, it was a favourite October gathering spot. He jumped out of the car and stood, sighing the way men did when they had a full bladder and the stream began to flow.

"Better?" I asked when he returned to the car.

"Almost."

"Almost—?"

He smothered my question with a deep kiss, exploring my mouth with his tongue while one hand slid behind my neck, drawing me closer into him, and the other fumbled with the buttons of my shorts.

"Now I feel better," he whispered, his hand having found my cock. "You're hard," he said, looking right into my eyes, as if he was searching for something.

"I was hard the moment I saw you get off the train," I said.

We arrived at La Mensola a little late, the taste of his semen in my mouth and a grin on his as he shook hands with Alfonso, whom he addressed as Father Ignazio. We brought him up to speed, although not mentioning the reason behind my friend's *exclaustratio*.

"This is amazing, Damson," he said, standing in the bedroom we'd decided he should have, his hands in his pockets, doing a slow turn as he inspected the room. "And this is where the Nazi was hanged?"

"Yup, right above your bed. I hope you don't have nightmares?"

"Pht! If I do, I'll be in your bed before you know it."

"I hope you won't need an excuse?"

"As long as I know that Giancarlo doesn't mind. We aren't on the *Neptunia* now, Damson. This is your house, the place where you both live."

I chuckled. "We shared this house and our lives for two years with my army mate, Danny. He was in our bed more often than his own. Just play it by ear. Giancarlo is fit to be tied that he can't be here tonight, but he will arrive late tomorrow night. Are you sure you're ready to have sex with both of us at the same time?"

Kendall sat on the bed and patted the mattress next to him, so I sat down too.

"You're the only person I want to stick their dick up my arse, Damson. I've decided that. I'm inexperienced really—except for what we've been doing and my few encounters while I was in the army—and I'm doubtful there's anything left that you and I haven't tried, but I was very turned on in that hotel room in Sydney. If I've got your big cock in my hand or in my mouth, I'm happy to do anything, but I'm afraid my bunghole's off-limits to anyone else but you … and perhaps Giancarlo … I'm not sure yet; we'll see about that when we get to it."

"You seem to like it when I fuck you," I said.

"Like it? I fucking love it, you dingbat; something I never imagined possible. But, despite appearances to the contrary, the idea of getting fucked by other men feels too much like going down the homo route— if you don't find that term offensive. You know what a thing I have for mature ladies, and one day I plan to marry one. Agreed, I love cock, especially big ones, but yours is the only one that's ever been inside me. I'd rather like to keep it that way. However, I'm not insensitive. I know that Giancarlo wouldn't understand if I let you stick it in me, but not him … he'd be puzzled at the least, if not annoyed."

"You're right; he wouldn't understand," I said, wondering how I'd feel if the shoe was on the other foot.

I knew he was very much into older women and that he'd played around in the army. He was greedy in bed and had told me that the best sex he'd ever had was with me. I didn't know whether to be flattered or not, especially seeing as he'd had relatively so few partners. One night during the sea voyage, half-sozzled, in a moment of complete frankness, he'd confessed that he wasn't particularly interested in the sex he had with the women he slept with; he got off on their looks, their age and his ability to bring them to orgasm, something he didn't always want for himself when he made love to them.

I didn't really understand it; I'd had no experience with women. However, I'd been around long enough to realise that everyone was different and that no two men had the same tastes in partners or in what they did in bed. What I really didn't understand—and that was a conversation for another day—was how he would come to terms with his desire for cock when he eventually married one of his "mature ladies".

"What was that thought?" he asked.

I patted his knee, then rubbed the top of his thigh. "Giancarlo loves to get fucked, Kendall. These days, it's his preferred option and I don't mind because I love him and I'll do anything that gives him pleasure. I wouldn't worry too much. Just wait and see how the moment seizes you. He's a very generous lover and very in tune with what his partner needs."

"Perhaps you shouldn't put it in me while all three of us are in bed together?"

"So you *are* thinking of doing more than sitting back and watching."

He grinned broadly. "Perhaps."

"Just let it happen as it happens. Anyway, just think how nice it would be for you to have your dick in him while I'm buried up to my nuts in you."

"You dirty bugger," he said with a chuckle.

"Let's not make something out of a situation that might not occur. You might just change your mind once your juices start flowing."

"My juices start flowing? Such a wordsmith, O'Reilly."

"That's what they pay me for. Now, let's go down and eat. I'm starving, and poor Alfonso will be wondering where we are."

★★★★★

Dinner was delicious, even though I say so myself: the duck cooked to perfection, smothered in cherry sauce, accompanied by roasted vegetables and a dressed green salad. The sauce was Madame Tremeau's recipe. I'd worked as her gardener/handyman for eighteen months in Vence, in the south of France, before coming to Italy. She'd had a profusion of cherry trees of all sorts and a multitude of recipes for the fruit, among which was my almost most-favourite dessert: *clafoutis*, a baked cherry tart, Occitan in origin and absolutely delicious.

Tonight, however, with such an abundance of fruit on my trees, I'd prepared a fruit salad with apricots, nectarines, white peaches, plums and strawberries, all picked this afternoon and left to chill in the refrigerator. There was cream to go with it, courtesy of the dairy cow that Stefano kept at the guest house. Our foreign guests liked milk in their tea or cream in their coffee and butter on almost everything.

To use a hackneyed phrase, Alfonso and Kendall got on like a proverbial house on fire, despite my having to translate between them. Kendall shared the news that his meetings in Paris, Munich and Milan were to do with his father's publishing business. Several of his stable of authors were to be translated into French, Italian, Spanish and German and that included a proposal for *Living with Ghosts*, *The Road to Montepulciano* and *Living with Monsters*. He was due to telephone my London publisher at some point in the near future to work out a deal. I was gobsmacked at the news, especially when he informed me that his father had already come to an arrangement by telephone with the Americans that guaranteed I'd receive an advance of one thousand dollars for my next two planned books—*Living with the Enemy*, which I'd just started writing, and the children's book with Stefano. One thousand American dollars for each was a great deal of money; it made me think that they believed both would sell very well, even without having seen a word that I'd written or an illustration that I'd prepared.

We talked late into the evening, finishing off a second bottle of wine, before Alfonso begged off and went to bed. Kendall and I did the dishes and tidied up. We barely got to my bedroom door before he was pulling my clothes off. It was over far too quickly for my liking, but as soon as he rolled off me and pulled me into his arms, he whispered, kissing my ear, saying, "Let me catch my breath and let's do that again."

He slid his cock into me and pounded the bejesus out of me, his mouth glued to mine. I ejaculated at the same time as he did, but without touching myself. It was something that had only happened a few times in my life: twice with Randy, whose penis was so huge that I used to joke that my prostate had given up the fight and surrendered to the assault, then a handful of times with Giancarlo, whose cock, although not nearly the size of Randy's, always continually hit that sweet spot inside me.

I'd always preferred being the active partner; I just loved the feeling of the soft warmth inside a man and the tightness of his sphincter as it clutched the base of my dick. However, I had absolutely no problems when it came to being fucked. I didn't think that being the passive partner in a sexual encounter somehow made me less of a man—I didn't equate it with playing a "female" role. In fact, this time, just a moment ago, when Kendall had ejaculated inside me, my own orgasm at the same time— although I knew it was coming—had surprised me with its ferocity.

"Can I fuck you this time?" I whispered back.

He shook his head. "If you've got another sweet load in your nuts, Damson, I want it down the back of my throat while I'm pumping mine down yours."

"Cigarette first?"

"Sure."

I lit one for each of us, then lay in his arms while we smoked and chatted. Damn, this man! He got inside me—literally and figuratively— in a very special way. I guess I was in lust with him … and, if I was to be honest, a little in love with him. Giancarlo knew; we'd talked about it. He'd felt the same about Danny when he lived with us. He'd become besotted with my former army captain, the married man I'd had sex with while we'd been stationed in Japan during the Allied occupation. I hadn't minded, because I really cared for Danny too in my own way. Giancarlo had been devastated when Danny had moved to Rome with Alejandro, a Spaniard he'd met and fallen for.

Giancarlo and I had remained deeply in love during the period Danny had lived with us, and I assumed the same thing would continue for however long Kendall was around. Honestly and complete openness was what had made our relationship work, especially because we both slept with other men outside the relationship from time to time. We'd work it out, I was sure of it.

"Ready?" Kendall said, stubbing his cigarette out, then pushing me onto my back.

He turned around, straddled my chest, then leaned forward and swallowed my cock. I rubbed my hands over his buttocks, my eyes closed, enjoying the sensation of the softness of his mouth and the movement of his tongue over the shaft of my cock. He was very good at sucking dick; not all men were nearly as skilled as he was, despite his relative inexperience.

"Kendall?" I said softly, my nose pressed against his perineum. He mumbled a noise that was meant to be "yes?" while continuing to massage my dick with his mouth. "Please fuck me again."

He stopped what he was doing then swivelled to kiss me. "Greedy, O'Reilly, that's what you are. Nope, tonight you're going to do what I want you to do, and, like it or not, what I want is for you to squirt into my mouth at the same time as I unload into yours."

I laughed softly. "All right, boss, but in the morning you're mine."

"Deal," he said, returning to his former position. "Just make sure you get your timing right, okay?" he added over his shoulder before taking me in his mouth again.

I was usually very good at timing my orgasms to coincide with those of my partners—men I knew and had slept with more than once. Giancarlo's came in waves, preceded by grinding his teeth, muttering low in his throat then a gradual clenching of the muscles in his thighs. His actual ejaculation was silent, usually followed by a few quiet shudders as his muscle tension released. I could time myself to meet him at the exact same moment.

Kendall, however, was very different. When we masturbated together or fucked face to face, he stared into my eyes with increasing concentration as he neared his orgasm, licking his lips more and more frequently, then began to encourage both himself and me with very dirty talk, egging us both on to spurt at the same time. "Come on, you bastard! Give it to me!" was one of his most frequent urgings a few moments before he let go. It often gave me time to get myself into position with my mouth a few inches from his knob, ready to swallow his load.

As said knob was dangling a few inches from my mouth right this very minute, I ran my hands around the small of his back, grabbed his arse cheeks and pulled him down roughly, swallowing his cock right down to the root.

Damn, I loved having sex with him.

CHAPTER 5

The following morning, I woke with a start, opening my eyes to find Kendall standing at my bedroom window looking out over the garden, the early morning sun flooding over his body.

"Breathtaking," he said, then turned to me. "You're awake?"

I mumbled something in reply. It was unlike me to sleep through our rooster's dawn reveille. For some reason, it had taken me ages to fall asleep.

"No wonder you love living here. Do you ever get tired of it?"

"No," I said, beckoning him back to bed. He slid under the sheet next to me and ran one hand over my chest, pulling the hair between his fingers. "Do you remember the day I left you during the tour and went to visit the monastery I grew up in?"

"Yes, you came back quite sad, if I remember, although you didn't talk about it."

"Sad? Yes, I suppose I was. I was prepared for all the wonderful moments to come flooding back, to have the countryside inspire me again as it did when I was a kid. But I realised that I'd built up a fantasy ideal about my life there, most likely to combat the austerity and strictness of life at the time. Sure, they were all very happy to see me—

especially Father Justin and Bert, or 'Banana Dick' as I've told you I called him—but I realised I'd moved on. For some odd reason, I always imagined that the greatest thrill of my life would be returning to the place and the people I grew up with, a successful author and having found my place in life …"

"But obviously the reality was something altogether different."

"Yes. They were excited, genuinely, but I'm a different creature than I was when I walked out the monastery gates and got on the bus to go to town to put on the khaki."

"I think we all went through that same sense of reality shift when we came home."

"You never talk about your time in Korea."

"I've told you about the good bits. One day … perhaps."

"According to you, the good bits were mostly about encounters with fellow officers in the showers late at night," I said with a chuckle, kissing his cheek.

"You left out so much in *Living with Ghosts*, Damson. Reading between the lines made me realise your war was so much more than what was in those three hundred pages."

"True. Some day I'll show you the three hundred extra pages that didn't make it into the final version. Most of what was not printed was about me facing what I went through; it was never meant to be read by anyone else. At the time, I thought of it as something like trying to write away the demons."

"You didn't answer my question?"

"About the war?"

"No, about ever being tired of the view and your life here."

"How could I, Kendall? I love this house, I love my life, I love the community around me, and I love Giancarlo. Besides, my friends are all here. Father Justin and Bert are together now, did I tell you that? No, how could I have? I didn't talk to you about my visit. I'm glad they found each other."

"You're talking about the monastery back in Australia? Do you ever speak at length without jumping thoughts, Damson?"

I laughed. "My brain moves more quickly than my tongue."

"Room for one more?" Alfonso asked from the bedroom door. I must have left it open last night when I got up to have a pee.

"In you get," I said, pulling back the sheet. He wiggled his way between us, yawning before he settled against my chest, Kendall's arms around him.

We chatted and laughed for about half an hour before I decided that I needed to start my daily chores: let out the chooks, the ducks and the geese to forage in the orchard; light the stove; turn on the pumps to fill up the storage tanks from the spring. Hot water was instantaneous, generated by an electro-coil the moment anyone turned on the hot water tap. Years ago, when I had visitors, there'd be no end of heating up water on the stove and washing standing up in a large tin tub that was now relegated to storage in the shed.

As it was Friday, I took Kendall to the market at Montepulciano. Alfonso tagged along. We spent far too much time at the smallgoods stall, Kendall wanting to try a sample of every cheese and salami, marvelling at simple things like *mortadella* and *prosciutto crudo*, which he'd never seen or tasted before. I bought stuffed olives, several cheeses, a very nice *cosciotto di agnello* for dinner—Giancarlo loved the way I cooked a leg of lamb in the bread oven on the terrace, pricked with garlic and rosemary and basted frequently with olive oil—and some mascarpone to go with dessert; and then, at my favourite hardware stall, I picked up some drill bits that I'd ordered over the telephone when I'd first arrived home.

"Where's Alfonso?" I asked.

"Over there, talking to that man in the overalls."

It was someone I'd never seen before—nothing really unusual, we often had visitors from other small towns around the area on market days—but there was something about the hesitant way in which they appeared to be speaking that made me wonder whether the man might be his French friend, Gaspard. He wasn't what one would call handsome, but was very masculine in appearance, the attraction immediately apparent when he smiled at something Alfonso was miming. The smile lit up his face, revealing twin dimples; I could see them from even where we stood, some five metres away. I wondered whether I should wander over and introduce myself, but when Alfonso turned to see where we were, he shook his companion's hand then joined us. The man nodded to me and I touched my temple with one finger; a lazy type of salute that was common around here.

"You should have introduced us," I said. Alfonso coloured, then excused himself, saying he'd meet us in the Piazza Grande in half an hour for coffee.

Of course, I had to explain everything to Kendall, who'd not understood a word of our conversation in Italian and confessed that his five weeks aboard the *Neptunia* had been wasted as far as learning the language went.

"How long did it take you?" he asked.

"About four or five months to be able to string more than simple sentences together, then years after that, before I started to feel like I could talk about nearly anything. It wasn't so much the language but the culture that I embarrassed myself over."

"In what way?"

I put our shopping in the back of the Jeep; I wanted to show him San Biagio, the Sangallo the Elder church at the foot of the town, before we headed up to the Piazza Grande.

"Stupid things, like thinking Montepulciano d'Abruzzo was a local wine, when in fact the wine of Montepulciano, the *Vino Nobile*, is very famous. I once complimented the mayor of this town on his famous wine while drinking an imposter."

He laughed. "Hardly a transgression."

"But embarrassing. I also omitted to call the local *carabinieri* by their correct titles; they're a military-style organisation with the same ranks you and I had in the army. None of them was offended; it just shows how much leeway I was afforded when I first came here."

"Ah, you were probably so charming no one could be offended."

"Nevertheless, fitting in took longer than learning the language."

*****

I shouldn't have worried about Kendall and Giancarlo. After dinner that night, everything flowed naturally, Kendall at first sitting at the end of the bed watching, then with Giancarlo's encouragement, sliding up the bed to join us.

A few days later, on Sunday, I got up early as usual and left them in bed, wandering over the field to talk to Stefano. I knew that while I was out they'd get a chance to start to get to know each other without me being around, something that hadn't happened while we were in Australia.

Alfonso took Kendall on drives around the countryside to see some of the local towns and villages while I cracked on with my own work: writing, painting and researching on behalf of Giancarlo. I gave Kendall my Michelin guide in English so that he could at least read about the places he visited and what he was seeing.

I still, of course, had a heap of mail to plough through, so on Monday afternoon I sat down to tackle it. Halfway through the pile of letters, I swore. It was an invitation to do a book reading and to sign copies of *Living with Monsters* at the Cipriani hotel in Venice this coming Thursday. I quickly leafed through my at-home diary of engagements and saw that Giancarlo had entered it. It was so typical of him to forget to remind me, but then again, I usually checked the diary every day—I was obsessive about it—so I couldn't really blame him. I'd been so caught up since I got home that I'd merely glanced at last week's agenda and hadn't turned the page.

I phoned the hotel, thinking at first that I'd see if I could cancel it, but the hotel manager told me that not only had they booked one of the premier suites for me to stay in on the evening of the book reading, but they'd had over a hundred acceptances from the nearly two hundred invitations they'd sent out last Friday, and were expecting more to arrive today and tomorrow. How many guests would I be bringing? I knew Giancarlo would be in court, so he couldn't be there, but, as Kendall had just arrived and hadn't seen more of Italy than from the train window on his journey from Milan, I told the manager that we'd be two for dinner after the reception.

Damn! I phoned Giancarlo, who was at the office. Cosmo's wife answered the phone; I could hear Giancarlo and Cosmo arguing in the background—nothing unusual for Italians. Eventually, when he did come to the phone, my lover was contrite, apologetic, affirming what I knew he'd say: that I was obsessed with my diary and he thought that I'd already checked it. However, seeing as I was going to Venice, he asked if I could deliver some documents to Mario Celestino—important documents that needed signing and which couldn't be risked in the unreliable Italian postal system. I was about to remind him that he'd told me that Celestino was filming in Ostia when he informed me that the movie star had finished shooting the majority of his scenes and wouldn't be required for another week or more, depending on the weather, so he'd gone home to Venice to relax.

*****

Two days later, I was just reversing the Land Rover out of the driveway when I nearly ran over someone who wasn't looking where he was going.

"James? What the hell are you doing here?"

"I thought I'd come to visit for a while. You gave me an open invitation, remember?"

"How did you get here?"

"Trains and buses. Quite easy really. Oh—I see suitcases … where are you off to?"

"Venice," I said. "Book reading, I'm afraid. You're welcome to stay here. You haven't met Alfonso; he's in the garden. Tell him to put you up in the small upstairs bedroom. We'll be back by Friday. This is my friend Kendall, by the way, from Australia."

They shook hands.

"Can't I come with you?" James asked.

"Do you have a tuxedo?"

"In Florence. Surely you could stop on the way."

"We're not driving, we're going by train. I'm leaving the Land Rover at the station at Chiusi."

He threw his suitcase in the back next to ours and got into the car anyway, despite my protestations.

"I know you have an apartment in Venice; I've heard all about it. I'll rent a tux when we get there."

"With what? I know you haven't got any money."

"Well, 'any' is all a matter of perspective, wouldn't you say?"

I rang the Cipriani from the station at Chiusi, telling them I was bringing another guest to dinner and asking whether they could recommend somewhere he might hire a tuxedo. The manager calmly told me there'd be no problem; so many American visitors in recent years had neglected to bring appropriate dress for dinner that they'd made an arrangement with La Fenice, the Venice opera house, which had stores of evening wear in all sizes, tuxedos and tails suits as well, a great deal of it of very good quality, suitable for any Transatlantic gentleman who'd arrived without a complete wardrobe.

We had a thirty-minute delay in Florence. It was normally a direct service through to Venice with no stops—I'd caught this train myself several times. However, today for some inexplicable reason, they were upgrading five kilometres of the electric overhead lines this side of Bologna. The delay was caused by swapping the electric engine for a diesel engine. Nothing was simple in Italy; I heard a whole lot of shouting coming from the platform at the front of the train, but eventually we pulled out of Santa Maria Novella and headed north.

It was during this first leg of our journey that I discovered the version of James that Giancarlo had told me about on the night he'd taken him to dinner. He was extremely bright—I already knew that—and well read. It obviously hadn't only been Ovid and Virgil that he'd buried his head in while at university. I wished for the old days, when the train had compartments that seated six to eight people on seats facing each other with a sliding door that closed it off from the carriage corridor. These days, it was an open carriage plan, and although our first-class seats were very comfortable, there was, alas, no dining car until after we left Bologna, so we spent the time chatting in English, raising a few curious glances from those sitting across the aisle from us. I spoke to them in Italian and apologised, explaining that I was showing their beautiful country to visitors from overseas. There still existed a little mistrust of English-speakers in some parts of Italy and among people who hadn't fared well under the American occupation. Some soldiers had treated the locals like servants, promising much but delivering little. I'd heard many stories about good food that hadn't been consumed in servicemen's messes being buried in holes in the ground, and further stories of starving Italians digging up the food with their bare hands and gobbling it down, dirt and all, as they crouched on their haunches with buckets and baskets at their sides. Of course, it hadn't happened everywhere, or frequently, but there'd been enough unconnected people telling me the same story over the years that I sensed some truth in it. It was a subject I wanted to research further for my next book.

Until you got to know him, Kendall was a quiet man, not unlike me, believe it or not. I rarely sensed the larrikin within him except in private. It was in our Australian genes to be irreverent at times and say things that people from other cultures found inappropriate. I'd been too war-weary to find that person inside myself when I'd left Japan, gone to France and then on to Italy. I wasn't serious—I smiled a lot—but most of the time kept a lid on my native cheekiness.

However, there was something very contained about Kendall, as if he was keeping some great secret about life inside while quietly observing the rest of the human race. I found it immensely appealing, a real contrast to Giancarlo, who like all Italians, mostly wore his heart on his sleeve and could be both shut off and then volatile almost within the same sentence … though I loved that too.

We moved to the dining car shortly after the engines had been changed in Bologna. The line had been electrified from Florence to Venice in the mid-1950s. I remembered my first trip without a steam engine, revelling in having the carriage window open without the risk of smuts in my eyes and the sometimes thick, acrid and choking smoke filling the compartment when we went through a tunnel before I could close the window.

Before too long, we were passing through Mestre. I nudged Kendall and told him to put down his book and look out the window, because I knew what an impact it had had on me the first time I'd experienced the slowly approaching views of Venice as the train made its way along the railway causeway. I moved out of the way for James; he sat where I had been next to Kendall. He said it was his first time here too.

I hired a *motoscafo* to take us to the canal entrance to the *calle* that led to our apartment, then had to explain the different names for water transport in Venice to my friends. The *motoscafo*, or speedboat, was somewhat like a taxi; the *vaporetto* a public ferry, Venice's equivalent of a bus; then the *traghetto*, a gondola ride that crossed the Grand Canal, passengers either sitting or standing up in the narrow vessel as the *gondoliere* navigated from one side to the other.

"Oh, wow!" James said once I'd opened our apartment door. The first impression had taken my breath away too. It was a cavernous space, marble-floored, with frescoed walls that ran across the length of the building. It had originally been a reception room for a noble family, the ancestors of Giancarlo's mother, but these days, impossible to heat in the winter, it remained empty. Had the artist who'd painted the frescoes been someone of note, we would have had art historians banging on the door, but they were pedestrian, probably painted by some group of artists back in the sixteenth century who specialised in what Giancarlo called "cheap and cheerful".

"Is this tiny space the only place you have to cook?" Kendall asked me after I'd shown them around. Most of the rooms had been closed up for decades. We spent so little time there that only two bedrooms, a study, a large sitting room that opened to a balcony over the Grand Canal, a bathroom and a minuscule kitchenette were in use.

"We eat out. It's far less fuss and there are local places with excellent food everywhere. I'll take you to a *bacaro* tonight if you wish; we can drink excellent wine and eat *cicchetti* all night; you'll love it."

I then had to explain that a *bacaro* was a bar/restaurant where patrons usually sat at the bar and ate a selection of small plates of Venetian specialities—*cicchetti*—that kept coming until you'd had your fill. I took every opportunity I could to eat at *bacari* because, like most things to do with Venice, Giancarlo didn't particularly like them, mostly because they could be small, smoke-filled and very noisy. However, he knew how much I loved the lively atmosphere and great food, so I dragged him along as often as I could every time we stayed there.

*****

Right on nine o'clock the next morning, the man arrived from the Cipriani to take James to the costume storage of the opera house. Kendall said he'd like to go too, so we arranged to meet in St Mark's

Square at noon and I'd take them on a short *vaporetto* ride to the Arsenale to eat at a wonderful local restaurant I knew. Before that, I had an appointment to visit Mario Celestino, to give him the papers that needed to be signed, and to talk to him about finding a bodyguard, something that Giancarlo hadn't been able to convince him to do.

I walked to his apartment; it was a beautiful day and, although the end of July, there were very few tourists. I knew that would change. Air travel was still fairly expensive and only wealthy Americans—the majority of tourists in Europe these days—could afford eight or nine days at sea crossing the Atlantic to Naples or Genoa. Britain and France were far more popular destinations; the majority of American men who had served there during the war wanted to bring their wives to see the places where they'd fought. I found the idea disturbing; the last thing in my life I'd want to do was to visit the places I'd been at war, like Bougainville or Borneo … and if I never even saw a map of New Guinea again I wouldn't be unhappy.

Mario looked quite different from the way he did in the movies; although still strikingly handsome, he appeared craggier somehow, less polished. I put it down to being used to seeing him on the screen, where movie lighting and make-up would obviously make a huge difference. His apartment was very similar to ours, except that it didn't look out over the Grand Canal but over the Rio di San Maurizio, one of the canals that led off it. He wore espadrilles, shorts and an athletic singlet, over which an unbuttoned pale green shirt. He was far more muscular than I'd imagined, and had lost weight since the days of his swimsuit movies.

"I'm sorry," he said. "Perhaps I should have worn a jacket and tie, like you."

"Don't apologise. Whenever I do anything for Giancarlo that has to do with business I always make an effort, otherwise I'd be dressed just like you." He showed me into his living area, a very nicely appointed room with large, comfortable-looking sofas and low furniture. "I'll get you a drink. Beer?"

I checked my watch—it was only ten o'clock—but I shrugged and said yes, loosening my tie a little. It was very warm inside, unlike our mausoleum of a flat with its ridiculously high ceilings and marble everywhere, which was cool, bordering on cold, even at the height of summer.

The document signing was very quickly done and he invited me to stay and chat for a while. I knew from experience how irksome it was when people began to rabbit on about my books, so I purposely avoided talking about his films, even though when he showed me his office, I saw photos of him with his co-stars hung on the walls.

I stopped at a framed poster of *Nights of Terror*, the movie that had stoked my fantasies after a night-time screening under the stars on a beach at Salamaua on my way to the now-famous Battle of Wau, where so many Australian officers and men had lost their lives.

"I loved this movie," I said. The poster featured him in his bathing trunks, a knife in one hand and the other arm around a girl. "You've no idea what a difference it made during a terrible time for me."

"When did you see it?"

"During the war, a few nights before far too many of my friends paid with their lives fighting the Japanese."

"Oh …"

"I'm sorry. I don't usually mention my time in the war. It's just that this poster brought back memories."

"Not bad ones, I hope."

"Not at all, quite the contrary," I said.

"I'm coming tonight," he said, standing next to me, running his hand over the poster.

"I'm sorry … coming where?"

"To the Cipriani, of course. Don't worry, it will be a low-key visit, I don't want to steal your thunder." His English, which we'd been using since I arrived, was very idiomatic although heavily accented. "I have all your books. Yes, even the cookbook, although I freely admit I can't boil water. Would it be an imposition if I asked you to sign them for me?"

I blushed very heavily, something that made him laugh. I decided to switch to Italian. "I will, of course, but you must return the favour. I have your biography at home. If I post it to you, I'd like you to sign it for me."

"Ah, Mr O'Reilly, Signor Manetti omitted to tell me how fluent your Italian was."

"Ten years of speaking it has certainly helped," I said.

He led me into the kitchen, a spacious room with a magnificent double stove and ovens, workbenches, everything stainless steel, gleaming and up to date.

"This is impressive," I said.

"A friend of mine used to cook for me," he said a little wistfully.

"Used to?" I was prying, I knew, but the way he looked at me made me realise he'd wanted me to ask.

"My stunt man, Stewart. He was an American, did my body doubles on all the movies I made after the war. He was a GI. We met in Rome in 1944 and became friends, then he returned after the war. He'd been a circus acrobat before 1941; it was me who talked him into becoming involved with the movies."

"Is he still …"

"No. Broke his neck in a stupid accident while we were on holiday in Sicily two years ago."

I saw the shadow cross his face and knew that my suspicions had been correct. Stewart had been his lover. I was so used to the openness I enjoyed between my friends, all of whom knew which side of the sheet I lay on, so took a slow breath before speaking.

"You must know that Giancarlo and I are … together."

"I didn't, but thank you for telling me."

"If you want to talk about your friend, please understand that I'm someone who understands loss. All of us who lived through the war are only too familiar with it."

"Did you lose someone special?"

"They were all special," I said. "But no one I was in love with."

I had lost someone very close to me whom I'd had feelings for: Renzo. But not on the same scale as Mario and Stewart. Lorenzo and I hadn't spent fourteen years together sharing our lives. Mario revealed that he'd never spoken to anyone about his relationship and how the death of Stewart had affected him. He was completely alienated from his family, his father never having forgiven him for going to Switzerland and not fighting for Mussolini. He had brothers and sisters, but they were all so cowed by their bully of a father that they'd never reached out to him.

I invited him to come to stay with us in Florence some time. I explained that we had a close coterie of queer friends who knew how to hold their tongues and he could perhaps experience the freedom of what it felt like to be in the company of non-judgemental, intelligent and accepting men who'd lived the same life as him and me. However, he seemed very reluctant; his studio would fire him if the merest hint of scandal ever came out and he'd never work again.

"Perhaps someone else will come along," I said. "You're still very young, Mario."

He smiled and patted my hand. "I can trust you, Damson?"

I pulled the chain out from around my neck and kissed the crucifix.

"You're religious?"

I nodded. "But my religion doesn't bind me in iron chains."

"There are two men in my life at the moment. One is a policeman here in Venice, the other a carpenter in Rome. I'm not looking for another relationship; I pay them both."

"Why do you need to pay?"

He shrugged. "The transaction makes it feel like less of a sin."

"Did it feel sinful when you made love with Stewart?"

"Occasionally … but no, not really."

"Then the only difference is something you've created in your mind. Sex is sex; everyone does it. Every member of the human race is the result of sexual intercourse. The priests just want to make you feel guilty because they're not supposed to have it themselves."

"Everyone says that."

"But not everyone says it from first-hand experience."

He sat back on the sofa, staring at me for a moment.

"I promise I'll share more about my own experiences," I said, "but not right now. I have to meet my friends at the Piazza San Marco; I'm taking them to Domino's at the Arsenale for lunch."

"Domino's? I love that place. Can I come too?"

"Of course. Do you have to put on a blond wig and wear dark glasses?" I asked.

He laughed. "No, not there. Venetians are very respectful of my privacy."

"Well, then, seeing as we've talked for ages, let's go down to the Zattere and see if we can't grab a *motoscafo*."

"Thank you, Damson. I really mean it. Thank you for listening."

"One moment," I said, then retrieved my document case, in which I always kept a sketch pad, pencils and a few charcoals. I made a quick sketch of him, then shook his hand as I gave it to him, crossing my heart, the way Australian kids did when we promised to keep a secret. "What I heard from you this morning will remain in here, Mario," I added, tapping my chest.

His eyes welled up briefly, and he thanked me effusively for the sketch.

"Wait—before we leave," he said, having found his hat and a light, cotton jacket. "You haven't signed my copies of your books."

"I hadn't forgotten. I thought it would be an opportunity for you to invite me back here again."

He hugged me quickly. I'd be lying if I said I wasn't tempted to turn my head and try to steal a quick kiss. He was still one of my favourite wartime pin-up boys and he oozed masculinity. *Che gran schiantò!*, as my friend Renzo used to say about handsome men. Mario Celestino was a knockout, for sure.

★★★★★

The hotel manager rearranged the seating for the dinner that would follow my book reading and customary signing of books so that Mario could sit with us. James, of course, being only twenty-three and a university swot who probably never went to the pictures, had never heard of him, but said discreetly to me in Latin while Kendall was shaking Mario's hand that he'd "give him one on the house". *Pro bono* wasn't quite the same as the English translation, but I had to stop myself from nudging him and scowling, forgetting that we were probably the only two within hearing distance that actually spoke a dead language.

I left Mario and James, Kendall accompanying me as the representative of the American and Southeast Asian publishers of my book, to join the Venetian distributor, a rather faded Italian man from a noble family who ran an English bookstore just off the Sotoportego e Calle del

Cappello Nero, as near to St Mark's Square as you could get without actually being in it. I had half an hour to sign over one hundred and fifty copies, two-thirds of them with requests for dedications.

Kendall was an old hand at this, having travelled with me all over Australia, so we set up at a large table, making sure first of all that our fountain pens were filled with the same coloured ink. He printed the dedication in block letters, passing the book to me, which I signed, then I grabbed another book and began on its dedication, which took far longer than my practised "official" signature. We'd worked out a production line months ago, and although we were running late by the time we finished, every copy had been signed and or dedicated.

Shortly before the time for me to do the book reading, Mario found us and apologised, saying he was going home.

"Why? Is there a problem?"

"Yes, Scavola has turned up."

I spoke to him in Italian, not wishing to involve either Kendall or James, who'd followed him to the room in which I'd been signing the books.

"You shouldn't let him intimidate you, Mario. Many people might know about your court case and the fact that he's suing you, but you shouldn't show any sign of guilt, which would happen if you left. People will notice. Ignore him. Enjoy the book reading, have dinner with us, then go home as if nothing had happened. There's no reason for your paths to cross."

He looked doubtful, but then, after a moment, slapped me on the shoulder with a bright grin. "I suppose you're right," he said. "I'll see you after your moment in the spotlight."

"*Fellatisne eum?*" James asked quietly.

"No, I'm not sucking his dick, and not every friendship between men is about sex," I replied in Latin.

Of course, Kendall was far too polite to ask what I'd been saying to Mario and then my very short conversation with James, who was giving me a far too knowing and rather suspicious look. It was obvious he didn't believe me; he could be exasperating at times.

The reading was held outside on the terrace next to the swimming pool. A rostrum had been set up with a microphone. When I was asked to do a reading, I nearly always used the same passage from chapter four of *Living with Monsters*. It was the section in which I'd been led to a charcoal burner's hut in the dead of night, discovered one of the would-be victims being tortured, then chased one of the killers through the trees on a moonless night, finally being knocked out by his offsider then found bound and gagged the following morning.

I still relived the moments when I was reading the twenty-minute-long excerpt, even ten years after the event.

> *"He's here! He's here!" someone above me called out, then whistled loudly.*
>
> *I heard scrabbling above me, then a pair of boots landed near my face and the rifle was withdrawn from under me.*
>
> *"Damson!" Fabrizio yelled, desperately trying to pull the gag from my mouth …*

There was loud clapping when I finished reading the last words of the chapter and closed the book. I guessed from the many people who stood to applaud that there were a lot of Americans in the audience.

I always invited questions, and during the years that I'd been reading from this story they were nearly all the same. Yes, everything in the book was factual. No, I hadn't used the real names of all of the people in the story—many had asked for their identities to be concealed. Was La Mensola a real house and was it now a museum of some sort? That question came up time after time and it always puzzled me; perhaps it was the story of the family that had been massacred in my stable and the shrine I later built there, dedicated to the local victims of Nazi occupation, that made people think that.

"I believe you're still very close friends with former Inspector Manetti?"

The question came in accented English, and, before I had time to gather myself, I realised that it had been asked by Giovanni Scavola. He was sitting in an aisle seat in the second row—the chairs had been laid out as if it were an auditorium. I could see the calculating smile that accompanied his question. Immediately I wondered if he was trying to disclose the nature of my relationship with Giancarlo and humiliate and discredit him—homosexuality had been legal in Italy since 1890, but these days, especially among Catholics and those who held extreme right-wing ideals, queer people were considered somehow inferior and lesser human beings. It would only take a judge who had the same views to put his thumb on the scales of justice. I needed to be circumspect.

"Yes, I am. During the course of the investigation we became friends, and after his retirement from the police force we became business partners in a few real estate ventures." I replied. But before I could ask for more questions, he quickly asked another.

"Did Avvocato Manetti live with you at La Mensola during the investigation?"

"Avvocato Manetti rented a house at Bivio San Biagio, seven kilometres from La Mensola. Anyone else have something to ask?" I asked, casting my eyes across the other guests, cutting him off before he could say anything more. He merely sat back in his seat, lit a cigarette and listened while I answered other questions, the same irritating smile hovering at the corner of his mouth.

I hadn't lied; merely omitted to elaborate. Giancarlo *had* rented a house at Bivio San Biagio while his investigatory headquarters were in Montepulciano; but then he'd moved in with me when Pienza became the centre of operations and he'd never really left.

*****

Instead of staying the night in the room that the Cipriani had set aside for me, we decided to take a *motoscafo* home. The driver pulled up at the end of our *calle*, dropped us off, then headed down the canal to let Mario off near his house.

"How much do they pay you for an evening like that?" James asked.

"Nothing. I get book royalties, that's all."

"Who'd be an author?" he said.

"I ask myself that same question nearly every day."

"What a great evening," Kendall said, a few minutes after I closed the front door behind us and James wished us goodnight.

"The meal was delicious, for sure."

"What about that arsehole Scavola, though? He seemed to be smiling—or was it smirking—at you all the way through dinner."

"I didn't notice," I said, helping him out of his jacket. "I didn't look at him once. He was seated behind me and I couldn't be bothered turning around."

"Well, let me tell you that he glared every so often at Mario's back, but his gaze kept flicking towards you. I could see him easily from my chair. Why's he got it in for you?"

"I've never met him. I can only surmise that he's trying to get at Giancarlo through me."

"Surely there's something you could—"

The phone rang. I glanced at my watch; it was two in the morning.

"*Pronto?*"

"Damson, it's me, Mario."

"Is everything all right?"

"No. My apartment has been trashed. The place is a ruin."

"Call the police. Unless I can hail a speedboat somehow, we'll be there in fifteen to twenty minutes. In the meantime, don't touch anything."

I phoned home. Alfonso answered; he'd fallen asleep in the kitchen. I asked him to rouse Giancarlo.

"Damson, what is it?"

"Scavola attended my book reading tonight. Mario was my guest at dinner and he's just phoned to tell me someone's done over his apartment. I've told him to call the police and not to touch anything. We're on our way there now."

"Jesus, Damson. We have to get him somewhere safe. Fucking Scavola ..."

"Look, I won't bore you with details now; I told Mario we were on our way to his apartment. I'll call you in the morning, all right?"

"Just one thing, sorry, before you hang up. I know this isn't the right moment but I have to tell you. It's been on my mind and driving me crazy."

"Go on."

"Is James in the room with you?"

"No, he's not here and we're speaking in Italian, Giancarlo, so even if he was it wouldn't matter. What's the problem?"

"I lied to you when you asked. I did fuck him, and not just once either. It's been going on since I got back from Australia."

"You pick the strangest times to tell me the oddest things. Is it something I need to worry about?"

"No, of course not."

"Then I don't care. Sleep well," I said, then hung up the phone.

CHAPTER 6

I was the first to wake the following morning. I picked up my watch from the bedside table—ten o'clock.

We hadn't returned until nearly four, after spending two hours with the police, who seemed to be there only because they'd been told to attend. Fed up, I asked for the name of their supervisor, telling them that I worked for Mario's lawyer and was making notes on their treatment of the crime scene. They went about their business a little more briskly but with semi-disguised reluctance. We made a list of every single thing that had been broken. Whoever had done over his apartment had taken their time and had been very thorough: mattresses slashed, curtains torn, his collection of photographs ripped apart.

"Doesn't this look like a personal attack of some sort?" I asked the more senior of the officers.

"*Che ne so io?*" he replied with a shrug. It could be translated as "I don't know", but from an Italian, accompanied by that slight shrug, it was more like "I don't give a shit".

I made him sign the list of breakages, which I'd written in very careful Italian, Mario double-checking that I hadn't made any errors, and told him that the head of Cinecittà would contact the chief of police the next morning to check how the investigation was going before he released news of the break-in to the press. And, before wiping it off the wall, I told the smirking policeman that if he, or either of his two other men mentioned one word of what had been written on it, they'd have their arses sued from here to Palermo.

Frocio was a derogatory word for a homosexual, one that was very offensive.

Mario had gone white when he saw it and then had exploded. "Can't you now see this is personal? Someone is trying to blacken my name and ruin my reputation!" he'd yelled.

The policeman's smirk had faded very quickly when I told him that his reaction would go in my report. Although corruption, accompanied by a *laissez-faire* attitude, was still very common among many law-enforcers, the one thing they never wanted was to be named personally, unless it was a commendation for something they'd done. Everyone was aware that most of them were in the pocket of someone else; it was just a disgrace for it to be made public.

We almost descended into a shouting match, him basically telling me to fuck off out of the apartment otherwise he'd arrest me. Arrest me for what? I'd yelled back at him. And then, when he'd grabbed my arm, I'd pulled him close to my face, telling me that my two friends would attest that he'd assaulted me and that both Kendall and I had killed men with our bare hands during the war. Did he really want to force me to defend myself?

We'd brought Mario back to our apartment. I thought we could put him in one of the unused bedrooms, but when I unlocked the door, the smell of mould and the coating of dust over everything made us change our minds. He slept in the bed between Kendall and me, both of us, unusually, sleeping in our underwear.

When I eventually woke this morning, the sun streaming into the room, I smiled as I looked at my two bed companions. Mario was lying on his stomach, his head in the crook of his arm. Kendall, however, had woken when I sat up, smiled at me then glanced at Mario.

"Did you …?" I mouthed to him, making a groping motion with my hand.

He shook his head and grinned.

I showed Kendall how to make coffee then went down to the local *pasticceria* to buy something for breakfast, or rather, brunch. I roused both Mario and James and we ate outside on the balcony, watching the canal traffic and listening to the sounds of the neighbourhood.

"I'll speak with Giancarlo," I said to Mario. "But after we return to the police station to countersign the police statement, I think we have to find somewhere else for you to lie low until you have to return to Ostia for filming. There's our apartment in Florence, or we could always put you up at La Mensola. Do you have anywhere else you could stay?"

"I could stay in the flat they provide for me in Rome. It's very quiet."

"By yourself?"

"I can look after myself, Damson."

"I don't doubt that, but Giancarlo was beaten up by two men. Can you handle two at once?"

"Giancarlo was beaten up? When did this happen?"

"Just over a week ago, in Trieste. And, before you ask, yes, we think it was Scavola."

We'd been speaking in Italian and I'd been completely oblivious to the fact, so apologised to James and Kendall and told them what we'd been discussing. Both of them agreed that it would be a better choice for Mario to come to La Mensola. However, none of us believed that Scavola would actually harm him.

"But … if he's behind the destruction of your apartment, as well as arranging for Giancarlo to be assaulted, as I suspect, it would appear that he's becoming worried," I said. "If there was no proof of what you wrote in your letter to the press, he wouldn't be bothered; he'd just sue you for slander and there'd be none of this other, more sinister stuff going on. Apart from the death threats you said you received before you wrote your letter, have you had any other contact with him?"

"I've already spoken about all this with Giancarlo, Damson. Thank you for your interest, but perhaps it's best to leave it to him. You don't need to get involved."

"Damson's investigative skills are beyond question," Kendall said. "Why do you think his first book about what he did in Japan and *Living with Monsters* have become best-sellers?"

"Giancarlo and I share everything," I added. "I'm investigating Scavola's background for him; I'm already involved."

"Let me think about it, Damson."

"You said in your accusation that you had proof—"

James grabbed my knee. "Leave it, Damson. You're like a dog with a bone. Talk about it later; give Mario a chance to catch his breath."

I held up my hands in a gesture of surrender and then apologised to my three friends. Kendall winked at me over the rim of his coffee cup. Yes, I did get over-focused from time to time, despite my assertion that I was basically very laid-back.

Mario had brought a small suitcase with a few changes of clothing. While he showered, I phoned Giancarlo at the Pienza office. He was getting ready to drive to Siena for a magistrate's hearing. He was furious when I told him about how the police had behaved but calmed a little when I said that, when I got home, I'd type out a statement in both Italian and English from the notes I made at Mario's apartment while the police were there. I'd get both Mario and Kendall to sign it and Cosmo to witness our signatures.

"Will you find somewhere for Mario to stay? He can't go back to his apartment," Giancarlo said.

"I've invited him to stay at La Mensola with us until he needs to go to Ostia. I'm not expecting Scavola's thugs to accost him in the street like they did you, but I think it's best he's somewhere quiet, out of the way."

"We have a houseful already. Where will we put him? With Stefano and his family at Il Fornaio? We don't have guests for a few weeks yet; he'd be fine there."

"I think I'd prefer him to be somewhere we could keep an eye on him, just in case. James just told me he's staying on here in Venice for another week and I said he could use our apartment. Something to do with the local museum and a collector of curse tablets and his research. He said that he'll come to La Mensola after Mario's returned to Cinecittà to start filming again. I think we should put Mario in the new guest wing and Alfonso can move back upstairs; he seemed happy enough in the small bedroom opposite ours."

I sensed he was about to say something else—knowing him, it had to do with James—but as Cosmo was probably sitting close by and neither of us were entirely sure how much English he understood after years of us teaching him, I knew he'd tell me once we got home.

"When will you be back?"

"The day after tomorrow. We could catch the first train early tomorrow morning, but Kendall and James have a dinner invitation tonight and have also accepted a trip to the Lido tomorrow with a couple they met at my book reading."

"You weren't asked?"

"I was busy signing books when they were invited. An American couple; he's a new consulate member at the embassy in Rome. They've just arrived in Italy and decided to have a week in Venice then another in Florence before he takes up his posting."

"How did you get on with Mario, Damson? He's very charming and I—"

"Did you know about his personal life?" I asked him in my laboured Arabic.

"If you tell me you've had sex with him, I may not ever forgive you," he replied in the same language with a laugh in his voice.

I switched back to English. "Do you mind if I ask him about what happened in Rome in '44?"

"Of course not. By the way, Venturi has agreed to do some snooping for us."

"I love it when you say 'us'. When is my name going on the door next to yours and Cosmo's?"

"Very funny, O'Reilly. Do you want me to pick you up at the station?"

"I left the Land Rover at Chiusi. I'm looking at the 1.40 service, which gets in just before six." I had to use American time descriptors when I spoke with him, because even after ten years of me saying things like ten to six, he still didn't quite get it.

"Alfonso and I will get something ready for dinner."

"See you on Sunday," I said.

*****

It was a very pleasant relief to finally sit down to dinner. We'd chosen one of the more upmarket restaurants in Torcello. It catered mainly to well-off Venetians and visitors from other parts of Italy; very few foreign tourists ever went there.

Mario, Kendall and I had slept in the afternoon after returning from the police station. I'd called in a favour from the lady who cleaned our apartment once a fortnight. She and a team of other local women arrived, aired and cleaned out one of the spare bedrooms. We were only staying a couple more days, but I thought Mario needed to have a room of his own. Kendall had then set off with James for their dinner with the American couple, leaving Mario and me alone.

Once he'd signed autographs and had posed for the restaurant's photographer with a few of the diners, we toasted each other with a delicious local pinot grigio, then spoke with the waiter about the house specialities.

"Thank you for all your help today, Damson, and your hospitality."

"It was my pleasure. I hope you didn't feel uncomfortable sharing the bed."

"You were so out to it that I don't think you noticed that I put my arms around you in my sleep. I woke at one point to find the three of us all spooned up together."

"I'm sorry, I—"

"Please don't apologise. It's been over two years since I've been held or … what do you call it in English … *coccolato* …"

"Cuddled," I said. "Don't either of your companions …?"

"No, it's a physical thing. There's no affection."

"Don't you miss that?"

"Of course I do."

"Well, you're very welcome to a cuddle any time," I said. "I'm told I'm very good at it."

He laughed then beckoned the waiter. We both chose local dishes as our starters. He picked *spaghetti alla busara*—pasta with what we called *langoustines* in French, *scampi* in Italian; I, however, chose one of my favourite Venetian dishes: *sarde in saor*—battered, fried sardines left to bathe in a slightly sweetened vinegar and onion marinade.

Giancarlo told me I was boring because I invariably ordered the same starter nearly every time we ate out in Venice.

"I'm very curious about aspects of your letter to the newspaper that kicked this whole thing off," I said. We were seated in a small annexe away from the large dining area to give Mario some privacy and to escape people staring at him all night. Erring on the side of caution, we spoke in English, which remained relatively unknown in Italy.

"What part of my letter?"

"The story about the murder of the nuns. How did you know Scavola was involved?"

"Because I was there."

"I'm sorry? I've read Giancarlo's notes and there's no mention of your being there."

"That's because I haven't told him yet."

"Why on earth not?"

"Because we've only had two meetings and both of those were about legal representation, trying to get the case moved to another jurisdiction away from Scavola's influence in Venice. I was also moving between Rome, Ostia and Trieste—where we did some outdoor shooting for the movie—so there's been little time. I only engaged him at the beginning of the month and these legal things move slowly. We were due to have a long meeting shortly; he's tied up in Florence and Siena for a few more weeks."

"Well, perhaps you can have that meeting when you come to stay with us."

"But you're curious, aren't you? I can tell."

"I don't want to pry, but yes, I am curious."

"May I propose a deal? I'll tell you about what happened during my war if you'll tell me about yours."

"You've read my book," I said.

"Ah, yes, but you skimmed over so much. The real detail started when you got to Japan. Don't forget, I fought during the war too."

"I haven't spoken about what I did to anyone, except my brother," I said.

He held out his hand, waiting. "What did you say to me in my kitchen, Damson? Wasn't it 'What I heard from you this morning will remain in here'?" he quoted, touching his chest as I had done.

Very tentatively, I shook his hand, just as our starters arrived.

"I've never told anyone about this," he began, "not even Stewart. When Italy sided with Hitler, I went to Switzerland. I loathed the fascists and everything they stood for, even though I'd been an early member of the party and when it had initially seemed like we could build a new world. But then the hatred started and the persecution of people for what seemed to be no good reason, something that in the long run turned out to be greed … I became very disillusioned."

"What did you do in Switzerland?" I asked.

"Most people thought I sat around with my finger up my bum," he said. I laughed. "But I'd already belonged to a group that was anti-fascist and which actively worked against Mussolini's Italy."

"Partisans."

"Yes, there were networks all over the country. Well, on the twenty-fifth of July, 1943, news broke that the king had summoned Mussolini, removed him from office and had him arrested. I knew instantly what would follow: the Germans in my country would be ordered to take control. I had to be part of that struggle, so I packed up and returned to Rome. Our group had already established contact with Marshal Badoglio, who by then had started clandestine negotiations with the Allies to switch sides, so one day I found myself in the garden of a country house near Tivoli, offering my services."

"Services? Services as what?"

"You call it a spy; I call it a patriot."

I could have eaten my starter three times over, but, as soon as our plates were cleared, I offered him one of my cigarettes and we lit up.

"I know that it wasn't until early September that Badoglio capit ulated to the Allies, which is when the Germans took control of the country," I said. "What did you do in the intervening time?"

"You're well informed about what happened on this side of the world," he said.

"We were information sponges when it came to the European war, Mario. Can you believe that nearly all of us wished we were fighting the

Germans instead of the Japanese, whose code of honour valued neither their own lives nor those of their enemy? On the whole, there were better conditions for imprisoned Allied soldiers and airmen in Germany than the forced labour camps, torture, starvation and misery for those of our men unfortunate enough to be captured in the Pacific theatre of war. I can't tell you how our hearts sank when we learned about Stalags where officers were treated with a modicum of respect and there was proper housing and regular, if not always wholesome, food. The con trast was almost too much to bear. The Japs just treated us, the Brits, Kiwis and the Americans like human cattle, worthy of nothing but a certain death, all because the idea of being captured or surrendering was the most shameful thing a soldier could do."

He studied my face while I talked; I knew I was a different Damson O'Reilly when I spoke about those times.

"But you were never captured, Damson."

"No, but I saw the results of it with my own eyes. Men beheaded, disembowelled, used as bayonet practice, impaled on bamboo stakes, their eyes put out, their fingernails torn off, most of them castrated before they died and left to bleed to death … sorry to get so stirred up; it's one of the reasons I never really talk about it."

"We had atrocities here; mainly in the form of mass shootings of men, women and children in retribution for some minor crime against the Nazis, but nothing like what you've just described. I'm not surprised you didn't mention any of that in your book."

"Thank you, Mario. I try hard to keep those images out of my mind. Believe it or not, some men—fellow soldiers I believed to be very resilient—went mad. They just couldn't continue after seeing what we encountered day after day … I'm sorry, let's move on for the moment. You were starting to tell me what you did for Badoglio."

"There's no need to apologise; I understand completely." He leaned across the table and patted the back of my hand, his eyes full of concern. "What I did for Badoglio? Well, very soon after my meeting with him, I recruited my brother Emilio to work alongside me. When the fascist government fell, the Milizia Volontaria per la Sicurezza Nazio nale—whom you know as the Blackshirts—was dissolved and members were absorbed into the military. Emilio and I were moved around; our 'secret' job was to sort out who were true converts and which of them were still working undercover to destabilise the new regime in the hope that after the war another fascist dictatorship would once more take control of the country. But it was before Mussolini's downfall, when the Blackshirts were at their worst, that we first met Scavola."

"My research revealed that he was already a member. I read that he joined the organisation in 1930."

"Much later, after Mussolini had been rescued by the Germans and had been put in place as the 'puppet ruler' of Northern Italy, my brother and I were assigned to a group that worked alongside Scavola's in Jan uary 1944, when the fascists and Germans were getting worried about the Allies, who'd already taken Sicily and were steadily moving north ward. After the landings at Anzio, and despite Mussolini's braggadocio and confidence that they'd be driven back to the sea, everyone knew that the Allies would eventually prevail and that ultimately Rome would fall. That was when those thugs decided to get really vicious."

"What do you mean, *really* vicious?"

We were interrupted by the arrival of our *secondi*, or main courses.

While we were eating, I had to force down unwanted visions of what I'd seen far too frequently in the jungles of New Guinea, Bougain ville and the Solomon Islands. It wasn't until I was in Japan that I found I'd become hardened to the sight of what one man could do to another, and that was when I'd discovered a group of orphaned children, all suffering from the hideous after-effects of radiation burns, adopted by an elderly widow who'd lost all of her own family in the fireball that enveloped Nagasaki, where I was stationed. The woman knew that the four children were most likely due to die—as was she—and it haunted me that we were ordered to separate the kids and take them to a field hospital for children, leaving her alone and distraught, still waiting for medical aid for herself. I had felt unmoved until a few days later, when the person inside me whom I'd hidden away for so long during the conflict tapped me on the shoulder and gave me a wake-up call. I visited the old woman the next morning, my rucksack filled with food imposs ible to obtain for the local Japanese people, and sat with her and grieved, tears pouring down my face, confronted with my own loss of humanity. We didn't speak a word of each other's language and yet I'd sensed that we both were mourning for what we'd lost.

"How's your fish?" Mario asked, drawing me out of the hole in my mind I'd fallen into. I'd ordered *bacalà mantecato*, creamy salted cod served on toasted bread and accompanied with grilled polenta—normally a starter, but it was another Venetian dish I couldn't get enough of, so I'd ordered a double portion as my main course.

"Absolutely delicious," I said, signalling the waiter and requesting a bottle of sparkling mineral water to help wash it down; I didn't want to get sozzled, and the wine was already starting to give me a slight feeling of inebriation.

Mario spoke while we continued to eat, telling me about his early days with his brother, getting to know Scavola's team and the members of his own group, of which there were about thirty. He'd discovered that several were diehards, men so committed to the fascist cause that they could only be described as fanatics. They belonged to a separate, secretive, smaller unit made up of men in Mario's group and some of Scavola's. As hard as Mario and his brother tried to find out what they got up to, it was impossible to break into their inner circle. He reported it, of course, but nothing came of it.

"Report it? Why did you report it? Were you suspicious about what they might have been getting up to?"

Mario pushed back his plate, by now emptied and the juices cleaned up using a piece of bread—*fare la scarpetta*, we called it in Italian—then suggested we take a break before dessert and have a cigarette outside.

The moon was a waxing crescent, a sliver of light in the sky on an otherwise cloudless starry evening, a slight breeze coming across the lagoon; it made for a perfect summer evening. A small park stood adjacent to the restaurant and we leaned against the waist-high railings, smoking, watching the fireflies blinking in the trees and among the bushes.

"In answer to your last question, there were a number of unexplained murders and kidnappings: whole families found shot in the back of the head; Jewish people who'd been hidden by the Church or by sympathetic families rounded up for deportation; the rape of women believed to be against the fascist regime—and not only women, men and boys too—and looting of business premises and shops. We couldn't prove it, but we suspected that it was Scavola's group behind many of these outrages, so we decided to follow them—not just Emilio and me, but a few others that Badoglio had introduced us to."

"And did you find anything?"

"Plenty, but never once were we able to witness them doing anything, only the results of what we believed were their actions."

"Until …"

"How do you know there's an 'until', Damson?"

"I recognise that look in your eye. I've seen it so many times in my life."

"Very well—*until* the evening, Emilio and I followed four of Scavola's men to the Holy City, four nights after the Americans occupied Rome and when we were all supposed to report to military headquarters for reassignment to the army to fight with the Allies against the Germans. We were stopped by guards at the Borgo Santo Spirito entrance."

"This story is about the nuns, isn't it?" I said.

He nodded. "Sister Ursula was very well-known for protecting the children of families who were susceptible to blackmail or threats—a common *modus operandi* of Blackshirt thugs. She also hid Jewish families and other political dissidents. We later learned that on the night of the ninth of June, the nuns were bound for Naples, well away from any possible attacks from the fascists who, although in turmoil, still had scores to settle."

"But surely they were safe in Vatican City?"

"There was a lot of arse-covering at the Vatican at the time and anyone who was politically sensitive was moved to different parts of the country. She was advised to leave by a papal nuncio—we believe he was French but have no proof—and given permission to take three fellow sisters and four children with her, go to a convent in Naples, and wait until things had settled down."

"But the fascists got to her first."

"Yes: she and the other three nuns were shot in the carriage of the train while it was waiting to leave Vatican City."

"And the children?"

"We didn't know at the time what had happened to them until a few weeks later, when three of their bodies were dumped at the door of the convent in Rome where Sister Ursula had lived."

"The fourth child?"

"A boy. Everyone assumed he was dead too."

The waiter appeared outside the restaurant and signalled that our desserts were ready. I pointed at my watch then held up five fingers.

"The station staff witnessed what took place but were powerless to do anything. Because they were standing on the platform, they didn't see the actual shooting, but they heard the gunshots, then found the bodies."

"And you believe it was Scavola who was responsible?"

"We'd been tailing the group on the night that it happened but had given up the moment they entered St Peter's Square. The Vatican guards were stopping everyone, checking permits and asking their business—those same guards were conveniently nowhere to be found when questions were later asked. Also conveniently, no one was able to pinpoint exactly who had been on duty that evening. But there was a man waiting for the men we'd been following, and I'm absolutely positive that I recognised him. He was standing about five metres away, and, despite his cloak and the scarf wound around the lower half of his face, I knew it was Scavola. There's was no doubt about it; I recognised his distinctive walk."

"Yes, he limps; I noticed that at the book reading."

"Shot in the foot. Story has it he discharged his own gun while cleaning it."

"Five metres away from where you were standing? He didn't recognise you? You'd been working with him at the time."

"We mingled with the crowd of people waiting to be processed by the guards and it was very dark."

"So, what did you do?"

"We tried to follow them, insisting we had official business, but without a specific permit the guards wouldn't let us pass. I asked about the men I'd just seen walk through with a wave, no papers asked for, but was told to fuck off."

"But you have no actual proof that Scavola was responsible for the murder of the nuns and the kidnapping of the children."

"None of us witnessed it, but one of the station staff, who was bludgeoned with a rifle butt and told to mind his own business, signed a statement saying they all had their faces covered. However, he swore that the man who appeared to be their leader walked with a limp."

"Circumstantial," I said as we headed back towards the restaurant.

"Perhaps, but the next morning my brother overheard a conversation between Scavola and the head of our group—a man we never trusted either—in which the answer to the question, 'How did it go last night?' was answered with, '*Tutto apposto; sono sfatte*'."

I hesitated in the doorway. *Everything went well; they're done* could mean anything except for the feminine ending on the word *sfatte*, which meant the things that were "done", or had been dealt with, as we'd say in English, were female things … such as women.

Still circumstantial, but I couldn't let it go. Once inside and seated again, a massive *fugassa Veneta* was delivered to the table, cut by the waiter and shared by us with a pile of whipped cream to help it slide down. Similar to a panettone, the *fugassa* was an enriched, leavened, cake-like bread, usually served at Easter, but much loved by the locals at any time of the year.

"Mario," I said, between mouthfuls, "what you've told me is indeed very suspicious, but it's not actual proof. Everything is deduction from conjectures. You're unlikely to win your case on circumstantial evidence."

He smiled. "I'm not entirely reckless, Damson. As I said in my letter to *La Nazione*, I have proof."

"Proof? What sort of proof?"

"That boy I told you about, the one who disappeared? He turned up a few months ago at Cinecittà asking to see me, saying he wouldn't go away until I spoke with him. Said it would only take a moment and that he wasn't a fan asking for an autograph, it was something important about the war."

"Why you? I don't understand …"

"Last year, there was a *processo*, a hearing, in Rome, in which Scavola and a few of his henchmen were questioned about links to other murders during the war and illegal goings on after it that were linked to pro-fascist underground organisations. I was called as a witness to talk about what happened in 1944. The story of the nuns never came up and Scavola and his friends were released for lack of proof, despite what was offered up at the hearing. I'm afraid the whole thing was nonsense. Three judges were all former members of fascist groups during the 1930s … from day one it was obvious which side they were on."

"And the boy was a witness?"

"No, Damson. He attended, but was far too frightened to come forward and give testimony about what he saw and experienced. He sought me out after the trial, thinking that someone with a high public presence like mine might be able to help him."

"Have you told Giancarlo about him yet?"

"No. I don't have his permission, and no one must know he even exists. If word got back to Scavola or any of his cronies—"

"You have to tell Giancarlo. He can arrange protection for him—"

"He's well hidden, and I'm the only person who knows where he is."

"And that in itself is a danger, Mario. Giancarlo was beaten up, your apartment trashed … if Scavola is behind this and anything happens to you, justice will never be served if the lad remains unknown and something happens to him."

"He's not a lad anymore, Damson. He's twenty-six years old."

"And you're not going to tell me where he is?"

"I'm thinking about it. I'll tell you before we leave for La Mensola, I promise. I need to run a few things through my mind first and then speak with him when I return to Ostia for filming, to get his permission to meet with Giancarlo."

"So that's where he is, I suppose?"

He laughed. "Always playing the detective, Damson. He could be there, or in Rome, or in any of the towns between your house and Ostia. Italy is a big place, my friend. All I can tell you is that you and he have something in common."

"He's Australian?" I asked with a grin.

He laughed. "No—he's a carpenter by trade."

"He's not …"

"One of the two men I have sex with? No, mere coincidence, Damson, and *my* carpenter lives in Rome."

"Ah, gotcha," I said, in English. "That rules one place out."

"I'll tell you, I promise. Let me sleep on it."

*****

I woke to someone fondling my dick.

"Hello," I whispered groggily to Kendall, who was still wearing his tuxedo. "How was your dinner?"

"Very pleasant and interesting. Yours?"

"Eventful."

"What do you mean, eventful?"

"I ended up sitting in an armchair with a bottle of brandy at my side, watching James eat out the wife while the American fucked him."

"What?"

"You heard me. He told me he'd arranged it on the night of your book reading. I was expected to join in, but she wasn't in the age bracket of women who turn me on. I have to put my hand up to admit that I felt very aroused a bit later on while watching James slide his big cock in and out of her while he bucked his arse back against her husband."

"You weren't tempted?"

"No, not really. I don't know how many times I've told you that I'm basically a voyeur. It was erotic to watch and I got hard in my pants, played with myself with a hand in one pocket, but if I'm to be really honest, my eyes went mostly to your young British friend's fat cock."

"If you want to take that somewhere, go for it."

He shook his head. "He's far too young and skinny. I'd like to know what it feels like in my hand, but that's about it. They're paying him over a hundred American dollars … that was supposed to include me, by the way."

"Did he let you know beforehand that you were expected to join in?"

"Not until we arrived. I said then that I wasn't interested but I was happy enough to watch as long as they agreed. When I eventually left, he followed me to the door and asked me to tell you that he was staying there for the night and not to worry about him."

"Worry about him? He's his own man. Why should I worry?"

"I'm not sure, Damson. But there's something about him …"

"Oh, so you did notice something more than his big cock."

He laughed. "There are times when I catch glimpses of someone different in his eyes. Only momentarily, you understand. That doesn't mean that I don't trust him, but I'm still wondering why he thought I'd have sex with the American and his wife and didn't tell me until we got to their hotel room door."

"Maybe it was a way of seducing you."

"If he really wanted to get me into bed, I'm pretty sure he wouldn't pussyfoot around. You know how direct he can be when he wants to. But …"

"But what?"

"I have a feeling it wasn't his idea."

"What makes you think that?"

"The American, while he was fucking James, couldn't take his eyes off my cock."

"I thought you said you were playing with it in your pants?"

"Most of the time I was, Damson," he said with a chuckle. "I had to let it free before I shot."

"Oh?"

"Yeah, I didn't have a handkerchief so I spurted into my whiskey glass."

"You created a new cocktail," I said with a grin.

"Jizz on the Rocks."

That made me laugh loudly.

"I gave it to the Yank after I'd zipped up and said I was heading off to bed."

"And he …?"

"Toasted me, slurped it into his mouth, then shared my spunk with James while James fucked him."

"And what did his wife think of that?"

"Oh, she'd gone to bed by then."

CHAPTER 7

"James is quite the character," Kendall said later that morning while we were having breakfast near the church of San Vidal. He'd decided to give the trip to the Lido a miss.

The owner of the "café" was an old friend of Giancarlo's mother. She had two tables outside her front door, each seating two people, at which she served coffee made with the moka pot on her stove and home-made pastries. If she didn't like you, she'd curse in Venetian and tell you to piss off.

"Both Giancarlo and I have spent time with him when he's not trying to impress by being catty or smart," I said. "He's highly intelligent and what the Italians call *furbo*, which means something like clever or crafty. I like that side of him. The other side makes me laugh, but once you realise that he's only craving attention …"

"I suspected that already. But, even when he's talking to you, you get the impression that he's aware of everything going on around him at the same time. Despite all that, he's charming. Did you know he's a viscount?"

"No, I had absolutely no idea. I know his parents. When I say 'know', I'm acquainted with them—his father's an earl or something or other.

They own the flat above ours in Florence. Did you know that he and Giancarlo have been fucking?"

"Really? I hope Giancarlo's not having to pay?"

I waved the idea away with a flick of my hand

"And you don't mind?"

"Why should I? You might find this hard to understand, but we're still basically monogamous. We might have sex with different partners occasionally, but we always tell each other, and we never sleep with anyone at the expense of time with each other."

"And you and me?"

"It's what you said it is, Kendall. You and I have become the best of friends and we enjoy sex together. Giancarlo knows about it; he doesn't care because you seem happy to share with him too."

"You just need to promise me one thing, Damson."

"And what's that?"

"If I start to get in the way, you must tell me."

I laughed. "The last person who said that to me was my friend Danny, and he ended up living with us for two years."

Half an hour later, we rang Mario's front doorbell. Having been given the green light, he'd returned to his apartment to sift through his belongings and to put things to right. With him was a man in his late twenties, whom he introduced as Alvise, and who, later in the day, Kendall and I worked out was most likely his Venetian policeman. He was a very taciturn man, strong in the upper body, with thighs that could crush a walnut. Every so often, he'd laugh at something—a laugh that lit up his face and made me understand the attraction. Despite what Mario had said—that the relationship was sexual only—there was far too much going on between them for me to believe that there wasn't more than a small amount of affection on Alvise's side.

As for his other lover: much of the furniture had come with the apartment when Mario had bought it, but there were one or two beautiful modern pieces, all bearing a small, hidden brass plaque bearing the name of the maker and his studio: *Gregorio Vaccarello, Piazza del Drago, Roma*. He'd told me his second lover was a carpenter in Rome; it wasn't hard to put two and two together. "This is beautiful work," I said to Mario, stroking the surface of a wonderfully crafted blanket chest. "And eucalypt too. The workmanship is outstanding and there's not a nail in it. Hand-sawn tenon and dovetail joints … lovely. I'd be very keen to know where he got the timber. Have you any idea?"

"I could ask him for you, Damson. Does it make you feel homesick?"

"A little. I've planted a grove of ironbarks and blue gums not far from Il Fornaio, our guest house. Father Benedict, my art teacher at the monastery, sent me the seed capsules about five years ago. The trees are growing well, but it will be some time before any are ready to be cut for timber. I'll wait until they flower and set seed before I start chopping any down; that way, I can replace them. They have very dense, almost woody capsules that only release their seeds after a bushfire. Our country relies on fire to propagate a lot of our native vegetation."

I studied his face while he told me about his visits to the atelier in Rome, watching the pieces of furniture take shape, and how much he loved to see men working with their hands. I told him he'd get to see me doing the same sort of thing when he came to La Mensola. I'd chosen some beautiful elm for the louvred bathroom cabinets and the doors for the two linen closets, which I intended to start putting together as soon as we got home. There was something about the way he spoke about his visits to the workshop that made me think that perhaps the carpenter meant more to him than Alvise, who followed him around like a spaniel. A big, burly spaniel, but a spaniel nonetheless.

When I suggested that we have a break for lunch—the apartment mostly put back together—Mario said that Alvise had brought enough for us all to share. We sat on his living room floor, tearing off chunks of bread from the two loaves Alvise had provided and stacking them with slices of mortadella, salami or cheese. There were *also olive all'ascolane ripiene*—olives stuffed with seasoned meat and deep-fried—and *peperoni sott'olio*—slices of capsicum skinned and preserved in olive oil. We washed it down with a bottle of white wine from the Soave region.

"Did you notice Alvise's wedding ring?" Kendall asked me later that afternoon while we were stretched out on the bed, ready for a short siesta.

"Yes. What about it?"

"It made me think."

"About when you marry someone yourself?"

"Yes. Would you and I still be able to … you know?"

"It would depend on a few things. Are you expecting to marry for love?"

"Nope. I don't want kids either. I want a sexy woman about twenty years older than me. Someone with style, money of her own and a life of her own. I'd really like a woman who was good at kissing and preferred me to take care of her orally."

"Well, that's pretty specific," I said with a laugh. "And me? What would I be for?"

"Your mouth, O'Reilly. You've spoiled me."

"You're forgetting something."

He grinned. "Oh, yes, your big fat cock in my mouth and my arse; I couldn't survive without that."

★★★★★

I decided to show Kendall around Venice while James was at the Lido with his Americans.

My Australian friend had never displayed much emotion—he was Mr Cool, Calm and Collected on the surface—but I'd learned, over the three-plus months that I'd known him, that from time to time it was his eyes that betrayed him. He stood in front of the carving of the Tetrarchy on the portico of St Mark's Cathedral for a good twenty minutes, occasionally reaching out to almost touch it while telling me the story of the four rulers of the empire: Diocletian, Maximian, Galerius and Constantius. I already knew its history but said nothing, mainly because I loved to see the fire in his eyes when he talked about anything to do with antiquity. Equally riveting was his story of the Triumphal Quadriga, or Horses of the Hippodrome of Constantinople above the façade of the cathedral. It made me determined to show him around Rome, or better, get Alfonso to guide us, who was born in the city and also trained there for the priesthood.

"Just before we left Mario's apartment today," he said, "you and he disappeared into his office, then Alvise was summoned a few minutes later. It's none of my business, but …"

"He'd written out a statement outlining what had happened during the war. I suppose he did it some time ago and you don't need to know the details, but it had to do with the squad he belonged to back then and what he saw on the night of a massacre a few days after the Americans took Rome. He asked me to read it and to witness him signing it; he asked Alvise too, but his mate didn't even want to look at it and said he wasn't going to get involved with anything that had to do with Scavola."

"I could have signed," Kendall said.

"It was in Italian, my friend. Anyway, it's in my attaché case and I'll give it to Giancarlo when we get home."

"Does that mean Mario's worried?"

"Wouldn't you be? I think it's unlikely that Scavola would try to harm him; he's too famous. But after Giancarlo's black eye and then the do-over of his apartment ..."

Kendall nodded. "And we made a detour to the railway station for what reason?"

"I wanted to buy the London and New York newspapers to see what's going on in the rest of the world. The Italian press, even the major press, is parochial by our standards. Then, while I was there, I phoned Giancarlo to tell him about the conversation I had with Mario last night and let him know that I was bringing the signed statement with me."

"Was there a need? You'll be seeing him tomorrow."

I nodded. "The one thing I've learned since my time working with the American military police in Japan, and afterwards with the detectives here during the serial killer case I was caught up in, is that one should never rely on a piece of evidence that's unique. Too many things can go, and have gone, missing. Giancarlo's assistant took down every word I said in shorthand in case the written statement somehow gets lost—a euphemism for stolen."

"Damson, for the rest of the afternoon, in between our sightseeing, I'd like you to tell me exactly what's been going on. I hear bits and pieces about Scavola and Mario, and then there's the business of Giancarlo's black eye ... how are these things connected?"

"I'll have to ask Mario's permission first. It's not that I don't trust you, but some of these things are not only confidential but also his own personal business."

"Here's an idea. How about I take you and Mario out to dinner, somewhere special tonight? I can ask Mario this afternoon and, if he's agreeable, we can talk about it over a good meal and a few bottles of wine."

"You won't get into anywhere special at this late notice," I said.

"Wait and see, Damson. Money speaks very loudly, no matter where you are in the world."

He was such a normal bloke that I often forgot that his father was the richest man in Australia and that Kendall had personally inherited millions from his grandfather.

Our final stop before lunch was the church of San Giorgio Maggiore to see the paintings by Tintoretto: his *Last Supper* was breathtaking. We ate at a nearby osteria then took a *motoscafo* back to the apartment.

Mario and James were there when we arrived, Mario with his feet up on the sofa, reading a book, and James spread out on the floor with books from the shelves in the library. Giancarlo's mother had amassed a large collection of what we now called art books: large volumes with glossy pages filled with photographic prints. I'd occasionally pull one out and peruse it. There were also many novels, some going back as far as the mid-nineteenth century, but despite my relative fluency in Italian, my head still hurt when struggling through flowery, prosaic stories for more than an hour or so.

Kendall threw me a look, one that told me that he wanted to speak with Mario alone, so I extended a hand to James and invited him out onto the balcony to have a cigarette. He looked puzzled, so I spoke in Latin, telling him I wanted to talk to him about Giancarlo.

He looked momentarily startled, so followed me outside. "Am I in trouble?" he asked.

"Not really. Kendall wanted to talk to Mario about something in private."

"Look, Damson, about Giancarlo. It was me—"

"I don't care, James. Honestly, I really don't … that is, unless he's paying you with our money."

He laughed. "I'm only a prostitute eighty per cent of the time."

"The Americans? That seemed very convenient."

"Convenient? In what way?"

"Well, you just arrived and—"

"I was to meet up with them in Florence, but then when I saw them at the reception at your book signing, I thought I'd say hello."

"Sorry, I'm confused."

"You don't need to know the details, but there is an organisation that makes these sorts of arrangements. I recognised the Americans from photographs in magazines and introduced myself to them at the bar. They were as surprised as I was; it was a total coincidence, I assure you."

I said nothing; I had little to say, to be honest, trying to get my head around what appeared to be an international organisation that arranged sexual partners for what I presumed to be wealthy, high-profile people who had certain tastes.

"It's been going on since I was at Oxford," James explained. "I was introduced by another student; it was a good way of earning a few extra pennies."

"Liar," I said with a chuckle. "Your family is very wealthy; you didn't need the money. You do it because you like it."

"Perhaps …"

I changed the subject. I rarely used Latin these days except for talking with Alfonso from time to time, so asked James if he minded if we talked about his project in that language. He was only too keen and I soon realised that it was a passion, not a rich-boy folly or a transient new *divertissement*. He was intending to meet up with Randy's wife, Helen, and her sister and join them at their dig in late August for a few weeks. He'd just started telling me about some of the curses that had been found in Ferento, not far from Viterbo, when Mario interrupted our conversation.

"Well, I don't know how your friend Kendall did it, but we're dining at the Danieli this evening."

"You've agreed to tell him your story?"

"How can it hurt now? James can come too, but he must promise to keep what I say a secret. If word gets out about the young man I told you about, then both our lives might be in danger."

"Surely Scavola wouldn't—"

"This is Italy, Damson, not England or Australia. Things happen. Now, tell me, shall I invite James or not?"

I glanced at James for a second, who'd turned away and had lit another cigarette while we'd been speaking in Italian. Somehow, I intuited that he was perhaps very good at keeping secrets. There was a side of him, the serious, earnest side, that helped me make up my mind.

"Ask him yourself," I said, in English.

*****

During dinner, both Kendall and James listened attentively while Mario and I unravelled the whole Scavola story, including the murder of the four nuns and three children, the beating up of Giancarlo, and the sudden reappearance of the missing child after the court case Mario had testified at. Despite Kendall's suggestion that Mario should at least tell someone else where the now grown-up lad was, Mario insisted that he'd have to ask his permission first.

Around midnight, we decided to walk home. It was a beautiful evening, and as many Italians ate late, there were people still wandering around the Piazza San Marco. When we reached the square, in front of the opera house, Mario said he'd arranged to meet Alvise at his apartment and would be home in about an hour. I lent him a spare front door key. We walked with him and said goodbye outside his building; he told us that he would bring Alvise back with him to our apartment.

I was awoken by a furious bashing at the front door. I had no idea what time it was. Perhaps Mario had forgotten that he had the key. "One moment," I called out, racing across the large, empty reception hall while pulling on my dressing gown.

"*Signor Damson O'Reilly?*" a policeman asked me.

"*Si, sono io,*" I replied.

"We'd like you to come with us," he said, and then, before I could say a word, his two companions grabbed my arms.

"What's going on?"

"I'm arresting you on suspicion of the murder of Mario Celestino."

"Mario is *dead?*" I couldn't believe what I was hearing. "No! This can't be true!"

"He was found floating face-down in the Grand Canal this morning at four o'clock and we have reason to believe you are responsible for his death."

"No, that's impossible! I was with friends all night," I shouted, trying to shrug off the policemen's hold on me. "They're here, they can vouch for me."

He spat in my face and slapped me hard; I kicked him in the groin and elbowed one of the policemen in the face.

In retrospect, it wasn't the wisest thing to do.

*****

I was locked up in a small, damp room with a bucket in which to do my business and a tiny window up high, which over the course of the day had allowed a shaft of light to navigate across the wall and the steel door of the cell.

After arriving at the police station, the detective and his two uniformed friends hadn't figured on a man who was still able to dredge up his combat experience from the war. So, when the cops restrained me while the detective tried to use my gut as a punching bag, I'd ended up being the last man standing.

I'd claimed a Pyrrhic victory for a few seconds, until someone poked their nose into the interview room to see how things were going—most likely expecting to find me a bloodied mess in the corner— and half a dozen policemen had swarmed into the interview room, beat the shit out of me, then literally sat on me to stop me breaking any more noses. The Irish in me had boiled over with odds of six against one, but I'd given as good as I got.

I had expected more beatings later that day, but oddly enough I'd been left alone, until a few moments ago, when the cell door had swung open and Cosmo had walked into the room then waited silently until the policeman who'd opened it for him departed. I recognised the cop as one of the uniformed police who'd sat on me in the early hours of the morning.

"Dear God, look at you!" Cosmo said, his eyes wide. "Strip off, quickly, before they come back. Hurry up, Damson, take everything off."

"Strip off? Why?"

He opened his briefcase and showed me his camera. I got the idea and then did as he asked. "We're suing them?" I said.

"Giancarlo has been on the phone with the Minister of Justice."

"He's spoken with Guido Gonella?"

"You were in France doing a book signing at the time so you don't remember, but our office represented his son in court in Rome. It was a falsified charge of dealing illicit drugs; one of Gonella's rivals set it up. You know the sort of thing: unwarranted police raid, drugs found conveniently …"

"How did you get him off? Never mind, that's beside the point."

"Holy Mother of God, what did they use to beat you?" Cosmo asked, taking photographs of the marks all over my body and my face. "Did they touch any intimate parts of your body?"

"They tugged at my scrotum so hard I nearly threw up, then three of them forced me to bend over and another one spread my buttocks: he shoved two fingers up my arse."

"That's sexual violation; we could argue rape. Do you by any chance remember who it was who did this?"

"Oh, yes, I do. The same arsehole who tried to assault me in Mario's apartment. Kendall was there to witness it at the time … oh, damn! Did they go through our apartment?"

"Yes. I'm sorry, it's a bit of a mess. However," he added, taking a close-up of the dried blood around my ear and whispering, "your Australian friend Mr Travert and Viscount Langley were very thoughtful. Mr Travert hid your attaché case and the viscount phoned the British ambassador and the Australian consul in Rome. The police here are frightened beyond belief. This has now become an international incident: famous author falsely blamed for murder by inept and corrupt Venetian police. Giancarlo sent a press release to *La Nazione* this morning. It's already headlines all over the country."

"But what about poor Mario? Is he really dead?"

"I'm afraid so. Your arrest is not a byline to the stories about his murder; you and he together take up the entire front page of every news-paper I've seen. You wait until I leave here and talk to the reporters. I intend to hold up my camera and tell them that you've been raped while in custody. As Giancarlo is fond of saying: 'Just wait until the shit hits the fan'."

The phrase in Italian was *quando verrà fuori tutto il casino*, something that didn't have nearly the same pithiness as our equivalent in English.

I started to feel the beginnings of a white-hot heat in my belly. Mario was dead? I smelled Scavola behind it. I'd been feeling uneasy since learning that Mario had revealed he had proof of Scavola's involve-ment in the murder of the nuns. With him out of the way, the whole slander case would be dead and buried … or would it?

Cosmo finished with the photos, including what he told me were spectacular bruises on my buttocks, I put my clothes back on. "Is Gian-carlo on his way?"

"He left a message with my wife. I called her the moment I got off the train here. He's asked the judges for a break in the proceedings of the trial he's defending in Siena. Mario's murder was a good enough excuse and he'll be catching the late train tonight, which leaves at about half past six and gets in at eleven. They only gave him one day off, though."

"Okay. But there's something we have to do right now and it's quite urgent. Do you know of a local notary? One who's completely trustworthy?"

Cosmo didn't reply immediately but pinched the bridge of his nose while he thought. "No, but I do have two friends I was at law school with who live in Padua, which is only fifteen minutes away by train. Why?"

"Last night over dinner, Mario related the whole story of Scavola and his involvement with him during the war, including the events surrounding the massacre in the train carriage at the station in Vatican City. Call your friends, offer them whatever outrageous sum you think that will get them here as soon as possible. Kendall, James and I need to write statements recording our memories of every moment of the conversation last night. You and the two notaries can sign them. We can be in separate rooms so that no one can hint at collusion."

"Excellent idea. Giancarlo can take the statements to the local courthouse tomorrow morning and have them lodged."

"Better still, you can travel to Rome on the six o'clock train tomorrow morning and give them to our friend Salvatore Venturi, who has plenty of associates in the judiciary. I'm certain there'll be no problem getting one of them to countersign his affirmation. It can't be here; it must be in another city. Another reason to avoid any suspicion of our having worked the system."

"I'll get straight on to it."

"Now, what do you know about Mario's murder? It's heartbreaking and I can't quite get my head around it yet, but—"

There was a knock at the door of my cell and then, when it was pushed open, I saw two men wearing white coats, one of them holding a stretcher.

"What's going on?" I asked.

"Ah," said Cosmo, "it's a theatrical event ordered by Giancarlo. There's a huge pack of reporters waiting outside the jail. You're to be carried out on a stretcher and put into a water ambulance, taken to the hospital and examined for injuries. I'll take your clothes. We need you to be seen on the stretcher wearing nothing but your undershorts. The reporters and their photographers will go crazy when they see the blood on your cheek and neck, and the state of your torso and legs. Give the 'V for Victory' sign as you're being carried out, but don't lift your head; you have to look beaten to within an inch of your life ... a few loud moans might help too."

I chuckled. It was, as Cosmo had said, pure theatre and I realised that Scavola's plan to frighten me had backfired. Kendall's father owned a newspaper chain on the other side of the world, but he had contacts everywhere. I'd have bet anything that my Aussie friend had been on the blower to his dad and not only would the pictures of my beating be on the front pages of all the Italian papers tomorrow, but most likely syndicated across the globe.

Stick that in your pipe and smoke it, I said to myself as I waved weakly to the throngs of excited press members packed in the forecourt of the police station, calling my name and shouting over each other.

There was not a policeman to be seen.

*****

By nine o'clock the following morning, not only had the chief of police resigned, but six policemen had been arrested and a crowd of journalists was waiting on the walkway of the *calle* outside our apartment.

Our statements had been signed last night and Cosmo was already on his way to Rome with them. Giancarlo had returned from the courthouse, where he'd lodged a motion to sue the Venetian police force and the mayor. I was ready for breakfast, very surprised to find that James had cooked it in our tiny kitchenette. He'd accompanied Giancarlo to the Palazzo Cavalli, after which they'd stopped at the market across the Rialto and bought fresh bread, ham and eggs.

"I've taken care of the press," Kendall said. "That phone call in the middle of the night was from my father. He's arranged an exclusive interview with a journalist from *The Times* in London, who arrived early this morning on a chartered flight, paid for by our organisation."

"Damson can't be paid for the interview," Giancarlo protested. "It would look terribly bad—"

"It's all right," I said, taking his hand and squeezing it. "I discussed it with Kendall while you and James were away this morning. The fee is to be donated to the Italian charity that supports the widows and orphans of servicemen who lost their lives in the war. That should thwart any naysayers who think I'm trying to profit from the circumstances surrounding Mario's murder … I still haven't heard anything about that yet. Do any of you know? I'm sick to the stomach thinking about it and not knowing what happened."

"We'll all have some information very soon," Giancarlo said. "After your interview, which will be at ten this morning, the head of the police force of the Veneto region will be here at midday to talk to you and to officially apologise. That won't stop me suing the local cops who beat you up; I need to keep Scavola on his toes. I'll telephone the Danieli and confirm your dinner reservation and what time you left. Do you know how to contact Alvise, Mario's friend?"

"No. Mario was very tight-lipped about him. But both Kendall and I could describe him easily."

"It's important we find him if he was the last person to see Mario alive, Damson."

"We need to figure out a strategy to avoid difficult questions."

"What sort of difficult questions?"

"The questions with answers like Kendall stating that he knows I didn't leave the apartment after we got home because we were in bed fucking until three in the morning."

"Only until three, Damson? I'll have to trade you in; you're getting old," he said with a laugh.

*****

"And you say you left Signor Celestino at the front door of his apartment building?"

"Yes, we three said goodnight to him at the door and he replied that he'd be back here in an hour."

Alessandro Pellegrini, the police supremo for the region, turned out to be a surprise. He was a striking-looking man with a wonderful smile, probably closer in age to Giancarlo than to me.

"What I don't understand," he said, "is why he would have been meeting a member of the local constabulary at midnight at his apartment."

"His house had been ransacked, many items broken and his personal belongings and papers trampled underfoot. He had made arrangements to meet with his friend earlier to help with getting things back into order, but then Mr Travert invited us to dinner at the Danieli and he postponed it until later in the evening."

"The Danieli? How lucky you are. My wife and I have only eaten there once, on an anniversary. This policeman—Alvise, you said his first name was—do you know the nature of their relationship?"

"They were very good friends, that's all I know about the man, other than that he's local and that he's a policeman."

"Local? How do you know he's local? There are policemen here from all over Italy. I'm originally from Sinalunga, not far from where you live."

"He and Mario spoke in Venetian dialect once or twice."

"But Signor Celestino is from Rome."

"And I'm from Australia, but I can give you a pretty good mono-logue in Tuscan if you wish," I said, using the local dialect that was common around Pienza and Montepulciano.

He laughed, then apologised, saying the situation was far too serious for him to be so flippant, but that he was of a cheerful disposition by nature.

"I have to tell you that I've made enquiries and there are no serving policemen stationed here in any of the four stations in Venice with the first name of Alvise, nor have there been for the past twenty years. Can you describe him?"

"I can do better," I said, passing him several sketches I'd made of Alvise.

"These are extraordinary, almost photographic. Signor Travert can verify that this is this Alvise?"

"Of course. Here's a written description to go with it, including his estimated height compared to my own, the clothes he wore on the day, which are in accord with the sketches I've given to you, and the bent little finger on his right hand. You can see that I've provided three views of his head, clearly showing the three distinct moles on his face: one on the left-hand side of the cleft in his chin, the second on the cheek parallel with the bottom of his earlobe and under his eye on the same side of this face, and the final one just in the hairline on his right temple."

"How did you get him to pose for these sketches, Mr O'Reilly?"

"I didn't. I made them from memory this morning."

"Well, I can't honestly—"

"Please, indulge me," I said, then retrieved my sketchpad and pencil from the desk drawer and did what I'd done countless times in my life. I wished I'd joined the circus and charged for each time I'd had to prove my photographic memory when it came to faces and people.

"This is extraordinary," he said once I'd finished and had passed him the portrait I'd done with my back turned to him. "You've made me look very handsome."

"My friend Giancarlo Manetti said exactly the same thing ten years ago when I drew his portrait with my back turned."

"You and Signor Manetti are …?"

"Business partners. We own several pieces of real estate in common;

we also run a retreat for artists and co-manage my farm. Now, can you please tell me about Mario's death? I think I deserve to know what happened to him."

I mentally put on my combat-veteran hat while I listened, prepared for any gruesome details. According to the forensic pathologist who'd examined his body, Mario had been dead for about four hours when his body was found floating face-down in the Grand Canal at four in the morning, which would mean that he was killed shortly after we'd left him. He'd been beaten severely before death, his jaw fractured and a hairline fracture of the skull caused by a blow with a heavy object. But the cause of death was not drowning. He'd been stabbed in the throat, the blade passing through the hyoid bone just above the thyroid cartilage in his larynx. There was no water in his lungs, so he'd died before he could be thrown into the canal.

"That sounds like a professional hit to me," I said, gritting my teeth in an effort to contain my fury. "It's the way one kills another human being that will allow the victim to understand what's happening to them and know that there's no hope … to suffocate and drown in one's own blood is a terrible way to die."

Pellegrini nodded sadly. "Although my English is rudimentary, I've read two of your books, Mr O'Reilly. I suppose what you say is drawn from your own experience during the war?"

"I'd rather not talk about it, Signor Questore," I said, using the title I remembered for the chief of police for a province.

"I don't like to talk about my war either, Mr O'Reilly … which leads me to ask a sensitive question, which you may choose not to answer."

"Please, go ahead."

"Can you think of anyone who would like to see Mario Celestino dead?"

I knew that if I spoke my thoughts I could get myself into trouble. However, Giancarlo had briefed me on Alessandro Pellegrini before he arrived; he'd known him for years while Giancarlo was still a detective in the police force based in Florence. *He's as straight as an arrow*, Giancarlo had said, which was as good a character reference as my lover could give about anyone. So, I voiced my thoughts.

"In view of Giancarlo's beating and—"

"Signor Manetti was assaulted? When did this happen?"

"Two or three weeks ago, in Trieste. He can fill you in on the details."

"Very well, please proceed."

"As I said, taking into account Giancarlo's beating, the attempt to publicly humiliate me during question time after my book reading at the Cipriani, and the death threats Mario received, I assume it's one person, the only person who could substantially profit from his death."

"And who is this person?"

"Giovanni Scavola," I said.

He opened his cigarette case and offered it to me. I took one and he lit it for me, then sat back in his chair, his brow furrowed and his eyes closed. I waited for him to speak.

"I really hope you wouldn't speculate without some proof, Mr O'Reilly."

"You're right, I wouldn't."

"Would you care to share your reasons? Signor Scavola is a very powerful man."

"Who is running for mayor."

"Yes … among other things."

"I suggest you speak with Giancarlo, who was representing Mario in the case Scavola brought against him for defamation."

"A case which will 'conveniently' disappear now that Signor Celestino is dead," he mused.

The slight pause before the word "conveniently" made me aware that he also wasn't a fan of Scavola, a man with enormous power, prestige and wealth, who on the surface appeared to be basically untouchable.

"What makes you think the case will disappear?" I said.

He sat upright in his chair. "What do you mean?"

"What happens if the defamation was based on the truth? Then it's not slander, it's a matter for the court on a completely different charge."

"Which is unlikely to ever come to pass if tried anywhere in the Veneto region."

"Isn't it fortuitous, then, that Giancarlo is based in the Tuscan jurisdiction, with a licence to also pursue high-profile cases in Lazio."

"A case in Rome would need enormous support, even for someone like Giancarlo Manetti."

"I understand you've known Giancarlo for way longer than I have. Have you ever known him to be reckless—to take up a case where there's no foundation or reasonable chance of success?"

"No, you're right, I haven't. But if it proves that there's any substance in what you're saying, I only hope that I can be involved. I'd love to nail that rotten piece of shit and spit on him when the jailor locks the door of his cell."

"Then I suggest you speak with Giancarlo," I said.

CHAPTER 8

Funeral gondolas in Venice were not an uncommon sight. Rowed by four oarsmen, the casket under a canopy, everything draped in black, they navigated through the canals, passers-by crossing themselves and men removing their hats as a mark of respect.

However, Mario's funeral procession up the Grand Canal was a different thing altogether. The Doge's official barge, swathed in black, eight oarsmen per side in mourning uniforms, the coffin on a raised dais over which was a canopy, its corners bearing plumes of black ostrich feathers. Thousands of mourners lined the canal, throwing flowers into the water, women weeping and teenage girls wailing.

We three stood on the balcony of our apartment, dressed in hastily borrowed black suits, courtesy of the costume storage of La Fenice, watching as the barge passed by accompanied by police *motoscafi* and a flotilla of smaller vessels. The city was so quiet we could hear the slow drumbeat of the bass drum that I knew would continue playing until the cortège reached the quayside in front of the railway station, where it would be raised on to the shoulders of six of Venice's notables and then, accompanied by the town band, carried to the train that would take Mario's body to Rome.

It was Tuesday, two days after his body had been found, and we'd remained in Venice. The national grief had been enormous: front-page stories on every Italian newspaper and reporters from all over the world clamouring to learn whatever they could. However, Pellegrini had personally taken charge of the murder case and had been very tight-lipped, providing me with a way of escaping the press: he forbade me to talk with reporters about my personal connection with Mario, though he gave me *carte blanche* to speak about my treatment at the hands of the local police force. It made me realise that there were old scores to be settled and my maltreatment gave him the perfect opportunity to achieve just that.

Giancarlo had returned to Siena for his court cases. He had three cases over two days, then a hearing in Florence on Thursday afternoon. He then intended to try his best to get to Rome on Friday morning for Mario's funeral there, but he promised me he'd be home at the weekend. I'd suffered a split lip, a fractured rib, an open wound on my scalp and a bruised kidney at the hands of the police, which gave me a great deal of pain. Yesterday evening, before he'd left on the overnight train, we'd sat by ourselves in one of the previously locked *salotti* in our apartment, pulling the dust sheet off one of the sofas and curled up together, he holding me carefully in his arms. I'd asked him if he wanted to spend time with James before he left and said that I didn't mind, but he had shaken his head, telling me it was me he loved. Men like James would come and go, he said, but I was his forever. Despite my infatuation with Kendall, my love for Giancarlo was immutable too, and I told him so.

"What's that they're singing?" Kendall asked now. The orchestra, soloists and chorus of the opera house were amassed on the forecourt of the station. I realised the coffin had finally arrived there.

"'*Va Pensiero*'," I said. "It's the famous chorus of slaves from Verdi's opera *Nabucco*, and very moving for all Italians."

"I should like to go to the opera sometime—will you take me?"

"I know nothing about the opera, sorry. Perhaps Giancarlo could go with you. He's quite passionate about it."

"I'll take you," James said. "My family is quite keen. We go often when in London."

"I'll keep that in mind. Perhaps there'll be something showing when we get to Rome—which reminds me, Damson, are we leaving this afternoon?" We were planning to go back to La Mensola first, then attend the funeral in Rome on Friday.

"I think it's a better idea if we wait until tomorrow. Mario's funeral train is due to take nearly ten hours to get to Rome. The train will be stopping at nearly every station on the way for mourners to pay their respect and the timetables will be in disarray … more so than they usually are, that is."

"He's that well known?" James asked.

"Compare him to someone like Rock Hudson or Richard Chamberlain. If either of them were murdered, can you imagine how important that would be?"

"Never heard of either of them," he said quite genuinely.

"Then Prince Charles, or Richard Burton," I replied. "I'm sure you've heard of them."

"If the next King of England were to be murdered, there'd be an enormous hoo-ha."

"Well, the Italians haven't had a monarchy since 1946, so movie stars, just like in America, are their new royalty."

The phone rang, so I excused myself and went to answer it.

"Hello, Damson, it's me."

I recognised Alfonso's voice. "Hello there, how are you?"

"I'm well, thank you, Damson. A telegram has arrived for you."

The wonder in his voice was so strong it made me smile. Telegrams, unlike in English-speaking countries all over the world, were few and far between in Italy and usually held news of the highest importance.

"Open it and read it out to me."

I heard him opening the envelope.

"I can't. It's not in Italian."

"Read me out the name of the person who sent it. It will be the word right at the end. If you can't pronounce it, spell it."

"It's from David."

He then tried to slowly say each word in a very strong Italian accent, pronouncing each letter separately as one would do in Italian. It sounded like gibberish, but I got the gist of it. My brother had read news of my beating in the newspaper and wanted to know how badly I was injured. I thought of replying straight away, but then checked my watch. It was just after twelve-thirty. There was a nine-hour time difference, so I rang the operator.

"Australia?" she said incredulously.

I gave her the number and promised her a copy of my cookbook if she could put it through as quickly as possible.

We were lingering over coffee after a late lunch when the call finally came through. My brother told me he nearly had a heart attack because my phone call had roused the family at almost midnight. He calmed a little once I'd told him the extent of my injuries and that I was doing well, ready to return home tomorrow.

"How is your brother?" Kendall asked after I got off the phone.

"He sends his best to you and says that he hopes to see you again next year."

"I'm not entirely sure that I'll be going home next year, Damson."

I replied with a broad grin and I'm sure what sounded like joy in my voice, "No, he's coming here. That money I gave him for the trip? He hummed and hawed about whether to use it to buy new farm machinery or the acreage abutting his spread, but it was the kids who convinced him. They're sailing next May and will be here for the summer."

★★★★★

The next morning, I woke with shooting pain down the side of my body and into my leg, so crawled out of bed and tried to stretch it out.

"What's up, Damson?" Kendall called out groggily from the bed.

"My bloody ribs."

"What can I do?"

"Nothing. I'll call the doctor."

Although it was very early in the morning, the doctor arrived soon after I called him. Of course, he demanded to know exactly what the police had done to me while I'd been in custody. I could see his eyes light up; most of the citizens in Venice had a gripe with the cops.

"Have you ever taken these before?" he asked, handing me a phial of tablets. I nodded. I recognised them as the very same painkillers our local doctor, Signor Ambrosio, had prescribed me when I'd been clobbered during the serial killer hunt ten years ago.

With a warning not to drink alcohol while I was taking them, he told me to pay a visit to my doctor when I got home, and asked for Dr Ambrosio's number in Pienza so that he could call him as a courtesy to inform him of his treatment regimen. I didn't roll my eyes, but got the feeling that the call was unwarranted; the nosy Venetian doctor obviously wanted to know more about me. Gossip was currency in Italy, no matter where one lived.

Kendall drove the Land Rover after we arrived at Chiusi. As he'd never driven a left-hand-drive vehicle, I was rather nervous that he might start drifting to the other side of the road, but then he told me he'd ridden numerous times as a passenger in American Jeeps towards the end of his war in Korea.

As I hadn't warned Alfonso exactly when we'd be home, I wasn't surprised to find that he was out; the Jeep was missing. I stoked the fire in the kitchen range, then headed for the shower while Kendall took our bags upstairs. I didn't like baths; I always felt that when I got out of the water, my body was coated in the soap and muck that came off me while I bathed, that's why I hadn't installed one in the new bathroom. However, with an aching body, I wished I could just immerse myself in water up to my neck and soak away the aches.

"Coffee's ready!" Kendall called out from the kitchen.

"Bring mine in here."

No matter how many times I saw him naked, he still made something leap inside me. I watched him walk into the bathroom with a cup in either hand, then lean forward to kiss me at the same time that he handed me my coffee.

"Aren't you getting in?" I asked, placing my cup on the tiled seat.

"If I do, I don't know if I'll be able to control myself," he said.

I laughed. "There's nothing wrong with my cock, Kendall."

He grinned. "I was hoping you'd say that."

About an hour later, while I was flat out on my bed upstairs, Alfonso arrived home. I heard him bounding up the stairs. "Holy Mary, Mother of God," he exclaimed.

"You've seen me naked plenty of times," I teased.

"But Damson, those bruises …" He sat on the edge of the bed and ran his hand over my shoulder.

"Where's Kendall?"

"I don't know, I've just arrived."

Kendall turned up halfway through my explanation of what had happened during our visit to Venice: the book reading, Mario's death, my arrest and what subsequently happened to me in the interrogation room at the police station. He stretched out on the bed next to me, listening without interrupting.

"Alfonso, can you do me a favour, please?"

"Of course, anything. What do you need?"

"I'm not going to push myself and go to the funeral in Rome. Would you mind accompanying Kendall? Perhaps stay for the weekend and show him around the city? He's still got my Michelin guide, so he can look things up without you having to try to explain to him."

"Well … of course I'd be happy to spend some time with him. But how will you manage by yourself?"

"I'm not actually incapacitated, just very sore. Besides, I'm sick and tired of journalists following me everywhere, hounding me, some of them still insinuating that somehow I'm involved in Mario's murder. I doubt things would be different, and they might be even worse were I to be spotted at his funeral."

*****

The following day, I stood at the front gate and waved them goodbye. Alfonso drove the Jeep, Kendall saying he was happy to sit back and watch the countryside go by. It was only a three-hour drive on a good day, so they left at about two in the afternoon. The funeral was tomorrow, at ten in the morning. Giancarlo had postponed his Friday appointments and was due to catch the train to meet them in Rome.

Part of me wanted to go with them, but I needed some space and time to myself. A few days would do it; I called those days my recharge-my-battery time. I didn't do anything different from what I'd normally do; I just wanted to have time to reflect. It was part of my upbringing at the monastery, where we boys were taught to pray and to meditate. I didn't do much of the former these days and hadn't for years, but I did try every day, if I could, to spend ten or fifteen minutes trying to find my inner peace. It wasn't always accessible, but I missed that silent communication with myself … and with God. It was something that Giancarlo was aware of, was supportive of but never commented on; he didn't really understand. His religion was just something that all Italians did, like eating, breathing, sleeping … mine was more profound, no doubt due to my brother's and my own upbringing by a religious order.

I watered the vegetable garden and checked on the progress of the apples, pears and quince trees. They needed copper spray; I'd do that next week—it could wait. After that, I threw a cake together using one of the small jars of apples that I'd put down last year. Once it was in the oven, I went upstairs to my study and pulled out my sketch pad and the notes for the next episode in the children's book that Stefano and I were writing together and started to draw a few quick outlines. I began to wonder what it would be like if our mouse held a party for his pals in his hidey-hole behind the kitchen stove, then made a quick sketch of the mouse, his friends the vole and the beetle wearing party hats and sharing a meal of crumbs for the mouse, grubs for the vole and bits of fruit for the beetle. It made me chuckle; I thought it looked charming, but decided to show it to Stefano's children, the arbiters of what appealed and what didn't.

I'd barely taken the cake out of the oven when the phone rang. If it was another reporter, somehow having found the phone number of La Mensola, I was prepared to let forth more than a few angry words. However, what I wasn't prepared for was a man stumbling in Italian, asking for Alfonso. I recognised the accent, so I replied in French.

"You must by Alfonso's friend, Monsieur Masson," I said. "I'm sorry but he's gone to Rome."

"*Ah, mon dieu,* I can hardly believe my ears. You must be his land-lord, Mr O'Reilly. He told me you spoke French, but didn't tell me you actually were French?"

"I'm not." I told him my story: that I'd been brought up in a monastery run by an order of French priests, then had lived for eighteen months in the south of France. When I'd first arrived in Vence, the locals had

smiled at my turns of phrase, thinking my language very old-fashioned—
and of course, it was. The older fathers had left France in the nineteenth
century and spoke with the accent and precision of the times; the newer,
more recently arrived ones had modified their own speech to reflect that
of their superiors. However, after some time in Vence, mine had
loosened and had become more contemporary. I'd often been mistaken
for a Frenchman during the time I'd lived there.

"So," I concluded, "I'm not from France, but thank you for the
compliment. Is there a message I can pass on?"

"Ah no, it can wait until he returns. Perhaps you can help me? Do
you know anyone who can look at my tractor? The engine turns over
for a few moments, then it stalls. Is there a mechanic that you use?"

"You're in luck. I know a very good mechanic. Your farm is somewhere off the road between my house and Bivio San Biagio?"

"Yes, about two kilometres from there."

"I'll be there in about ten minutes," I said.

"You have a mechanic at hand so readily?"

"I do. See you soon. Now exactly where is it?"

"I'll stand at the edge of the road at the front entrance and look out
for you."

Dressed in shorts and a white T-shirt, my work boots and with my
large tool kit in the boot of the Maserati, I got there in no time at all.
Gaspard waved as I slowed down, then whistled at the car, patting the
bonnet when I pulled up next to him.

"But where is your mechanic?" he asked.

"Right in front of you," I said.

"I thought you were a writer?"

"I am, but I'm also a trained carpenter and a vehicle mechanic, a
trade that I learned in preparation for the war."

"*Vous avez eu de la chance*," he said. "I spent my war fighting the
Boches."

"And I the Japanese," I said. "But it doesn't mean I still can't fix
anything that runs on petrol or diesel."

An hour later, the tractor up and running—it was a partially blocked
fuel line—Gaspard showed me around his house and his land. The house

was far larger than La Mensola and in far better condition than my house when I'd bought it. The great beauty of it was its view. Built on a small rise, it had amazing views to the south. I immediately suggested to him that he move his sitting room upstairs and construct a balcony to take advantage of the vista. He shrugged, saying that sort of work was far beyond him, but then smiled when I told him that I'd be only too happy to help build it whenever he was ready.

The fields, he explained, hadn't been cultivated since before the war. Tenants had rented the house until five years ago, neglecting the land. I stood at the edge of what had been a large field, one hand on my hip, the other around the back of my neck. It was the pose that Giancarlo said was my version of scratching my head.

"Do you have a harrow attachment for your tractor?" I asked him. Then, when he said that all he had was a three-pronged plough, I offered to drive my tractor here when I'd recovered enough, then help him fell the few trees that had grown over the past twenty years, use my tractor chains to pull out the stumps, and then, using both of our machines, we could plough and furrow the field in a day, all things going well.

He shook my hand and thanked me, offering me coffee and a slice of his *tarte Tatin*. The kitchen was far more modern than my own, boasting an electric stove as well as a wood range. He made coffee in the French style in a *cafetière*, something that brought back memories of my days in France. How wonderful it was to speak the language again with a native speaker. It was obvious that Gaspard was well educated, his French cultured and with a slight accent that I did not at first recognise until he told me that he'd been born in Lille, in northern France, his mother from Brittany and his father a Walloon, from the French-speaking area of Belgium.

He was effusive in his thanks and asked time after time what he could do to repay my offer of help. I told him that we should just be friends and neighbours, and invited him for dinner the day after tomorrow, when Giancarlo was back from Rome.

"Giancarlo is your business partner?" he asked.

"And my bed partner," I said.

That was all that was spoken of about our situations. I felt that if I told him about me and Giancarlo, it would leave a door open for him in case he wanted to talk about his relationship with Alfonso.

He asked me if I'd mind helping him with his mail. Much of it turned out to be official letters about the land and taxes. He spoke not a word of Italian except for very simple everyday phrases, explaining that many of the words looked similar to French words because of the common Latin roots, but that he struggled.

Before I left, I shook his hand, told him I'd look forward to seeing him on Saturday evening and saying that if there was *anything*—I emphasised the word—that he wanted to talk about, I'd be only too happy to lend an ear and that I was good at keeping confidences.

On the way home, I realised I was driving with a gentle smile on my face, the result of spending a pleasant afternoon with a new acquaintance, renewing my love of the French language and lending a hand to someone who was in the same situation I had been in when I'd first arrived in Italy. How he and Alfonso communicated was beyond me, but if their relationship was merely a physical one, then nature had a way of making words unnecessary.

*****

"How was the funeral?" I asked Giancarlo as he kissed my cheek.

"Packed. There were thousands of people outside the church. It would have been much too tiring for you; I hope you've been resting since you got back."

"I have, yes, but I've also had an interesting encounter." I explained that I'd spent Thursday afternoon with Gaspard—and that I'd invited him to dinner tonight.

"Oh, God," said Giancarlo. "Can we speak in French for the rest of the day before he gets here? Mine is so poor."

"You'll do fine," I said. "I can always translate if you get lost."

"I had such a good teacher," he said, drawing me closer into his arms. I recognised where this was going, so began to unbuckle his belt. I kissed him, a quick peck at first, which then turned into a longer, more exploratory kiss. "I still hurt," I warned him, "so you'll have to be careful."

"Tell me what you want, Damson."

"Whatever makes you happy."

Despite the shooting pain in my chest as we lay side by side on the floor of the new breakfast room, sun shining through the open doors, his cock in my mouth and mine in his, I still managed to stay hard. We even managed a second round, this time in the shower. He wanted to wash off the grime of travel; I wanted to run my hands over his body. Despite our years together and my infatuation with Kendall, Giancarlo did things to me that no one else had ever done. Not so much sexually, but his very manner, the sheen of his skin, the blond hairs on his chest and his groin were all things that, put together, made my motor purr.

"Scavola went to Greece the morning after Mario was killed," he said, standing between my knees, facing away from me while I sat on the bench in the shower recess, soaping up his back with a flannel. He bent forward cheekily as I ran my hand between his legs and massaged his scrotum with my soapy fingers.

"That was convenient. Who told you that? Have you been speaking with Pellegrini?"

"No, it was James, actually. He found out."

"How on earth did James find out where Scavola was?"

"I've no idea. Perhaps he heard it from his American friends."

"He's still seeing them? I suppose he called you."

"No, I called him. Mainly because you always forget to tell people who stay in the apartment to leave the key with the baker when they leave."

"Did he say when he'll be back?"

"He's staying a few more days. He said sometime around the middle of next week."

He turned then kneeled on the floor, laying his head on my lap, the water from the shower playing over his back. "Damson?"

"Yes."

"How incredibly stupid it would be for Scavola to arrange to have Mario killed, if that's what happened."

"I've had those same thoughts."

Giancarlo sucked on the skin above my hipbone, drawing up a love bite.

"Why did you do that?" I asked with a laugh.

"Just marking my territory."

"Are you jealous?"

"No, I've already told you that I'm not."

It was one of those playful moments I was loath to spoil, but there were things on my mind I needed to tell him. I sighed.

"I recognise that sigh, Damson. What's up?"

"I phoned the carpenter in Rome this morning—"

"Oh, shit!" Giancarlo said. "The statement!"

"What? Which statement?"

"The statement you told me about, that you and Mario's policeman friend witnessed. That's how we can track him down."

"Track who down?"

"This Alvise character," he said. "The Venetian policeman that no one can find. If his signature's on Mario's statement, then—"

"Whoa! Settle down. You must have forgotten. I told you … no it wasn't you, I told Kendall. And Pellegrini, of course."

"Told them what, Damson?"

"Alvise wouldn't even look at the statement when he came into Mario's study, said he wouldn't sign it; he said he 'didn't want to get involved with anything that had to do with Scavola' … Wait! Are you thinking what I'm thinking?"

"You'd better tell me what you're thinking first, Damson."

"Mario said he'd been seeing Alvise for about two years … perhaps this Alvise was in Scavola's pocket? Bedroom secrets could prove invaluable to Scavola."

"If that's the case, then it was extremely stupid of Alvise to have refused to witness the statement. He could have learned exactly what Mario had on Scavola."

"Maybe he got too involved?" I said. "I had the impression that he had more than just a passing interest in Mario; I'd say he was besotted with him. That would muddy the waters if Scavola did have him in his pocket, and could explain why he didn't want to read what Mario had written."

"We'll never know, until or if we ever find him," Giancarlo said.

"True, but then there's the carpenter I phoned this morning."

"Which carpenter, Damson? Must you always speak in riddles?"

"The man Mario said he was having sex with in Rome."

"You phoned him? How did you know who he was?"

"The tags on his furniture. Every high-class cabinet maker signs his work discreetly. In this case, like many other furniture artisans, he inscribes his name and address on small brass plaques. I found a few in Mario's apartment on the underside of chairs and in the corner of the interior lid of the blanket chest. His name is Gregorio Vaccarello, and he lives in Piazza del Drago in Rome. It was easy enough to get his number from the telephone exchange. His wife answered the phone, saying that they were closed today and that her husband was away. He'd gone to Aranova to source some timber and wouldn't be back for a day or two."

"A *day* or two? Aranova is what, twenty minutes by car from Rome?" Giancarlo said. "I wonder if he, too, could be on Scavola's pay list."

*****

The next morning, I was aching all over. The priests at the monastery would have said that my bruises were "starting to come out", hence the discomfort. Perhaps last night, when Gaspard had come for dinner, an evening filled with good cheer and laughter, I'd overdone things. So, I woke Giancarlo early, told him I was going to six o'clock mass and that, when I got back, I was going to the Bagni di San Filippo, about forty minutes away by car, to soak in the hot springs. He said he'd come with me—not to mass, he'd become a lapsed Catholic, but to San Filippo.

Situated halfway between Pienza and Lake Bolsena, the beauty of the natural hot springs was one of the wonders of the area. Infrequently visited, except for men—women preferred to travel to Chianciano Terme, a vast, almost industrial thermal bath complex—the springs were isolated and tranquil. The string of pools just outside of the small town of Bagni di San Filippo was a refuge; I loved it there. During a difficult time in our relationship, Giancarlo used to go there to meet men, more often than not returning grumpily because no one else had turned up.

We parked just on the outskirts of the town and wandered down through the forest to the main pool, which was a startling azure blue, then followed the concatenated pools downhill until we arrived at my favourite spot, a smaller, shallower pool, hidden from view from above by a rocky outcrop and surrounded by dense pines. The water here, unlike some of the other adjacent mineral springs in other parts of Tuscany, didn't stink, and the mud at the bottom of the pools was renowned for its supposed healing properties. We stripped off, and Giancarlo sat at the edge watching me as I eased myself into the water and sighed. I pinched my nose and sank under the water, revelling in the slight effervescence and the warmth of the water.

"Mud?" he asked when I surfaced, handing me a cigarette.

"Only if you smear it on me."

He grinned. "Why else do you think I came?"

"On the lookout for lost boyfriends," I said, then kissed him.

I stood in the shallows while he scooped up handfuls of the rich ooze from the floor of the pool then smeared it over my shoulders and chest, asking me to turn so he could do my back. The next handful of mud went over my buttocks and between my legs.

"Oi! What are you doing back there?" I said with a laugh.

"How'd you like to be fucked with my muddy cock?"

"No, thanks, the mud is very gritty."

"You're a pervert, Damson. You'd love it."

I knew he was teasing, and laughed into his mouth when I turned to kiss him.

"You've got that look," I said.

"What look? Oh … when I'm thinking about a case. Yes, I'm trying to fit pieces together."

"I'm happy to talk about it," I replied, sitting next to him, waiting for the mud to dry before I hopped back into the pool.

"There are three men we need to find."

"You mean three men *Pellegrini* needs to find, Giancarlo. You're not the detective in this instance, merely the lawyer who represented Mario before his death."

"Ah, I may have forgotten to tell you something, Damson. When we last met, Mario signed a *procura speciale*, which I had notarised in Venice. So, you see, as the *esecutore testamentario*, I'm still involved. I can't execute the will until I'm satisfied that everything is legally in place and his murderer can be found."

"You got him to sign a power of attorney and you're also the executor of his will?"

"As it turns out, very handy, wouldn't you agree?"

I didn't know what to think yet, but it was just like him to have covered every base. "Why did you do that?"

"I thought it would be easier for me to find out things for him using the power of attorney rather than have him expose himself by searching for legal documents, which could lead to Scavola finding out. After I was beaten up, I was worried something could happen to him, famous or not. It seemed a prudent thing to do, and he was happy enough to agree."

It was prudent, and, in light of what had happened, fortuitous. "All right, tell me who the three men are you need to find … you *and* Alessandro Pellegrini together. I don't want you to get into any more trouble, Giancarlo."

"First off, this mysterious man Alvise. I'm thinking I might send Onofrio Manfredi to Venice to do some digging."

"Onofrio? The detective from Florence who worked on the serial killer murders with you? How would he get away from work?"

"He left the police. Didn't I tell you?"

I shook my head.

"He's working for the courts now as an official and sometimes does some *ad hoc* work for me, preparing documents and helping my secretary in Florence with her mountain of work. He and his wife have five children now, can you believe it? I know the extra money would come in handy."

"All right. So I suppose the second man you need to find is Mario's partner in Rome. Leave that to me; I've already contacted his wife and I'm going to follow it up. That leaves the third man you need to find: it has to be the survivor of the massacre in Vatican City."

"Yes. I'll spend some time—"

"No need," I said. "I already have a fairly good idea of where he may be."

"Where?"

"Aranova," I said. "The carpenter told me her husband had gone there to search for wood for his cabinet-making business. I told you in the shower yesterday and, like me, you thought it odd that he was intending to stay so long. I know that timber mill; I've bought bits from them before. They have an enormous stock of reclaimed timber from buildings demolished after the war, stuff that's impossible to find unless you travel to France or Germany. I bet anything that Mario entrusted the missing boy, now a man, to the care of his Roman lover."

Giancarlo stared at me for a few moments, evaluating the situation. "I'm coming with you," he said.

I patted his knee. "I think not this time. I'm a carpenter by trade, remember. I also know all about his relationship with Mario, because Mario told me about it."

"Very well. When will you go?"

"The middle of the week; hopefully, I'll be less uncomfortable by then. I have things to do here and I'd like to speak with Alessandro Pellegrini first, to tell him what I'm up to."

"Why does he need to know?"

"Because I'm trying to avoid any unnecessary surprises. You're used to working on your own, the way you did when you were the hot-shot detective who first shared my bed ten years ago. We need to be transparent, Giancarlo, and if we do anything, it really needs to have approval by the police, otherwise we might both end up in hot water."

The mud now caking on my neck, I plunged back into the pool, then dived under and swam around for a while.

I couldn't blame Giancarlo for wanting to go it alone—I'd been the same when I was in my twenties—but so much had happened since we'd first got together that I'd vowed I'd never go off on my own without someone knowing where I was or having someone to cover my back. The last time I'd done that, I'd nearly been killed and had ended up in hospital with a fractured skull.

Giancarlo had plenty to get on with—his legal practice was very busy—and he realised that what I'd said made sense. I'd visit the carpenter's workshop in Rome to check whether the carpenter was actually there and his wife had been covering for him, and if not, then I'd go to

Aranova. As for back-up, I'd take Kendall. As much as I loved Giancarlo, I knew who'd be the strongest and most deadly should I find myself in trouble.

Trouble? I didn't expect to have trouble with the carpenter, but I had a bad feeling about Scavola and what he might get up to in the aftermath of Mario's murder. The press hadn't held back, speculating on the days leading up to Mario's murder and my close friendship with the now-dead film star.

If I were Scavola, I'd be keeping a close eye on Damson O'Reilly.

CHAPTER 9

Aranova was perhaps thirty minutes from Fiumicino, where we'd dropped off Kendall.

He'd been summoned to a meeting in London as his father's representative in discussions about royalty-sharing between the various publishers who were to reissue translated versions of some of the Travert Pty Ltd books—among them, by arrangement with my publisher in London, my own. He'd decided to fly, and as Rome's airport, Fiumicino, was close to where we were headed, we'd driven him there after visiting the carpenter's wife.

I'd wanted him to go with me to Aranova, as a just-in-case back-up. Perhaps I was being overcautious, but both he and Giancarlo had thought it a sensible option. Now, with Kendall away, I'd asked Alfonso if he'd like to come with me. He was a far better boxer than I was; I tested him out and he had me nearly on my back after three punches. Besides, I'd seen how level-headed he was in action one night ten years ago in the darkness of an olive grove in Pienza when we'd been confronted by the two murderers we'd been chasing.

"There's still time to back off ..." I said to him as we drove from the airfield to the small hamlet about thirty kilometres to its north.

"Shut up, Damson," he said with a small laugh, one hand on my knee in the front seat of the Land Rover.

"Light me up a smoke, will you?" I asked, glancing at him. How he'd changed over the years I'd known him. He wasn't a man who'd make heads turn, but there was something incredibly attractive about him, especially when he smiled. He'd become my closest friend during the time I'd been in Italy; we'd played sport together, laughed, spent time in my garden, and he'd almost lived in La Mensola over that time.

Initially, there'd been a very strong yet unrequited sexual attraction between us, which had been replaced over the years by a bond of friendship the like of which I'd never experienced before, the type of friendship that I could only describe as love.

I hadn't had time to foster close, intimate friendships. At the monastery my brother had been my world, and then, during the war, the wisest of us had made friends, sure, but with the knowledge that perhaps that person wouldn't be alive to see the next day. In Japan, I'd got close to Danny; however, he'd outranked me, and our meetings were infrequent and usually involved sex, me fucking him in all sorts of awkward places at ridiculous hours of the day and night.

After that, I'd lived the life of a loner in France, working for Madame Tremeau in Vence, writing, painting and looking after her garden and her house. Alfonso, whom I'd known then as Father Ignazio, was not only one of the first friendly faces I'd met on the first day I'd arrived in Pienza, but he'd also translated for me by the use of Latin, which I'd learned alongside French from the age of six at the monastery.

"What were you looking at?"

"The handsome man sitting next to me," I replied, squeezing his hand. He gave a soft snort then passed me the cigarette I'd asked him to light for me. "Don't mock. You are handsome," I added in response to his snort. Dressed in khaki-coloured shorts with a white shirt and wearing Kendall's aviator sunglasses, he looked more than just attractive.

He leaned across and kissed my cheek, his lips lingering a little, as they always did. "You and Giancarlo do wonders for my self-confidence. Thank you, Damson."

"You've never appeared to me to be a man who's in need of self-confidence. I don't mean that you come across as overconfident or cocky …" I used the word *vanitoso*, which had slightly different subtleties than our English word "vain".

"In my role as a priest, you're right. But, over the past month or so, now that I'm a private citizen, I feel that I'm judged differently. I feel far more vulnerable as a human being."

"Why?"

"I think it's something to do with feeling I no longer have that direct connection with God, that I'm no longer His mouthpiece or His representative on earth, doing His will."

"Every one of us has a direct connection with God, Alfonso. He's still there, guiding you. Perhaps it was His wish that led you to your decision to approach the bishop and take your *exclaustratio*. Did you think of that?"

*****

Aranova was a rural, predominantly farming community, similar to thousands of such small towns scattered across the country. I parked the car in one of the side streets and led Alfonso to the café I'd eaten at, the few times I'd been here to source timber. The wife of the owner was an excellent cook and, every time I'd visited, had eaten very well.

This time was no exception. Alfonso had spoken to the owner in Roman dialect so thick that I barely could follow the conversation, which led to us being presented with two large steaming plates of *trippa alla Romana*, one of my favourite dishes; one that, when I prepared it, I would leave overnight on the back of my fuel stove for at least twelve hours on the barest of simmers.

I'd always equated tripe with poor people's food back home in Australia. As a child, it had often appeared on our table as the only meal of the day, rubbery because of the short cooking time my mother had spent preparing it, serving it with her wallpaper-paste-gluggy white sauce with parsley. However, since coming to Italy, I'd discovered this wonderful regional dish, the tripe slow-braised for hours in delicious, rich, thick tomato sauce and served smothered in Parmesan cheese. I complimented the *signora* effusively on her tripe. Over the years I'd lived here, I'd discovered that compliments on a woman's food were appreciated far more than those on her looks—something I'd never do; it would be outrageously bad-mannered and would probably end up with her husband confronting me, asking me what the fuck was going on.

It had been a number of years since I'd last eaten here and she didn't seem to recognise me. When she asked me why we were visiting Aranova, I explained that I was a carpenter and had come to buy timber. She told me that a lot of people who ate in her trattoria had come to the town for the same reason. In fact, two had eaten breakfast here for the past five or six days: a man she recognised from his frequent visits, and his apprentice. They were from Rome, she said.

"I have a good friend who's a cabinet maker in Rome who comes here with his apprentice," I said. "Wouldn't it be an extraordinary coincidence if it was my friend Gregorio and his young helper … what's his name again? It escapes me …"

"Luca."

"Yes, that's right, Luca. Gregorio has a shop in Piazza del Drago; we were going to call in to visit him after I've made my purchases."

She wasn't to know that we'd already visited Gregorio's wife at his atelier. She'd been close-lipped, merely asserting what she'd told me over the phone: her husband had gone to Aranova.

"Well, catching up with your friends here will save you a journey to Rome."

"Do you perhaps know where they're staying? Oh, don't bother, I'll ask the owner of the timber yard."

"Save yourself the trouble, *signore*. They're staying at my brother's farmhouse, just outside town. Take the main road out to the west and it's the second house on your right, perhaps a kilometre away."

"Smooth, O'Reilly," Alfonso said when we were out on the street, the owner's wife's tripe doubly praised again by us both before we left.

"She couldn't take her eyes off you," I said.

"I'd have preferred it had it been her husband," he said, then refused to catch my eye when I stared at him, rather surprised that he'd say such a thing. It made me realise that I'd still not come to terms with this new version of my old friend. Maybe he was just voicing thoughts that he'd carried for years in silence.

I recognised Gregorio, the carpenter, from the photograph Mario had of them together in his office. He was playing bocce with an older man, whom I took to be the restaurant cook's brother, and a young man in his mid-twenties. Without any proof yet, I immediately assumed that that was Luca.

They paused mid-play, turning their heads when we called out *"Buongiorno!"* I noticed Gregorio's knuckles turn white when he saw me, and for a moment I thought he might throw his bocce ball at me; he looked poised to either fight or flee.

"My name is—" I said, holding out my hand and approaching him.

"I know who you are, Signor O'Reilly," he said. "Why are you here?"

"I wonder if we might talk privately. I'm not here to cause trouble, I came with a message from a mutual friend in Venice."

The young man's head turned, and he stared at me anxiously. I smiled at him and offered him my hand too, but he backed away a little.

"We can talk down in the vegetable garden," the carpenter said.

"Wait! Can't you wait until our game is over?" the older man asked.

"I'll play for him," Alfonso said, using the same thick dialect he'd used in the café.

I followed Gregorio behind the house, turning to see that Alfonso had already made himself acquainted with the other two men.

"Mario sent you?"

"No, not specifically, but I was with him on the night he was murdered, and we spent a few days together before that."

"They really did you over, didn't they?" he said, inspecting the bruises on my face.

"Who, the police?"

"Yes, I read about it in the *Corriere della Sera*. How did you find me? I doubt Mario would have given you my name."

"He told me all about you, without mentioning your name. I'm a carpenter by trade and I saw the plaque inside that beautiful blanket chest you made for him. He told me he had a special carpenter friend in Rome. It wasn't hard to put two and two together."

"Look, Mr O'Reilly, I'm a married man, and—"

I pulled my crucifix on its chain out of my shirt collar. "I kissed this and swore to Mario that I would tell no one about you and him."

"But why are you here? What do you want from me?"

I nodded my head in the direction of the three men playing bocce. "I think Luca might be in danger."

"Mario told you about him? I can't believe it. He swore me to secrecy …"

"If I could find him so easily, others could." I offered him a cigarette and lit it for him, noticing how his hands were trembling ever so slightly. "Let me tell you what happened," I said.

"Luca deserves to hear this too."

"Maybe not all of it, Gregorio. He doesn't need to hear about Mario's private life."

We sat on a low stone wall while I revealed to him the various connections: Giancarlo's and, therefore, my involvement; Giancarlo's presumed beating at the hands of Scavola's henchmen; the ransacking of Mario's apartment; the attempt to frame me for his murder.

He dropped his head, the expression on his face immeasurably sad. "Did he tell you about Emilio?"

"His brother? Only that he'd been killed in a street fight some time towards the end of the war."

"Is that all he told you?"

I nodded. "Is it relevant?"

"I'll tell you later. What do you intend to do with Luca?"

"Mario told me when we last spoke that he was going to ask Luca's permission to tell me or my partner, Giancarlo, exactly what happened on the ninth of June 1944. There's no record of his account except for a verbal one, an account he related to Mario, who's now dead. I need Luca to be able to tell his own version of the story, have it written down and witnessed. It's a precaution. If Scavola got one whiff of the fact that he was the sole survivor of the massacre …"

"You think he …?"

"Yes, I think he was behind Mario's murder. Who else had the most to profit from his death? Scavola's in Greece, probably thinking that now Mario's dead, the whole thing will disappear and he'll get away with it; not only what happened on that night in Vatican City but also the other things he got up to during the war."

"I brought Luca up here as soon as I heard of Mario's murder. You've risked his safety by coming here, Signor O'Reilly."

"I didn't tell anyone I was coming," I said.

"Then how did I recognise you? Your photograph was all over the front pages of the newspapers. You must have known where we were from someone in town."

"Yes, the cook at the café told me."

"No one would have said anything, but you can bet that everyone recognised you. Gossip; it's the local currency. Soon news will spread."

"Then we need to relocate Luca."

"But where?"

"Do you know whether he's at all religious?"

"Yes. He was an orphan, and you presumably already know that he was brought up by an order of nuns."

"He and I have something in common. My brother and I were brought up in a monastery by an order of monks." I had somewhere in mind but needed to discuss it with Alfonso first.

When we returned to the others, I joined in the game, teaming up with Alfonso and playing in pairs, the owner of the house watching from the sidelines. It took a while, but eventually I could see that Luca had warmed to me. I spoke quickly with Alfonso while we were standing at one end of the pitch, while Gregorio and Luca took their turns. "I need some time alone with them," I said, nodding at our opposing team pair, then explained that we needed to find somewhere safe to hide Luca, saying that perhaps I had an idea but would discuss it with him when we were alone.

After two more games, Alfonso begged off and started to engage in conversation with the owner of the house. I took the opportunity to speak with Luca and Gregorio, expressing my concerns to the young man, who still seemed reluctant to trust me.

"Alfonso, my friend—did you get on well with him?" I asked.

"Yes, of course. I liked him a lot."

"He's a priest. Will you trust him?"

Both men turned to stare at Alfonso, who at the moment looked far from priestly, his shirt open to the waist, showing his hirsute chest, his hair unruly, wearing shorts and sandals with sunglasses perched on top of his head, a gold chain around his neck on which hung a crucifix. He looked all the world like some Neapolitan gangster.

"He's having a sabbatical," I explained.

★★★★★

The four of us arrived at La Mensola at about seven that evening. Giancarlo, just back from Arezzo, looked surprised at first, but he was the perfect host. Bedrooms were arranged—there was room for everyone—he sorted them out while Alfonso and I started to get something ready to eat.

Pasta was the quickest and easiest and I made it nearly every other day. Using jars of *passata* from my pantry and rummaging through my dry goods store and the contents of the refrigerator, I created a tasty sauce for my *pici*—hand-rolled local pasta shapes. I sent Luca out into the garden with Alfonso to pick salad greens. It took me no more than a few minutes to throw together the ingredients for soda bread rolls. There wasn't time to get the outside bread oven hot enough, but I stacked the firebox of our wood range full, knowing that in about twenty minutes the oven would be ready for the rolls I'd form from the dough I'd prepared, and they'd take no more than ten minutes to bake.

In the meantime, Giancarlo set the table outside and bought out bottles of wine and some cheese and olives from our pantry to munch on while we waited for dinner.

It was he who finally convinced Luca to open up and to share his story. It was after dinner, everyone feeling mellow with tummies full of good food and a few bottles of the local red, that he interrupted our chit-chat, announcing that what I'd said was right: that, if Luca didn't tell someone what had happened to him, the story of the death of Sister Ursula, the other nuns, and his three childhood friends would be lost and perhaps the perpetrators get away unpunished. "Perhaps not now," Giancarlo added. "Tomorrow, in my office, with my assistant present.

He can take shorthand and we can have a statement typed up quickly then witnessed.

"This is going to be very hard to talk about," Luca said. "I've only told Mario and I had nightmares after telling him. I'd prefer to do it first here, so you can ask questions; that will prepare me for the formality of your office tomorrow, Signor Manetti."

Giancarlo understood, saying that it was a good idea, so while everyone settled back I went to find my notebook—and one for Giancarlo from his study—then returned, to find that Alfonso had served up a blackberry jam *crostata* that he'd made earlier and which had been baking in the oven while we'd been eating our pasta.

*****

"Although you might find it hard to believe, I have very clear memories of the time leading up to what happened," the young man said.

"Ease into it, Luca," Giancarlo said. "Start wherever you like. Tell us a bit about yourself, perhaps how you came to be looked after by Sister Ursula?"

It was incredibly painful for me to listen to Luca's story, which was in many ways similar to my own. Although I was older, so had memories of my mother and father, David and me and our two sisters sitting at the table for meals, Luca had none of these. His father had disappeared, presumed kidnapped by fascists, in 1938 when Luca was just four years old, and his mother had left him with the nuns, unable to cope by herself and shunned by her devoutly religious rural family, who blamed her for her husband's disappearance. Luca didn't even know his own real name. He'd been given a new Christian name and a new surname, which he later learned was that of Sister Ursula's before she'd taken her vows. He'd only ever known himself as Luca Rinaldo and he was too afraid to go back to the convent to ask for his records … there were still nuns alive there who presumed he'd been murdered, along with their fellow sisters and the other three children.

At the trial, he'd heard stories of mounting pressure, of threats to the Mother Superior and the convent itself by fascist groups, furious that the nuns were harbouring dissidents and others deemed to be against the regime. All he remembered from that time in the early years of the war was the lack of food, sharing a tiny, cramped room with half a dozen other children of all ages, and fear and secret whisperings between the nuns. However, he'd been shown true kindness and love by the women, especially Sister Ursula, with whom he'd had a special relationship. He still didn't understand why, but suspected it was something to do with his natural mother. There were so many children, and he'd always wondered why she and he had formed such a close bond.

"The week before we left, Sister Ursula asked me to sit with her in the cloister garden. I was very shy in her company, I do remember that. She told me she wanted me to gather my possessions, enough to fit into a pillowcase, and have it ready to take with me when we left. When I asked where we were going, she simply smiled and kissed me on the forehead, saying it would be somewhere safe, and that the Pope had given us his blessing."

Gregorio sat next to him, one arm around his shoulder. "Take a break if you need one," he said. "I can hear this is difficult for you."

Luca nodded then stood, lit a cigarette and walked to the end of the terrace. "May I visit your shrine?" he asked me.

As it was such a still night, I gave him a candle to light his way and we sat and watched the flickering light as he walked down the driveway towards the stable until my fig trees blocked him from sight. "Shall I go to see if he's all right?" Gregorio asked. We told him it would be better to wait. He returned perhaps five minutes later, his expression no longer anxious but calm. I wished I still had that ability to find inner peace so quickly by prayer.

"One night, she woke me up, shushed me and told me to fetch my bundle. Four of us children and four nuns climbed onto the back of a covered truck that took us through the streets. I had no idea where we were; all I remember is tall buildings all around, everything still in darkness. But what I do remember the most was that there was no sound of gunshots, bombs or people yelling. We were so used to it that it hit me as being strange, as though we were living in a different world."

"Do you remember the names of the other nuns, the children?" Giancarlo asked, looking up from his notepad.

"The children, yes; the nuns, not really. I was the oldest of them by far. The other three were just babies, perhaps two or three years old. Gianetta, Elisabetta, Carlino … those were the children. As for the nuns, Sister Benedetta was one… and the other two I didn't really know and if I did know their names, I've forgotten them. One worked in the library, the other in the kitchen, that I do remember."

My stomach turned. Gianetta, Elisabetta, Carlino … names of innocent children … what could have been gained by their deaths? I wondered. It was too terrible, and Luca could easily have been one of them. The worst of my memories were not of the battlefield but of the towns and villages we fought through. I was no stranger to dead children; they, and women, were the most frequent civilian casualties of war.

"Sister Ursula had brought a sandwich for each of us; she and the nuns nibbled at tiny bread rolls. If I close my eyes, to this day I can still taste mine: dry with a few slices of cucumber and some sort of cheese— we were still under rationing back then. I was desperate for something to drink. We'd been told not to before we'd left the convent by the nun who worked in the kitchen; she said that she didn't know when we'd next be able to use the lavatory."

"Were you all together or spread out?" Giancarlo asked.

"I was right at the back, all the others at the front near the entrance to the carriage. I'd opened the window to get some air. It was warm and there was a breeze. That's when we heard the shouting."

"Shouting?"

"Yes—there were men outside, all dressed in black. I was sitting on the side of the carriage opposite the platform, so moved over onto the bench seat across from mine to look out of the window. Sister Ursula motioned to me to keep down low. Men were arguing. I pulled down the train window shutter, just like everyone else. Sister Ursula had told us to, but I could see through the slats. The yelling got louder and a fight broke out; it only stopped when there was a gunshot."

"A gunshot?"

"Yes, a man fired a pistol into the air. The men formed into two groups—one in railway uniforms, the others dressed in black. A man who appeared to be the leader of the 'blacks' moved into the middle. It was he who'd fired the pistol; I could still see it in his hand, held high up in the air. He started shouting, then pulled one of the railway workers from their group, knocked him to the ground and began to kick him. That's when I noticed the leader's limp. It all went by so quickly, the limping man and another from the black-clothed group tried to get into our railway carriage while the railway workers were trying to stop them. There was shouting and yelling … someone blew a whistle …"

Then he stopped and crossed himself, swallowed deeply and drained the last of the wine in his glass.

"Sister Ursula ran down to me and told me to climb out of the window and hide. There was a bar on the outside about halfway down. The space was far too small for an adult to crawl through, but I managed to squeeze through and stood outside waiting for her to pass the other children down to me … that's when the screaming started and shots were fired."

"Fired where?" I asked.

"Inside the carriage. I was so scared that I flattened myself on the track underneath the train behind one of the wheels."

"Dear God …" Gregorio said, crossing himself.

"That's not all, though, is it?" Alfonso said, very quietly.

Luca shook his head. "I could hear the children still screaming loudly, then their screams became muffled. I heard one of the men say, 'There are only three. Where is the other one?' Then I knew I was in trouble. So, I got from under the train and climbed up the outside ladder at the back of the carriage and hid on the roof in the dark. Although the Americans had taken control of the city, there was still a blackout in place."

"How much could you see?" Giancarlo asked

"Enough, without exposing myself," Luca replied.

"What happened next?"

"Time seemed to have stood still, but it could only have been a few minutes before the two men who'd been inside the carriage came into view, dragging bundles behind them. I could hear the muffled sobs and screams of the babies; they'd been tied up in sacks."

He took a very deep breath and clutched at the edge of the table before continuing.

"That's when Scavola and his men left, taking the children with them."

The hatred in Luca's voice as he said the name was visceral. I nearly grabbed the edge of the table myself.

"Are you absolutely sure it was him?" Giancarlo asked, carefully.

"Yes! How could I forget the face of the man who killed the only person who'd ever been truly kind to me? And there was that limp. Although it was dark and I was on top of the railway carriage, his image was seared into my mind."

"But from what Mario told me, they had covered their faces," I said.

"Yes, they wore hats and scarves covering the lower halves of their faces. But just before they left, Scavola seemed to be trying to wipe his eye. At first I thought he was crying, but then he turned his back on the other group of men standing on the platform and pulled his scarf down and wiped his face with it. He wasn't crying; he was wiping blood off his face."

"How did you know it was blood?"

"It was a full moon and there was enough light to see what it was: dark-coloured and glistening on his face. His handkerchief came away stained. I might have only been a child, but it was wartime, Mr O'Reilly; I'd already seen too much blood not to recognise it, even in a situation like that … do you mind if I stretch my legs for a bit before we continue?"

Giancarlo and Alfonso started to clear the table while Luca lit a cigarette and disappeared into the orchard. I could see the glowing tip of his smoke as he moved among the trees.

"You're really a carpenter?" Gregorio asked me.

"Yes, let me show you my workshop," I said, then led him to the end of the terrace and pulled open the double doors of my workspace.

"This is lovely work, Damson," he said, picking up one of the louvre-fronted doors I'd already constructed for the bathroom cabinets. "You could come to work for me any time."

He was very charming and open. I thanked him.

"May I use your phone to call my wife?"

"Of course."

He ran his hands over my treadle lathe, smiling at the simplicity of its construction, remarking how well it was made. I shrugged a little; not because I didn't appreciate his compliment, but merely because it was a utilitarian piece of furniture, nothing that I'd laboured on with love. One day I'd buy an electric lathe, but until then this one would do me for the time being.

"Mario was not my lover," he said quite suddenly.

It took me aback for a moment. "That's not what Mario seemed to indicate," I said. "He said that he had a man in Venice and another in Rome. Forgive me … seeing as he seemed to be so fond of you, I just assumed—"

He laughed, then perched on one of my sawhorses. "Mario and I never had sex. You have to understand that he was a complicated man."

"Did he lie to me, then?"

"No, not really. He gave me money, that's true. We kissed a lot and slept together when he was in Rome, but we never had sex."

"I'm astonished. Why did he give you money?" I asked. "I'm sorry, that's none of my business."

"I struggled after the war to get my business going. It was very hard. No one had money for luxuries like new furniture. I got work on building sites, but in my heart I was a craftsman, and he knew it. He wanted to help me found my own atelier."

"So, he's not a new acquaintance?"

"No, Damson. I grew up with him and Emilio, his twin brother. We're from the same town." He didn't speak for a moment but then reached over and tapped on the cigarette packet in my shirt pocket, smiling. I gave him the packet then lit his cigarette. "Emilio was my lover," he added in a very matter-of-fact tone. "From the age of seventeen we were together."

"Oh … I'm terribly sorry. Mario told me he'd been killed in a street brawl during the war."

"It was right at the end of the war, Damson. On the nineteenth of April 1945. Scavola shot him."

"What?!" I couldn't believe what I'd just heard, or Gregorio's seemingly calm delivery of such an astounding piece of news.

"It was only quite recently, just a few months ago, that we learned that he was responsible. We were told by a former member of his squad. Did Mario tell you about the group he and Emilio belong to that was tasked with keeping watch on Scavola before the liberation?"

"Yes, he did. He put it in writing, actually."

"This former squad member confessed to Mario one night in the Chiesa di Santa Maria della Luce; said he couldn't continue keeping the secret to himself. At the time, Scavola thought that he'd shot Mario, but it was poor Emilio who died."

"I knew they were twins, but Mario didn't say they were identical."

"They weren't, they were fraternal twins, but very alike in looks and in manner. Mario was a true beauty; Emilio was a handsome man with all the self-confidence that Mario lacked."

"Why did Scavola want to kill Mario?"

"Scavola was sent to Sicily in late 1944 with a lot of other members of the army to work on reconstruction and to help keep law and order. He was furious that he had to go and was burning with jealousy—Mario had been seeing someone else regularly. He could put up with the promiscuity, but the man Mario had met was something very different. Mario was in love with him and made the mistake of telling Scavola."

"Wait … you said Mario was seeing someone *else*? Mario and Scavola were …"

"Giovanni Scavola has the biggest cock in the universe, Damson. Had you known Mario longer, and going by what he'd already confided in you, I'm sure he would eventually have told you everything. They weren't lovers; it was a pure financial transaction for sex, and Mario … well, to be perfectly blunt, he liked both Scavola's penis and the money he gave him. He was perverse in a way, despite having fallen for—"

"Stewart."

"Oh, he told you that too? Then he must have trusted you. As I was saying, despite having met Stewart, who'd arrived with the first group of Americans in Rome, he continued to lift his legs for Scavola. Money was everything back then, Damson. People died of hunger, even during Mussolini's so-called 'golden age' before the war. We were brought up dirt-poor in a tiny village south of Rome. Mario had the face and a willing arsehole; he kept us all in food—his family and mine. His father disowned him when he found out what he was doing, though he continued to hold out his hand for more money—which, as far as I know, he still has done to this day, despite having cut his son out of his life."

This was one of those times I knew to keep silent, so moved to sit on my sawhorse next to him.

"My wife knows everything. We're happy together these days. Emilio was the great love of my life and he was the only man I've ever been with. She's given me enormous support and a huge amount of space after I told her what I learned had happened to Emilio."

My mind was working overtime. Mario had said he had proof—proof of Scavola's murder of the nuns, supported by Luca's information—and now, after his former comrade's confession in the church, proof of the murder of his twin brother at Scavola's hand.

"They made up, you know," Gregorio said.

"Who is the 'they'?"

"Mario and Scavola."

I stared at him in disbelief. "This was before Mario knew Scavola had killed his brother, of course?"

"Yes. After Stewart died in that stupid accident, Scavola turned up with a huge bunch of flowers, his eyes filled with tears, saying that despite the past, he still cared for Mario."

"And Mario fell for that?"

"No, but what he did fall for was the promise of Scavola's immense wealth to get him to star in an American movie, made in Hollywood."

"In exchange for …?"

"Mario's arsehole, of course. And he did, for ten million lire."

"How much? Ten million? That's almost ten thousand American dollars," I said, currency conversions still fresh in my mind after discussions with Kendall about my book deal in the USA. It was a great deal of money.

"That was just the teaser—the deposit. He was to get ten times that much to star in the movie. I suppose you have misgivings about the morality of the arrangement? I certainly did, and advised him against it."

"I'd never go that far. It's not something I'd do, no matter how much money someone offered me. But sleeping with Scavola? He knew what had happened during the war and knew in his heart that Scavola was responsible for the murder of the nuns … and other worse things, from what I understand."

"Mario and Emilio were the polar opposite of each other, Damson. Emilio was gentle, kind and a natural lover in bed. Mario, however, was a sex addict. He was totally passive, and he couldn't get enough of it. You wouldn't believe the people he slept with—many of whom I wouldn't cross the road to say hello to—just because of his craving for penis. The only time he wasn't sleeping around was when he was with Stewart, from the end of the war until two years ago; during that time, he swore to me that he'd been faithful. Stewart, like him, was a great beauty, you know. Not so much in the face, but a rugged he-man type who oozed masculinity. They were made for each other."

Life, and men in particular, were complicated. One never knew what went on behind closed doors. Of course, I'd met people like Mario before, men who had a public face, a face for friends, then another face that they kept quiet, hidden away, a face that they only acknowledged to themselves in times of extreme sobriety; a face that reminded themselves of who they really were.

I'd liked Mario Celestino very much and I considered myself a good judge of character. He'd been honest with me on the day that we'd sat in his apartment and he'd told me about Stewart. Perhaps the face of the man who opened his heart to me on that day was Mario's real face. What a complicated life he'd led, like so many of us who'd also lived through the biggest upheaval in the history of mankind.

CHAPTER 10

I didn't hang around the next morning while Luca gave his statement to Giancarlo, taken down by Cosmo in shorthand. Alfonso and I went to the Bar Azzurro, promising to return in two hours to co-sign the statement after it had been typed up and to witness Luca's signature. We sat inside at the back; Alfonso wanted to avoid the locals asking him where he'd been and why he wasn't saying mass.

As it was only half past eight in the morning, I ordered a cappuccino, Alfonso, who'd missed breakfast because he'd gone for a run, had pastries with his coffee.

"I'm sorry we didn't get any time alone yesterday," I said.

"Me too. You promised to tell me so many things. I thought you might have come to see me last night after I got into bed."

"I was too tired, to be honest, and Giancarlo wanted to talk. Eventually, I fell asleep while he was telling me something. I got a slap for my trouble," I added with a chuckle.

"Well, then. You said you wanted to talk to me about Luca."

"I've had an idea. He needs to be somewhere no one would think of. My idea was perhaps your old rooms here in Pienza. We could talk with the bishop, tell him it's a matter of sanctuary—"

"Stop! Father Milanese is a terrible keeper of secrets. Haven't you learned that yet? He's perfectly honourable when it comes to confession, but the man loves to gossip."

"What if I asked him in the middle of confession?"

Alfonso screwed up his nose at me and shook his head. "Are you crazy? No, it's a terrible idea … putting him up in my old rooms, that is. But I can see why you thought of it."

"Gregorio told me he was very religious, brought up by the nuns. I thought it would be ideal. He would be close enough for us to keep an eye on him and to occasionally spend time with him. It would be very lonely, I know."

"Damson. For such a worldly man, you are sometimes a total innocent. You know this town. Can you imagine for one second that every *zitella* in town wouldn't be wondering who the handsome young man was who was occupying the rooms I lived in? No, let me think for a moment."

He seemed very preoccupied, so I went down to the counter and bought a packet of cigarettes. Returning to our table, and while tearing off the seal around the top of the packet, I had an idea. "That monastery that Cristoforo Baldi was going to train at to become a priest—"

"No, I've thought of that too. Buonconvento is too far away. Besides, our involvement in Baldi's death—not that we were; he was killed in prison—still lingers there. I got a very cool reception last year when I last visited, more or less told that we should have just shut our mouths and let the Church deal with it."

"What? Cover up how many murders and the fact that Lorenzo's brother Giorgio had not only gotten Lorenzo's fiancée pregnant, but had molested dozens of his younger female parishioners?"

"They've covered up worse. Not Buonconvento—the Church as a whole, I mean. I'm still furious at the cover-up of what happened to Sister Ursula and her fellow nuns, not to mention the children … the fact that it happened in Vatican City and that the records have been sealed says it all, don't you think?"

I leaned across the table and rubbed his shoulder. "Don't tell me your *exclaustratio* has disillusioned you about Mother Church," I said wryly.

"I've never been disillusioned about the politics of the Church,

Damson. Just the magnitude of self-preservation when the truth would have served a better purpose. Now, about Luca. Not far from here, to the east, there's a tiny collection of buildings that used to be a hamlet, now mostly abandoned, but which never had a name. The locals call it Lepri, because of the number of hares that live in the area. My order in Rome has a retreat about a kilometre from it. It's only small, three or four houses clustered together, all occupied by a dozen or so brothers of all ages who spend time there for reasons of their own. No one knows why they're there; it's their own business."

"Is it for penance?" I asked.

"For some, perhaps. For others, it could be a place to reflect. Who knows? Not even the father who runs it knows why men are there. I'm sure they could do with a handyman; the place was a bit of a wreck when I last visited."

"You should have told me; I could have fixed things up for them. But it might be ideal for Luca. How far from here is it?"

"No more than fifteen minutes by car, and the road that leads there is more of a track than what you'd call a road. I used to walk sometimes. It's an hour on foot, but the scenery is glorious."

"It's an idea. But there's one problem: Luca's not a priest."

"But Father Green, who runs it, was my Latin teacher while I trained for the priesthood. He's going to love you, Damson."

"Father Green? Is he English?"

"No, his real name is Grün. He changed it during the First World War."

"Why didn't he change it to Verdi?"

"Because his first name is Josef, which, as you know, in Italian is Giuseppe."

★★★★★

Although Alfonso and I thought the idea of Luca going to Lepri was a great solution, the young man himself was very hesitant.

"How long would I have to stay? What would I do there? I love the work I do for Gregorio; besides, we have orders coming in that we're already finding it hard to complete."

Alfonso calmed him by saying he didn't have to go if he didn't want to, but then asked whether he'd like to see what it was like. I'd drive the two of them in my Jeep. We could see the retreat, talk to Father Green—who, after all, might not agree to the idea—and then, if Luca didn't like it, we'd come up with another solution. Besides, Alfonso said, Giancarlo had informed us that, with Luca's statement in his possession, he could now speak with our friend Salvatore Venturi, and see whether a preliminary hearing might be held in Rome as a matter of urgency. Giancarlo was also positive that, with the statement, Venturi would be able to force access to the Vatican archives with the threat of exposing more of Pius XII's collusion with Mussolini's thugs and the Nazis.

Giancarlo phoned Venturi in Rome, who was excited to hear the news and promised that as soon as he saw the statement and lodged it with the local court's notary, he'd contact the Vatican and make his move. In the meantime, Alfonso and I would take Luca to Lepri while Cosmo had both copies of Luca's statement officially signed by our local notary. One would be kept in Giancarlo's safe, the other entrusted to Gregorio, who, about to return to Rome, promised to deliver it into Venturi's hands.

We left the office while Giancarlo was on the phone to Alessandro Pellegrini in Venice. I was about to get in the Land Rover to take Gregorio back to La Mensola to pick up his car when Giancarlo came out into the street and waved to me.

"Alessandro is coming here tomorrow. He's bringing his wife and children so that it appears to be a simple family weekend away in the countryside."

"Is there room at the hotel?" I asked. In 1955, a large hotel had opened just outside town. It was mostly used by tour operators, who were starting to take Americans on guided tours of the hillside towns of Tuscany.

"They can stay at Il Fornaio. I'll call Stefano and let him know."

"Don't forget we have to harvest sunflowers on Saturday, Giancarlo. Everything's been arranged with the locals."

"Well, I'm sure his kids will love to be part of it; there'll be children everywhere and they're sure to find someone to play with. I'll tell him about the harvest. It's a great cover story, and he'll be close enough for us to talk shop while it's going on."

"Talk shop? I need every pair of hands at the harvest, Giancarlo. Don't forget this business is half yours too. You can talk your hearts out on Sunday once it's done, but don't expect to go skiving off and leaving it all to me."

He held up his hands, then apologised. "Sorry, of course you're right, Damson. The 'us' must come first." He spoke in English; we knew no one else would understand.

I gave him my half-hearted smile; the one that said *all right, do what you will, I'll cope*, then put the car into gear and headed off.

*****

Father Green was a delight. He was my idea of Friar Tuck in the Robin Hood adventures, although somewhat older. A rosy-cheeked, portly man in his seventies, of impressive height, he also spoke exemplary Latin. It made me realise, as it had done while speaking in the same language with James, that mine was conversational, less "Pliny the Elder" grammatically precise.

He'd invited us into the refectory and treated us to a *merenda*, or late morning snack, of freshly baked bread, their own cheeses and salami, accompanied by excellent coffee. We'd spoken in Italian, he telling me he'd recently read *Living with Monsters*. When I switched to English, he coloured, saying that although he'd been able to read my book, having studied the language in the 1920s, he'd never really spoken it. I promised I'd help him remedy the situation in the future if he wished to learn, but he laughed and said that he feared he was too old to really master the spoken language.

After about twenty minutes, he asked one of the other priests to show Luca around the retreat. They had their own bees, vines, olives, goats and chickens and grew everything they needed to eat, even milling their own flour. I'd seen Luca's eyes, as mine had been, roving over bits and pieces of furniture and fixtures that desperately needed care. If Luca decided to stay, there'd be no end of jobs to keep him busy.

That's when I heard Father Green's excellent Latin for the first time. "*Nunc soli sumus. Potesne causam veram cur hic sis narrare?*" he'd asked.

"The young man we brought with us needs sanctuary. He's done nothing wrong, Father," Alfonso said in answer to the priest's question about why we were really here. "But his life could be in danger."

"Has this anything to do with the bruises all over your face, Mr O'Reilly?"

"Peripherally," I said. "But it's better for everyone that no one knows why we feel it's important that he's protected."

"I understand, and no one is ever asked why they're here. Of course, the only problem is that every man here is subsidised by the Church, their places paid for by their local diocese, and every one of them is either a priest or someone from a religious order. It would be quite out of keeping."

I glanced around the room again. "He's a trained carpenter, Father. It looks like you need help on that front. Besides, we'd be only too happy to contribute to his upkeep."

At the mention that Luca was a tradesman, the priest's eyes lit up. "We could never afford a handyman. Does he do anything else besides carpentry?"

"I'm not sure, you'd have to ask him, but there's one thing I do know: he's very devout. I'm sure he'd fit in with whatever regime you follow here."

"Well, we'll be saying Sext shortly and you're welcome to join in if you'd like. He can see at first hand how we conduct things here. And then, of course, you're also welcome to stay for lunch afterwards. However, I should warn you that everyone is expected to lend a helping hand."

"Suits me fine, Father," I said. "I was brought up in a monastery and lived my entire life there before leaving for war. I can turn my hand to anything."

"My, my, Mr O'Reilly, you are such a surprise."

Alfonso gave me a wink. I knew there'd be no problem now; it just depended on Luca.

"Perhaps you'd like to officiate, Alfonso?"

"You know I can't, Father."

"I know about your *exclaustratio*. But I won't tell if you won't. I know it will give you an enormous amount of pleasure. The Church may have excluded you for the time being, but God will forgive; He knows the good in your heart."

I swear that my own eyes filled up as Alfonso's had done.

*****

Alfonso insisted that we go down to the pool when we got back. It was hot and the road had been very dusty. We stripped off and dived into the cold, clear water. I loved to run my hands through the mud at the bottom even though it was quite deep.

"That went well," he said once we'd dried off and had stretched out in the sun.

"I'm not going to tell Giancarlo where Luca is," I said.

"Why on earth not, Damson?"

"Let's see if he fits in first. All I told him was that you and I had an idea and if it worked out, we'd let him know, but the fewer people who knew where Luca is, the better."

"What about Gregorio?"

"Better he doesn't know either. I know I'm probably being over-cautious, but as we say in English: better safe than sorry."

"Where is he now?"

"Giancarlo said he was taking him on a tour of the area after lunch."

"And what are your plans for the rest of the week?" Alfonso asked.

"Kendall is due back tomorrow, sometime in the evening he said. Will you be around during the day?"

"I have nothing to do; why do you ask?"

"Because I promised I'd help Gaspard clear his field, but I need someone here to be able to take Kendall's call to let me know when to pick him up from the station. I was thinking I'd drive the tractor down the road and start slashing, perhaps pull out the stumps. I'd like to get that field cleared and ploughed before we start on our harvest on Saturday."

"Perhaps Gaspard could help here over the weekend, Damson? It would be an opportunity for him to meet more people in the community, and, if the harvest is anything like it is every year, every extra hand is always welcome."

"That's an idea … I might ask Andrea Gagliardi to join us for the day, too. I know he won't be any use with his hands, but it would be good to have another French-speaker so that Gaspard doesn't feel totally at sea."

"Are you sure you should be doing something like this?" he asked.

"What? Helping Gaspard? I'll be all right—"

"You say you'll be all right, but I see the way you wince every time you bend or raise an arm."

I reached over and tweaked the hair just below his navel. "You sound like my mother."

He mock-protested then laughed, moved his towel next to mine and his head on my bicep. "Go on, ask!"

"Ask what?"

"You really want to know about him and me, don't you?"

"It's none of my business," I said.

He sighed heavily then sat up quickly, searching for my shirt. "Your cigarette pack is empty."

"I expect that's because you smoked more than me and didn't bring your own when we took Luca to Lepri."

Alfonso snorted and lay back down next to me.

"All right," I went on, "it's not about Gaspard, but I do have a question. That man, the café owner's husband in Aranova—you said to me that you'd have preferred him giving you come-hither looks rather than his wife."

He chuckled. "I have a type."

"Big and burly, rather unkempt-looking, with dimples."

"Ah, so you noticed too."

"I wouldn't be surprised if he was amenable; he spent a lot of time looking at us both. Italian men! I think they're all sexually available under the right circumstances."

"Isn't it the same in your country?"

"This is my country now, Alfonso. But in Australia? The society is so different. Giancarlo noticed it immediately. We're still joined at the hip to Britain, so social etiquette is far more formal than it is here. Men get close, very close, one could almost say lovers, except that the physical goes no further than the occasional arm around the shoulder and rough-housing. You'd never see men walking down the street arm in arm as you do here, for example. Not even fathers and sons or brothers."

"But what about in private?"

"During the war, I saw many of those close 'mateships'—that's what we call them—cross the line. Men showering together, washing each other's backs, sharing a cot, even kissing in the back rows of the outdoor cinemas in the dark. I'm sure more went on."

"And you?"

"There were places … beaches at night, groves in the palm trees where men met and had sex. Everyone pretended that they didn't know each other and never spoke about it again. It happened everywhere. And, of course, there was a lot of relief masturbation after days of fighting."

"What's relief masturbation?" he asked.

"I'm sure you can work it out. Men taking care of themselves after battle for the mere joy of knowing they were alive and had survived for another day. More than once I had sex with men in dugouts or in quiet places; it didn't mean anything more to them than the touch of another human being. We'd masturbate together, sometimes each helping the other out, but never any oral sex or fucking—that was left for the beaches and palm groves."

"I really need a cigarette," he said, sitting back up again. "I won't be a moment. I'll fetch a pack from my bedroom."

"Grab a packet of mine from the pantry while you're at it," I said, then dived back into the pool again and breast-stroked around. Despite the sometimes indescribable pain in my side from my beating at the hands of the police, my mind was filled with images of hot summer nights, needy men with fires in their bellies having unrestrained sex, all of us with the thought that perhaps tomorrow would be the last day of our lives.

My most vivid memory was the last time with anyone before I met Danny in occupied Japan. It was in Borneo a week before I shipped out. I'd woken about one in the morning with an ache in my balls and wandered down the path behind the ablutions tent to a clearing near the beach. I hadn't expected to find anyone there at that time in the morning, but I ended up with a man on his knees sucking my dick while another fucked me and the startlingly good-looking new lieutenant feeding me his tongue while I pulled on his cock. He spurted into my hand at the same time that I unloaded into the mouth that was sucking me off, the fellow behind grunting his release almost immediately after.

The memory made me hard, so I rolled onto my belly on my towel. Alfonso had seen me with an erection before; he'd watched Giancarlo and me have sex. I'd also seen his. Men often woke up hard.

"Here you are," he said, throwing me my smokes.

I lit up while he jumped into the pool again.

"What are you looking at?" he asked when he came out of the water, towelling himself dry in the sun.

"You. Is there a problem with that? I keep forgetting you're two years older than me, Alfonso. You seem at times to be ten years younger."

"Is that a good or a bad thing?"

"Neither really. Besides, I think you're very handsome; what's wrong with looking at you?"

"Nothing, Damson. I look at you often enough too."

I turned over and rested my head on his thigh, my erection now subsided. "I think you were on the point of telling me something about Gaspard before you ran off to get a smoke."

"That wasn't an excuse; I really needed a cigarette. Yes, you were right in what you said. I do have a type, and yes, big and burly and—how did you put it, rough around the edges?"

I laughed. "I didn't actually say that, but yes, that was my implication."

"I didn't have sex with anyone after I entered the seminary at the age of eighteen, not until my first lapse in 1944. I spent four years alone in my cell, surrounded by other monks, praying to God to put a halt to my wet dreams and to give me the strength to stop wearing the skin off my penis by constant masturbation several times a day. It wasn't as if there wasn't a lot of temptation, but we were at war, and if you were caught you'd be kicked out of the seminary, have a gun put in your hands, and be sent off to fight."

"So, what happened in 1944? You must have been twenty-two at the time?"

"A Canadian happened."

"Oh? Do you want to share the story?"

He fiddled with the edge of his towel for a moment before speaking, his other hand now resting on my chest, stroking it gently.

"The Canadians came with the first bunch of Americans to enter Rome. We billeted several of them; housing was at a premium and the seminary asked for Catholics. He shared my cell, sleeping on a canvas stretcher bed that he'd brought with him. I couldn't take my eyes off him when he undressed in front of me. It was June and so very, very hot. He smiled—he knew I'd been staring at him—then ran his hand over his belly, pulling the hair between his fingers. I was sitting on the edge of my cot and couldn't hide what happened. I leaned forward to try to hide my erection, but he kneeled down and took my hand. 'It's okay, buddy. There's just you and me,' he said, the head of his penis poking out from the leg of his very short undershorts. I couldn't stop what happened next. We had sex at least twice a day before he was shipped out. I went to confession at a church on the other side of Rome, was given absolution and penance, then, after he was shipped out, told my Father Superior that I was ready to go out into the world, that I wanted to go somewhere quiet, away from Rome, to begin my ministry. That's how I landed in Pienza."

"And this Canadian, he was …?"

"Big and burly and rough around the edges. He still writes to me, you know. Settled down in Manitoba with a family now, but he writes. I saw him a few more times—he came here twice to see me right at the end of the war before he went home. His family was Italian and he worked as an interpreter. He spoke very old-fashioned Italian and knew no swear words or had vocabulary for what we did, but his letters still make me feel aroused with the memory of those few weeks we shared, even though he never talks about anything intimate in them."

"And Gaspard reminds you of him."

"In some respects, yes. The way he kisses. The way he smiles while he looks at my body and runs his hands over me."

"And you say it's just sex?"

"I have to keep it that way, Damson. I do intend to return to the Church. The choice between the flesh and my ministry is eating me alive from the inside."

"You'll probably think this is completely crazy, but is there any reason you can't have both?"

He looked at me strangely for quite a while before shaking his head, as if he didn't believe what I'd just said.

"Alfonso, what Father Green said about God knowing the good in your heart. Do you think you're the only priest who's ever suffered the same dilemma? I didn't tell you this, but do you remember my friend from the monastery, my sports teacher, Father Justin? I told you about him."

"He's the priest you and your brother fooled around with?"

"Yes. When I visited while we were in Australia, he told me that he'd settled down with another man, a farm worker who I also used to sleep with just before I left for war. Father Justin gets on with his life, his religious duties and has Bert as his companion. That's one example. I can't imagine that there aren't hundreds, if not tens or hundreds of thousands, of priests all across the world who have women or men as their special companions yet still continue to be exemplary leaders of their flocks. For heaven's sake, even St Peter was married."

He rolled on his side, put one arm across my chest and lay his head on my shoulder. I flinched. My rib was giving me holy hell.

"Can you tell him something?"

"Who, God?"

"No," he said, chuckling against my neck. "Gaspard."

"Of course. What do you want me to tell him?"

"Just tell him that I'd like to fuck him once in a while too."

He looked up at me with a huge grin. I kissed him. "Any more sexual positions you'd like me to mention?"

"Not that I can think of right now, but if I do, I'll let you know."

I was about to speak when Gregorio appeared from the track that led to the pool. He stripped off quickly and dived into the water, yelling out, "*Cazzo, fa caldo!*"

Yes, it was fucking hot, as he'd just announced to the world very loudly.

*****

By Sunday, I was exhausted. As always, I'd done too much. "Damson the Martyr", Giancarlo had frequently called me over the years we'd been together. I liked to be in control, and, although I never complained, he always sensed my internal griping.

"Why did you have to do Gaspard's field on the day that Alessandro and his family arrived to stay and Kendall returned? Couldn't you have left it until next week?" he'd said late on Friday night. We'd almost gone to sleep without a goodnight kiss, but I'd rolled him onto his stomach and fucked him brutally. "You should get angry more often," he'd said, laughing into my mouth, my ankles next to my ears as he returned the favour. We didn't make love as frequently as we had done when we first got together, but these times, when having sex was a form of making up after a disagreement, were very special.

Fortunately, he was up with me early the next morning, the Mori brothers arriving at half past five in the morning. I fed them coffee and fresh bread, which I'd left to prove overnight in the refrigerator then thrown into the oven thirty minutes before they were due to arrive.

Alfonso helped, promising to drive to the station at eleven to pick up Kendall, who'd been delayed. I'd told him over the phone when I got back from Gaspard's that he should buy some work clothes if he didn't have any, because it was going to be all hands on deck.

He arrived, wearing American blue jeans, boots and a short-sleeved, red-checked shirt, just as the second truck left the field. "Eyes on the crop," Giancarlo said, perched next to me on the tractor, concentrating on the sunflower-harvester that trailed behind us. Gaspard had driven his tractor up the road and brought his furrowing attachment to till the soil and plough in the stalks and leaves of the harvested sunflowers. Normally that would have been my job after the initial harvest had been done. But, with his help, we'd finish mid-afternoon instead of in the early hours of the evening.

Giancarlo had been to the bank yesterday and, while I'd been getting the tractor ready early in the morning, had counted out wages for every-one who'd come to help. We paid fifty per cent more than the other neighbouring farmers but were very careful to stagger our harvests so that they didn't overlap with anyone else's. We didn't want to cause dissension or steal labour.

Even Alessandro Pellegrini pitched in. He'd told me he came from Sinalunga, a little more than twenty kilometres from Pienza; what he hadn't told me was that he also came from a farming family. Kendall had also got to work immediately, even without more than a few words of Italian. His camera around his neck, he'd helped with the other men who followed after Gaspard's tractor, pulling out any lengths of stalk that had not been cut into short lengths by my harvester and piling them into hand carts, to be added to our compost heap. He later explained that the photos were for an idea he had for the documentary the film crew were to make after the Olympic Games about my life in Italy.

Although I loved entertaining, the continuing pain in my side and the stupidity of doing too much had taken its toll on me. I went to mass with Alfonso in Orvieto on our way to Rome to pick up Luca's belongings. I'd intended to go by myself, or to take Kendall with me, but both he and Giancarlo were still sound asleep when I woke up and I didn't have the heart to wake them. I left a note on the dresser, where I knew Giancarlo would see it.

"You didn't have to do this today," Alfonso said after mass, when we'd broken our fast in Orvieto at a small café on the Piazza del Duomo, the distinctive striped cathedral our backdrop.

"Everyone keeps telling me what I could have done and what I shouldn't have done, Alfonso. I love you very much …" I used the term *ti voglio molto bene*, which meant something more like *I love you dearly* or *I'm very, very fond of you*, in English "… but you know I don't like things that are left undone. Besides, today will give Alessandro and Giancarlo a chance to talk about the case."

"Will you take Giancarlo with you when you and Pellegrini go to visit Luca?"

"No. I've asked Giancarlo to take Kendall to look at a house that's for sale in the Piazza Grande in Montepulciano."

"Montepulciano? I thought he wanted to buy somewhere in Florence."

"He does. But I think he wants to compare what's on offer and the prices they're asking. Did you know he's bought a car?"

"No. When did he tell you that?"

"Last night in bed."

"It's a wonder you got to talk; you made so much noise fucking I could barely concentrate."

"I'm sure Gaspard was enough of a diversion. It was nice that he stayed over."

"He left quite early in the morning; that's why I was already up and about when you got up."

"How was it?"

He blushed.

"Come on," I said, "I'll tell you mine if you tell me yours."

"After what you said to him, he was very amenable."

"Ah, so you fucked him?"

Alfonso winked at me over his coffee cup. "You were saying that Kendall bought a car?"

"Yes, in Paris. It's coming this week sometime. He's having it driven here by the dealer."

"The dealer is driving his car from Paris to Pienza? What the hell sort of car is it?"

"It's a Mercedes-Benz 220S Cabriolet," I said, vainly trying to keep the envy out of my voice. "The latest model and I'm sure it cost a fortune. That's all he would say about it. He intends to keep it in Florence when he eventually buys something there."

We made Rome in good time and were able to park in Piazza Sonnino. I spent rather too much time in Gregorio's workshop admiring his furniture and the beautiful set of German precision woodworking tools he told me that Mario had bought for him. We rudely ignored both his wife and Alfonso while we swapped stories of projects that we'd built and exchanged tips on where to find the best timbers for inlays.

Eventually, back on the road, Luca's small suitcase in the back of my Maserati, I suddenly felt extremely unwell, and pulled over to the side of the road. No sooner had I got out of the car than I vomited, falling to my knees.

"Damson!" Alfonso yelled, jumping out of the car, then holding my shoulders as I continued to spew up my guts.

I didn't remember much of what happened after that except that

Alfonso flagged down another car. I heard a vague conversation and then something about hospital. The next clear thing I remembered was lying somewhere cool and quiet, someone holding my hand.

"Damson?"

I recognised Giancarlo's voice and opened my eyes.

"You have to stop doing this," he said. His forehead was creased with worry.

"What happened?"

"You had a rupture of the spleen."

"What?"

"The doctor told me it's not entirely unheard of to happen even a few weeks after a fracture of one of the lower ribs, like yours."

"Did they operate on me?"

"No, but they said you were exhausted and sedated you to force you to rest. You were also extremely dehydrated. You should never have done the harvest, Damson. Had you been honest with me about how you were feeling … Alfonso told me you said you'd been in bad pain—"

"Please, Giancarlo, no admonitions. You know me by now."

"This could have been very serious," he said, then bent over to kiss me.

"I bet you've told the press," I said with a laugh.

"Of course," he said, kissing my hand. "And there are a lot of very, very nervous policemen in Venice who've been told you're hovering between life and death as a result of their mistreatment."

I laughed, but then the pain made me break out into a hacking cough.

I listened as he told me how Alfonso had telephoned Stefano at Il Fornaio to go to Montepulciano to fetch Giancarlo and Kendall, who were inspecting the house for sale, then had spoken with Pellegrini. Alfonso, once he knew I'd been stabilised, had then driven my car back to La Mensola, picked up Pellegrini and taken him to Lepri to interview Luca. Giancarlo and Kendall were staying nearby in a hotel. I had no idea even where I was.

"We're in Orvieto; you'd got about halfway home," he informed me, then told me that Kendall had gone to get something to eat.

The surgeon arrived and told me that the bleeding was relatively minor and that I'd have to stay in hospital for two more days, then do nothing but light work around the house for a minimum of two weeks after that. Then he scolded me when Giancarlo told him that I'd been ordered to report to our local doctor after my beating at the hands of the police, but that I hadn't. He told Giancarlo he could have ten minutes more before I was sedated again and that he suggested that I go somewhere quiet for a week or so after I was discharged from hospital. Somewhere quiet, away from home, where I wasn't tempted to do stupid things like spend two days in a tractor ploughing fields and harvesting sunflowers.

"I think I know the perfect place," Giancarlo said, as Kendall's face appeared around the door. He sat on the edge of the bed opposite Giancarlo and they both held a hand each, only interrupted by the arrival of a nurse in a starched white veil, carrying a stainless steel kidney dish covered with a linen cloth. I recognised the type from my previous hospital stay; in it, I was sure, was a syringe.

"The doctor will be here in a moment, gentlemen. You can come back later this evening. Now, Mr O'Reilly, this needs to go into a big muscle; we usually inject into the gluteus maximus. Have you ever had anything injected into your buttocks before?"

I imagined the looks that might have passed between Giancarlo and Kendall if they'd heard what she said.

"I served in the tropics, sister. I've probably had more needles in my arse than you've given all year."

She gave me a pretend frown, but she was young enough to attempt to smother a smile.

CHAPTER 11

Castiglione del Lago was a small town right on the edge of Lake Trasimeno. I'd discovered it in 1950 on the day I'd picked up my Jeep from the army surplus store at Pontassieve. I'd stopped there to have lunch at a tiny trattoria and had eaten the most glorious, memorable meal. Over the years, I'd returned over and over again, taking Giancarlo and other friends who'd stayed with us at La Mensola. Randy, who'd been very interested in buying a rural property in the Tuscan countryside near us, had fallen in love with the area and had instead bought a run-down villa outside the tiny hamlet of Rigutini, five minutes by car from Castiglione del Lago, with four bedrooms on two floors and two hectares of land right on the lake. He'd turned it into a magnificent retreat just over an hour and a half by car from Florence, where he lived. We'd visited it very often and it was here that Giancarlo had taken me to recuperate. He left me with strict instructions not to do anything more than swim, take walks, read, sketch and paint.

I'd sighed over the fuss, fighting the whole idea until, beaten down by the relentless nagging—which I knew was for my own benefit—I'd given in and promised I'd stay for a week, but no more. Among the books I'd brought with me was some of the research I'd been doing on

Scavola, Giulio Evola and Mario, and a copy of Luca's statement that I'd asked Cosmo to make for me; I wanted to go over it in detail.

Despite the grumpiness I felt at my enforced isolation, I'd never minded my own company and had always found something to keep me busy. Kendall had told me he was going to Florence to look at a house on the road to Fiesole, not far from Giancarlo's sister's art gallery. It was she who'd told Giancarlo it was up for sale and she had promised to meet Kendall and to accompany him. He said he'd telephone, and he had, on the first day I arrived here, not long after Giancarlo had left me with enough food to feed an army for a week.

I'd found it very hard to still my mind on the first night. The power went out at about seven, nothing unusual for rural Italy; it happened at La Mensola quite frequently. It was often caused because many people had hooked up to the electricity grid illegally so they didn't have to pay bills. You'd often see jury-rigged power poles in even large cities, festoons of electrical cables leading off every which way. However, Randy had a store of old-fashioned kerosene lamps, so I lit a few and placed them around the house and, despite it being warm, laid the fireplace and lit it, opened a bottle of wine and lay back listening to the news on the battery-powered portable radio that I'd thought to bring with me.

The following morning, I went for a swim in the lake then returned for breakfast, pleased to find that power had been restored. I was pottering in the kitchen in my swimmers when I heard a car drive up.

"Morning!"

I recognised Randy's voice. "In the kitchen."

"I finally get you by yourself and you've been knocked about, Damson. Holy Dooley, you're a mass of bruises still. Are all of those from—"

"The Venetian cops? Yes. They're fading, but those bastards really got stuck in."

He pulled me carefully into his arms and kissed my neck. I'd always been more than fond of him. Over the ten years we'd known each other, and despite both of us being in committed relationships, we had still found time to be together. It wasn't all about sex; we shared a lot in common and I still counted him as the handsomest man I'd ever met, despite his age. I kept reminding myself that I'd be in my early fifties before I knew it and hoped to God that I looked half as good as Randall McCall did.

"You must have left early to get here," I said. "Have you eaten yet?"

"Thought I might eat you," he said with a wink.

I laughed. "I'm about to have something myself. Eggs?"

"Yes, please. I stopped and bought provisions in case you hadn't stocked up."

"You know Giancarlo; we should put up a sign on the road saying: *Free food. Help yourselves.*"

We chatted while I cooked breakfast, after which we went for a walk along the shore of the lake.

"Are you still going to the Olympics next week?" he asked, watching me scud stones across the still surface of the lake.

"I wouldn't miss it for quids," I said. "I'll be there even if I have to walk from La Mensola. Giancarlo's annoyed that I won't stay home and 'get better', but I've been looking forward to it for years, ever since it was announced that Rome was getting the Games. Do you have tickets?"

"For the diving and the swimming, the opening and the closing ceremonies. Arnie and I will be going together; the girls aren't even vaguely interested. My wife and her sister are head down and ass up in their dig. Nothing will pry them away from that."

"We're staying in Salvatore Venturi's apartment in the Campo de' Fiori. Do you remember him? He was the lead prosecutor at Cristoforo Baldi's trial."

"Yes, good-looking man who spoke with you in French all the time despite the rest of us drumming our fingers in annoyance."

"That's him. Well, Alessandro Pellegrini, the head of the provincial Veneto police force, has been staying at Il Fornaio to talk with Giancarlo. He brought his family to make it look like a holiday, but it's really an excuse to talk about the murder of Mario Celestino and the case Scavola had brought against him. I suppose that our stay with Venturi in Rome is an opportunity for Giancarlo to let him know what's been discussed with Pellegrini."

"That will be boring for you."

"Not really. I'll have Kendall with me, and if I get too fed up, I can always take him sightseeing between events. Besides, I'm used to it. As much as I love him, Giancarlo can become intensely focused on some things."

"And you can't?"

I nudged his ribs and smiled. Yes, I could also become obsessed, usually when I was writing or painting. "Actually, do you mind if I use you as a sounding board?" I asked. "It's something that should remain between you and me."

"Sure. What's eating you, Damson?"

"It's about Mario Celestino …"

"My lips are sealed."

He listened without comment while I spoke, nodding every so often, only reacting at the last thing I revealed.

"Mario Celestino was having sex with Giovanni Scavola?"

"Right up until a few months before he died. It stopped abruptly when he learned that Scavola had murdered his brother. Not long afterwards, Mario started to get death threats, then decided to write his letter to the press denouncing him."

"If it had been me, I'd have killed the bastard."

"Probably what I'd have done too, Randy," I said. "But who knows if that's not what he intended to do after the trial, once he'd produced his star witness."

"There's something still bothering you about Celestino, Damson. I heard it in your voice when you were telling me about him. Did he say something that makes you think he wasn't telling you everything? Could he have been lying about something?"

"No, it's not that; I honestly believe he was telling me the truth. It's what I later learned that he left out about his personal history … he just turned out to be a different person than I thought he was."

"Everyone keeps some secrets up their sleeve, even you and me. But what was it about Mario?"

I then revealed what Gregorio had told me about Mario's extreme promiscuity and his obsession with Scavola's cock, the only reason he started sleeping with him again, even knowing what he did during the war and his conviction that Scavola was personally involved in the murder of Sister Ursula, her companions and the three children. I couldn't reconcile it with the person I'd believed him to be.

"Maybe he was wilier than you give him credit for, Damson. Did you ever think of that? Perhaps he was having sex with Scavola to gain his trust and find out more about what went on during the war."

I hadn't thought of that, and I supposed it showed on my face.

"Please don't tell me you judged Celestino for what he did privately?" Randy said.

"No, I don't judge him. Surely you know me better than that? It's just that, when he told me about Stewart, I simply got the impression that he was someone else altogether."

"He was an actor, Damson. That's what they do. He was probably very honest with you about that relationship. All he did was leave out things that he probably considered none of your business. You did say that he was petrified about people finding out …"

"Perhaps you're right, Randy. Maybe I've just blown the whole thing out of proportion in my mind. That's why I wanted to use you as a sounding board. You always—"

"Look, stop for a minute. I've got something to say."

"Go on."

He took me by the hand and led me into the shallows of the lake, where we sat side by side. It was a glorious day, birds scudding barely over the surface of the lake, not twenty yards away from us.

"You were going to say something?"

"I think you're obsessing over the wrong things, Damson. You may not want to hear this, but I'm going to tell you anyway: I don't like this situation one bit."

"What part of it don't you like?"

"The assault on Giancarlo, the ransacking of Mario Celestino's apartment, followed by his murder, then a nonsensical police arrest resulting in you being beaten senseless at the hands of one of the most corrupt police forces in Italy. I'm being quite serious."

"I understand—"

"Do you, really? If Scavola manages to get the merest hint that you're hiding a witness to what went on in that train carriage in Vatican

City, then you, Giancarlo and everyone close to you might find your-selves tortured and then most likely killed just to find out where that young man is."

I looked at him calmly. It wasn't anything I hadn't thought of myself. "Don't forget, Randy, that as of this morning, you also know too much."

For a moment, the World War Two army captain stared me back in the face, grim determination in his eyes. "Just let them try," he said. "Now, can we go back home so you can fuck me, Damson, or are we going to just sit here up to the waist in the water while the skin of our ball sacks puckers?"

He had such a way with words.

★★★★★

Randy had barely left and I'd just started to go through my notes on Scavola when Alfonso arrived in the Land Rover with Gaspard, whom he'd cajoled into taking a day off from farm work. If I were to be honest, despite my welcoming smile, I'd have preferred to be alone right then to go through my research, and they seemed to sense it, glancing at the piles of books and my notes on the kitchen bench, so said they'd leave me to it for a while and wandered off down to the lake.

I shook my head as I watched them walk down the track towards the *spiaggia*—what the Italians called a beach resembled nothing like the beaches on the eastern coast of Australia or those in Malaya that I'd seen. The sight of them laughing, the backs of their hands touching, made me wonder how much resolve Alfonso still harboured to return to the priesthood. I knew smitten when I saw it, and, from the way that Gaspard had been glancing at him while they'd been unpacking food and storing it away, I had no doubt the feeling was mutual.

I returned to what I'd been jotting down about Scavola. Married twice and yet he'd apparently had a very long sexual relationship with Mario Celestino. However, many, many Italian men were bisexual—to use the new word.

I felt that we needed to know more about the man himself. Someone with such immense wealth and links to other men of power and influence, not to mention the Ordine Nuovo group and Evola, would be hard to defeat in court, especially with the widely known corruption that existed in the judiciary.

Luca seemed like a nice lad; I wondered how he'd hold up under fierce interrogation in the hostile environment of a courtroom. I made a note in my agenda to visit him before we left for Rome. How had he survived the war? The story that he'd told us only went as far as having been spared the fate of his three young friends and the nuns. Where had he gone after that? How had he survived? How did he become a carpenter?

I picked up the phone and called Cosmo, who, after the expected social greetings and enquiries about my health, filled me in on Giancarlo's agenda for the week.

"Thank you, Cosmo. Signor Manetti doesn't always let me know where he is."

"You are not alone there, Signor O'Reilly."

I said that, if he had time, I'd like him to dig out the pathologist's report on the death of Scavola's two wives, with an emphasis on his second wife—death during the war was something that had happened only too frequently, but a diving misadventure was something altogether different. Newspaper clippings, anything he could find. I told him it was something I'd have loved to have done myself, but as I was currently sequestered in a tiny village miles from anywhere, with orders to rest …

I next phoned Salvatore Venturi in Rome. The moment he realised it was me on the phone, he switched to French.

He'd had no problems lodging Luca's statement with the court, ordering the document to be locked away under the seal of protection until he and Giancarlo were ready to go ahead with the prosecution, a case that would need the co-operation of the police. A matter of slander was one thing, but a major *causa* against an important Italian business-man for war crimes was another thing.

"Is there some doubt that the chief prosecutor will go ahead with the case?"

"I fear that palms may be greased, Damson. You know how it goes. However, I have thought of something that in this current climate might make it politically advantageous to him; something he'd find hard to resist."

"And what's that?"

"I have evidence that Scavola is tied up with the Camorra. The chief prosecutor and his associates have publicly expressed their mission to clean up criminal societies; therefore, mentioning that I have proof of Scavola's connections will probably convince him to take up the case and run with it."

That left me almost speechless. The Camorra was the criminal organisation run out of Naples, similar to the Mafia. If Scavola had used them to pull political strings—in the form of bribes or coercion—it might be hard, if not impossible, to get the case off the ground. And yet, as Salvatore said, the current political climate was focused on rooting out organised crime. Ultimately, it could depend on whether the public got to hear of a proposed court case were it to be leaked in advance, something I was sure that, with his great experience as former chief commissioner of police, Salvatore could easily arrange, perhaps with a little help from Kendall.

He informed me that, while we were staying with him at his Rome apartment during the Olympics, he had invited the chief prosecutor and his wife to lunch; they were old friends. No doubt Giancarlo would not be sitting with me on that day, watching the athletics or whatever other events we had tickets for. If I knew him, together with Salvatore, he'd be piling pressure on the chief prosecutor in order to get the case to court.

Alfonso and Gaspard returned while I was still on the phone. They got busy preparing lunch while I continued to speak with Salvatore, Gaspard covering his ears and miming that he was not listening. I switched to Italian, telling Salvatore that I had a French-speaking visitor, then asked him whether he'd had any luck accessing the Vatican documents that dealt with the death of Sister Ursula. He informed me that he'd run into obstacles at every turn, then said something very strange. I wasn't entirely sure that I understood, but it seemed that, with the right introduction, one of the archivists might be willing to be "distracted" for half an hour or so, and in exchange allow Salvatore access to, and free rein in, the particular section of the archive in which notes about that night might be kept.

"Are you asking me if I know anyone who might be amenable? I suppose you're hinting at an intimate distraction?"

"I believe you know someone who's associated with the 'Acquaintance Club'?"

"The Acquaintance Club? I have no idea what you're talking about."

"Someone who you know who's had … contact … with the new American legate to the embassy in Rome."

"How do you know about this, Salvatore?"

"Before you jump to conclusions, I have no personal experience, but my brother does. He and the archivist share a mutual interest in that particular organisation."

"Then why don't you get your brother to arrange it?"

"My brother had an unfortunate incident with one of the 'acquaintances' last time he availed himself of the service. I was rather hoping it could be arranged privately, without the organisation being involved."

"I'll see what I can do. The next time I see him, I'll mention it. However, I've no idea how I'll broach the subject—"

"Just say to him that the suggestion came from me. Say I mentioned a name."

"A name?"

"Yes. Rivet Wilson."

"Rivet Wilson?"

He wouldn't elaborate, instead telling me that he had to go. So, after hanging up, I returned to my guests, who'd set the outdoor table and had opened a bottle of wine. Alfonso had brought a loaf of bread that he'd baked at home using my sourdough starter and Gaspard's contribution was the most delicious-looking duck terrine, a trio of large roasted quail, and another of his fruit flans.

Although I spent most of the time translating between French and Italian, lunch was extremely pleasurable. The duck terrine was outstanding, lightly perfumed with lemon zest and tarragon—where did he get tarragon in Italy? I wondered—baked with a flaky pastry crust. Alfonso had brought a jar of my plum chutney to accompany it. By three in the afternoon, I was hoarse from laughing—mostly at the misunderstandings between Alfonso and Gaspard—and sleepy with wine and food, so begged off, saying I needed a siesta. I left them to clean up while I staggered upstairs to bed, exhausted, the pain in my chest nagging, so

I took a painkiller, drew the floor-length white linen curtains and lay on the bed watching them flutter gently in the breeze while I waited for sleep to come.

That strange name, Rivet Wilson, was the last thing I remembered before I drifted off.

★★★★★

On Saturday morning, two days after Alfonso and Gaspard's visit, I heard a car horn beeping at the front gate. I was in the living room reading and ignored it the first time. However, after successive beeps, I wandered up the front path to the gate to see what was going on.

James was standing next to a car, talking to a man I'd never seen before, beside him was a suitcase. I nearly didn't recognise my English friend; he was wearing shorts, a pale pink open-necked shirt and espadrilles, a straw hat perched on the back of his head.

"I've brought lunch," he said, holding up a large brown paper bag.

I watched him take out his wallet and pass over money to the man then shake his hand.

"Who was that?" I asked as he gave me a hug.

"No idea. He did tell me his name, but you know me and Italian. Hello, goodbye, thank you—all the necessities but nothing else. Gave him the piece of paper that Giancarlo had written the address on and offered him ten thousand lire to drive me here."

"Have you lost your mind?" I asked. "That's fifteen American dollars."

He shrugged. "Closer to seventeen, but it's just money. Anyway, he looked nice, let me feel his leg while we were driving."

I rolled my eyes; I knew he was exaggerating, but it was part of his charm.

"How was Venice?" I asked as I showed him his room.

"Busy."

"I heard you were in Florence too."

"Yes, a quick pit stop to see the olds."

"Liar: quick *spit* stop to moisten your dick more like it."

"Oh, you've seen Randall."

"Yes, he was here two days ago."

I led him into the house then upstairs to one of the spare rooms. "I have a favour to ask you," I said, sitting on the edge of the bed while he unpacked.

"Oh, really?"

"Not right now. It's hot; would you care to have a swim? We can have coffee afterwards and catch up. I'm interested to hear about Venice."

"I did some legwork for you and Giancarlo while I was there," he said.

"You're talking about Scavola, aren't you?"

"Yes. But after a swim. Are swimmers necessary?"

"No, this area is private property."

"Lovely!" he said, then stripped off quickly and ran down the stairs. I found him a few minutes later, lying on his back in the shallows, sighing as he paddled the water at his sides with his hands.

I sat down next to him, handing him a bottle of *chinotto* I'd retrieved from the fridge. We chatted briefly about his museum visits in both Venice and Florence and he assured me that he'd left the key to our apartment with the local baker, as Giancarlo had asked him to. I casually enquired whether he'd caught up with his Americans again.

"Yes—with him, not her. She didn't like how enthusiastic her husband was; she felt left out. That's the problem with threesomes."

"So you had sex with him again?"

"A few times, actually. He's very pleasant. No, that's a terrible word to use about someone. He's young, your age, Damson, handsome, ex-military with a knockout body and nice penis and absolutely crazy about mine."

"You always say penis; it sounds so clinical," I said with a chuckle.

"Penis, cock, dick, prick … they're just words."

"Talking of words, I have two for you."

"Oh, yes? And what are they?"

"Rivet Wilson."

His face turned from cheerful and bright to quite stern, almost hard. "Where did you hear that?"

"It's connected with the favour I said I'd like you to do for me."

He leaned closer to me, so close in fact that our faces were mere inches from each other. I thought he was going to kiss me at first, but then I noticed that his eyes were examining mine very closely. Without warning, he broke into a smile and gave my cock a quick tug.

"Coffee? I'll race you back to the house."

He stood then ran off without looking over his shoulder, leaving me open-mouthed, wondering about the powerful effect those two words had had on him.

I made coffee while he sat outside, drying his hair in the sun.

"Sit, Damson," he said when I joined him, offering me one of his cigarettes. "We need to talk."

His whole demeanour was quite different. An exaggeration, perhaps, but I felt it: less limp-public-school-British-aristocrat and more contained, somehow very "adult".

"I know about the Acquaintance Club," I said, without waiting for him to speak and while pouring the coffee.

"And that's all?"

"Yes, apart from the name Rivet Wilson."

"And where did you hear that?"

"From a senior police inspector, now retired—"

"Who lives in Rome and has a brother?"

"Yes. You know him?"

"I know the brother."

"Don't tell me you've slept with him?"

He didn't answer, but his eyes narrowed a little. "This favour and Detective Inspector Venturi …"

"He needs to gain access to private Vatican City files."

"And you want me to …?"

I thought blunt was best. "Have sex with the archivist, in order to give the detective inspector access to the archive for half an hour."

"Sounds like fun," he said after a very long pause, his face still serious. "Did he say anything more about …?"

"Rivet Wilson?"

"Yes."

"No, nothing."

His hard look returned. It wasn't aggressive, more steely-eyed. "There are some things that you're better off not knowing, Damson. I'd be very grateful if you'd promise me never to mention that name to anyone else—and I mean anyone. Not even Giancarlo. Can you do that?"

"I think I'd need to know why."

"Do you want this favour or not?" He leaned over, ran his hand down the side of my neck and fondled my gold chain, drawing out my crucifix, which he held up a few inches from my lips. "Kiss this and promise me you'll never mention that name to anyone and I'll do what you ask."

"But you won't tell me why?"

He shook his head, then his face softened. "It's best for everyone if I don't."

It took enormous effort, but eventually I kissed my crucifix and then crossed myself, saying a quick prayer to St Raymond Nonnatus, the saint who was invoked when needing help to keep secrets.

CHAPTER 12

It was good to be home. Even though I'd have been able to put my feet up just as easily in my own house, the change of scenery had been good. For five whole days, I hadn't had to worry about household chores or the farm.

We had a full house; James had, as he'd promised, prepared dinner for the five of us: me, Giancarlo, Kendall, Alfonso and himself. However, it took me just a split second to realise that he hadn't cooked any of it himself. I recognised Signora Marino's tortellini filled with spinach and ricotta, the creamy sauce easily made from my cookbook, which was on its stand on the kitchen counter, opened at the page for the recipe. Two roasted chickens—another quick and easy dish—with vegetables from our garden were followed by a scrumptious date and custard flan from the bakery in Montepulciano.

"It's the thought that counts," Giancarlo had whispered to me in Arabic halfway through dinner.

The fireflies were out, blinking and weaving through the grape vines above us and the fig trees on the eastern side of the terrace. It reminded me of the night I'd had dinner with Mario in Torcello, when we'd stood outside the restaurant between courses and he'd told me about the night he'd followed Scavola to St Peter's Square.

"What was that thought?" James asked. I'd felt a wave of sadness and he'd seen it.

"I was thinking about Mario."

"I contacted his family," Giancarlo said. "They were astonished to learn that I had a *procura speciale*. Although his father had cut him out of his life before the war, he was still venal enough to think that he was going to be the sole beneficiary of his estate."

I explained to Kendall and James that a *procura speciale* was our equivalent of a power of attorney.

"And now I'm the executor of his will. He left the bulk of his inheritance to a charity run by the same order of nuns that took in Luca as a child. There are small amounts to some of his fellow actors and a large sum to a leftist political party that is vociferous in its opposition to parties such as those Scavola espouses."

"I know you're going to say *but*, I can hear it in your voice," I said.

"Well, yes, the *but* is that he's left the royalties from all of his motion pictures to Luca, with the proviso in his will that Luca set up his own carpentry shop once he feels he's ready to stand on his own two feet."

"What about your fee?" Kendall asked.

"There's an unspecified, open-ended amount put aside for legal fees, which will also cover any argument over his will. I'm not expecting his father to contest it, but while we were drafting it he did say he'd like to have a sum put aside for each of his sisters, to be delivered on the day of their weddings."

"That's pretty generous of him," I said, "considering they hadn't spoken to him in decades."

"Maybe it's because they weren't allowed to," Giancarlo said, then turned to Alfonso and translated everything that we'd said. "They're both coming up to thirty. His father actually wrote to me asking if he could get his hands on their dowries if they didn't marry by forty, which in his eyes would be too late to bear children."

Of course, when Alfonso replied, the conversation switched to Italian, so then I had to translate to Kendall and James.

"Does Luca know that Mario has left him money?" he asked.

"No. I've yet to tell him."

"I can let him know when I visit him tomorrow if you wish," I said.

Giancarlo said he didn't mind if I did, and would brief me on the exact terms of the bequest before I left. I intended to park the car in Pienza, take Kendall and Alfonso with me and walk to Lepri. I felt I needed to stretch my legs. Giancarlo informed me that he was going to Rome in the morning to meet with Salvatore Venturi and that he'd see me there late on Wednesday night, two days from now, when I arrived in time for the opening ceremony of the Games the following day.

★★★★★

The walk to Lepri was quite beautiful. We trekked through the country-side rather than following the roads. In the back of my mind, I knew that I'd decided to go that way not only for the scenery but also, perhaps being overcautious, so that no one could follow us.

Kendall was finally making an effort to speak Italian. Although he'd skipped nearly all of the on-board classes on the *Neptunia*, he had a primer and had been using that since arriving at La Mensola. Living with us, he'd been forced to learn the most common phrases to communicate with Alfonso—and with us, because these days Giancarlo and I spoke in Italian more frequently than in English.

As we walked, I tried to make a comparison of this lush, green landscape to that in which I'd grown up on the western side of the Great Dividing Range. There, the fields were vast, covered in bleached, straw-coloured grasses, studded with clumps of bushes and stands of eucalypts. Behind them ran a low range of blue hills that was usually distorted by the shimmering heat of outback Australia—summer or winter, there was no difference in the middle of the day.

I also loved the Italian countryside where feet other than mine had trod for millennia—the Romans, the Etruscans before them, Latins, Samnites, Umbrians and Celts, all of whom had civilisations of their own, now mostly long forgotten. In the vast spreading grasslands of my home, no such settled civilisations with buildings and agricultural pastures had ever existed until white men had arrived not quite two hundred years ago. But there existed a semi-nomadic group of peoples who'd inhabited my country for tens of thousands of years, handing down their culture and traditions from generation to generation. All of us who'd been brought up in the bush—black, white or brindle, as the Father Superior at the monastery was fond of saying—shared the same love of the land, the connection with nature around us and the soil beneath our feet. I sometimes had extraordinary pangs of homesickness, wishing to simply run my hands through the newly ploughed furrows of Australia's rich, red soil so that I could feel that connection again. I'd brought a jar full of iron-rich dirt back with me so that when I felt those pangs I could open my jar and take a deep whiff. Of course, it smelled of earth, as did dirt everywhere in the world, but to me it was a special balm for those times I wanted to revisit the home of my birth.

I walked behind Alfonso and Kendall, smiling as I listened to them conjugating simple verbs in each other's language, just as I had done with Renzo, ten years ago when I was first learning Italian. I noticed that Alfonso had placed a buttercup behind his ear. High summer wasn't the season for wildflowers, but it was the best time to gather aromatics; the heat brought out the volatile oils. As we'd been walking, I'd been picking allium heads and wild garlic to infuse in bottles of our olive oil. A few months ago, the countryside would have been a sea of red, especially in the wheat fields that surrounded us. Poppies—for those of us of British heritage, they symbolised the fields of Flanders and the carnage of the First World War. In many parts of western Europe, they covered the land for as far as the eye could see in early summer.

On my previous visit, Father Green had insisted that although he'd studied English, he'd never spoken it much. But less than half an hour after we arrived, he and Kendall were sitting in a corner laughing. Alfonso also disappeared, leaving me alone with Luca, who asked me if I'd like to see the project he'd been working on. I'd seen the retreat's rather miserable collection of tools and had brought a present for him: a roll of six high-quality German chisels and a wooden mallet that I'd made myself.

He'd been restoring a lectern that he'd found pushed to the back of the small chapel, so I offered to help him while we talked. He wasn't as skilled as Gregorio, but I could see that he knew what he was doing. When I asked to take over a particularly fiddly bit of work, he watched as I worked, asking questions, wanting to know more about my technique.

"I barely knew Signor Celestino," he said, after I'd revealed Mario's bequest to him. "But he was very, very kind to me."

"Obviously he was, Luca. The income from his movie royalties will be quite considerable, especially over the coming months. Since his death, I've noticed a big revival of some of his earlier films. Did you know there's even a festival devoted to him in Naples?"

"I don't deserve this."

"There must have been something that made him think of you."

I wondered if there had been some sort of sexual relationship going on between them. Maybe it was actually Luca and not Gregorio that Mario had meant was his Roman "lover". However, Luca had given no sign of being interested in any of us—not that that proved anything—and I didn't think it the time or the place to enquire. What did it matter anyway?

"You had a hard time … after the war, I mean?"

He nodded, so I encouraged him to tell me a bit more about himself.

"Where to start?" he asked.

"Perhaps start at the night when Sister Ursula was killed, if that's not too hard for you to talk about. I'm interested to know how you survived. The Allies were in Rome, but there were still many pockets of resistance—collaborators, fascists, German soldiers. From what I heard, battles still raged through the streets."

"Can I have a cigarette?" he asked. "Outside, I mean, not here."

There were two men praying in the chapel. I was sure their minds were on the Lord and they hadn't been listening, but Luca had been glancing at them from time to time while we'd been speaking and looked a little nervous. I followed him outside into the olive grove. We sat on a low stone wall, lit up, then I waited for him to speak.

"I was scared out of my wits that night, hiding on the roof of the train carriage. I had no real idea of what had happened beneath me, but still I pissed my pants in fear," he said, blushing heavily and glancing at me sideways from under his eyelashes.

"You're not alone, Luca. I did that more than once myself during the war. Leave out anything that's too difficult to talk about."

"No, I don't mind. No one's ever asked me what happened after she … not even Signor Celestino or Gregorio. I don't know why you're so interested, but I'm sure you have your reasons."

"You know I write books, don't you?"

"Yes. Father Green told me he'd read two of your books."

"I'm writing one now about people who survived occupation by the enemy, and the stories of others who were captured and lived to tell the tale."

"I'm not sure I—"

"I don't intend to use what you say. I promise you won't be in the book, don't worry," I said, crossing myself. "However, I am interested in knowing what it was like at that time in Rome. Please … you were saying you were hiding on top of the railway carriage …"

"Yes. I don't know how much time I stayed there, but it was until long after the men in black left, taking the other children with them. I couldn't move; I felt frozen, clinging to the top of the carriage. But then I heard shouts and cries of anguish: the station staff had found the bodies inside, below me. At that point, I didn't actually know what had gone on. I'd heard the shots but thought that they could perhaps have been warning shots and the sisters might still be alive, maybe hiding behind the seats or crouched on the floor. It wasn't until I climbed down and peered through the slats of the window shutters that I saw the men tearing their hair and sobbing. I couldn't see the floor of the carriage because of the way the slats were angled, but I heard everything. I realised that the nuns were dead."

"So, what did you do next?"

"You might think it was stupid of me, Damson, but, as I said, I was petrified. I should have asked the station staff for help, but then I thought that if those men who'd left found out that I hadn't run away, and had seen not only what had happened but also Scavola's face …"

"But surely you'd have been safer to have stayed—"

"Those men, the station staff, are all dead! Didn't you know that? All of them bar one: just one man, who emigrated to America after the war."

"Dead? All of them?"

He shrugged. "I found this out much later, but they were all transferred to Albano Laziale, the station closest to Castel Gandolfo, the papal palace, a few weeks after the massacre of the nuns. Didn't you hear what happened there? It made news headlines, even during the war."

"No, sorry, I was fighting the Japanese in Southeast Asia. We didn't get all the news from Europe. Please, tell me."

"Although the Allies had cleared most of the country south of Rome, there were still pockets of German troops fighting for control. The staff room of the station, which was packed at the time, was blown to bits; only two survived. One of the survivors was the man I told you about who went to America. The rest of his friends from the Vatican City station were killed outright, alongside a dozen other local station staff. They were having a union meeting. Can you believe it? A union meeting in the middle of a war. They thought he would die, but he eventually recovered. The British who liberated the area sent him south to a field hospital, which was far out of reach of Scavola and his henchmen."

"So, you think Scavola was responsible—?"

"I'm certain he was. No witnesses left, no one to point fingers. It was far too convenient. They said it was Allied artillery that had hit the station; but, as far as I've been able to find out, the fighting was hand-to-hand in that area. The British were far more respectful of our heritage; unlike the Germans, they didn't use their big guns to turn everything that was worth preserving into rubble."

I pulled the notepad out of my shirt pocket and scribbled a few notes. "Do you know the name of the man who went to America?"

"Don't bother looking. He met some woman in 1956 and took her name when they got married. I've written to so many places but never received satisfactory replies."

"You've been researching all of this, Luca?"

"Wouldn't you? I'm the sole survivor of, and witness to, what happened that night. If Scavola were ever to discover that I existed before this case goes to court, I might as well swallow a pill myself and save him the trouble."

"Don't say that. We'll look after you."

"But who will look after you?"

"I've lived through worse, Luca," I said.

He gave me the name of the man in America—his name before he got married—and the month and year that he'd sailed across the Atlantic. He knew that it was one of two ships, but, without any authorisation, hadn't been able to gain access to the passenger list of either. I told him to leave it to Giancarlo; he'd find out.

"You know that if this case does get to court, Scavola's lawyers will do everything they can to discredit you, to say you weren't there at all."

"Of course. But I can prove that I was there."

"How can you do that?"

"Topolino," he said.

"Mickey Mouse?"

He smiled, the first time that day. "I had a Mickey Mouse watch. Not one of the expensive ones. It had a tin face, the kind that they gave out to kids as souvenirs at cartoon screenings before the war. Sister Ursula took me to the cinema and got one for me. There's a picture of her and me taken three days before that night. I'm standing in front of her, her arms around me and my left hand clutching her forearm. You can see the watch clearly in the photo. Everyone knew about it; the children all called me Topolino because of it."

"And how will that watch prove you were there?"

"Because I buried it beside the railway track. I thought those men might come looking for me and I didn't want anyone to use it to identify me."

"Thousands of children must have had the same watch, Luca."

"But I was the only one with the woven blue band. It came with a red plastic band, but Sister Ursula changed it. She said the ribbon was one she'd tied around the head of her son when he was born."

"She had a child?"

"She hinted that he had been taken away from her before she became a nun. That was why she worked at the orphanage."

"And the watch?"

"It's still there as far as I know, Damson. I've never been back, nor do I really want to."

"The defence would say you could have come back and put it there at any time," I suggested.

"But why there? No news was released about Sister Ursula's death at the time, and all the witnesses were killed; why would someone bury a watch at the site if no one knew what had happened there?"

"Well, it did hit the news later. I've seen newspaper clippings."

"Wait here a moment, Damson. I'll be right back."

He left me running through his story in my mind, trying to pick holes in it as Giancarlo would have done with any witness about to face a lawyer for the opposing faction in court. The major one was establishing the veracity of his statement and whether he was, within reasonable doubt, at the scene of the massacre when it happened.

"Here you are," he said a minute later, passing me a scrapbook, already opened.

"What am I looking at?"

"This is me," he said, placing his finger on one of the photos that had obviously been taken in a police station. It was of a scrawny, dirty-faced kid. I barely recognised him. He was holding up a chalkboard with his name on it, his face streaked with tears, his hair a dishevelled mess. "Look at my left wrist; there's no watch."

"Maybe the police took it before they photographed you?"

"You watch too many American movies about crooked cops, Damson. They didn't pocket my valuables. I was a dirt-poor street kid, arrested for stealing bread from a barrow at the market."

"Still …"

"Look at the date on the slate," he said.

It read *10 giugno, 1944*. The tenth of June, the day after the nuns were murdered. It would be easy for Giancarlo to get a copy of the arrest statement, which would include a list of Luca's valuables … if the Mickey Mouse watch was not on that statement, then there was no reason to doubt that he'd been at the scene … as long as the watch was still there. There'd have to be a documented, official search and we'd probably need Luca to show us exactly where he'd buried it.

There were too many variables. It might have been uncovered during trackside work or washed away by rain … my thoughts were many, but at least this was a fair chance of scotching any attempt to discredit the fact that Luca had been where he said he was in his statement, and therefore what he saw and heard.

We wandered back into the refectory and made ourselves a pot of coffee. There were freshly baked bread rolls covered with cheesecloth and a selection of jams laid out on the kitchen bench. Luca told me that everyone just helped themselves. I longed for butter on my bread before I slathered it with blackberry and apple jam, but the Italians didn't do that. A lot of our Italian friends had given me weird looks over breakfast when they'd stayed at La Mensola, watching me butter my toast before adding jam then a thick slice of cheese.

We sat in the corner, near the door that opened into the courtyard overlooking the olive grove and not far from where we'd been seated earlier. Luca told me about his life after that night, how he'd trained as a carpentry apprentice and then, years later, had found himself standing outside Cinecittà, demanding to see Mario.

The police hadn't thrown him in jail after he'd been arrested for theft. Too many people, both young and old, were starving. Food had been almost impossible to find before the Allies finally liberated Rome, and there continued to be problems with not only supplying their own troops but also feeding the population. He'd been given a plate of watery chicken broth from the pot that had served the policemen for their lunch, a slice of bread and a cot to sleep on until the following morning, when he was booted out on the street to join the countless thousands of other children who'd been displaced or had lost their parents.

He'd spent weeks hiding behind the bushes in the front garden of a house opposite the orphanage, fretting over whether to knock on the door but fearful that perhaps someone inside had been complicit in the abduction of the nuns and the children. He still didn't understand why Sister Ursula and her companions had been shot; there seemed no reason. And, as for the children, it still tormented him to this day, wondering why such unnecessary cruelty had been inflicted on innocents, their bodies dumped outside the convent at night while he slept in the bushes of the abandoned house. He hadn't even heard the screams of the nuns when they'd discovered them in the morning. He'd been so hungry and exhausted that he'd slept through it all, and had only learned what had happened by overhearing talk of it in the market when he'd gone to scrounge for scraps and to beg for food.

The rest of his story, up until the end of the war, was miserable to listen to. He had lived on the streets, sleeping in abandoned buildings, surviving mostly on handouts from Allied soldiers. He'd even begged one of the kinder British lads to take him home with him, to adopt him. For a while he'd become the mascot of an office set up for American intelligence, but then a visiting colonel had told them to get rid of the scruffy child who spent his day sitting on the doorstep waiting for pats on the head and sandwiches from their mess. "Get a dog," the colonel had said. "Far less future trouble and, as you know, there should be no fraternising with the natives."

He'd joined a gang of street kids—scavengers, pickpockets and petty thieves—learning how to look after himself. It was a wonder that he'd never been arrested again. He told me he was basically a loner, a quiet lad tormented by what he'd been through. The death of Sister Ursula had haunted him. The other children had eventually kicked him out of their group. They couldn't cope with someone who woke them in the middle of the night thrashing and screaming, caught up in an endless, repetitive nightmare.

Then, one day, when he was fifteen, he'd run across an old man sitting on his front step, whittling. He was fascinated and perched on the roadside opposite, watching, unable to tear his eyes away. Of course, the man noticed him, but didn't look at him directly until he put away his carving and held out a piece of wood to Luca, beckoning him to cross the road.

The man's wife appeared with a bowl of stew for them while he was teaching Luca how to use a penknife to turn a piece of wood into something else. He had a natural eye for it and asked the man if he could come back the following day, which he did for weeks, the two of them making pegs, small figurines and carved animals.

"You are very good at this," the man said one day. "My son is a carpenter in Civitavecchia, on the coast. I'll write to him. Perhaps he needs someone to help him in his workshop."

Luca thanked the man but then lied, saying his parents would never let him go away far from Rome. The man simply fingered the frayed edge of Luca's jacket, then wetted the corner of his handkerchief with a little spit, wiping the dirt from Luca's cheek.

"Ask them nicely," he said. "It might only be food and lodgings, but it would be better than the life you're living here."

So, Luca went to Civitavecchia.

He worked first as a carpenter's monkey, sweeping the workshop, running errands, sleeping in the loft but eating with the family. They encouraged him to become friends with their children, but he remained aloof. Over time, he was taught the basics of woodworking and given chores that were simple, but he did them with such ease and skill that he graduated on to more difficult tasks until one day he was offered a job as an indentured cadet carpenter. He cried with the generosity, falling on his knees and thanking the man and his wife, asking them to write to the man's father, who years before had taken him to the train station, given him the ticket to Civitavecchia and then stood on the platform waving goodbye.

"I was very happy for the first time in my life, Damson," he said.

I had to admit that I found his story quite moving.

"I came to Rome to attend the *processo* after reading about it in the newspaper. It was there that I saw Signor Celestino and knew that I had to share my story. Of course, I knew who he was, we all did. Everyone had seen his pictures. He is … or rather was … a star!"

"You were very lucky that he agreed to see you. I can't imagine how many people must have been waiting at the gates of Cinecittà to see their favourite actors come and go."

"It was only when I said to the guard that it had something to do with his brother that he came."

"His brother? Emilio? Mario never mentioned that to me; all he said was that you had some important information about the war."

"Emilio had once been very kind to me. I had no idea he was Signor Celestino's twin; the surname isn't that uncommon. It was only at the hearing that I discovered the connection."

"Did you know that it was Scavola who'd killed him?"

"No! How did that happen?"

Luca was genuinely shocked, so I explained that Mario had learned that Scavola had mistaken his brother for him and had shot him.

"Dear God! That's awful. Poor Signor Celestino. I can't imagine how he coped hearing that news … he had a terrible reputation back then, you know."

"Who? Mario or his brother?"

"Neither. Scavola. They called him '*l'uomo dall'anima nera*'."

L'uomo dall'anima nera literally translates as *the man with the black soul.*

"Was what you had to say about Mario's brother important?"

"Not really. I just wanted to share a memory of him; he was very kind. He used to come to the camp we'd set up when I was a member of the street gang. He'd bring food, and a bottle of wine for the older teenagers. There were perhaps a dozen, at times more of us. He'd sit around and talk, make us laugh. I was very upset when I heard he'd been killed. Had we known at the time it was Scavola who'd shot him, then perhaps you and I wouldn't be having this conversation right now."

"Why not?" I asked.

"Because we'd have done everything we could to slit that bastard's throat and dump him in the Tiber."

I nodded, understanding. "I know Mario arranged for you to work with Gregorio, to keep you safe. Had you been intending to return to Civitavecchia after your visit to the film studio?"

"Yes. I phoned and said that I would be back but didn't know when. I didn't want to say where I was. Signor Celestino impressed upon me the importance of secrecy. I knew he hated Scavola, but until you just told me about his brother, I had no idea exactly how much."

"He only discovered that fact two months ago."

"I hadn't seen him for three, nearly four months. Maybe in time, he might have told me. I'm not sure."

"Scavola is in Greece right now. He left Italy in the afternoon of the day that Mario was murdered. Up until a few days before that, Mario was the only person who knew you existed. Now there are a few of us, all trustworthy and keenly aware of what might happen should Scavola learn of your existence, so you're safe here. If anything changes, we'll make sure to look after you."

"Thank you, Damson. I'm not afraid, if that's what you're thinking. I may seem retiring and shy, but don't forget I was a street kid. I can look after myself."

I was tempted to reach across and ruffle his hair but held back. He didn't come across as a young man who'd be comfortable with physical gestures of affection.

I told him the details of Mario's bequest, informing him that over time he'd end up being a very wealthy young man. Together with the royalties of Mario's motion pictures and an income from his own future atelier, he'd hopefully be more than comfortable for the rest of his life.

He listened to me carefully then turned his head and vomited into the lavender bush behind us, before breaking down into racking sobs. I'd seen men do that when hearing something momentous—the news of the death of a brother or a father during the war for example. Human beings reacted in such different ways. I put an arm around him and held him until he stopped crying.

He pulled away from me. "I'm sorry, Damson, I don't like being touched. It's not you, please believe me. I'm sorry that I reacted like that but—"

"There's no need to apologise, Luca. I lived and fought through the war, remember. I've seen stronger men than you and me crumple and fall to their knees at both good and bad news. You're a lucky young man. But, as I said before, Mario must have felt that you deserved it."

"I really don't understand," he said, wiping his nose on the handkerchief I passed him.

"He didn't explain it to me either. Perhaps Giancarlo knows more, but he said nothing to me other than what I've told you."

"This is life-changing," he said with a smile, his face still streaked with tears.

"It is, Luca."

"Now all I have to do is survive, to reap the benefits of such an extraordinary gift."

This time he allowed me to replace my arm around his shoulder and didn't shrug me away.

CHAPTER 13

I could barely hear myself think as the crowd roared, watching the bearer lift the Olympic torch triumphantly before lighting the cauldron, the signal that the Games of the XVII Olympiad had begun.

The Stadio Olimpico was packed to the rafters, all seventy thousand seats fully subscribed for the opening and closing ceremonies. We'd arrived very early in the morning so I could meet the Australian crew who were filming the Games and then would also be following me around for a few weeks for the television programme Kendall's father had arranged.

I was introduced to Wesley Arnott, the young man who'd be writing the article for *Housekeeper* magazine. I'd originally expected it to be a female journalist, but I'd been informed that young Australian women needed the permission of their husbands or fathers to get a passport and travel abroad. It seemed that nineteenth-century mores still persisted in my home country and, as the magazine would not fund the travel of a male companion, none of the suitable ladies was able to travel alone to cover the story.

It was a subject I intended to broach with the journalist during the course of our interview. He was rather nonplussed when I told him that due to unforeseen circumstances, he wouldn't be staying at La Mensola, as I'd arranged with Kendall's father in Sydney. We now had a houseful, and the guest house was hosting its first ten-day group of overseas visitors. I told him we'd put him up with the film crew in Montepulciano, where Kendall had rented a house with a cook and cleaner to look after them.

He appeared to be a rather shy man, who, when I met him, was wearing fashionable fawn slacks and a white button-down-collared shirt with a lemon-coloured unbuttoned cardigan. His black-rimmed eyeglasses gave him a serious look, despite his bright smile when he shook my hand.

Kendall seemed very protective of him. I later learned that although Wesley had come from humble beginnings, he'd won a scholarship to the same private school Kendall had attended and they'd become close mates. After high school, Kendall had joined the army and Wesley had won a bursary and had gone on to study economics at Sydney University.

It was great to see Kendall in his element again. During my Australian tour, he'd been very much in charge. Obviously his background as an army officer had given him not only a sense of authority but also the ability to marshal resources and to get things done. Since we'd arrived in Italy, he'd taken a back seat, allowing the world to flow around him. However, here he was the boss's son, and the film crew and journalists complied with his every direction. I got the occasional wink from him behind their backs but was happy just to see him with his "I'm in charge" hat on.

He was seated in the special VIP section of the stadium with other major donors and the Olympic committee. His father had donated ten thousand pounds: a fortune! Giancarlo and I had very good seats on the other side of the arena. I'd brought my binoculars and a small aluminium cool box that we used for picnics, packed with snacks and mineral water. No alcohol was allowed, otherwise I'd have brought beer.

The teams marched out in alphabetical order of the name of their country, with a bearer carrying the flag of the nation of the team that he or she represented. As A for Australia was right near the top of the list, I jumped to my feet when I spied the Union Jack in the corner of our blue flag bearing the stars of the Southern Cross, yelling my head off and holding a very large Australian flag behind my back by its corners. I'd brought it home with me from the tour; Giancarlo had wondered why I'd bought it. Now he knew.

Of course, Giancarlo was embarrassed, tugging at my belt, but I ignored him. I was hoarse by the time the team arrived in front of where we were seated. I recognised so many of the athletes, having met them earlier this year. They looked so smart marching proudly in their uniforms. It brought tears to my eyes.

However, despite his admonitions not to make a spectacle of myself, Giancarlo joined the countless thousands who jumped to their feet when the host nation, the last team to enter the arena, finally appeared. It was then that I realised that I had split loyalties, because I was up beside him yelling just as loudly.

The rest of the week passed by in a flash. I felt like a teenager again, excited non-stop every minute of the day, attending events at the track and field and at the swimming arena, cheering for my favourites, wet-eyed when Australia's or Italy's medallists stood on the podium to receive their gold, silver or bronze medals while the appropriate national anthem was played for the winner of the event. How I wished we had our own national anthem and not "God Save the Queen", which accompanied medal finalists from not only Great Britain, but also South Africa, New Zealand, Canada, Australia and the other nation members of the Commonwealth.

It wasn't just sporting events but a whole social calendar of parties at embassies, private residences and official receptions. I'd brought two dress shirts to go with my tuxedo, but they weren't enough. Salvatore's poor washerwoman was a godsend; every morning our previous day's clothes appeared freshly brushed down or washed, our shirts starched and brilliant white, and even our underwear and singlets spotless and ironed. More than once I told Giancarlo that I could easily get used to the life of a member of the nobility with acres of cash to spare and staff to sort out my every problem.

One evening during the second week, we had a late supper at Randy's Rome apartment with Helen, her sister and Arnie. James arrived unexpectedly, invited by Helen, and they spent a lot of the evening talking about the dig the sisters were working on. None of us minded; it was very informative.

In fact, we saw James quite a lot; he was at all the embassy parties. However, there was one in particular that struck me as being out of the ordinary. It was at the British embassy, where he stood in the receiving line with the ambassador and his wife and the senior embassy staff. It was explained that his father, the Earl of Penwyth, was a member of the Olympic committee and James was standing in for him. However, during the course of the evening, I became aware that he was very friendly with the embassy staff; it was as if he knew them very well. When I remarked on it to him, he shrugged, telling me that the "old boys' network" was alive and well back in his country and they were all friends of friends or of his father's.

However, nothing prepared me for his appearance seemingly out of the blue at the American embassy. It was a very swish event with other heads of legations, and quite formal. I didn't own a tails suit but I'd hired one in advance over the telephone, calling in at the tailor first thing in the morning to have it fitted. Although the upright starched collar chafed a bit at first, both Kendall and Giancarlo assured me that I "looked like a million bucks".

James seemed very at ease in his formal wear, an order on a ribbon around his neck and a large decoration on the left-hand side of his jacket. I was immensely curious, but he fobbed me off, saying it was part of British upper-class nonsense and really meant nothing. There were cocktails first, followed by a sit-down dinner in a massive room, with so many guests that the tables were joined together in a U-shape so that the sixty diners could fit around it comfortably.

I found myself sitting next to a striking-looking man whom James had pointed out earlier in the evening as being the American, the husband of the pair he'd slept with in Venice. I didn't quite know how to react when I felt his hand on my knee but turned to him and said under my voice that, although I was flattered, my dance card was definitely full up.

"Pity, Mr O'Reilly," he said with a gleam in his eye. "We could swap war stories."

I stared at him in disbelief until he winked.

"Oh, those sorts of war stories," I said with a grin. "I'm very happy to do that sometime in the future, but as for the rest …"

"I'd be quite content to even watch you and that handsome brute sitting next to my wife," he said, indicating Kendall. "I could be very generous," he added, his hand moving further up my thigh.

I gently replaced his hand. It was rather fun, because I sensed that he was playing games, not entirely serious, even though I felt quite flattered. "I'm afraid you've confused me with Viscount Langley."

"Oh, my generosity wasn't meant to be insulting; I meant it in terms of information, not money. I wouldn't be that crass."

"Information?"

He turned in his seat, his face quite serious. "I know you and your partner, Mr Manetti, are seeking information about Giovanni Scavola."

That really got my attention. "Do tell?"

"After dinner, perhaps, when the gentlemen repair for cigars and brandy and leave the ladies to freshen up, we'll find a quiet spot away from everyone else."

"He says he has information about Scavola," I said a little later, between the cheese remove and dessert. I'd found Giancarlo in a huddle in one corner of the room speaking with an Italian couple that I'd met once or twice at official gatherings and had drawn him aside. I was still, after all these years, getting used to formal dinners in Italy, where people often got up from the table between courses and either went outside to smoke or chatted about other issues before returning to their seats.

"What sort of information?" he asked, replying to me in Arabic, the language I'd spoken in.

"He seemed quite serious."

"Then what's the problem?"

"I think he wants to have sex with me first."

He grabbed my arm and led me into one of the window alcoves, then spoke in Italian. "So? He's very good-looking and James told me he was a great fuck; what's your problem?"

"I wasn't asking for your permission," I said, annoyed at the tone he'd used, as if I was wasting his time with something of no consequence.

"Well, honestly, Damson, what's another notch in your belt going to do? The world won't end if you let him suck your dick. What he has to say might be important."

"Oh, for fuck's sake, Giancarlo. Another notch in my belt? If we look back over the past ten years of our relationship, who's fucked more people outside it? My meanderings have only been with people we both know and—"

"Look, this isn't the time or place. If you have problems about what you and I do outside our bedroom, then let's talk about it some other time."

He turned on his heel and left me standing like an idiot, wondering how the conversation had taken the turn it had. I was about to return to my seat when I caught Kendall's eye. He gave me a very slight head tilt, beckoning me to follow him, excused himself from the American's wife, then headed off to the restroom.

"What's up?" he asked once we were standing in the vestibule. There was no point actually entering the men's room because at all these functions there was always an attendant.

I explained the situation.

He laughed softly, then kissed me quickly. "I'll watch, if that makes you feel any better."

"I haven't made up my mind yet," I said. I was still feeling a bit cross after my conversation with Giancarlo.

"Of course you have, Damson. I can see it in your eyes—"

We were interrupted by the door opening. "What are you two up to?" It was, of course, the American who'd obviously seen us leave together and had followed.

"Came for a quick chat," I said.

"Why not inside, in the can?"

"There are ears."

"I'll fix that. Wait here for a second."

A moment later the attendant appeared, the American having given us warning that the man would stand outside the men's room and direct gentlemen to another on the floor below while a "spill" was cleaned up.

"So, what's up?" he asked when we were inside with the door closed behind us.

"All right: the information you said you had. What do you want me to do for it?" I asked.

He glanced at Kendall with a raised eyebrow.

"I'll just be the audience, like I was last time," Kendall said with a broad grin.

"What do I want you to do? That depends …"

"Depends on what?"

"Show me your cock," he said.

I shrugged, unzipped and pulled it out, giving it a tug to allow it to lengthen. He whistled softly. "Good grief, it's big," he said, reaching over to squeeze the shaft. I felt myself fattening up. Despite my reservations, he was very handsome, and I could feel Kendall's dick pressing against my arse.

"Not as big as when it gets hard," Kendall said, a slight gravel in his voice, standing behind me then running his arms around me.

"Will you fuck me with it?"

"That depends …" I said, echoing his previous hanging sentence.

"On the quality and value of what I have to tell you about Scavola, I imagine."

I shrugged, my cock by now hard in his hand. He stared at it, licking his lips, his glance flicking back and forth to my mouth. I knew what he wanted.

"Kiss me," I said.

"I don't kiss men," he said. The statement was out of his mouth almost like a snap; it cemented my belief that it was exactly what he wanted.

"Sure you do," Kendall said from behind me, then reached over and drew the American close to us with one finger underneath the knot of his starched white tie.

I found myself leaking as soon as the American started to explore my mouth with his tongue, alternating kisses with Kendall.

"Fuck, I want that in me," he whispered hoarsely into my ear, his thumb smearing my ooze over the head of my cock.

"Later, Tiger," I said, extricating myself from both his mouth and his arms.

I allowed him to settle my dick back into my underwear, watching as he carefully patted it in place then slowly zipped up my trousers.

★★★★★

"Wake up, sleeping beauty," I whispered into Giancarlo's ear as I slid into bed next to him and wound my arms around his chest, last night's contretemps forgotten. In the scheme of things, I'd decided, we both might have overreacted.

He made mumbling noises then settled back against me, rubbing his arse against me then feeling for my penis. "Damson?" he muttered. I laughed. It was a game we'd played for years.

"No, it's the milkman," I said, gently biting his ear.

He laughed, then coughed into the pillow. I supposed he'd had a lot to drink last night, as we all had.

"What time is it?"

"Just gone eight. We're going to have to get moving if we're to make the ten o'clock men's relay."

"You go. I'm tired; I'll see you there at lunchtime."

"Are you hungover?"

He nodded "Aren't you?"

"Dreadfully, but I wouldn't miss this for the world."

He yawned, stretched then tried to sit up. "Ouch!"

"What's wrong?"

"Sore asshole," he said with a grin, reaching for his cigarettes on the bedside table.

"James?"

"He was one of them." He passed me his packet and I lit up too.

"One of them?"

"The other was a young guy, the ADC to the military attaché."

"American?"

"No, a Brit, and it seems one of James's old pals from Eton. Cock on him the size of a donkey and a prizewinning fuck machine."

"A fuck machine?" I laughed. I knew just what he meant, though.

"How was your evening?" he asked.

"Eventful."

I then described how we'd gone back to the suite that the American kept at the Hotel Excelsior for visiting dignitaries. During the Games, however, he'd kept it empty as a pied-à-terre and for what I expected might be dalliances. In fact, it looked like he lived there; there were personal items placed around the room and a desk with photographs of him in his naval uniform during the war.

We'd drunk champagne and brandy, smoked and laughed ourselves hoarse until we'd fallen onto the bed, still dressed; despite some drunken attempts to undress each other while swapping tongues, we'd fallen asleep, only waking at six in the morning when his phone rang. He'd returned to the bedroom stark naked, his erection showing that he was ready to get down to it. My attempt at resistance dissolved when he pulled off my pants and swallowed my cock, Kendall feeding me his, his trousers still on and his dick jutting out of the fly. He knew that I found having sex with him while he still had his clothes on very erotic, as I also did when he started to talk dirty, slapping my hand away when I tried to unbutton his trousers so I could get his balls out too and suck on them.

"Swallow that fat cock, you Yankee cunt," he grunted at the American, reaching down to grab a handful of the man's hair and pushing his head down onto my dick, his voice thick with either feigned or true lust. One never knew with him.

The American raised his head and grinned. "Say it again," he said, a thick rope of saliva dripping from his chin. He'd obviously loved the use of a word he'd heard more often than he'd had hot breakfasts during his time in the navy.

"Say what?"

"What you told me to do and what you called me … a cunt."

Kendall obliged, using his military voice.

The American squirmed, grinding his cock into the mattress; his grin became broader. He did as he was ordered, sliding further down on the bed to lie face-down between my knees, choking on my dick. Kendall started to fondle his arse; I winked at him then nodded at the bedside table. On it was a jar of Vaseline and a large black rubber phallus. Randy had one exactly the same size, but his was a dusky brown colour.

It was very arousing to first watch Kendall grease up his thumb then massage the American's arsehole with it, before crossing his index and middle fingers and easing them into him. I smiled as the American raised his hips and pushed back against Kendall's very expert finger-fucking. Kendall passed me the dildo and I greased it up for him, his fingers still working the American who, by this stage, was moaning loudly, his arse in the air and choking on my dick.

"Put it in me," he said to Kendall in a thick half-whisper, having released my cock from his mouth.

"How much of it do you want, Yankee?" Kendall asked.

"Don't go easy: shove it all in as far as it will go; get me ready for Damson's cock."

I'd stripped off my pants, but still wore my shirt and jacket, my socks, shoes and garters. The scene looked like something from the new American pornographic magazines that were starting to make the rounds, handed from one man to another.

"Impressive, O'Reilly," Giancarlo said after I'd finished describing the evening.

I put my arms around him and kissed him. "It was fun, but you're the man I love."

"What about Kendall?"

"You know I have feelings for him, but he's eventually going to marry, Giancarlo. You and I might be his best friends and fuck buddies—to use a term Randy says all the time—but you're my forever man. I intend to spend the rest of my life with you."

"And if I decided that I wanted us to be monogamous?"

"You?" I asked.

He laughed.

"Then that's what it must be," I replied. "Despite your having turned into a cranky old bastard, I can't imagine my life without you."

"Aw ..." He kissed my nose. "Now, all this talk of sex has me wanting you inside me."

"After last night? I thought you said you had a sore arsehole."

"Hair of the dog, Damson. Can you manage after your morning?"

"I'll try," I said. "Although it might take me a while to squirt."

"Perfect. Now lie back, let me suck you for a while, then I want you to take as long as you like stretching my hole with your big cock."

I laughed out loud. "Dirty talk, Signor Avvocato? You've been taking lessons from Kendall."

He winked, then pulled back the sheets and got to work. I ran my fingers through his hair; there was something about the familiarity of his mouth and the way that he worked his tongue that had me rock-hard in no time at all and before long I found myself turning him on to his stomach then trying to fuck him right through the mattress.

Despite everything I felt for and enjoyed with Kendall, making love to Giancarlo was another thing altogether, on a higher level. I knew it was the love between us that made it so.

★★★★★

"He's what?" Giancarlo said later that morning, my attempt to go to the track and field abandoned after our vigorous interlude in bed. We sat outside on the terrace that ran along the front elevation of Venturi's Rome apartment, eating a late breakfast and taking in the sunshine.

"An intelligence agent. I bet he works for the CIA. I suspected when I saw the pictures of him in his navy uniform on his desk. It figures, doesn't it? You know the diplomatic comings and goings better than me; your father is a diplomat. Distinguished military career man in his late thirties, man with a 'trophy' wife, now a diplomat … bears all the hall-marks of a secret service agent."

"He told you that?"

"He said as much, but without the actual words."

"And the information he said he'd give you? I hope it was worth the sex marathon?"

"The sex marathon, as you called it, was well worth it, and to be perfectly honest, I wouldn't mind a return visit."

"How was your evening?" said our host, Salvatore Venturi, appearing from behind us. I had no idea how long he'd been there, but it didn't matter; he was non-judgemental and extremely discreet.

"Whose, mine or Damson's?" Giancarlo asked, patting the seat of the empty chair of our table.

"Your evening with the American, Damson."

"Ah, you know about that, Salvatore?"

He nodded. "I hope you came away with more than memories of an interesting evening?"

"You know there's more to him than meets the eye?"

He nodded. "He reports to General Walter Smith."

Smith was the head of the CIA in the United States, so my assumptions were correct.

"Luckily for us, the Americans are also very interested in Scavola," I said.

"In what manner?"

"Their interest is twofold. First of all, there are his believed connections with Italian organised crime in Chicago; and, secondly, he's suspected of war crimes against American military personnel in Rome during the liberation."

"That's interesting," Salvatore said. "Was that all?"

"He wanted to enlist my aid."

"He wanted you to help him? I thought he wanted to share information."

"And he did."

"In exchange for an evening of intimacy?"

I shook my head. "That was something personal, Salvatore. It was something he wanted anyway. He would have told me what he did without the rest, enjoyable as that was."

"So what did you learn?" he asked, signalling to one of his footmen, who'd been attending to our breakfast, to bring more coffee.

"Three months after the liberation, there was an assassination of a group of American servicemen in Rome. It's believed it was carried out by Scavola's gang of crooks."

"While he was supposedly working for the Allies."

"Yes. Had the Americans known about Mario Celestino's surveillance of Scavola's group before and after the liberation, they might have asked him what he knew. However, the job to handle Scavola was only recently tasked to our American, who's just arrived in Italy too late to interview a dead man."

"But there's—" Giancarlo started to say.

"Yes, there's Luca. Perhaps he knows something. One of us must ask him when we get home."

"If it was Scavola's gang, why would they want to murder Americans?" Venturi asked.

"Each of the victims was shot, then spread out naked on display in a public square."

"Reminds me of you know who," Giancarlo said. He was referring to Joseph Gemello, the serial killer, a man I'd befriended before meeting my lover ten years ago.

"Yes, but Gemello was flying bombing raids over Germany at the time. I know it sounds suspiciously like his *modus operandi*, but there was something about the way the bodies were posed that made me think of him."

"And what was that?"

"All the men were posed exactly like Da Vinci's *Vitruvian Man*, a black ribbon tied around their genitals under the scrotum and behind the base of the penis, lifting them up into prominent view."

"What on earth …?"

"No one has any idea why. There was one thing the American shared, something his superior suggested, and it had to do with all of the men being circumcised."

"That's nothing unusual as far as Americans are concerned," Giancarlo said.

"According to our American," I explained, "roughly sixty per cent of men in the US in 1944 were circumcised; it seems recruitment medical examinations and records were very thorough. So, his superior officer proposed that it's either a random fact—a few at least should have been intact—or, more sinisterly, it was meant to say something."

"There was a lot of hatred of the Yanks before we switched sides," Venturi said. "Do you think that's what your friend was implying—that it was antisemitic?"

"As I said, it was his boss's theory, despite only one of the men being Jewish. The American thinks it could be something else altogether. When he asked me what I thought about what he'd told me, I just shrugged and said that I wouldn't go focusing my investigation on some tenuous link to antisemitism."

"And what did he say?"

"He said that those were his thoughts too, but his boss in Washington had a bee in his bonnet about the circumcisions and was obsessed with the idea of a Jewish connection."

"Interesting," Giancarlo said.

"News of the massacre got out just after the war and it just won't go away. There are families in the USA who are clamouring for details of what happened to their sons and husbands."

"Surely something like that would have been kept secret," Giancarlo said.

"It was so shocking that it was on every US serviceman's lips at the time. No way you could keep something like that secret. Anyway, as I said to the American, the truth of what happened and the reason for the massacre could only come from Scavola, or one of his group at the time."

We were briefly interrupted by the appearance of Salvatore's young wife, wearing a two-piece swimsuit over which was a see-through cotton robe. When she saw it was us, she wiggled her fingers in greeting, then, with a toss of her long copper-coloured curls, turned and went back inside.

"I need to tell you about my visit to the Vatican archives," Venturi said after she'd gone. "You can thank your friend James, who kept the archivist busy for well over an hour, which afforded me extra time to root around."

"What did you find?"

"A lot. Unfortunately, all it does is verify what we already suspected: that Scavola was directly involved in the murder of Sister Ursula, her companions and the children."

"Why do you say 'unfortunately'?" Giancarlo asked.

"Because none of it would ever be admissible in court. How would I explain that I had access to one of the most closely guarded sections of the archive without exposing either the archivist or my brother—something I'd never do? And if I did lay out in court what I'd found, I'd end up in jail myself, for trespass first, then probably for theft."

"Well, you'd better tell us what you discovered."

"The place is a rabbit warren. There are many doors, gates, enclosures, each of them more secure than the one before. The archivist opened each, sometimes with a key, at other times using a combination lock. He pointed me to the section I needed to search. Fortunately, the files are double-referenced by date and by subject matter. Anyway, I eventually found what I was looking for. There was a meticulous record. I was not allowed to take anything in with me to record what I found. No writing implement or paper …"

"However?" I asked, noticing the rather smug look on his face.

"However, as you both know, I was a senior investigating officer for decades. Both the Americans and the Russians have developed technology that is nigh undetectable unless you know what you're looking for, and although the archivist was quite thorough in his pat-down, he failed to detect the wire that ran from my jacket pocket through its front seam and into the lapel, where I had an excellent buttonhole camera."

"You took photos?"

"Yes. My memory isn't good enough to remember everything. But, as much as I trust you both, I'm not going to give you copies of what I photographed. It would be a calamity for me if they ever came to light. The photographs are locked in my safe. What I can give you, however, is a transcript of the most important parts."

"But what you found directly implicates Scavola."

"It does—him and his cronies who murdered the nuns."

"Then we can track them down?" Giancarlo said. I sensed his excitement.

"No, we can't, my friend."

"And why not?"

"You probably won't be surprised to learn that Scavola is the only survivor of the group. The other three men who accompanied him that night are all dead."

I sank back in my chair a little. Not really surprised, just disappointed. The more I learned about the man, the more I realised he was the type who wouldn't leave loose ends, just like the Vatican City station staff killed in the explosion at Albano Laziale.

"The names of the guards who met them when they arrived and then prevented Mario Celestino from following were also in the file. I haven't been able to trace them. One of them was Swiss, the other a Brazilian. Perhaps they returned home after the war; it's another piece of the puzzle that needs sorting out. I'll get on to it, don't worry."

"Did the file give any clue as to the reason the nuns were murdered?"

"The language was opaque. I didn't have access to the section in which personal files were kept, so was unable to read about Sister Ursula. However, at the end of the report on that night, there was a handwritten margin note that at first I took as being enigmatic, but upon reflection, gives me the idea that Scavola did not act independently."

"The remark?" I asked.

"You're the Latin scholar, Damson. How would you translate *quaestio soluta*?"

"It's a shorthand two-word phrase for something longer. Quite common in manuscript notations."

"Yes, but the meaning?"

"Basically it means something like 'problem solved'."

Giancarlo stood from the table and walked to the balustrade of the terrace, leaning on it while he smoked and looked out over the people in the Campo de' Fiori. Venturi and I joined him after a moment.

"I suppose her death was ordered by the Vatican," my lover said, rather sadly.

"That's my assumption too," Venturi replied.

"How does a scumbag like Scavola get such a high level of protection?" I said. "The brothers at the monastery who'd brought me up were immensely devoted to each other. Surely the Vatican would accord some sort of loyalty to the nuns."

"You aren't Italian, Damson, otherwise you'd know about Sister Ursula's history. She was very well-known both before and during the war. There's a group of campaigners who want her beatified for the work she did saving orphans, protecting Jews, speaking up about the atrocities of the Nazis and blaming the Vatican for turning a blind eye to, if not colluding with, the enemy. Had she not been a nun, the Gestapo would have taken care of her long before the Allies liberated Rome."

"So, the note at the end of the file would seem to indicate that someone was rather glad that the 'problem was dealt with'."

"So it would seem."

"But the children?"

Venturi shrugged. "Scavola would have to tell us. I, for one, have absolutely no idea why the children had to die. I can only surmise they were witnesses."

"But Luca was the only one of them old enough to really know what was going on …"

"True. But what you said before, about 'a scumbag like him' and his level of protection. I have an answer for that, too, but it has nothing to do with what I discovered in the Vatican archive; it was in our own police files. You asked Giancarlo's assistant, Cosmo, to find out what he could about Scavola's first wife, the woman who was killed during the bombing. She's the reason."

"I don't understand," I said.

"Her godfather protected her, and therefore by extension her husband, during the war."

"Her godfather?"

"Yes, Damson. Her godfather, Eugenio Maria Giuseppe Giovanni Pacelli."

"Who is?"

"Who *was* His Holiness Pope Pius XII."

"That fucking Nazi?" I said more vehemently than I should have, then crossed myself.

"Don't waste your time with benedictions, Damson," Venturi said. "I hope that old bastard is writhing in the flames of hell."

He spat on the ground next to his feet.

*****

Monday, the twelfth of September, was the last day of the Games, and in the evening, after the excitement, we attended a cocktail party at the Australian consulate.

It was a rather low-key affair, but I was delighted to be among the people who'd represented my country and had made me feel very proud.

Around ten o'clock, as the evening was winding down, Kendall tugged at my sleeve and told me to follow him.

"Grab your jacket, O'Reilly, we're going for a quick ride."

"Where to?"

"Don't ask questions," he said, then slipped a tube of Vaseline into my pocket, patting it in place.

"More adventures?" I asked.

He winked.

We were in the car that he'd hired for no more than ten minutes, pulling up in the darkness outside the Colosseum.

"Are we playing Emperors and Gladiators?" I asked with a grin.

He beckoned me to follow and we made our way up through the deserted structure to one of the top rungs of the seating area, behind an arched portico. A figure appeared from the darkness: it was the American.

"Evening, fellas," he said, shaking our hands. "Exactly what are we doing here?"

"Well, get on your knees, Yankee. First, you're going to suck Damson's cock, then he's going to fuck you."

"What? Here?"

"No, down there," Kendall said, indicating the ruins of what had once been the floor of the gladiatorial arena below us. "Just in case there are any other perverts hanging around in the dark, I want them to see you having your arsehole stretched open by my pal here while you blow me."

I knew my eyes were round with surprise, but the American slowly broke into a grin.

"Both of you fuck me and it's a deal," he said, holding out his hand.

To my surprise, we both shook it, then wandered down the stairs with our arms around each other's shoulders.

It didn't take long before a few other figures appeared from the darkness: a couple of young men and one about our age. They stood there masturbating, watching while I fucked the American while he gobbled Kendall's dick. It was easy to see that he found it immensely arousing, as did Kendall: voyeurism was his thing after all.

A young man with a cock that almost rivalled the size of Randy's took my place, causing the American to stop what he was doing and turn his head to see who'd invaded his arsehole. His half-closed eyes and slightly opened mouth indicating that lust had taken over and that he didn't mind at all.

Eventually, other men having taken our places, Kendall and I left the American to it, finding a quiet place to ourselves among the shadows.

"How did you know about this place?" I asked.

"Wesley, the reporter who's going to interview you. He told me about it. Says he's been here most nights. I told him to stay away this evening, then phoned the Yank at the embassy. We met up in the VIP stand at lunchtime and I told him to meet us here. Didn't say why, though."

"You're a bad boy, Kendall Travert," I said, then kissed him.

"Fancy fucking a bad boy in the ruins of Ancient Rome?" he mumbled back to me in between kisses.

"What if someone else comes along?"

"Depends on who they are and what they want, O'Reilly. You need to live a little."

It made me laugh. Really, it wasn't much different from the parties Randy's South African pal held, except that this was outdoors and I'd had fun at those. He began to strip.

"What, naked?" I asked.

"Just in case anyone cares to watch," he said, lying on his back on the ground and pulling me down to him with one hand.

I unbuckled my belt and undid my flies with one hand, the other behind his neck while we kissed. Somehow I managed to get my strides down to my ankles.

"Looking for this?" he asked, holding up the tube of Vaseline.

"I thought you gave that to the American."

"Thought I might need it myself," he said, one hand between his legs, greasing himself up as he lifted his legs, then wound them behind the small of my back. I watched the glow in his eyes as I slid into him; he smiled and sighed with pleasure, fondling my balls, urging me to thrust deeper.

"You are such a bad boy," I said.

"You have no idea, Damson, and it's all your fault."

I laughed against his mouth, then got down to the serious business of fucking.

CHAPTER 14

James returned to La Mensola the day after I got back from Rome. Following him was the hired van bringing the film crew and with them Wesley Arnott, the reporter who was to write the article about me for *Housekeeper.*

He'd been hovering around in Rome during the Games but had kept a low profile. After our evening at the Colosseum, I'd asked Kendall whether he'd ever fooled around with him but had been told that as far as he was concerned business and pleasure were two entirely different things and the line between them should never be crossed.

"Do you mind if I ask questions while you go about your business?" Wesley asked, watching me as I screwed the lid on the moka pot then put it on the stovetop after stoking the firebox.

"As you wish. I'm fairly laid-back but there are times when I'll have to concentrate. The Irish in me might come out, but it will be nothing personal; I'll tell you if you're being obtrusive."

The telephone rang while I was stretching out two large *focaccie* ready to go in the outdoor oven. It was a detective. He told me that our apartment in Florence had been broken into. James's parents had reported sounds of crashing and, when our building supervisor had gone to investigate, she'd discovered that the front door had been smashed open. The detective wanted to know when one of us could go there to inspect the damage and to see whether anything had been taken.

I asked him why he'd called me and not Giancarlo. He said that he'd phoned the office in Pienza first. Cosmo had answered and told him that Giancarlo had arrived at the office at half past seven that morning, answered a phone call, then left, saying he'd be gone for twenty minutes, but hadn't returned.

I was about to give him Carla's number, but then remembered she'd gone to Naples after the Games to see an exhibition by a local artist she hoped to hang in her gallery. Randy had been in our apartment dozens of times, so I told the detective to phone Randy and ask him to have a look; he could report to me after he'd seen whatever damage had been done.

Where the hell was Giancarlo?

I cursed under my breath then started issuing orders when Kendall, James and the film crew, having settled in at the rented house in Montepulciano, arrived. I'd already informed them that I wasn't going to either entertain or feed everyone every day, but that our first meeting was to discuss scheduling. I'd invited Stefano to join us; I needed to co-ordinate activities at the guest house around filming. Giancarlo's absence started to really grate. I depended on him to translate for the non-English speakers while we worked through schedules.

We'd just sat down when the phone rang again. Hoping it was Giancarlo, I answered with an abrupt and angry-sounding *pronto*. It was Randy, who informed me that the only damage was in the office. The desk drawers and the filing cabinet, normally locked, had been forced open and papers were scattered everywhere. As far as he could tell, nothing else seemed to have been touched. Hanging up, I then phoned the Florence office. Giancarlo's secretary was just as puzzled as I was. She went through the shared agenda she kept with Cosmo and assured me that Giancarlo had left a week free to attend to "personal matters". In fact, when she'd last spoken with him, he'd said he was looking forward to time at home looking after the farm while I was otherwise occupied.

I returned to the crew with what I was sure was a worried look on my face, but I wanted to get the scheduling organised, so I didn't tell anyone what had happened. Randy had offered to have the locks changed on our front door and clean up the office. I told him to leave the mess, because only Giancarlo would know what was either missing or was what someone had been looking for … once he showed his face, that was. I suspected Scavola or his men were behind it, or maybe the legal representatives of the cops in Venice whose case was due to go to court next week. The scenarios that played over in my mind when something went wrong always had a flair for the dramatic. I made a mental note to phone Salvatore Venturi in Rome, to see whether Giancarlo had returned there unexpectedly, and to call Alessandro Pellegrini in Venice for the same reason. It wouldn't be the first time that Giancarlo had decided to go off without telling me. I glanced at my watch. Besides, I said to myself while trying to clear my mind and pay attention to what was being said around the table, it was only half past twelve, five hours since Giancarlo had told Cosmo that he'd be back in twenty minutes.

My annoyance at his absence had me making mountains out of molehills, or so I thought until the phone rang again. The film crew all stopped talking; I guessed my anxiety hadn't been quite so well hidden as I'd thought it had been.

"Damson? It's Salvatore Venturi here."

"*Commissario*, I was intending to phone you myself. What a pleasant surprise; how can I help you?"

"I'm looking for Giancarlo. Is he with you?"

"Wait one moment; I need to move to the upstairs telephone. Can you hold?"

I signalled to Alfonso and asked him to hang up after I'd taken the call upstairs in the study.

"No one's seen him all day," I continued once I'd picked up the receiver. "I was going to phone you to see whether he'd returned to Rome."

"I think we may have a serious situation," the former police commissioner said.

I listened carefully, making notes while he explained what had happened. Last evening, he'd received a call from a friend of his who worked in the section where he'd lodged Luca's statement along with the rest of the information that the public prosecutor would need, when and if a case was launched against Scavola. This friend had informed him that there'd been a break-in and several document boxes had been opened, the seals of several envelopes within them broken and the contents missing.

Venturi was furious, explaining to me that the area was somewhat like a bank vault, the walls lined with recessed steel boxes, each numbered and requiring a key to open.

"An inside job, then?"

"Yes, and of the four keyholders, only one is missing. The police are trying to find him now."

"I suppose you're looking for Giancarlo because our document was in one of the boxes that was robbed of its contents."

"Yes, and I think we are all in danger. Your, my, Giancarlo's and Inspector Pellegrini's names are all on statements by Mario Celestino and Luca Rinaldo. I fear that it was our documents that were the target; the other boxes were opened as a diversion. Scavola is bound to be behind it."

"If the documents are gone, then he's already won," I said, my mind starting to worry not only about Giancarlo's safety, but also Luca's.

"No, my friend. I'm a *vecchio saggio*: what you call a 'wise old bird', in English. Of course I took precautions. Photographic copies were made and witnessed of every scrap of paper. I made two copies; one is here in my safe, and the other in my bank. There's no way that either of those places can be compromised. However, it does mean that once the contents of those stolen statements reach Scavola, then—"

"We could be in trouble. He killed Mario, so what's to stop him coming for Giancarlo too? I have to get Luca somewhere else; I can't have his presence imperilling the people who are keeping him safe."

"And what about you, Damson? Pellegrini and I are basically untouchable, but you?"

"Let them try, Alessandro. I can look out for myself. However, having worked alongside Giancarlo for ten years, I'm no stranger to how these things work. I need to look out for the people close to me. If Scavola can't get at me, there are others whom I'd do anything to protect."

"I understand. But first, we need to find Giancarlo."

Excusing myself from the film crew, I drew Kendall and James outside and then explained the situation. "I know you've got a filming schedule organised, Kendall, but—"

"But we have to find Giancarlo and do something about Luca."

"Yes, I—"

"Leave the production crew to me, Damson," he replied. "Wesley and the producer have a list of background shots for the documentary. If I can't find someone who knows the countryside to show them where to go and can also speak English, then I'll eat my hat."

"I'm drawing a blank, sorry," I said, running through my friends and contacts in my mind. "I can't think of anyone local who might help." It was then I realised that I'd become fully Italianised. Apart from Randy and his circle in Florence, I had no other English-speaking friends.

"There were official translators at the Games," he said. "I'll contact the agency we used. It will be easy enough to fill a few days with outdoor shots, but before you go running off, I'll need you to speak with the Marinos and others in Pienza to get their permission to film their premises."

"I can sort that out for sure—"

"May I use your phone?" James interrupted. "I'll pay for the call."

I told him to go ahead. "I'm sorry to muck up your production schedule, Kendall, but—"

"You just do whatever you need to do, Damson. I'm going to organise a few things then take Alfonso with me to pick up Luca and take him somewhere safe."

"Where's safer than Lepri?"

"Come on—you know what would happen if someone found out he was there. If Scavola is behind this, no one there is safe. I'll take him to Rome."

"Kendall—"

"You have no idea of the power my father wields, Damson. No one is going to try to do anything to Luca while he's staying at the Australian embassy, and, if my dad can't wangle that, we'll have him on a private plane to London within the hour."

"I've no idea whether he even has a passport, Kendall."

"Don't worry about that. I'll organise it all; James will help if we need to get him to London."

"Help with what?" James said, returning from his phone call.

"Arranging to have Luca looked after by the Yanks in London."

"What makes you think that I—"

"Our—I mean, your American," Kendall said. "Your CIA buddy. I know you have traction with him, and I also know they're just as eager as the Italians to pin some dirt on Scavola. With an ace card like Luca and his testimony ..."

"CIA buddy? Great imagination, Kendall." Even I could see the slight moment of hesitation in James's eyes before he spoke.

"Sorry, my friend—you may consider me a colonial with buckets of money and perhaps a little rough around the edges, but I still have contacts."

"I have no idea what you're talking about."

"I know who runs the Acquaintance Club."

James merely raised an eyebrow, then sighed deeply, reached over and took the packet of cigarettes from my shirt pocket and lit one. The silence seemed to stretch on forever, so I spoke.

"All right, I have no idea what the hell is going on," I said. "Who runs this 'Acquaintance Club'? Anyone care to tell me?"

Kendall ran a hand behind the small of my back then leaned in close and kissed me behind the ear. "MI6 runs it, Damson, and that's who James works for. He and our American do more than share their spunk. They're both field agents for their respective organisations."

★★★★★

An outsider might have called it an argument—I'd have described it as a heated discussion—but for about ten minutes, there was a lot of yelling between the three of us. So much so that Alfonso, Wesley and the documentary producer came out into the garden to find out what the fuss was all about.

Four hours later, we found ourselves sitting outside a small café in the main square of Magliano Sabina, a small hilltop town about seventy kilometres from Rome and about one hundred and twenty-five from Pienza. James had refused to talk about his situation until the American arrived; he'd phoned him immediately after Kendall's revelation. We did, however, discuss Giancarlo's disappearance, which I continued to argue was not yet anything more than him having gone off on some work-related issue and forgotten to tell anyone. He did it so frequently that I'd considered it part of his normal routine.

I'd sent Alfonso to Lepri in the Jeep to warn both Father Green and Luca about Kendall's plan and impress upon them the necessity of keeping calm: to reassure them that we'd protect everyone at the retreat, and say that Luca shouldn't do anything rash like running off in the night. Alfonso promised he'd stay with him until Kendall arrived to collect him tomorrow morning.

The American drove up into the square in a very nice Citroën DS convertible, not a strand out of place in his American preppy-style combed and brilliantined hair. He folded up his sunglasses, placed them into his shirt pocket, lit up a cigarette then waved to us.

"You two are a mammoth pain in the ass," he said, ordering a coffee and a Campari soda then plonking himself heavily into the chair opposite me.

"Aw, you say the nicest things," Kendall said with a grin.

The American smirked. "I've had to report this up the chain."

"I expected as much."

"How did you find out about the Acquaintance Club?"

"It was James," Kendall said.

"Me?" James seemed surprised.

"Yes. I know how vulgar you Brits find the talk of money, but my father could buy your father's estate twenty times over and still have enough for Buckingham Palace as a weekender. You weren't indiscreet; it's simply that I was able to pay enough to do some digging about your escort agency and then speak with one of my former army friends who's a senior advisor in ASIO. I simply told him that you and I had been in an 'intimate situation'—don't worry, I didn't mention our American friend here—and, as I didn't want my personal life compromised. I wanted him to find out what he could, to protect us both."

"Protect you both?" I asked. "What, you and James?"

"Yes, James and I had to lie, say there was some sort of physical relationship going on between him and me. That was the only way I could get the man to dig deeper than he normally would."

"Why would he do that for you?"

"It was a personal favour, one that benefited both him and me; besides, he's up to his neck in debt. I offered to pay it off."

"A personal favour of such magnitude? I don't understand." I said, aware that James and the American were listening intently.

Kendall sighed heavily, then leaned closer to me, his hand on my knee under the table, then whispered in my ear. "Think Malaysia, Damson. Me, in the showers, my officer mate late at night ..."

I remembered his story of the man he'd played with during the war.

The others had overheard, despite his whisper. James smirked a little; the American looked as if he was about to ask for details. No doubt he, like me and so many other men, had shower stories from the time during the war.

"What's ASIO?" I asked, moving the conversation along. Wartime sexual escapades could wait for another time, when there wasn't this sense of urgency.

"The Australian Security Intelligence Organisation. It didn't exist before the war ... it was before your time, Damson," James explained, looking quite annoyed.

"But what about me?" the American asked. "I'm not admitting to anything, by the way, but what on earth made you think I might be working for the CIA?"

"Ah, that was my fault," I admitted. "You shouldn't keep pictures of yourself in naval uniform on public display in your private quarters. I told Kendall."

"And my buddy at ASIO spoke to someone he's 'seeing', a man who works at your embassy in Canberra," Kendall explained. "Anyway, your turning up here has pretty much confirmed what Damson suspects."

"You know you can't tell anyone about this, either of you," James said. "It would have serious repercussions if word of my involvement with MI6 got out. My bosses know about him and me," he said, glancing at the American. "But if that information fell into the hands of enemies of either of our countries ..."

"How long has this being going on between you?" I asked. "I'm fairly certain, with what I know now, that it didn't start in Florence at my book signing."

"Before I got married—" the American started to say.

"My first year at Oxford when I was recruited," James said over the top of him.

"Whoa! So you two have been getting together for how long now? Five years?"

"Give or take," the American said.

"And the display you put on for me in Venice?" Kendall asked. "You said it was the first time—"

"I had to say that for my wife's sake, buddy. It was she who'd always hankered for a threesome with another man, but she isn't so keen anymore."

"She thought she'd be the centre of attention, I suppose."

"My mistake, to be honest, but I'm so used to having James stretching my asshole that I couldn't resist."

"So that display? That thing when you said you'd pay James more money to fuck you harder …?"

"I was playing the game but got carried away. I was really turned on. It was the straw that broke the camel's back for her, though. She hit the roof the next morning, saying I could do whatever I wanted but not to involve her anymore. We had to have a very civilised conversation and set some guidelines. I also had to tell her a few truths about my past history—nothing to do with James, though; she still believes we'd just met. We're planning on having kids. Callous or not, I need that semblance of stability, of the typical American family, for my job and my future prospects."

"You're planning to have children? So you still have sex with her?"

"Of course I do, and I enjoy it when she's in the mood. We've agreed that we won't talk about my other activities unless it interferes with our lives and her social standing. If word got out that I—"

"Her social standing?"

"She's more worried about that than she is upset about learning that I like to get fucked in the ass. Her father owns Preston's Pharmaceuticals. Appearances are everything, for her and her siblings. Besides, I have to play ball. Her money landed me the job in Rome, and I have to do whatever she or her old man tell me to do."

I turned to James. "And what have you got to say for yourself? Any more secrets up your sleeve I should know about?"

He fiddled with the teaspoon on his saucer, then looked me in the eye. "Plenty, Damson, but I'm sure you know that I can't talk about much of it."

"And meeting Giancarlo and me?"

"Pure accident, I assure you. I didn't know either of you existed until I grudgingly packed my bags and was dragged off to Florence to see Pater's latest bit of real estate. Imagine my delight to find out I had two handsome homos living on the floor below me."

"We weren't so happy to learn of your father's purchase. We wanted that apartment for ourselves. Anyway, you were saying?"

"My interest in my PhD is genuine. It serves the agency well that I have a sound cover, and they're only too happy to provide support whenever I need it. However, some of the other things I get up to are best left unspoken. If any of them were to impact you or your friends, I guarantee I'd let you know. However, there is something that I've been feeling very guilty about ever since we met."

"Who have you been sleeping with now? If you tell me it's Alfonso—"

He chuckled. "No, nothing like that. He's well and truly madly in love with Gaspard."

I gaped. He'd said it in French; perfect, flawless, unaccented, colloquial French.

"You little—"

"German, Spanish, and—"

"If you say Italian, I might just jump over the table and punch your nose."

"I'm sorry; it's part of my cover," he added in that same language.

"And what about you?" I said to the American, exasperated at the thought of how far I'd gone out of my way, suffering extreme frustration, to translate everything to someone who probably spoke Italian as well as I did.

"Only French and Italian … some Spanish and Portuguese, Damson. It goes with my job."

"In the CIA."

"My public job is in the diplomatic corps; the other is, well, you know, private shit."

"Who else knows you two are swapping bodily fluids?" I asked.

"Just you and Kendall, the *chargé d'affaires* in Rome and my direct boss in Washington."

"This is so fucking complicated," I said, puffing furiously at my cigarette before stubbing it out angrily.

"It's only as complicated as you want it to be, Damson," he said. "I've slept with all three of you, so you and Kendall have something over me if you really wanted to make trouble."

"I'd never do that—"

"I know. You're an honest guy. James and me? Well, our jobs allow us to be honest about some things. I had no vested interest when I had sex with you and Kendall; that was personal. You can trust me on that. I wasn't doing it as part of my job; it was for pure private pleasure. However, I'm being polite, as I'm sure James is, answering your questions about our personal lives when what we should really be discussing is the problem of the stolen documents from the prefecture in Rome, what Scavola's next move will be when he gets his hands on them, what to do with Luca, and most importantly, where Giancarlo is."

The café owner interrupted us, saying that he was closing up for the evening. None of us had eaten lunch, so the American gave him a bundle of lire so large it made the man's eyes bulge and asked if his wife would mind cooking something for us, even if the café was closed. He offered his back room, used for card games and probably some illegal goings on, the money disappearing into his pocket so quickly it was almost a blur.

Although I was mildly annoyed to realise that, ever since we'd met him, James had overheard and understood some very personal conversations between Giancarlo, me and Alfonso, once we began to talk business, it became apparent that he wasn't the passive Pommy egghead that he cultivated as his public persona. He was—as I should have suspected with an education like his—very competent, quick, and, if not forceful, then quite blunt.

Kendall's idea of housing Luca in the Australian embassy and then, if that was not possible, sending him to England was quickly dismissed, the American assuring us that the US bureau chief in London was an idiot and would no doubt stuff everything up by trying to manipulate Luca for his own personal advancement. Instead, he proposed one of two possible locations, both safe houses: one in Rome, the other in Florence.

The Rome house was on the outskirts of the city and would require not only someone to look after Luca, but also security. There'd have to be two guards at all times. However, the location in Florence was somewhere I knew very well and not only very close to our apartment but also to Randy's. It was a private guest apartment in the American consulate in Lungarno Amerigo Vespucci, right on the Arno. No one, except consulate staff, would be able to enter the private quarters, and we'd be able to visit him easily.

When Kendall asked if this was possible and whether the American had clearance to arrange it, we were told that the consul general in Florence was a close pal. In other words, the CIA had something over the man, and he'd require little encouragement to put Luca up and look after him.

"He really likes it where he is at Lepri," I said sadly, thinking how disruptive another move would be for Luca. "He's busy, working with his hands, and he gets on very well with everyone there."

"He wouldn't get on well with them if they were all killed in front of him," the American said. "Do you think a minor problem like a dozen priests would stop Scavola from getting rid of a major thorn in his side? He didn't baulk at murdering one of Italy's most famous film stars, and so far he's got away with it."

"Do you know something I don't about Mario's murder?" I asked.

"No. But we've got an eye on the case too. It's in our interest to have Scavola in court."

"In what way would it be in your interest? I thought you were after him for links to organised crime in Chicago?"

"If he got to court, we could do a deal with the Italians, promise him some leniency, perhaps exile, in return for information that would lead to the arrests of crime bosses back home."

"No!" I protested. "No fucking way is Scavola going to get away with Mario's murder and the nuns during the war. Why, this is fucking outrageous—"

"Hold your horses, Damson. There's absolutely no way we'd go through with it. It would be 'encouragement'. We'd promise him the world and then say there were obstacles at the last minute, after we'd got everything out of him we needed."

"What?"

He gave me a very frank look. "Behind the scenes, we don't care if our hands get dirty as long as the job gets done, my friend. It's not as if every intelligence organisation in the world hasn't done something similar, ever since there were such agencies. We'd promise Scavola anything he wanted then cheer once we heard that the person we hired to take him out had succeeded. Dead men don't tell tales."

I supposed that was the way all agencies worked: play seemingly fair and square in public and then arrange for the disposal of unwanted or politically uncomfortable players by using a third party so it appeared that they'd kept their hands clean.

"Wow, that's hard to hear," Kendall said.

"That's life, believe it or not. I bet your father didn't get where he is without being ruthless."

"Maybe not, but he'd never kill anyone."

"Different levels of the same game, my friend. It's all a matter of scale. Besides, if justice is done while we're sorting out our problems with an Italian gangster, the murder of innocents, nuns, American soldiers and a much-loved international film star, then everyone's happy."

The *signora* had cooked her heart out. We'd heard her and her husband clattering in the kitchen while we spoke, delicious smells wafting into the back room. We'd polished off a bottle of wine made with the local *dolcetta* grapes. The owner had left us with small bowls of preserved olives and cheese with some breadsticks to munch on while he went to help his wife in the kitchen. Large bowls of *umbricelli al tartufo* then arrived for us: delicious home-made pasta with a cream and truffle sauce;

the aroma made my mouth water as soon as the plate hit the table. With a warning that there were *braciole di maiale in padella* to follow, we tucked in. Even while eating the pasta, I could smell the pork chops being tossed in the pan with garlic, sage and rosemary in the other room.

It was at the same time unsettling and very pleasant hearing both the American and James conversing fluently in Italian with the owner and his wife. It made me very focused on giving James a piece of my mind in French, just to test out how resilient his knowledge of the language was. I'd been brought up speaking it and had none of the common problems most foreigners had with a language, like Italian for me, that they'd learned later in life.

*****

Luca had looked petrified when I'd arrived the next morning with the American. When I'd driven down the dusty track to the retreat, Father Green had appeared with a shotgun cradled in his arms.

Neither Luca nor Alfonso had met the American before, and we'd spoken in Italian on our way back to La Mensola to drop off Alfonso and pick up James before we headed off to Florence. I was very impressed with the American's use of the language and his accent. His French was pretty good too, joining in a conversation with me, James and Gaspard, who'd been at La Mensola when we'd returned from Magliano Sabina last night and was still there this morning when we arrived back from Lepri.

I was immensely torn over the decision whether to accompany Luca to Florence or to start looking for Giancarlo, who still hadn't either reappeared or phoned. Cosmo had reminded me once again that this wasn't the first time he'd gone off on his own, walking back through the door days later and looking surprised that anyone had missed him. But it was the timing that had me slightly anxious; he knew how much was going on and how much he was needed to keep an eye on things while the documentary crew was here. Had his disappearance not coincided with the break-in at the records office in Rome …

The decision was made for me when the phone rang. It was the detective from Florence, insisting that I come as soon as possible to sign off on his report about the forced entry and disturbance to Giancarlo's office. Also, Onofrio had returned from Venice with information that he didn't want to discuss over the telephone; his wife was in labour with another child and he was at the hospital. I told the detective that I was heading to Florence and I'd be there later in the day. I'd track down Onofrio when I arrived.

I spoke with Kendall and Alfonso first, asking them to take James to translate for Kendall, go to Pienza, speak with Cosmo and try to discover more about Giancarlo's movements before he left the office.

That left the American and me to take Luca to Florence. As Giancarlo had taken the Land Rover to work yesterday morning, and the Jeep was assigned to Kendall, Alfonso and James, that had left us three to squeeze into the Maserati. It was a two-seater sports car, but it was not uncommon to see overloaded vehicles on roads in Italy. The two-seater designation for most Italians was an indicator rather than a rule.

The car park lot attendant's face lit up when he saw me drive up in the sports car. I'd dropped the American and Luca outside the embassy a few minutes beforehand and had phoned the detective to let him know that I'd arrived and that I'd meet him at the apartment.

Randy had arranged for the door locks to be replaced, this time with stouter fixtures than had previously been in place. I wasn't surprised to see him chatting with our caretaker when I arrived. She was endless in her protestations and commiserations, almost wailing and beating her breast, as if it had been her fault that someone had broken in. I'd packed a small box of white-fleshed nectarines for her and she wouldn't let go of my arm, protesting that she didn't deserve them. Randy's behind-her-back eye rolls were spectacular. I found it very hard not to burst out laughing.

The study was a mess. I checked both the detective's written report and the photographs he'd taken when he first arrived, signing off that nothing had been changed in the intervening period. He tipped his hat to us both, informing me that Onofrio was anxious to speak with me and was at the Hospital of Santa Maria Nuova, and then left.

"So, alone at last," Randy said, pulling me into his arms. "Any news of Giancarlo?"

I explained what I'd done and that Kendall was due to phone me at one in the afternoon, just an hour and a half from now, to let me know whether they'd discovered anything.

"So, do you want to stay here or come back to my apartment? Arnie's out of town for the day, but I can fix us some lunch."

"Is that another of your euphemisms?" I asked. "Because we can have lunch here …"

He chuckled then kissed me.

Men were such odd creatures. No matter the circumstance, sometimes even in quite dangerous or inappropriate situations, their gonads could take over and their minds go blank. No wonder heterosexual men could be so easily manipulated by honeypots. We queer men had far more readily available opportunities to have sex, so perhaps were less tempted, but still, I found myself lying flat on my back on our bed, my pants around my ankles and choking on Randy's cock, him on all fours over me, sucking on my balls, when someone knocked at the front door.

"Don't answer it, Damson," Randy said.

"It's the American; he's expecting me to be here."

Randy sighed, got off the bed and began to pull up his strides. "Well, this will keep," he said, tugging on my dick. "What's his name again?"

"Benjamin Smollet," I said. I'd learned his name when I was introduced to him at the embassy party, the night he'd followed Kendall and me into the men's room and had offered me information about Scavola.

"Have you …?"

I winked, then, buckling my belt, went to answer the door.

I haven't often gaped in my life, but this was one of those few times, the American's voice drying up as we walked into the living room.

"This is my great friend Randall McCall …" I said, my voice faltering as I saw the deep red blush on the American's face and at the same time Randy's broad grin, his hand extended, waiting for the American to shake it.

"You two know each other?" I asked hesitantly.

"Oh, yes, we know each other," Randy said, almost laughing. "How's it going, Rivet?"

Rivet? I was speechless.

CHAPTER 15

Rivet? Rivet Wilson? I was very confused.

Randy looked fit to burst with laughter while Benjamin Smollet shook his head, muttering something and red to the roots of his hair.

"Who'd'a' fucking thought it," Randy said.

"It's a small world, captain," the American replied.

"Whatever happened to you, Rivet? Last I heard, you got promoted then disappeared off the radar. Arnie and I went looking for you after the war, you know."

"Sergeant Black? I haven't thought of him in years."

"Well, if you're still around tomorrow, you'll get to see him again. Him and me? Let's say we're as close as two guys can be. He lives here with me most of the time, going on ten years now—"

I interrupted. "If you tell me that Benjamin Smollet is the guy you and Arnie both fucked in the deserted farmhouse near Salerno during the war, I might—"

"You told him?" Smollet said, his eyes wide with surprise.

"Well, as Damson's was only the second asshole I stuck my dick into after yours—"

"Oh, damn, sir. It's so long ago. I figured you might have forgotten."

"Wait, just stop everyone, let's just all take a breath," I said. "Pour us a drink, Randy. I think I need one—and I need to have a serious talk with whatever-your-name-is here," I added, turning to the American diplomat.

"Benjamin Smollet is the name I've gone by since just after the war," he said, "and it's the name everyone knows me by. Wilson is my real surname. 'Rivet' is the nickname I was given as a teenager, and, along with a few of the guys I grew up with, it followed me into the army."

Randy, like Kendall, had an easy ability to handle difficult situations. He chuckled, clapped us both on the back, asked us what we'd like to drink, and then more or less instructed us to go out onto our terrace. A few minutes later, he joined us.

"I'm interested in your story, as I'm sure Damson is," he said to Smollet, as he handed him his gin and tonic. "Want to fill us in and tell us why you're going by a different name from the one I knew you by in the army?"

"This is difficult for me, sir," he said, staring into his drink. "Mainly because it's sort of classified."

"It's been fifteen years since the war, Rivet. No need to call me 'sir'. Randy will do just fine. Now, 'sort of classified' or not … Benjamin Smollet … where in hell did that name come from?"

"It's a long story."

"I've got all day. If you tell me it's embassy-level secret and you can't talk about it, we can—"

"Okay, it's complicated, and I'll have my balls handed to me on a plate if the office learns I've told you how I've ended up with a new name."

"The office?" Randy asked. "Which office? You mean the embassy?"

"I think he means the CIA," I said, lighting a cigarette, then throwing the packet to Randy.

"Oh, wow! Now I'm all ears."

During the war, on the first day of three weeks' leave back home in the USA and intending to visit his family, Rivet had been standing outside his base in uniform with his thumb out trying to get a lift when Joe, a brawny, good-looking officer, also in uniform, had pulled up in his convertible and offered him a ride. The visit to the family never eventuated; he ended up on his back on the bed of the officer, who'd offered him hospitality for the duration of his leave, fucked him twice a day and offered to be his "daddy" when the war was over.

Late in 1945, after being shipped home, Rivet had phoned Joe, who was only too happy to offer him bed and board again. Joe had confessed that he'd been in the OSS during the war when he'd picked him up at the side of the road. Of course, at the time, it was something he hadn't been able to talk about. Just a week after the war, the OSS was dissolved and Joe had been seconded to the Bureau of Intelligence and Research as a recruiter. Keen to foster Rivet's career and future presence in his life and his bed, Joe had arranged for him to be interviewed.

It had worked well for a while, until late one night in the men's room of Whitehall ferry terminal in New York, Joe had sucked off a man who, as he was zipping up, had revealed he was an undercover cop. "You're under arrest," the cop had said, smearing the last of his semen across Joe's face with his thumb. His bureau had saved his arse, but in exchange Joe had had to give up the names of his queer contacts, Rivet among them.

Even though Joe was reprimanded, he was still anxious to look after his "protégé" and suggested to the CIA that Rivet might turn out to be an asset for the agency. It was how he came to their attention and then, after a lengthy process, ended up with a shore-based commission in the navy, working in intelligence. One day, he was summoned to E Street in Washington for an interview with a man who'd introduced himself as a recruiter for "Liaison Affairs", a department Rivet had never heard of, but which he later learned didn't actually exist. It was a front for the CIA.

During the interview, he was asked whether he'd be interested in working in the diplomatic service. Rivet had hated his current job and had jumped at the opportunity; he was invited outside to a back alley to continue the conversation, where what they spoke about would be "off the record". The recruiting officer offered him a cigarette then revealed he'd be working for the CIA if he accepted the position. Rivet had shrugged, said yes, held out his hand to shake on the deal. The interviewer hadn't released his hand but continued to hold it, telling him that there was one condition.

"What was it?" Randy asked.

"That, in view of my past activities, I might at some time be expected to use my dick and my arse in the service of my country."

"What, really?" Randy asked.

"In so many words."

"I'd have been worried it might have been a set-up, a way of getting you to confess what you got up to during the war."

"I thought about that at the time, until the recruiter drew me into a doorway in the deserted alley, pulled his dick out and asked me to show him what I could do."

"You're kidding me …"

"This was before the McCarthy days, Randy; you have no idea how many homos worked there. The intelligence agency would have come crashing down if all of them had been fired. Anyway, I was signed up before I knew it and inducted the following day."

It was then, after he came to work for the CIA, that he was given the new identity of Benjamin Smollet, handed the keys to a house in Poughkeepsie and a brand new car, then sent to the UK to swap spit with an Oxford undergraduate whom he was to cultivate as a contact. The undergraduate? James, of course, newly recruited by MI6 and told to offer his cock to the visiting Yankee businessman in a suite at the Savoy Hotel.

"Samuel Arthur Wilson is my birth name," he said once he'd finished telling us the story.

"Your nickname, Rivet—that's pretty random." I was curious.

"You know what rivets are? Steel plugs that go into holes. As a teenager, I was very popular with the sports jocks and it became a bit of a secret war cry among them; they all wanted to 'rivet Wilson' after school. The name stuck."

"So, what shall I call you?" I asked.

"Ben or Benjamin. I'll answer to either. Rivet is a name from the past and I'm so unused to being called by my birth name, Sam, that I'll wonder who you're talking to. I'm sure that you, like me, have moved on since the war, which was the last time anyone called me Rivet Wilson. Do you mind telling me how you learned that name?"

"An old friend of mine, a retired Italian inspector, told me."

"A retired Italian inspector who speaks French?"

I smiled without replying, then asked if either of them was hungry.

★★★★★

"Hey!" I said, answering the phone. Kendall had called from Giancarlo's office in Pienza right on time.

"You get to Florence safely?"

"Yes. Luca is at the embassy and I'm just about to have lunch with the American; I've ordered in from that restaurant you like so much."

"I could say I'm jealous, but Signora Marino has promised to cook something special for us once you and I have finished speaking."

"Any news of Giancarlo?"

"He took a phone call just after seven, not long after he'd arrived in the office. Cosmo said he didn't know who it was, but heard Giancarlo flipping through documents in his room while talking on the phone. He left at about twenty past seven saying he'd be back in twenty minutes."

"Anything else?"

"Well, here's the strange thing. We called into the Bar Azzurro because I needed smokes. That waiter, the one I keep saying fancies you, said that he'd seen Giancarlo heading off to the bus station. There was a bus at twenty to eight that left for Chiusi."

I was about to state the obvious—why would Giancarlo take the bus to Chiusi when he had a car?—but held my tongue.

"I got Alfonso to phone the depot and ask to speak with the driver. He was told that our friend Franco, who'd been rostered on the Pienza to Chiusi route that morning, would phone us back. He was due to return to the depot from Chiusi in about ten minutes. Franco said that he remembered Giancarlo getting on the bus, but swore he wasn't still on it when it arrived in Chiusi, where most of the passengers changed on to a service to Orvieto, and he didn't remember Giancarlo getting off on any of the stops beforehand. There was something, though."

"Go on."

"Wait, here's James; he was listening while Alfonso spoke with the driver."

"There was a minor accident, just before Chianciano on the way to Chiusi," James said. "A car clipped the rear end of the bus while it was overtaking. No one was hurt, but everyone piled out of the bus to see what was going on."

Alarm bells started to ring. An accident?

"I need to speak to Franco," I said.

"I knew that would be the case. He's waiting for your call. Phone us back when you've spoken with him," James said, then gave me the number.

Franco had gone home for lunch, so I called him there. He explained to me that he was extremely puzzled when Giancarlo boarded the bus because he'd made him wait while he told one of the local lads to keep an eye on the Land Rover until he got back—it had seemed odd that he hadn't appeared to want to drive to wherever he was going.

"Was he carrying anything?"

"Just his briefcase. I glanced up once or twice and he had it on his knee."

I thanked him very much, making sure that before I hung up the phone, he'd given me the exact location of the accident, a description of the car that had clipped the bus, and the name of the driver and his passenger. I was about to place the receiver in its cradle when I heard him ask if I was still there.

"I meant to tell you, Signor O'Reilly, that you might want to talk with Signora Gagliardi. She was on the bus too. You know her husband can't drive at the moment." Andrea had fractured his ankle playing football with his senior students. "She told me she was going to Chiusi to catch the train to Rome to visit her sister. I saw her and Signor Manetti chatting for a while. She was sitting in the seat across the aisle from him."

I hung up the phone just as I heard a knock at our door.

The restaurant Randy had ordered from was the same he'd used to cater for his birthday party. We knew the staff very well, and more than once they'd catered in our apartment for clients of Giancarlo's. We'd even hosted a small exhibition of my watercolours for invited guests, for which they'd provided the food.

I left Randy to chat with Benjamin—they were swapping stories of their war experiences after they'd parted ways in Salerno—and spoke briefly with the sous chef and waiter about lunch. Randy had ordered up a huge meal. I wasn't sure I had the stomach to eat anything after what I'd learned, but while they prepared the *primo—pappardelle al cinghiale*: ribbon noodles with a ragù made from wild boar, their speciality and always delicious beyond belief—I used the phone in our bedroom and called the Trattoria del Mercato. Signora Marino answered the phone. We spoke for a few minutes before she called Alfonso to talk to me.

I relayed the information I'd got from Franco and asked him to drive to the exact spot where the accident had happened. It would take me at least four, if not five, hours to get there from Florence and I thought time was of the essence. I also asked him if he could call in to see Signor Gagliardi—James could chat with him in French, which he'd love—to find out how to contact his wife in Rome and get the phone number of his wife's sister so I could call her this evening. I told him I'd be here at the apartment in Florence, that he should call me if he found anything at the accident scene, and that the only time I wouldn't be here was after lunch, when I would be at the hospital to find Onofrio, to see what was so important that he couldn't tell me over the phone.

The phone rang just as I wiped my lips, having smeared the last of the ragù onto a morsel of bread and popped it in my mouth. It was Onofrio.

"I was coming to see you straight after lunch," I said. "Any news on the baby?"

"Not yet, Damson. Another hour or two. Our babies always take time coming into the world."

"Can you tell me anything over the phone?"

"I've sequestered the head physician's office to call you. I can't go into details with a civilian present, I'm sure you understand. But you need to meet Pellegrini in Venice as soon as possible."

"I'm not sure why—"

"Remember the sketch you made of Alvise? The Venetian cops think they've found him. You and your Australian friend are the only two who've actually met him. Someone needs to make sure it's actually him."

"I'll be at the hospital in about an hour," I said.

He told me the name of the hospital ward in which his wife was in labour and said he'd be there all afternoon. I hung up the phone, found

Alessandro Pellegrini's phone number in my wallet and called him. His secretary told me that he was on his way to Venice from his office in Treviso. I asked when she thought he might be arriving there and asked for a contact number. I smiled: he was staying at the Danieli. I could hear the envy in her voice.

"If he doesn't answer in his hotel room, this is the number you should call. He might be there."

I jotted it down, hung up, checked to see how long it would be before our second course arrived. I had ten minutes, so excused myself again from Randy and Benjamin, who were so engrossed swapping stories and laughing that they barely looked up. I decided to phone both the Danieli and the other number his secretary had given me, and leave a message for Alessandro with my movements for the afternoon.

I could barely eat my food when the main course arrived. The number in Venice that Alessandro's secretary had given me was the morgue.

*****

Onofrio was semi-distracted, his wife in the late stages of labour, but we found a quiet corner to have a smoke. Giancarlo had sent him to Venice to see what he could do to trace Mario Celestino's policeman, Alvise. The local cops had already done a lot of footwork, but finding him wasn't high on their list of priorities. Although Onofrio didn't know Venice well, he knew how to find the sorts of places that someone like Alvise might have hung out. Giancarlo had provided not only my detailed description of him but also a copy of the sketch I'd prepared for Alessandro Pellegrini.

It had been Alvise's bent little finger that had provided the first clue—that, and the scar in his hairline. "*Potrebbe essere 'Il Mignolo'?*" a labourer at the Arsenale's former foundry had asked his companion after looking at the sketch. *Il mignolo* was the little finger, or pinkie finger, as the Americans called it, and Alvise's bent digit had stood out to me. The other fellow had scratched his head and had replied, "*Può darsi,*" which meant "perhaps". Onofrio said both men were very drunk at the time.

However, they weren't drunk enough to forget his visit, because two days later a stranger had approached Onofrio asking him whether it was he who'd been looking for Il Mignolo at the Arsenale and how much information to find him might be worth. Seemed word had got around, and not in a good way either, because a few hours after Onofrio had handed over a thousand lire note, been given an address and turned up at the boarding house, he'd found two policemen standing outside the apartment building and the occupants outside spread along the *calle* wondering why they'd been evacuated.

Onofrio was fairly certain that the body he'd been shown was Alvise. Stabbed multiple times and with his right hand severed: the hand with the distorted finger that had given him his nickname.

This had only happened yesterday, and he'd tried to phone me just after he'd had news that his wife's waters had broken. The line had been busy, so he'd called Alessandro Pellegrini. When he'd arrived in Florence early this morning, he'd gone to the courts to report that he was back from Venice and to check schedules to see whether he was needed over the next few days. That was when he'd run into the detective who'd phoned me to tell me that our apartment had been broken into. He'd asked the detective to pass on the message that he needed to speak with me face-to-face.

I told him about the stolen documents from the safe deposit boxes in the Rome courthouse and Giancarlo's puzzling disappearance.

"Scavola must be behind it," he said, then, noticing my slight frown, added, "I'm sure there's a logical explanation for him leaving his car and taking a bus."

"Well, if you can think of one, I'd be only too happy to hear it."

"Have you spoken with Pellegrini yet?"

"No. I rang the hotel and the morgue and left messages at both for him."

"You must go to Venice and identify the body, Damson. You're the only one who's actually seen him with Mario Celestino."

"Not the only one; my Australian friend Kendall and I both had lunch with him and Mario."

"You're going to send him instead?"

"I'm thinking of it. I'm still trying to juggle what's more important: going to Venice to identify Alvise's body or returning to Pienza to start looking for Giancarlo."

"Giancarlo has been missing for how long now? One day? I worked with him for years when we were detectives together. He was always running off by himself, not letting anyone know where he was going. The bus episode sounds strange, but you need to speak with this French teacher's wife first to find out what she knows before you start letting your imagination run riot."

"I suppose you're right," I answered with a sigh. "Giancarlo *is* prone to go running off by himself, as you just said, and you're also correct: he's only been missing for a day. But it's coincidental with too many other things ..."

Onofrio went to find out whether there was any progress with the birth of his child and, while he was away, I sat on a bench seat in the corridor in which we'd been chatting to have another cigarette and to think about what I'd just learned.

Alvise could only have been killed because word had got around that there was a picture and a description of him and a cop was looking for him. Even though Onofrio wasn't a detective anymore, Giancarlo was fond of saying "Once a cop, always a cop", and any lowlife worth his salt could spot one a mile away, active or retired. Onofrio had shown the sketch to dozens of people and enquired after Alvise. Word was bound to have spread. Alvise was linked to Mario's murder and presumed to be the last person to see him alive, despite the efforts the Venetian police had made to pin that one on me. Mario had told us that he was going to meet up with Alvise at midnight. If he'd been working for Scavola, his true identity could be very problematic for the industrialist. Ruthless thugs were more likely to do away with the evidence rather than rely on the word of someone who merely promised they could keep their mouths shut. I'd learned that while hearing about cases Giancarlo had handled over the years. He'd prosecuted many criminal cases in courts all over Italy.

My thoughts were tangled. On one hand, Alvise's murder; on the other, worry over Giancarlo. He'd told Cosmo he'd be back in twenty minutes and yet he'd left his car and had, for some unfathomable reason, taken the bus to Chiusi ...

"Damson, I have to go," Onofrio said, having run down the corridor. "The baby's on the way. I'll phone you later. Where will you be?"

"I'm not sure yet. Phone Giancarlo's office in Pienza. I'll make Cosmo the go-between for the time being. He lives in an apartment behind the office so he'll be able to take phone calls no matter the time of day or night."

I wished him good luck and watched as he hurried back in the direction he'd come.

*****

There was no sign of Benjamin Smollet when I got back to our apartment and Randy had crashed on our bed. I spooned up behind him. He snuffled softly in his sleep but didn't wake up. Two minutes, I promised myself, and then I'd try the morgue in Venice again.

I woke up wondering where I was. I checked my wristwatch. Two minutes had turned into nearly two hours. Randy was nowhere to be seen; he'd left a note on the pillow:

> *Didn't want to wake you. I've invited Sam for dinner to catch up with Arnie, who decided to drop everything and drive here. Come for dinner at seven (clothing is optional).*

Sam? Who was Sam? Then I remembered it was the American's real name: Sam Wilson. I smiled at the "clothing optional" business. I was sure Randy, Arnie and Benjamin—the name I'd decided to call him—had a lot of catching up to do … even perhaps recreating that day in the abandoned farmhouse outside Salerno? Maybe I'd leave them to it. I needed to phone Pellegrini in Venice to speak about Alvise's body, and then Cosmo in Pienza to see whether Kendall, James and Alfonso had returned from the accident scene. They might have called earlier while I was at the hospital. I'd decide about Randy's invitation for dinner later when I knew how things stood.

Eventually, after a bit of phone passing, I was patched through to Alessandro at the police station in Venice. After a few exchanges of pleasantries, I asked about the body.

"Stabbed twenty-four times with a short knife, perhaps only about four centimetres long. It would have hurt badly. There are rope marks around one of his wrists and his ankles. The other wrist was probably bound too, but that hand has been severed. He didn't die from the stab wounds or the amputation; he bled out. The *medico legale* said that the cause of death was apparently the last two stab wounds, both of which severed the popliteal arteries behind each knee. He would have been dead in between two and five minutes, depending on whether his leg was extended or bent."

"Did you get to see the crime scene? Were there signs of a struggle? Any clues left to who might have killed him?"

"Nothing. I don't think it was the crime scene; otherwise, there would have been blood everywhere."

"What do you mean, there *would* have been blood everywhere. You're saying he wasn't killed where he was found?"

"Not a drop of blood, despite the severity of the wounds that killed him. It's safe to say that he was killed elsewhere and then moved. We need you here, Damson. Either you or your Australian friend. You're the only two who can actually identify Mario Celestino's lover. It would cause mayhem and an enormous investment of police resources if we started looking for acquaintances and connections of the wrong man, if this isn't Alvise. Can you come now?"

I then had to explain Giancarlo's disappearance and the bus accident outside Chianciano. There was much I wanted to talk about, but I didn't want to speak to him using our telephone or via the Venice police telephone exchange. He needed to know about so many things.

"Have you heard from Salvatore in Rome?" I asked in a tone that I hoped suggested there was more to it than a simple query.

"Yes, and I'm very anxious to speak with you about several matters pertaining to the conversation I had with him."

I glanced at my watch. It was half past four. I leafed quickly through the copy of the Thomas Cook train timetable we kept in the telephone stand.

"There's a train at nine-twenty tonight that gets in at a quarter to midnight."

"I'll meet you at the station and we can go straight to the morgue."

"Your secretary said you're staying at the Danieli?"

"Yes, in a suite. There's a spare bedroom if you don't want to stay at your apartment."

"Any excuse to stay at a five-star hotel. I'll look forward to catching up. I warn you, I may fall asleep on the train, so you might have to wander down the platform and wake me up."

He laughed then hung up the phone. I dialled Cosmo, who passed me to Alfonso.

"He was definitely on the bus when it arrived at the bus station in Montepulciano, but a few passengers told me that Franco had to help an elderly passenger with a large crate that was in the side locker of the bus—"

"Franco didn't mention that to me—"

"But he wasn't on the bus by the time it was involved in the car accident and there were no stops between Montepulciano and where the collision occurred. One of Giancarlo's clients lives in a farmhouse on the road where it happened. His wife was in the garden and saw the accident. She said Giancarlo was definitely not on the bus, because everyone came out onto the road to see what had happened."

"So you think he could have gotten off the bus at Montepulciano while Franco was busy with the other passenger's crate?"

"It's likely; he could easily have got off the bus without Franco noticing."

"I know that Giancarlo was speaking with Signora Gagliardi when he first got on the bus. I tried to—"

"Phone her—yes, I know. Her sister picked her up at the station and they drove to a cousin's house in Ostia."

"It was on my list to try her sister today …"

"I saved you the trouble. I spoke with her on your behalf."

"What?"

"The biggest gossip in Pienza is who, Damson? Your friend and mine, Andrea Gagliardi, who'd heard of Giancarlo's disappearance—I should warn you that half the town already knows, thanks to him. He came into the office just after we'd returned from the site of the accident, trying to see if there was any more news. He gave me the sister's phone number, so I called and spoke with his wife."

"And what did you learn?"

"Giancarlo got on the bus with another man. They sat together and appeared to be talking *sotto voce*."

"Could it have been a client?"

"Perhaps. Perhaps not."

"Why do you say that?"

"She described him as being a tall, thin man wearing a white polo shirt, dark glasses and with a pale green sweater draped over his shoulders. He was distinctive because of his 'very well developed biceps' and his brilliantined ducktail haircut, a curl over the forehead, just like an American rock-and-roll singer. She said she sat in the seat on the other side of the aisle and chatted with Giancarlo whenever he wasn't talking with his companion, but mostly had eyes for the young man, who she kept saying was very handsome and muscled. They both got off the bus in Montepulciano."

"Did she say whether Giancarlo appeared anxious or not?"

"She said he was a little flushed. There's more, though. She wanted to confess over the phone to me."

"Confess? Confess what?"

"She couldn't take her eyes off the man's crotch; it seemed to be either packed with socks or the man was very well endowed. She was mortified at her own behaviour."

In some ways, that gave me both a sense of relief and, at the same time, a feeling of potential danger. It wouldn't be unlike Giancarlo to make an assignation with some handsome man with plenty of meat and potatoes in his pants and then go off with him, but it was extremely unlikely that he wouldn't have phoned me to share what he'd got up to. It was one of our rules—he loved to share, and I didn't mind hearing about his conquests.

Alfonso passed the phone to Kendall. I told him that I was going to Venice and explained what I'd learned. He asked if he'd like me to join him. I said I didn't mind if he wanted to, but I didn't intend to spend more than a day there. I suggested that someone needed to speak with the man who ran the snack bar at Montepulciano bus station, who was almost as nosy as Andrea Gagliardi, to see whether he'd seen Giancarlo and the American rock-and-roll lookalike and perhaps had remembered in which direction they'd headed after getting off the bus. He said he'd ask Alfonso to do that.

As an aside, Kendall said he missed me and offered to drive to Mestre in the morning so he could pick me up late tomorrow afternoon, after which he'd drive us to Florence so I could pick up the Maserati, which I'd left with the parking attendant near our apartment. I told him that instead of him traipsing all over the country, I'd just catch the train to Florence, pick up my car and see him back at La Mensola. I said I'd phone him from Venice tomorrow morning, but that if Alfonso learned anything from the kiosk attendant, he should phone me tonight at Randy's before I left to catch my twenty past nine train. I gave him Randy's number.

★★★★★

"It's him, definitely," I said later that night in the Venice morgue.

Alvise, like a great number of dead men I'd seen during my life, looked almost as if he was asleep. I'd never studied his face when I'd met him at Mario's; staring at someone, no matter the culture, was considered impolite, if not rude. But now I took note of his features: he was handsome, something I hadn't really noticed over lunch at Mario's apartment. My artist's eye had been more intent on studying how firm his musculature was and how well-proportioned his body. At the time, I thought he'd be a great charcoal study. It had been an idle thought, but now, with him stretched out naked on a slab before me, the thought was vaguely obscene, his torso peppered with knife wounds, the lips of each slightly puckered as if he'd been underwater for some time.

"No water in the lungs?"

Alessandro shook his head. "The medical examiner has yet to identify the weapon used to inflict those wounds."

"I'd say an oyster knife; the type used to open shellfish. We had a case like this in Japan."

"Japan? What case?"

Of course, Alessandro was a new acquaintance. He had no knowledge of my time with the group that investigated crimes by Allied soldiers in occupied Japan. I gave him a quick rundown of my time there and what I'd done, then told him about a particular case that had made me think Alvise had been stabbed with an oyster knife. A young woman had been brutally murdered by an American soldier who'd first sexually assaulted her then gone on to stalk her, she always rebuffing his advances. Her husband owned a restaurant; she worked in the back, gutting and filleting fish and shucking oysters. The soldier had sneaked in the back door, pleading with her to run away with him, then said something snapped inside him when she'd told him to go away, and the next thing he knew was that she was lying dead on the floor, and her husband and his friend were beating him with an iron bar.

"They obviously didn't kill him," Alessandro said.

"Not until after his court martial. He was sentenced to be dishonourably discharged and sent back home with no prison sentence. But there was a riot when news got out. His prison van was attacked, the soldier dragged out and ripped to pieces by the mob. They nailed his penis to the newspaper broadsheet posted on the wall outside one of the American bases. It was very ugly."

"I'll let the doctor know about your suggestion. It would make sense: a short, wide blade, just like an oyster knife."

"Was he sexually violated?"

Pellegrini looked startled and puzzled at the same time. "Why would you ask such a thing?"

"Mario's apartment wall had the word *frocio* written on it. I erased it and told the police to keep their mouths shut. Whoever killed him knew he was a homosexual and perhaps that Alvise was his lover. Have you asked yourself why he was murdered? It's not a robbery gone wrong; there's intent, violence in the way he was stabbed. My theory was that Alvise was …" My Italian dried up; I had no vocabulary for the word I was searching for.

"*Piazzato?*" Pellegrini suggested.

Planted! I did know that word in Italian but had completely forgotten it.

"Yes, *planted* by Scavola to spy on Mario, but I think the plan failed."

"Why would you say that?"

"Because my observations were that Alvise couldn't stay objective; he followed Mario around with his eyes like a puppy. He was besotted."

"And Signor Celestino?"

"Look at the size of this man's cock, *Questore*. Even in death it's impressive. I've passed on the information to you that I learned about Mario's private life; he loved men of all ages, shapes and sizes and was fixated on the reported enormity of Scavola's penis, the only reason he initially had a sexual relationship with him. I can only surmise that he found this man convenient for the times he needed to be …"

"Fucked? You can say the words; I'm not a prude. I'm a police officer and a man with a world view, Damson."

"Mario Celestino was in love with Stewart, his body double and stuntman, who died a couple of years ago. I got the feeling that, although he lied to me about his other supposed carpenter lover in Rome, Stewart was the great love of his life. I was told that the time they were together was the only time in Mario's life that he didn't stray."

"Getting back to this body: you asked whether he'd been checked for sexual violation? In my experience, it's not something that's routine when it comes to male victims in this country."

"Done by heterosexual men, it's the ultimate defilement; or that's how they see it. Multiple rapes or penetrations with weapons, anything that could be inserted that the perpetrator believes would be painful and shameful. I saw it done so often that I barely turned a hair. Japanese ex-servicemen habitually raped local men and boys … men and boys who hadn't fought for whatever reason. They saw it as punishment meted out on those they believed had helped the enemy by not taking up arms. However, most of them admitted when caught and questioned that it was a way of dealing with the shame of having lost the war. There's plenty of documentation in the literature; Germans were just as guilty during the war in Europe, but for other, usually sadistic reasons."

"I'll make a note to get it done tomorrow. I sent the doctor home; it's one in the morning."

I yawned; I hadn't slept on the train as I thought I might have done and was feeling tired. One in the morning wasn't an unusual time for me to go to bed, but there'd been a lot going on today and I was beat.

"Did you eat on the train? My stomach is growling. We could order room service."

"I had dinner with friends in Florence before I left, but I'm happy to keep you company while you eat."

"Surely you could manage something, Damson. It's the Danieli after all, and all expenses are covered."

"Very well, maybe some dessert. I left my friends' house after the main course."

I had left before dessert, mainly because the dinner had descended into something far more physical. Normally, I'd have joined in. Randy and Arnie were long-term bed partners and I'd really liked Ben's arse and mouth the two times I'd slept with him, both with Kendall, of course. So, I'd poured myself a drink after the main course when clothes started to come off and sat in an armchair watching the proceedings. Despite myself, I got very hard, but knew that in my current state of mind, distracted over Giancarlo's disappearance, I'd be an uncooperative cog in what appeared to be an otherwise apparently well-oiled machine. Another time, I'd promised them. I'd meant it too.

"Mr O'Reilly, such a pleasure to see you here again," the night manager said to me when we arrived at the Danieli. "I had no idea you were staying—there's been no reservation in your name—but a telephone call came for you from Signor Valentini. He said that if by chance you were here, to call him at your home, no matter what time. He said it was urgent."

"Who is Signor Valentini?" Alessandro asked as we collapsed into armchairs in his suite.

"You know him as Alfonso."

"Ah, the priest who's staying with you at La Mensola. How does he know you're here at the Danieli?"

"I've no idea," I said. "He knew I was coming to Venice to meet you. I suppose he tried our apartment first and then, when there was no answer, the local police station, and they told him you were staying here."

"Well, make yourself at home," he said, kicking off his shoes and pouring us both a large scotch from the complimentary drinks cabinet.

"Do you want to order food first, or may I call home to see what's up?" I asked.

"Let me call room service first; I'm starving. What shall I order you?"

"Tell the night chef to choose. Something with chocolate."

He handed me the phone after he'd spoken with the concierge. I asked the operator to put me through to La Mensola.

"Hey, it's me," I said to Alfonso, who answered the phone. "What's the emergency?"

"Damson, I have disturbing news," he said.

My heart nearly stopped in my chest. "Is it Giancarlo?"

"No, not him. They've found the man he was with on the bus, the rock-and-roller."

"Well, that's something. What did he have to say?" I could see Alessandro hovering, smoking a cigarette and looking anxious.

"He said nothing, Damson. That's the problem. He's dead. They found his body on the portico of San Biagio with his throat cut."

"And Giancarlo?"

"No news, I'm afraid, Damson. But they're starting a different kind of search first thing in the morning."

"A different kind of search?"

"Yes. I didn't want to tell you this, but the police will, as soon as you're in touch with them. Giancarlo's disappearance case has ratcheted up a notch: they've decided to start looking for his body."

CHAPTER 16

The new local chief of police had been appointed by the deputy mayor, who'd hastily taken up his former boss's position, anxious to avoid any association with the corruption and greed of his predecessor. He was extremely co-operative, to say the least. He'd answered the phone at his home at half past two in the morning after we'd finished eating, promising to send out squads of officers as soon as he got to work to try to discover the location of Alvise's murder and therefore perhaps get a clue as to who had killed him. My bets were on Scavola's men.

I said goodnight to Alessandro just as someone knocked at the door of our suite. Thinking it must be an emergency at this time in the morning, I opened the door carefully. It was Kendall.

"I've been waiting outside your apartment," he said.

"Why? I thought we'd agreed that you'd stay at La Mensola."

"I wanted to surprise you."

"I'll leave you to it," Alessandro said after shaking hands with Kendall. "I've arranged for an eight o'clock wake-up call, Damson. There's nothing much we can do until I meet with the new mayor."

We waited until he'd left us, then I put my arms around Kendall. He smelled good: comforting and familiar. Something I needed right now.

"As delighted as I am to see you, how did you know I'd be here?" I asked.

"It was a guess. By half past one, I started to wonder where you were, so I called in at the morgue; the night attendant said you'd left with Alessandro, who'd left a message with him saying that he could be contacted here if there were any emergencies."

"Well, it's great to see you. How did you manage to get from La Mensola to Venice by ten o'clock? Mine was the last train of the evening."

"I drove. Left my car in Mestre. It was easy enough. Paid for a room for two nights at a very expensive hotel, had my car valet-parked, then asked the concierge to hire me a … what do you call it? A *moto* …"

"*Motoscafo*," I said.

"Yes. It dropped me on the canal at the entrance to the *calle* to your apartment. I banged on the door of the bakery where you keep the spare key, but he put his head out the window and yelled at me. I did recognise some of the swear words, but he wouldn't give me the key. So I waited in the *calle* until I decided you were probably still with the cops then went to the morgue."

"Silly boy," I said, knowing that, despite my attempt to sound stern, the light in my eyes showed that I was anything but displeased to see him. I told him about Alvise's body and what little we'd learned.

Twenty minutes later, he took my hand in his. We'd been standing out on the balcony of the suite, which overlooked the Grand Canal. He'd listened attentively while I talked about the anxiety I was feeling caused by the discovery of the body of the man Giancarlo had been with on the bus.

"There's nothing either you and I can do except wait and leave the police to do their job, Damson. But I'm willing to help in whatever way I can. Tell me, what do you need?"

"A hug would be a good start."

"Out here?"

"It's pitch black down there. Besides, you're the voyeur."

He held me tight and swayed a little, as if we were slow-dancing.

"How was dinner at Randy's with his pal Arnie and the American?" he whispered into my ear while running a hand down the front of my trousers. I chuckled into his neck as I felt him begin to undo my flies, one button at a time. My cock hard in his hand, he squeezed it a little. "The dinner? Come on, Damson, you know me; I want all the sordid details."

He pretended to be shocked when I told him that I'd simply watched and hadn't joined in. Bad move in retrospect because after all he was a voyeur, so I had to give him a very detailed description, which, of course, led to him to undoing his belt and allowing his trousers to drop onto his shoes.

"What, no underwear?" I mumbled in between kisses.

He merely shook his head, guiding one of my hands to his backside while pressing himself tightly against me. I felt comforted in his arms, despite my thoughts wandering to Giancarlo, worrying about his safety.

"Just let me take charge, Damson," Kendall whispered in my ear. "Giancarlo would understand."

I sincerely wondered whether he would, but then again, he was the person who'd caught a bus to Montepulciano with a muscled, good-looking young man with a large bulge in his pants. Dear God, I sincerely hoped the death of the rock-and-roller was a mere coincidence. There'd been a lot of transient violence in recent years, due mainly to the number of homeless men displaced from communist countries sleeping rough, looking for a better life, and resorting to violence when robberies went wrong.

I led him back inside, into the bedroom and undressed him, my own clothes flung across the room. He pulled me down onto the bed and blew a raspberry into my navel. I usually laughed, but tonight I merely grunted with amusement.

"Hey, Damson, are you too distracted?"

I sighed, then kissed him deeply before rolling onto my tummy and raising my hips. "Nah, can you fuck me please? It will do me good to have you inside me."

Of late, it hadn't been his thing; but more than once I'd expressed my frustration that, despite how much I loved fucking him, he seemed reticent to return the favour. He'd replied last time with an apology, explaining that this was all still new to him and he had to put his hand up to admit he was greedy for my dick in his arse.

Several minutes later, I couldn't have cared if the walls had collapsed and the hotel had fallen into the sea. His tongue in my ear in between bouts of dirty talk and his dick ramming into me relentlessly, I spurted into his hand. It was just the medicine I needed to help me sleep.

*****

"Damson! Wake up!"

Alessandro was shaking my shoulder. I turned sleepily in bed. Kendall was gone.

"What's wrong?" I asked, noticing the concern in his eyes.

"A group of men have stormed the American embassy in Florence; there are at least six dead."

"What?"

I jumped out of bed and ran into the living area of the suite. Kendall was speaking on the telephone. I could hear the radio blaring out the news.

"*In the early hours of the morning, twelve masked men broke into the American embassy building in Florence, killing as they went …*" the broadcaster started to say, then stopped mid-sentence and apologised, explaining that he'd just received an update: a seventh victim of the shooting had just died. He further went on to explain that American military forces were on their way from all over the country. The news-reader was so agitated that his words came out like a gabble; I had to concentrate very hard, especially as I was still half asleep.

"Luca …" I said to Alessandro, feeling my face cold, as if the blood had drained out of it.

"Luca? Do you mean Luca Rinaldo, the witness to the Vatican massacre?"

"Yes, that's where he was. We took him there yesterday for safe-keeping. Holy Jesus … Benjamin …"

"He's safe," Kendall interrupted, hanging up the phone. "I called La Mensola; the line was busy despite three attempts. No one is answering at the American embassy in Florence either, so I phoned your friend Randy, to ask what time Smollet left last night. Randy said he'd stayed over and had left perhaps half an hour ago, before any of them knew anything about the invasion, which happened at seven this morning. None of them had thought to turn on the news, although they could hear dozens of police sirens."

"Was that Randy you were just speaking with?" I moved to the phone to call him back myself.

"No, it was Arnie. Randy's gone to the embassy to see if he can help. Arnie said he couldn't stop him; he said that Randy sometimes forgets he's not wearing the uniform anymore."

"I need to speak with Benjamin. If Luca—"

"I'll arrange it," Alessandro said. "Tell me who I should speak with at the embassy in Florence. My English is bad, but not bad enough that I couldn't understand."

"Wait!" I said, then spoke slowly and clearly in English to Kendall for Alessandro's sake, only dimly aware that he was still wearing one of the hotel's complimentary guest robes which had become untied and that the three of us were naked. I was so focused I didn't even check him out. "Why would a gang of armed thugs storm the American embassy unless they were looking for Luca? It feels like too much of a coincidence to be anything else. So, assuming they attacked the place and killed people, they were either desperate to kidnap him, or, more likely, make it appear that he happened to be in the wrong place at the wrong time and got caught in the crossfire."

"Yes, but we're missing something: how would anyone know he was there?" Kendall said. "Only a few of us knew where he was: Kendall, me, Benjamin, James, and … oh, fuck, Alfonso …"

I jumped out of my chair and ran to the phone, asking the hotel switchboard to dial La Mensola. The line was still busy, so I asked to call again, three times in a row, just as Kendall had done. I then asked the operator to call the office in Pienza.

Cosmo answered. "Damson! Thank God! Where have you been? We've been trying to contact you. No one answers the phone in the Florence apartment—"

"Have you heard the news? About the shootings at the embassy in Florence?"

"Yes, of course. Don't tell me you were there?"

"No, I'm in Venice. I'm trying to call Alfonso at La Mensola—"

"That's why everyone has been trying to find you. Stefano phoned not long ago. He went to find one of the guests who'd gone wandering. She was standing in the open doorway of your kitchen. The house is a mess. The Mori brothers had turned up a moment after he arrived; they told him they'd come to do repairs to your roof. They've just got back and called in here to see where you were, to tell you what had happened."

Guests at Il Fornaio were told in no uncertain terms that my private house was out of bounds.

"Alfonso?"

"Nowhere to be found. I phoned the police. Did you know that Fabrizio Negri has been transferred back here after ten years in Siena? He's on his way to your house now."

I supposed that Alfonso was probably with Gaspard and luckily not at home when whoever it was had arrived to ransack my house.

"Fabrizio is an excellent detective. You said the Mori brothers had just returned. Are they there with you?"

"Yes."

"Put one of them on, please."

Marco, the younger of the two, spoke. It was mere coincidence that they'd arrived at the same time as Stefano, finding the elderly American woman standing in my kitchen doorway looking bewildered and calling out my name. The house had been ransacked, signs of struggle in the kitchen and living room. As far as they'd seen, there was no blood in either of the two rooms.

"Any idea why the phone is constantly engaged?"

"I think it's out of order. Stefano tried to phone Cosmo from there but said he couldn't get a dial tone. That's one of the reasons we came here to Giancarlo's office: to find out where you were so we could tell you."

Out of order? The local exchange couldn't be down, otherwise I wouldn't have been able to get through to the office in Pienza.

"I think the line has been cut," I said to Cosmo after Marco had passed back the phone.

"Cosmo …"

"Yes, Damson. The sound of your voice is making me feel anxious."

"Have you heard of Lepri? It's to the west of Pienza, not far away."

"No, sorry."

"Ask the Mori brothers."

Mario's brother, Ennio, knew where it was. I spoke with him; told him to go home, get their rifles and round up a few more men who weren't afraid to use their weapons and go to Lepri. I explained that they should be cautious; I didn't expect there to be any trouble, but I wanted some reassurance that Father Green and the rest of the priests were all right.

We spent the next hour or so listening to the radio for updates on the situation. "*The latest statement from political analysts is saying that, according to inside sources, this attack was a combined effort by the Camorra and underground fascist groups ...*"

"What?" I yelled, jumping from my armchair. "No! Who are these fucking political analysts—?"

"Clowns in the pocket of Scavola and his media interests. He's a major stakeholder in several of the important Italian newspapers," Alessandro said.

The phone rang. It was Cosmo. "The Mori brothers are back from Lepri. Father Green said no one had been there. He's sending most of the priests back to their parishes until this dies down and only he and the farm workers are staying to look after the retreat. They're all armed."

I asked Cosmo to stay on the line while I passed the news to Kendall and Alessandro.

"Kendall, who was at home when you left yesterday?"

"Just Alfonso and Gaspard."

I started to feel very, very uneasy. "Where was James?"

"With the production crew. I sent them to Siena yesterday morning to film some of the sites where the serial killer murders happened."

"When are they due back?"

"Tomorrow."

I didn't have Gaspard's phone number; it was in the address book I kept at home next to the upstairs telephone.

"Cosmo?" I said, returning to my conversation with him. "If the Mori brothers are still there, can you get them to go to Gaspard's farm to see whether, by chance, Father Ignazio has gone there?"

"Who is Gaspard, and why would Father Ignazio be there?"

I made something up. He told me that the Mori brothers had just left, so he'd get his wife to answer the phone and drive there himself. While I gave him directions and told him to be careful, asking him to find someone else to take with him, Alessandro went to see who'd knocked at the door of our suite. I could hear him talking with our room attendant, who followed him into the room, politely ignoring the fact that the three of us were naked. While speaking with Cosmo, I watched the attendant unlock a door and usher Alessandro through it.

"Benjamin has been calling while we've been on the phone. Alessandro's gone to the empty suite next door to speak with him," Kendall said, as I placed my hand over the receiver.

"Go, see what's up," I whispered.

A few minutes later, I hung up, having made sure that Cosmo had understood what I'd asked him to do. I suggested he call in at the gym and ask the weight trainer to accompany him; I could never remember his name, just that he was a burly Romanian who used to be Alfonso's boxing partner.

I was beginning to have very dark thoughts. I was convinced that Scavola was behind the attack on the US embassy and positive it had been an attempt to either kidnap, or more likely kill Luca. But I'd made a fundamental error: I'd assumed we'd been followed to Lepri. But Father Green had said no one had come to the retreat … so how would Scavola know that we'd taken Luca to Florence …? Then it hit me. My name and Giancarlo's were appended as witnesses to Mario's statement; the statement that had been stolen from the secure lockup in Rome.

If Scavola's men had kidnapped Giancarlo to find out where Luca was, that would have been futile, because I hadn't told Giancarlo where we'd decided to take him. As far as I remembered, he'd only heard talk of London, but didn't know that we'd kiboshed that idea. It would explain why his study in our apartment had been ransacked.

So, that meant they'd come for me at La Mensola for information; hence the disorder in my house. I crossed my fingers, still desperately hoping that Alfonso had gone to visit Gaspard and the mess was the result of someone looking for clues to Luca's location.

I made my way into the adjoining suite and listened while Alessandro spoke with Benjamin. Eventually, he held up the receiver. "He wants to talk to you, Damson."

Benjamin explained that all around him was chaos but that Luca was unharmed. The embassy was swarming with US military, who'd arrived from Camp Darby, near Pisa, a ninety-minute car trip. After speaking with the US ambassador in Rome, it had been decided to take Luca to the US Air Force installation at Aviano in northern Italy, where it would be impossible for anyone to reach him. I was about to protest that a car convoy could be hijacked when he told me that a helicopter was coming to transport Luca. There was a helipad on the roof of the building.

He asked me to tell him what I'd learned since I arrived in Venice, so I filled him in. He urged me to get a weapon—a small arms weapon preferably—but couldn't tell me where I could get one. I had an idea: there was a US Army surplus outlet at Pontassieve, just outside Florence. I'd bought my Jeep there, and was still in contact with the quartermaster who ran the place. I made a mental note to phone him once I got off the line.

I heard the phone ring in the other room; Alessandro went to answer it.

"I had too much to drink last night. Thank God your friend, Captain McCall, had a spare room," Benjamin said in a very transparent tone of voice that warned me to be careful what I said. I knew he was worried about the call being monitored. "Had I not stayed over, I might have been one of the unlucky ones. Four were Italian citizens, Damson. Two external security men and two local female cleaners leaving after their night shift. The other three were embassy security staff on guard at the front of the building, cut down before they could draw their weapons."

Female cleaners, probably on their way home to cook breakfast for their loved ones. What a nightmare. Fucking Scavola!

"Have you got a pen handy?" I scrabbled in the desk drawer and found a sheet of Danieli-headed stationery. He gave me a number to call in Rome, said that I should say I wanted to speak with him, and then, when asked, give them a five-digit security number, which I also wrote down. The operator would then patch me to wherever he would be. He said he'd catch up with us in person in a few days.

Alessandro appeared in the doorway just as I hung up. "A soldier has presented himself to the police, saying he has just returned from a military exercise to find his house turned upside down and his kitchen covered in blood. The dog's throat had been cut, but there's too much blood for that. His housemate, who was supposed to be looking after the dog, is missing and not answering his phone."

"Housemate?"

"Goes by the name of Alvise Fanucci."

Alessandro then told us what he'd learned. The pair, although they didn't live together, were obviously in a relationship. The soldier was beside himself with grief when told that we'd found Alvise's body. Alvise was a former corporal in the army who'd been discharged for multiple counts of drunkenness, something the soldier said he'd conquered over the past few years. Alvise worked as a security guard at the wharf at the Lido; he wasn't a policeman, something we'd already discounted. Alessandro said he was going to get dressed and go to interview the boyfriend, telling us to keep in touch with him once we'd decided what to do.

Ten minutes later, Kendall and I were in the shower when Alessandro barged into the bathroom. Fortunately, we were just washing ourselves.

"That was Giancarlo's assistant, Cosmo, on the phone," he said breathlessly. I hadn't heard it ring. "The Frenchman is dead. Cosmo said he took the man from the gym with him and they found Gaspard in his front garden with his throat cut. He said he was naked and had obviously been badly beaten, his body slashed. I'd guess he was tortured."

I crossed myself. Kendall's eyes were confused: he had no idea what we were talking about in Italian. "And Alfonso?"

"In a serious condition; the ambulance is taking him to Siena. He's been beaten to within an inch of his life."

*****

I'd never flown in a tiny five-seater plane before, and was initially astounded when Kendall piloted it. He could fly? When I asked him how he'd been able to hire an aircraft at the tiny airfield on the mainland just near Venice, he'd left me almost speechless when he'd simply said, "They didn't have any for hire, so I bought it."

He landed it expertly in the Pienza football grounds, a large group of spectators assembled because they'd been forewarned by Fabrizio that we'd be landing there. Cosmo waited for the aircraft to come to a halt before running across the field to join us. To my relief, James was standing not far behind him; he smiled when he saw me.

"News of Alfonso?" I asked before he could open his mouth.

"Too soon yet, he's just been wheeled out of the operating theatre. Pienza is crawling with cops already and Fabrizio has just told me that American soldiers are on their way too, plus a whole lot of senior police from Rome. Your house and Gaspard's are being searched by men in black uniforms. No one seems to know who they are; we suspect they're *stoppisti.*"

"*Stoppisti?*"

"Sorry, the past coming back to haunt me. It's what we called the Americans after they started kicking out the Germans during the war. The first word we always heard out of their mouths was invariably 'Stop!'"

Out of the corner of my eye, I could see Kendall speaking with some apparent urgency to Wesley. James appeared to be listening intently to their conversation.

Despite the crawling fear in my gut, which had now grown alarmingly over Alfonso's beating, I was genuinely pleased to see Fabrizio; I'd missed him over the years and we'd only caught up infrequently whenever I had need to go to Siena. We embraced fiercely, him muttering against my ear that he'd do whatever it took to track down Giancarlo and find the people who'd killed Gaspard and savaged Alfonso.

It was a muddle of a morning. Kendall told me he'd arranged to have his car brought back to La Mensola from Mestre. Who knew that a valet service in a hotel would extend so far? As for my Maserati, I phoned the young man who always looked after it in Florence at his house. I heard his mother screaming his name out the window and a few minutes later offered him ten thousand lire to drive my car back here. He nearly wet himself with excitement. I promised him that I'd drive him back home to Florence tomorrow. I had a chore to do: I had to call into the army surplus depot in Pontassieve and see whether I could buy a few hand guns, so it suited me to go to Florence anyway.

James, whom I'd told of my plans, offered to drive the young man back to Florence himself and then go to Pontassieve to choose weapons for Kendall and me. He said I should go to the hospital to be with Alfonso; he also needed to speak with Benjamin on some urgent matter but wouldn't tell me what.

I felt totally useless here—even though they'd rounded up hundreds of locals to scour the countryside around Montepulciano, the police wouldn't allow me to join in the search for Giancarlo—so I followed James's advice: I took the Jeep and headed off to the hospital in Siena. I was desperately worried about Alfonso, sick to the stomach about what had happened to him and Gaspard. I could have phoned, but I needed to see Alfonso face to face; that was, if the doctors would allow visitors. Fabrizio was my passenger; he, too, was inordinately fond of Alfonso and had been told to leave the local investigation to the Siena police, who'd taken over.

I'd seen hundreds of injured men during my war, but never anyone who was as close to me as Father Ignazio, a name I still called him in my mind from time to time. My guts gripped when Fabrizio and I were shown into the hospital room. It was the same ward that I'd been in and in which we'd interviewed Cristoforo Baldi, one of the two serial killers that I'd written a book about. Although ten years had passed since I'd last been in this hospital, a familiar face was leaning over Alfonso's form, muttering to him softly: my old pal, the French doctor who'd looked after both me and Baldi. His Italian had improved markedly over the decade and we spoke in that language.

Alfonso was semi-conscious, but not well enough to be inter-viewed. He had broken legs, both wrists and several ribs, and a fractured orbital socket—they also initially thought he might lose his left eye. He was uncovered down to the waist, the starched sheet folded across his body just below the navel; he was a mass of bruises and cuts. There might have been more severe internal injuries, the doctor said. His rectus abdominis muscles were very developed, the only explanation the physician could give for the lack of severe injury. I told him that Alfonso was a trained boxer; perhaps that was the reason.

"I was told that he had to be operated on?"

"He had a suspected ruptured bladder; it turned out to be a false alarm. He was only in theatre for no more than thirty minutes and not heavily sedated—"

"Damson ..." Alfonso called out weakly.

The doctor went to his bedside. Fabrizio grabbed my arm, shaking his head at me, urging me with his eyes to stay where I was until the doctor gave me the green light to take my friend's hand.

"I'll give you thirty seconds," he said to me, beckoning me over.

I grabbed Alfonso's arm, kneeling on the floor, feeling angry and distressed all at the same time.

"I'm sorry," he whispered. "I'm so terribly sorry. I held out for as long as I could, even when they were attacking Gaspard. They threatened to kill him if I didn't tell them where you'd taken Luca. I'm sorry ... I gave in. It was me who told them where to find him."

He burst into racking sobs and the doctor pulled me away, calling for the nurse.

Perhaps fifteen minutes later, outside in the corridor, the doctor told me what Alfonso had said to him before they'd taken him in for surgery. The men had tortured them both, but, as he'd just said, finally threatened to kill Gaspard if Alfonso didn't tell them what they wanted to know. They had a gun to his head, so he gave them the information. They slit his friend's throat anyway, then beat Alfonso almost senseless.

"If they killed his French friend ... why would they leave Father Ignazio alive?" Fabrizio asked.

"Probably as some sort of message," I said.

"As I said, he was semi-coherent when he was brought in and spoke with great difficulty," the doctor said. "My colleagues tried to pull me away but I sensed that what he had to say was very important. He seemed to indicate that they left him thinking he would die with his companion's death on his conscience."

"Jesus ..." I swore. Even to myself, my voice sounded brittle.

"You must realise that the police haven't interviewed him yet. I've made my own notes and you two are the only other people who know what he told me. Before you ask, he gave me no details of the men. That's all."

"Can we wait?" I asked. "Perhaps he'll be able to talk more later this evening?"

"I should go home, Mr O'Reilly. Give me your phone number and I'll call you when he's up to a visit. It probably won't be today or tomorrow. However, if he has a message for you, I'll be sure to pass it along."

"Anything he needs—please, don't worry about bringing in a specialist if that will help. I'd be only too happy to pay—"

"There's no need for that. He's getting the best care possible. The orthopaedic surgeon will be fixing his legs and his wrists in a few days. They're plastered for the time being but we didn't want him to have heavy anaesthesia too soon after this morning's relatively light sedation."

"What can I do?" I asked Fabrizio out on the street in front of the hospital, my arms spread wide in a gesture of despair.

"Go home and get some rest."

"They won't let me look for Giancarlo, La Mensola is a crime scene, and there are dead bodies everywhere."

"From what you told me, your witness is in very safe hands. No gangs, no matter how well armed they are, are going to storm an American military base to try to silence him. If I were you, I'd be speaking with Inspector Venturi in Rome to see if you can't have at least a preliminary hearing brought forward. You said there are copies of the young man's statement, and you are a witness to Mario Celestino's statement as well. A preliminary hearing with all the evidence that you already have will tie Scavola's hands behind his back. Where is he, anyway?"

"I believe he's still in Greece. I need to phone Pienza; where's the nearest bar?"

"I could do with a drink too. I'll ask someone."

We were directed to a small bar, of the type that was around every corner in every town in Italy. I phoned Cosmo to be told that Kendall had left a message saying he was taking Wesley and going to Rome; he was staying at the St Regis. He'd arranged a room for James and me in Montepulciano in the same *pensione* as the film crew, expressing regret that the only hotel in Pienza was booked out. I cursed. Normally, we could have stayed at Il Fornaio, but it was full of visitors at the moment.

Fabrizio and I had a few drinks at the bar; he offered to put me up in his spare bedroom, but, thinking of his four small children, I declined. I asked him to drive. My emotions were high and I was full of anger over what had happened to Alfonso, despair at Gaspard's death—a lovely quiet man who had nothing to do with anything—and extremely worried about Giancarlo.

However, I'd spent nearly ten years in the military, much of that time at war, so was no stranger to stressful and life-threatening situations. I'd learned that living for the moment was sometimes the best one could do; so that was what I decided to do. I hated feeling helpless, but tomorrow was not today, and I could do nothing at the moment that could influence the future.

★★★★★

James was playing with Cosmo's children in the street outside Giancarlo's office when we arrived in Pienza at about six o'clock.

When I asked, he said he hadn't eaten lunch and I admitted that I'd skipped it too. He told me that Kendall and Wesley had decided to fly to Rome instead of driving. There was nowhere nearby where he could keep the aircraft he'd purchased in Venice; the local World War Two landing strip that had been used by the German occupiers had long since been returned to cultivated fields and the nearest airstrip with hangars was at Asciano, a circuitous two-and-a-half-hour drive from Pienza. There was a field at Gracciano, perhaps thirty minutes away, but there was no provision for storing aircraft.

Kendall had left a message asking me to phone his hotel in Rome at eleven o'clock.

James suggested we eat something and catch up over dinner. I told him I needed to speak with both Salvatore in Rome and Alessandro in Venice. He told me he'd been in contact with Benjamin, who could be reached later that night at Randy's.

It was still a bit early for dinner, so, despite how hungry I was, I sat at Giancarlo's desk in his office and made my phone calls while James entertained Cosmo, his wife and their children. His Italian was incredibly vernacular; I made a note to ask him where and how he'd learned to speak so fluently and with so much current slang.

James was very sombre when we eventually got to the restaurant; I supposed his mood was a reflection of my own. Since leaving the hospital, I'd been almost shocked to realise how incredibly attached I'd become to Alfonso over the ten years that I'd known him. In many ways he was more of a kindred spirit than even Giancarlo, whom I considered almost part of my body. I couldn't bring myself to admit out loud how terrified I was that something awful might happen to my friend; he'd looked like a wreck in the hospital. I'd seen far too many men in similar physical condition not make it through the night.

"What are you doing, Damson?" James asked, looking up from his plate of pasta. I'd wolfed mine down.

"Promise me you won't laugh," I said. "I was praying. Praying for Alfonso's survival, for Giancarlo's safe return, and for our own well-being over the next twenty-four hours."

"Why only for the next day?"

"Because by this time tomorrow night I'll feel far safer with a pistol under my belt."

He hesitated for a moment, his fork, laden with *pappardelle*, frozen in mid-air. He spoke quietly in French, leaning over the table. "Your car will be here from Florence when? Around ten, you said? I'll give you my weapon when I leave to drive your parking lot attendant back to Florence."

"What about you?"

"I'll make a call after dinner and have someone meet me about halfway. Perhaps Chiusi will do."

Unlike many other people, I had an appetite when I was on edge. This evening I could have eaten for the Olympics, having scoffed my pasta then managing an enormous pork cutlet with two plates of vegetables and a double portion of strawberry tart. "I need to fuel the fire," I explained.

Our room at the *pensione* was at the end of the same corridor in which the film crew had their rooms. There was only one double bed, and when I made enquiries, I was told that all the rooms were the same and members of the crew were in the same situation, forced to share beds. The producer had shared with Wesley, who I was told had been almost grabbed by the scruff of the neck by Kendall and bundled into the aircraft to fly to Rome. The producer had absolutely no idea what was going on either.

Fortunately, there was a phone in our room. I knew that dialling Rome at that time of night would be outrageously expensive and asked the *signora* whether I might pay for it in a few days after I'd been to the bank. She crossed her arms and glared, so I phoned the hotel in Rome and asked them to get Kendall to call me back. *Signora* was not amused when the phone rang at eleven in the evening but I didn't give a hoot if she listened in. Even if she had some idea of American English, with Kendall and I speaking in Australian English, I doubted she'd gather much through our coppery, bright accents and local slang.

"Have you seen the fucking papers or heard the news?" he asked the moment I picked up the receiver. "Everyone's saying the hit on the US embassy was by the Camorra, a disgruntled band of fascists seeking payback for what they say the Americans did during the invasion of Italy."

"Well, what did you expect?" I asked. "Scavola, much like your father back home, owns most of the press and radio in this country."

He was about to explode, until I reminded him that I'd visited Alfonso in hospital. He sounded broken-hearted when I said that I thought he would be lucky to make it through the night and that I was going back to the hospital first thing in the morning.

"How's James?" he asked.

"Pretending to be asleep, but I can see him playing with his cock under the sheet," I said, loudly. James laughed and pulled the sheet back, holding his penis so that it pointed up into the air and giving me a sheepish grin.

"Do you intend to help him?" he said. I could hear the voyeur edge to his voice.

"Contrary to popular belief, I don't fuck absolutely every man I meet."

"Unless I'm there to guide you in and smack your arse, wishing you good luck."

I didn't laugh when normally I probably would have. I was too heartsick with worry over both Alfonso and the nagging possibility that Giancarlo, like the rock-and-roller who had been found with his throat cut, would also have come to grief.

"Why did you kidnap Wesley?"

"Ah, that. Well, it's nothing like the situation you seem to find yourself in with James. I'll tell you in the morning. The international phone bill for this room is going to be astronomical. Damson …?"

"Yes?"

"Look after yourself."

"I've got James here with me; there's nothing to worry about," I said.

"I'm so very, very sorry about Gaspard and worried sick about Alfonso."

"Yeah, me too."

"Anyway, I'll leave you to it. I've got a heap to get on with here. Where will you be tomorrow?" he asked.

"As I said, at the hospital in Siena, then back home if the police will allow it. How long will you be in Rome?"

"I'll drive home just after lunch. If you aren't at La Mensola I'll check in with Cosmo to find out where you are."

"Drive home? Are you hiring a car?"

"No. I rang the hotel in Mestre and told them there was a change of plan. One of the hotel's employees is driving my car to Rome overnight. Should be here in the morning when I get out of bed."

I shook my head, wondering what it would be like to be a person who never had to think about money.

"Sleep well," I said.

"I'd sleep even better if you were here. Goodnight, Damson, give one to James for me."

I smiled, a bare smile, then hung up the phone.

CHAPTER 17

It was such a warm night that I'd left the bedroom windows open, but the shutters closed. Our room looked out over Via Ricci, one of the main streets of the steep incline up to the main square of Montepulciano.

I woke to the sound of people yelling in the street outside. James was nowhere to be seen. I vaguely remembered holding him in my arms during the night with his head on my chest. It was pleasant rather than anything else. As I came to the surface, I heard excited voices, pulled myself onto the edge of the bed and scratched my head, yawning in an effort to wake up.

"Damson, come! Quickly!" The producer had burst into my room.

"What's the hurry?"

He looked at his watch. "Two minutes to nine. You need to listen to this."

"Listen to what?"

"The BBC international morning news."

I pulled on my briefs and the singlet I'd worn yesterday and stumbled down the corridor to the *salotto*, available for guests of the *pensione*. Over the babble of the film crew, I began to hear voices from outside and downstairs in the reception area; people lamenting. *Che miseria!* and

Vergogna! being some of the most common. What the hell was going on? I was about to open my mouth when the music announcing the nine o'clock news came on. "This is the BBC broadcasting from London …" Someone handed me a cigarette.

I couldn't believe my ears when I heard what followed. Fucking Kendall? What a ripper! That was why he'd disappeared with Wesley yesterday.

Newspapers and radio reports around the world were carrying the story that Wesley had written for the major London tabloid owned by Kendall's father, debunking the whole Camorra explanation for the invasion of the US embassy in Florence and laying out the case for pointing the finger at Scavola. Nothing had been left out: the mention of his war crimes; the suspicion that he'd arranged for Mario Celestino to be murdered; the torture of a priest and the murder of his friend, a newly settled French immigrant; the supposed kidnapping and—my heart stopped in my chest when I heard this bit—presumed assassination of Giancarlo Manetti, the famous Italian lawyer. Most startling of all was the revelation of Scavola's involvement in the murder of the nuns at Vatican City during the war and that the reason he'd attempted to storm the American embassy was to kill the only living witness to the crime.

I was flabbergasted. I ran downstairs to the *pensione*'s kitchen, still in my underwear, to hear the Italian news broadcast. The *signora*, her sister and the cook were huddled around the radio, crossing themselves endlessly and muttering prayers while they listened. My name was mentioned several times; for some reason, the news broadcaster in Rome suggesting that I was a major player in the investigation into Scavola. He finished at a few minutes before half past nine with the warning that this was "indeed a dark day for the country".

I had to drag myself away from the small gathering because the *signora* and her staff grabbed and held my hands, thanking me over and over for trying to solve the murder of Mario Celestino. Bugger the murder of the nuns during the war, Giancarlo's disappearance, the death of Gaspard almost on their doorstep and the torture of one of the district's most well-loved priests. The death of the nation's heart-throb film star and retribution for his murder was all they could think about.

I called the hotel in Rome; Kendall had checked out. I phoned Cosmo; the line was engaged, ditto Il Fornaio. On the off-chance, I phoned La Mensola. James answered; the swarm of Americans investigating the house had obviously found where the line had been cut and had reconnected it.

"Morning, sleepyhead," he said.

"Jesus! Did you know about this?"

"I may have," he said. "That's why I was on the phone to Benjamin last night. He was providing information to Kendall and Wesley for the newspaper article."

"Why didn't you tell me?"

"Kendall told me not to."

"What I don't understand is how the news got out so quickly if they only compiled the news story last night?"

"Special edition. Hit the streets of London at six this morning, syndicated across the globe. I bet the teleprinters at Reuters were running red hot most of the night. Your car is here, by the way. I've already washed it and put it under cover."

"What, at half past nine in the morning?"

"Seems your little friend from Florence wanted to get on the road early before there was any traffic and see what she could do on the open road."

"Tell him I'll cut his balls off if there's a scratch on my machine."

"I'll do better than that," he said with a chuckle. "I'll tell him he can take the wheel on the way back to Florence if he lets me suck him off."

"I hope you're joking …"

"Damson. What's the point of being serious right now? Kendall's on his way back here, and there have been a dozen phone calls this morning since I got here at eight. The leader of a very polite group of police told me they'd finished with the house, and the phone was working again. The police finished and actually tidied up before they left. Randall is desperate to talk to you, so is Giancarlo's sister, Carla, and his father phoned from Egypt. I told him who I was and that the British embassy in Cairo would keep him informed. I said that you'd be away for most of the day … that's a presumption on my part, but I guessed it to be the case. He left a phone number. Alfonso's parents called; I told them you'd visited him in hospital. You're going back again this morning?"

"Yes, as soon as I have a shower and have something to eat."

"I suggest you call them first, actually. Venturi and Pellegrini have also been on the phone, and when I spoke with Cosmo just before the nine a.m. news he told me that the phone hasn't stopped ringing in the office."

"Okay, I'll come to La Mensola first. I'll shower and eat at home."

"See you shortly, then."

My car minder from Florence had a rather stupid look on his face when I got home. I gave James a look from under my eyebrows; he merely raised an eyebrow and shrugged with a grin on his face. It was none of my business. Young Italian men: if it was warm and wet, they'd stick their dick in it.

James talked with me while I was in the shower. Surprisingly, the young Florentine prepared something for me to eat. While we were talking and I had my head under the shower, Stefano arrived, as did the Mori brothers a few minutes later, with Gino, Renzo's cousin, sent by Signora Marino to find out news of Alfonso. They informed me that cars had started to line the road outside and people were bringing flowers to the shrine to pray for Father Ignazio, as the locals knew him.

I became aware that I was stark naked in a room full of Italian men whose voices had started to rise in volume; such was the case with groups of Italians in a small space. I shooed them out while I towelled off, not blinking at the young Florentine's direct stare at my bits when he brought me in a cup of coffee. "*Complimenti, Signor O'Reilly!*" he said, his eyes fixed on my dick; his congratulations made me feel like a prize bull at the local agricultural show. I exchanged glances with James, who was trying not to laugh. No doubt I'd hear the story of what I believed had happened between them at some later date.

He'd made very passable scrambled eggs, Italian style, with finely chopped onion sautéed with garlic and sprinkled with fresh chives from one of the terracotta pots on the terrace outside the kitchen. He also knew how to make toast and had refilled the moka pot. I sat down to eat while listening to the Mori brothers' report on the search for Giancarlo.

Stefano reported that there'd been grumbles from some of the guests, who'd expected to see more of me, explaining that was why they'd come: to meet the author of the books I'd written. I told him that I'd call in to Il Fornaio this afternoon after returning from seeing Alfonso in Siena. James had checked with the hospital, and not only had he survived the night, but he was also in much better shape this morning, although very weak.

I got changed, phoned Carla and tried my best to calm her, but she was beside herself, wanting to come here to see what she could do. I explained that it would be impossible, and she would be better off leaving the search to the police and the *carabinieri* who'd been called in from Siena to help in the search. More American soldiers had also arrived, some of them from the same base as the men who'd turned up in Florence after the shooting at the American embassy. I expected that by midday today this whole area would be swarming with Italian journalists; then, by evening, the international press would arrive.

Kendall's front-page stories across the world were bound to stir up a hornet's nest.

★★★★★

Alessandro Pellegrini's interview in Venice with Alvise's soldier lover had proved interesting, although not particularly informative. I ran through it in my mind on the way to the hospital.

The soldier had been aware of the relationship with Mario and had been extremely jealous, but not jealous enough to want to kill either Mario or Alvise. Besides, he'd been away on exercises the night Mario died. He'd tolerated being cuckolded, as he put it, because the money that Mario gave Alvise for sex was needed to pay off the mortgage on the small farm they'd bought to live in when the soldier finished his military service. He'd always found it odd, however, that Alvise had never come home from Mario with the money in his pocket; instead, it had been delivered directly to the soldier once a month by a man he described as "weasel-like". Alvise had told him the money was safer with him than hidden in his room in the boarding house.

A large stash of notes—their savings, the soldier had told the police—had been found under a loose floorboard in the bedroom.

One of the policemen had identified the "weasel-like man" as an accounts assistant who worked in Scavola's Venice office—the man was well-known to the Venetian police. Alessandro had despatched two men to bring him in. I told him that someone should try to find a picture of the weasel taken during the war and ask one of the attachés at the American embassy to show it to Luca. Perhaps, if Luca did recognise him as being one of Scavola's thugs back then, the man might be an entrée into the inner workings of the gang during the war.

Just like the time that I'd visited Baldi in the same hospital ten years ago, there were guards outside Alfonso's door. He'd been moved to a private suite, something I hadn't even known existed during my time in the same ward. The French doctor came to find me once I left a message with the nurse saying I wanted to visit my friend. "The private room was paid for by a Mr Travert, said he was a friend of Signor Valentini's and yours. He's awake, but very weak. You can sit with him for a while, but he's semi-sedated. Be warned, he might fall asleep on you. If he asks for something to drink, there's a jug of water in the bedside stand and a glass drinking straw. Only three sips. If his condition deteriorates suddenly, we might need to rush him to theatre."

"He must be starving," I said.

The doctor looked at his watch. "It's half past eleven now. The specialist will visit him at one o'clock. If he thinks that he's out of danger, he can eat then."

"Tell me, doctor, is he likely to …?"

"Die? He's young and strong, and he's markedly better than when you saw him yesterday. I think it's unlikely."

"Can I see him now?"

"Shortly. There's a policeman with him right now?"

"A policeman? Just one …?" I started to get to my feet.

"No need to be alarmed. He's quite famous, from Rome, an ex-inspector who speaks excellent French. I thought he was a native until he told me otherwise."

"I don't suppose his name is Salvatore Venturi?"

"Well, yes. How would you know that?"

"He's an old friend."

Alfonso was asleep when I was eventually shown into his room. My breath caught in my throat when I saw him, his eyes closed, looking incredibly fragile. It became immediately clear that my heart was attached to this wonderful, fragile human being. In many ways, he was my *amico intimo speciale*, an Italian term for soul friend, the one special person in one's life who is connected by an invisible thread of the deepest friendship, transcending sexual or romantic attachments.

I spotted Venturi, who was standing outside on the small balcony smoking a cigar. I walked quietly to the bed and kissed Alfonso gently on the lips. He didn't stir, so I made my way out onto the balcony and stood next to Salvatore. He put his arm around my shoulder. "Filthy business," he said, squeezing the back of my neck while I lit up a cigarette.

"Was he able to talk to you?"

"One of the local priests gave him the last rites last night." My heart sank in my chest. "He was here again this morning, said mass next to the bed just after I arrived, anointed him again, then left saying God loved him. Alfonso wept. Why would he weep so bitterly, Damson?"

"I can't tell you that, Salvatore."

"Then I suppose my next assumption is that he and the Frenchman who was found dead next to him were more than just friends?" I said nothing. "He told me what happened. One doesn't give up what one knows is a very dangerous secret because someone who's a chance acquaintance is being tortured in front of them."

"I've heard of it happening," I said.

"It must have been terrible for him."

I brushed away the tears in my eyes with the back of my forearm. How my life had changed. Fifteen, twenty years ago, when I was at war, I'd have gritted my teeth and moved on after the news of a friend killed, maimed or tortured. Although I hated the feelings that were coursing through my body and mind, it made me aware that I'd finally started to become more human, that the horrors of the war were memories, not recurring realities. The unnecessary murder of a kind, generous neighbour, even after his lover had given the information he'd been tortured for, brought forth a vile, dark beast from somewhere inside me. I fought it; the anger was almost overwhelming, as was the sadness, the grief and the need for retribution.

"If I find those men …" I muttered.

"That's why it's best to leave it to the police … and the Americans. Think yourself lucky. Had you been at home when those two were snatched, it might be you either in this hospital room or, worse, in the morgue, waiting for my former medical forensic officer to arrive, inspect your body and write his report for a future court case when and if this comes to trial."

"But how can I trust the police to—"

"I don't believe you can be that naïve, my friend. Everyone has read or heard the news this morning. They all believe that this was surely ordered by Scavola in an effort to find the only person alive who can point the finger at him for the massacre of the nuns. I was listening to the wireless while I drove here this morning, tuning into local stations as I passed each new town to hear what was being said. People are furious, calling for Scavola's blood. The case of the nuns was so very famous and it was believed it would never be solved. Now? Your friend Kendall has ignited a passion that I thought was dead in my country."

"That won't help find Giancarlo," I said. My voice sounded threadbare.

"Perhaps Benjamin Smollet will help?"

"Why didn't you tell me about him?"

"Not my story to tell. I know about your friend James because of my brother—and Mr Smollet? Well, let's say even retired ex-inspectors have the ear of the international intelligence agencies. You've no idea how many people owe me favours. Besides, you forget that I inherited my father's title; a duke can do things that are almost impossible even for officials."

Alfonso stirred and we both looked over our shoulders. It was hard to tell whether he was awake or not: both eyes were swollen almost shut. I went to his bed and sat on the edge. Both forearms were in plaster, so I played gently with his fingertips. "Are you awake?" I whispered.

"*Sitio,*" he mumbled.

"What?" Salvatore asked quietly, having taken a seat next to the hospital bed.

"He said he's thirsty," I replied, opening the bedside cabinet to find the water carafe and a glass. I filled it, put the glass drinking straw to his mouth and said in Latin, "Only three sips."

"Poor Gaspard," he said in almost a whisper, a tear running from the corner of his eye.

"It's my fault, Alfonso," I said close to his ear. "They came looking for me."

"It's God's punishment. I turned away—"

I stopped him by kissing him again, leaving my mouth pressed against his until he settled. His lips eventually softened; I supposed that he'd heard too many confessions during his life as a priest not to realise that what he'd said was nonsense. I imagined I was just as much at fault; I blamed myself for Giancarlo's disappearance.

"I'm sorry, I shouldn't have said that …"

"Shh. God knows the love in your heart, my friend. There's no punishment here, no lesson to be learned, no *mea culpa*; it's simply man's lot in life."

I heard Salvatore snort. He might be a Catholic, but hadn't been brought up in a religious community as Alfonso and I had. There was no use explaining. Guilt was part of what the Church taught its followers: guilt meant devotion; devotion meant blind following; blind following meant power. Cynical? Perhaps.

He closed his eyes and turned his head away from me. I took the hint; he just needed time to himself to process things, as I would have done in his place. I gestured to Salvatore to follow me back to the balcony.

Always eager to speak in French, he said, "You should plan for the worst outcome, *mon petit*."

"It's a very long time since anyone called me a young man." It made me smile.

"When was the last time?"

"My landlady in Vence, Madame Tremeau. She came to a very bad end at the hands of her disgusting drunkard of a nephew."

My thoughts turned dark at the memory and I leaned on the balustrade of the balcony, watching the foot traffic in the square below.

"I hope he was held accountable?"

I shrugged. "The body was never found."

"I see …"

I thought the silence between us would go on forever. I smoked my cigarette down to the stub then flicked it into a small tin canister in the corner of the balcony.

"I expect you made him suffer," he said eventually.

"Not nearly enough."

"Then, my friend, I hope the opportunity never arises that you find yourself face to face with Scavola. As tempting as it might be to strangle him, he needs to be held accountable for his crimes. The entire Italian population needs to know what he did, even though the appetite for retribution for war crimes is unpopular these days. His empire probably controls half the country—"

"Do you remember what happened in the aftermath of Baldi's trial? Judges, politicians, businessmen fled the country by the dozen. It will be the same, except that I think that this time it will be worse. I know we've just had a change of government, but who knows how high Scavola's influence reaches?"

"Our prime minister, Fanfani, is a centre-leftist, anathema to Scavola's crowd. I can't believe he'd be involved," Salvatore said. "I'll phone him later today to explain the situation; he'll take my call. He'd be briefed anyway, but a lot of his administration is still staffed by remainders of the last government."

"When you said I should be prepared for the worst, what were you referring to? The doctor said Alfonso was improving. He just—"

"I was just thinking out loud, Damson. Don't listen to me," he said. "And I was referring to Giancarlo. He's my friend too; don't forget that."

I clasped my hands tightly together, my shoulders hunched and my teeth clamped. I felt fury and desperation behind my eyes, a feeling I hadn't had since visiting Renzo in hospital, when I learned that he not only had a few weeks to live but also that his so-called lover at the time had abandoned him in his sickness.

"I can't hear what you want to tell me, Salvatore. It's only been four days—"

"He would have contacted you, Damson. I'm not saying anything more than perhaps he's … there's only one way to say this … been kidnapped, or, like your friend here, roughed up to find out where the witness is."

"But it was Alfonso who told those men where Luca was, two days after Giancarlo went off with that fellow on the bus … besides, I never told him where I'd hidden Luca. He was kept out of the loop on purpose: his idea, not mine."

"You need to find out more about this man."

"Which man?" I asked.

"The rock-and-roller. The man he went with to Montepulciano."

"How on earth do I do that?"

"He isn't a local. He must have got to Pienza somehow."

"I'll get Cosmo on to it."

"Talking of Cosmo, I sent him more information on Scavola's two marriages."

"Tell me," I said.

"Now? Do you think now is the time?"

Alfonso coughed. I went to see if he needed anything, but he seemed to be dozing.

"It will take my mind off other things," I said, returning to the balcony.

"His first wife did die during the bombing of Rome. As you know, Pius XII was her godfather. She was from old money; Scavola inherited everything after her death. There was no foul play. A stick of bombs fell right through the square and obliterated their house. It couldn't have been planned. However …"

"The death of the second wife is suspicious."

"No one can prove anything, and the case was closed quickly by the local chief of police, who has now conveniently retired and relocated to Crete. I've had my old friend, the archivist at the police department, send Cosmo the file on the investigation into her death. There was plenty of motive. Scavola inherited an absolute fortune, close to nearly a million American dollars in today's money. Scarcely was her body in the ground than he bought that vast industrial estate outside Turin and launched his monopolistic pharmaceutical collaboration with the American giants, something he wouldn't have been able to do without her fortune. I—"

"Salvatore, why are you here? You didn't know Alfonso, as far as I'm aware, and as delighted as I am to see you, why are you in Siena?" I knew it was an abrupt and unconnected thought, but it had been hovering in the back of my mind ever since I'd arrived and found him out on the balcony.

"I knew you'd be here, and what I have to say to you I don't trust over the telephone."

I waited for him to speak.

"I will talk in English; bear with me please. I know your friend in there doesn't speak it, neither does the French doctor."

"We're out here on the balcony, fifteen metres from the ground. Who could hear us out here?"

I was aware I'd raised my voice. He placed a hand on my arm and spoke very quietly.

"I've asked for a special pre-hearing in Rome. My copies of Mario Celestino's statement and your written statement about what he told you will be presented in … how do you say it: *in camera?*"

"Yes, that's it: in private."

"Yes, to a small panel of judges appointed by the Minister of Justice, who is an old and trusted friend of mine so we can be sure that there will be no bias. I need to know whether you'd be prepared to testify and to answer any questions regarding the case. Some of it they may consider … what do you call it? *Testimonianza indiretta …?*"

"Hearsay."

"Yes, hearsay. You know, of course, that you are the only living witness to Mario Celestino's story, Damson. This puts you at considerable personal risk."

"Do I look afraid, Salvatore?"

"No one doubts your courage, my friend; we've all read your books. It will, of course, mean dropping everything here and coming to Rome. I can arrange for the initial hearing to take place in the late morning tomorrow. After that, if the judges agree that a *processo* could go ahead as a matter of urgency, you'll need to go into protective custody."

"I'm sorry, I don't trust the Italian police. You must understand—"

"The Americans will look after you. I've already spoken with an official and they've agreed."

"An official? Do you mean Benjamin Smollet, by chance?"

He placed his thumb and index finger together and "zipped" them across his lips.

"When do I leave?" I asked.

"You see those two black limousines that have just pulled up down there in the square?"

"You knew I'd say yes?"

"Your American friend and your British friend both said you would. Who was I to argue?"

"Kendall—"

"He was informed early this morning. He's still in Rome, and James Llewellyn, the Viscount Langley, by now should be on his way to Rome too."

I shrugged, just as someone knocked at the door to Alfonso's room.

*****

The "interview" the following morning was quite unexpected. I'd been told that it was informal, but what I wasn't told was that, besides the four judges, there would be three secretaries recording the conversation, one of them an American soldier in uniform, another a police officer, also in uniform, and the third a bespectacled young man from the British embassy, representing the Australian consul. All three, I was told, were fluent in Italian and English.

Another surprise was that the proceedings were to be tape-recorded on several machines simultaneously. There was also, strangely enough, an American naval lieutenant: the ropes of gold looped around the epaulette on his left shoulder signifying that he was an attaché at his embassy. I had no idea why he was there and hadn't been introduced. After a few minutes, he stood and gave his credentials to the judges. He was a lawyer, sent by his people as an "advisor", whatever the hell that meant. He caught my eye briefly and nodded perfunctorily; I decided at that moment that I didn't care who he was or why he was here, but I took an instant dislike to him. I didn't know why; it was a gut feeling.

It was a rather tedious process, the lawyer for the Americans interrupting a few times and asking me to repeat what I'd said in Italian in English, then double-checking with his American secretary counterpart to assert that my translation from Italian had been exactly what I'd told the judges.

The major problem was not that they didn't believe my account of what Mario had told me both at his apartment and over dinner at Torcello, but why he'd chosen me to confide in. I hedged carefully for a very long while until the American lawyer interrupted once more and asked to speak with his client privately. His client? I had no idea he was there to somehow represent me in the preliminary hearing. Usually, there would be some sort of briefing before anything got to even an interview. I guessed that Benjamin was behind it.

"What the fuck are you avoiding, O'Reilly? It's as plain as day that there's a whole heap of crap you're leaving out of the narrative. Sooner or later one of those judges is going to start to believe that the rest of your testimony is somehow tweaked."

"I'm trying to avoid mentioning Mario Celestino's private life. That's why he confided in me."

"He was a fruit; we all know that."

"Mind your fucking tongue, dickface," I said rather angrily. His manner had brought out the Irish in me. "You're talking to another *fruit* who could rip your arm off at the shoulder and stuff it up your arsehole."

"Whoa, buddy—"

"First of all, I'm not your buddy, and secondly, if as you say you're supposed to be representing me, why haven't you spoken up earlier?"

"Okay, settle down. Sorry, I'm just not used to—"

"You're probably more used to it than you know, buster. Mario Celestino unburdened himself to me after he'd let slip something about his long-time lover. We clicked and—"

"You fucked him?"

"Jesus Christ! Have you got even the modicum of respect? No, I didn't fuck him, but Giovanni Scavola had been since before the war. Happy now? There are also a lot of people who shouldn't become involved in this, and if you value your career working in the American diplomatic corps, I suggest that you don't antagonise me any more than you already have. I could not only report you up the line, but also have you named and shamed on the front page of every newspaper in the world when I do my interview for the press."

"What interview? You can't—"

"In case you haven't realised, I'm not an American citizen and you can't stop me from doing anything … unless you want to shoot me in the head."

"You've got me all wrong," he started to say.

"I've got you more right than you believe. Okay, despite my reservations, I guess I'm going to have to spill some milk … just don't cry if you get splashed as a result."

There were gasps of surprise when I revealed the longstanding relationship between Scavola and Mario, the sexual jealousy that was the reason for the assassination of Mario's twin brother during the war, and Scavola planting a spy lover in Mario's bed to find out what he knew about the events that had unfurled in a train carriage at the Vatican City railway station on the ninth of June 1944. The room became ominously quiet when I revealed that there was information in the Vatican archive that attested to the fact that the Holy See knew who had perpetrated the assassination of the nuns, but that, because of the relationship Scavola's wife had with the then pope, the whole business had been locked in the secret archive. Even the secretaries paused and stared at me in disbelief.

"You have witnesses to this alleged sexual relationship between Giovanni Scavola and Mario Celestino?" one of the judges asked me.

I nodded. I didn't want to reveal Gregorio's identity without warning him first.

"And the Vatican archives? How on earth could you—"

"It wasn't me. That's all I can tell you. The documents were discovered by a senior former member of the Italian judiciary whose reputation is beyond reproach. I know the copies could never be admissible in court—"

"Copies? There is material proof?"

"Photographs of the documents, and that's all I can say." I turned to the American lawyer, who suddenly seemed to remember that he was supposed to be on my side.

"This is new knowledge to me," he said to the judges, one of whom gave me leave to speak with him at the back of the room.

"Without conferring to a senior member of your embassy staff," I said before he could speak, "I can't tell you who it is who has the photographic evidence."

"Why on earth not?"

"Use your brain, lieutenant: the identity of that person could compromise US intelligence. How access to the Vatican archives was achieved could create not only an international incident but also have severe consequences for fellow members of your staff."

"Is there any other way of getting those documents from another source? A subpoena, perhaps?"

"I don't know how long you've been in Italy, or understand the way the place works, but the Vatican City is another country. It has its own passports and diplomats."

"Look, I'm a little out of my depth here …"

"I'm not quite sure why you *are* here, to be perfectly honest. I'm going to ask to make a quick telephone call to sort things out."

"What things?"

"Like the reason you're here. I'm going to phone my friend in intelligence and ask him."

"You have a friend in the US intelligence service?"

"Yes, Benjamin Smollet. You know him, of course?"

"Oh, fuck," he said, the colour draining from his face.

★★★★★

I used the number and the code Benjamin had given me. It turned out he was in Rome too, having just arrived. I quickly told him what had happened. He cursed over and over when I revealed the name of the lieutenant who'd been sent as the duty legal officer of the day without actually knowing anything about why I was testifying to a preliminary hearing.

After the lunch break, Benjamin turned up at the courthouse.

"Miss me?" he asked with a cheeky grin.

"I hope you brought back-up?"

"No need, Damson. I'm all the back-up you need, and I know just as much about the situation as you do. I've been brought up to speed by Pellegrini and Venturi. I missed you by about five minutes when I turned up at the hospital to see how Alfonso was getting on."

"Can you keep your puppy on a leash?" I asked, glancing over his shoulder at the lieutenant, who was now nervously smoking a cigarette and glancing in our direction while we were speaking.

Without breaking eye contact with me, he snapped his fingers and the lawyer joined us.

"Ever been to Nome, lieutenant?"

"No, sir. Where's that?"

"It's in Alaska. Didn't they teach you that at school? Now, you're going to forget every word you heard at the hearing so far, unless you want a permanent posting to one of the farther outreaches of our country. Bring me up to speed while Mr O'Reilly has something to eat, then I'll join him to corroborate what you've told me and you can leave. Your reputation for being on the wrong side of the fence more often than not has followed you even here, to Rome. With the wind of change in the air in Washington, you might find your hatred of the pink crowd and the commies comes back to bite you in the ass, just as it's doing to your homo pal Joe McCarthy. Are we clear?"

The man nodded and held out his hand. Benjamin ignored it, sneering at the gesture.

"I'm not your pal, lieutenant, and this wasn't a friendly conversation. Save your handshakes for someone who appreciates them. I'm your senior officer, not some buddy you've had a drink with at the embassy staff bar. You forget to salute me one more time and I'll have your ass handed to you on a plate. Understood?"

The lawyer's hand was trembling slightly as he snapped to attention and saluted. Where did they find these people? I asked myself.

"Now fuck off for five minutes while I talk with Mr O'Reilly," Benjamin continued. "No doubt once I learn what the hell you've done inside the courtroom, I'll owe him an apology on behalf of the US government."

I smiled then spoke in French to him. "That was tough talk."

"He's a cocksucker, Damson. No, not a real one; we could all deal with that. He's the nephew of a Republican senator and has ideas above his station. Why on earth he got assigned to you this morning, I've no idea."

I gave him a quick briefing on what had happened, the lawyer's inappropriate comments about Mario's private life and how I'd nearly put my boot up him. "Thanks for turning up. I owe you one," I said.

"Well, we both know how you could repay that debt," he said under his breath.

He sat next to me during the second half of the interview, the proceedings smoother for his presence and his ability to direct the conversation away from awkward topics, like how our source managed to gain access to the Vatican archives and photograph the evidence. He'd arrived prepared and passed around copies of what Salvatore had photographed, telling the judges that although they could read it, the copies had to return to him, as they were considered property of the US government.

Of course, I had to reveal the reason that Mario had confided in me and had told me so much. However, Benjamin had briefed me and I'd explained it in a way that did not disclose my own sexual identity.

Salvatore arrived at the end of the day, shaking hands with the three judges. It was he who'd convened the meeting, after all. We were asked to leave while he talked to them.

"Spoken with James?" I asked Benjamin while we stood outside, chatting.

"Yes, he'll join us when he can get away."

"Get away from what?" I asked. "Or is it something I'm not allowed to know?"

"He's meeting with some of his colleagues and the Greeks at their embassy."

"What's he doing there?"

"The Brits have a better presence in that country than we do. They've been there longer—stealing their treasures and shipping them home, that sort of thing. His team is looking for Scavola."

"Any leads?"

"Just before you phoned me, a message came through saying that someone who looked like him boarded a ferry in Patras heading for Brindisi."

"Looked like him?"

Benjamin shrugged. "It was from a very reliable source. Need I explain more? The ferry gets in at five tomorrow morning. We've sent people. So has Pellegrini. If it's him they'll get him. The ferry will be made to heave-to before it reaches Italian waters and will be boarded, the passengers and crew unloaded one by one and then the ship searched from top to bottom. If even one person is unaccounted for, they'll scuttle it."

"For fuck's sake, won't that kill Scavola if it's him? What happens if he's trying to hide and can't escape in time?"

"Slimy bastard like him won't drown. Rich people think they're immune."

We were interrupted by the return of Salvatore. "Success! We have a date in court next Monday to start the public proceedings; there's an order issued to arrest Scavola and hold him in custody. The main case against him will take months to prepare, but at least we'll have leverage to 'persuade' the Vatican to release their documents."

"How can you do that?"

"Ah, the shame of front-page stories revealing that they knew what had happened but covered it up to save any involvement by Scavola."

"Would the Italian press really do something like that?" I asked, knowing how much of a precedent something like that would be.

"Probably not, but the international press would be only too happy to. They could even print copies of the photographs I took from the archive. I'm sure my blackmail would work."

"Even the international press might baulk," Benjamin said.

"Ha! That's all been already discussed and given the green light."

Kendall. Who else?

"Oh, by the way. I nearly forgot; he's expecting you two for dinner tonight at his hotel. He asked me to pass on the message."

CHAPTER 18

Dinner that night with Benjamin at Kendall's hotel turned out to be a surprise for many reasons.

Kendall had booked an executive apartment at the Hotel Excelsior on the same floor as, but directly opposite, the suite that Benjamin kept and which he'd taken us to on the night we'd first slept with him after the reception at his embassy.

I learned shortly after James had joined us that I wasn't going to be put into protective custody in the American embassy, as I'd supposed, or at one of the US Army bases around the country, as Luca had been. Instead, Kendall and I had both been assigned agents to follow us around. When I queried the safety issues, I was told that we were basically confined to the hotel until the hearing started on Monday.

I'd spoken with Stefano, asking him to apologise to the guests at Il Fornaio, and was on the point of making up some story for him to tell them when he informed me that Fabrizio had paid them a visit to explain my unexpected absence. Of course, the news had already filtered through about my involvement in the current furore and there had been much excitement and requests to pass on best wishes to me after he'd told them that I had been put into protective custody until the case went to court. Stefano informed me that more than half of the guests had already booked for the first available dates in 1961, anxious to be on the spot, so to speak, after the trial had finished.

Benjamin had invited Kendall and me to spend the night with him, including James, of course, but my mind was full of thoughts of Giancarlo. I knew it seemed to others that I appeared to be blasé, unconcerned about what had happened to him. No one, bar Kendall and Randy, was aware that most of my waking thoughts centred on what might have happened to my partner, where he might be and how I could possibly be involved in the search, which I'd been told by Cosmo had not come up with any leads in the area around Montepulciano. I'd seen the lowered eyes of the people who lived in our community as they passed me by; they suspected the worst, but I was convinced that he'd be all right. I argued to myself that the dead rock-and-roller had nothing to do with his disappearance; that they'd had an early morning assignation and then Giancarlo had gone off on his own on one of his routine evidence hunts without telling anyone. Every time the thought crossed my mind that it was unusual for him not to have at least telephoned after being away for what was now five days, I forced it down, reminding myself of the time he'd once taken the train to the Puglia region without telling anyone to interview witnesses for a case and hadn't made contact for ten days. I'd been frantic at the end of that time.

However, I was acutely aware that everyone around me was walking on eggshells the moment his name came up.

James, after politely declining Benjamin's invitation for a foursome, left us at about eight o'clock, shortly after we'd finished our main course. He explained that his people were sending him to Brindisi to be part of the operation to check the passengers on the ferry from Patras.

I glanced at my watch, asking him how on earth he could get there in time to be part of the interception fleet. He informed me that he was flying. The British consulate had arranged for an aircraft to pick him up at Fiumicino and to drop him at the World War Two airfield of San Pancrazio, a mere four kilometres from Brindisi. He told us not to worry, he was travelling with company: four specialist soldiers from the British SAS brigade.

"You like him, don't you?" Kendall said to Benjamin after James had left us and the table had been cleared.

"I'm not allowed to get involved. But when he's doing the deed, I keep thinking that in another life … what about you two?"

I shrugged. "It is what it is. Kendall's aiming to get married, Giancarlo is my life, and if the two situations can coexist, then that's what it will be."

"Very stoic of you, Damson."

"Sorry about not staying with you tonight. My mind is too full of other things. It doesn't mean that I haven't enjoyed our times together. I'm sure there'll be other occasions."

Benjamin smiled and shrugged a little. "It's not the end of the world. Did Giancarlo tell you about the aide at the embassy he shared with James?" I nodded. "I might ask him and Wesley to come with me to the Colosseum later tonight."

"Well, if you do go, I expect a full report in the morning over breakfast," Kendall said, then leaned forward and spoke very softly. "And I want all the sordid details."

"Ah, yes, I'd almost forgotten how much you like plain talk."

Kendall chuckled a little. "I do remember you liked it when I called you a Yankee cunt …"

"Stop it," Benjamin said, his face split with a Cheshire-cat grin. "Say that again and I'll pull my dick out and do the business right here under the tablecloth."

"Put it in a spoon and I'll feed it to Damson," Kendall said with a wink.

"I think you'd need at least a shot glass."

Their laughter was interrupted by the waiter asking whether we were ready for dessert. I tried vainly to smile; but my heart and thoughts were elsewhere.

★★★★★

Before I got ready for bed, I had a quiet moment at the open window of our suite; it overlooked the Via Veneto. The street below was busy: *fare la passeggiata*—going for a late-night stroll—was an Italian tradition.

After a light night-time snack, people wandered around, greeting each other or just taking the air.

Kendall was, if nothing else, very aware of my mental state. He also knew that sex could calm me down, buoy me up, make me forget, make me remember, make me feel alive. But, foremost, he knew when to press the issue, unlike Giancarlo, who when in need didn't want to know about my morose moods or preoccupations. It had always been our understanding and arrangement that if one of us needed it, the other would always provide it, and never reluctantly either.

He appeared out of the darkness, wrapping his arms around me. I almost flinched. It was an odd reaction, but then I realised I'd been so immersed in my thoughts that he'd startled me a little.

"All right, Aussie?" he asked.

I nodded without turning around. Sometimes words didn't need to be said. He squeezed me gently, kissed the back of my neck then whispered that he was going to bed. I knew it was an invitation but I couldn't stop wondering where Giancarlo was. Maybe it was a lover? He'd had far more of those during our ten years together than I had. In fact, except for Randy and Arnie, and an on-again, off-again connection with one of the local builder's sons who was the same age as me, I was happy with the status quo. Giancarlo was enough for me. He was circumspect, never refused me anything if I needed him, even if he was fresh home from some conquest. His mind was what had initially drawn me to him, and it was his personality and intelligence that was the fuel for the fire that existed between us.

Kendall, however, lit a different flame, one that I continually monitored and starved of oxygen every so often so that I could keep what we had constantly alive. He made no bones about getting married. He'd recently told me he'd been seeing what he considered the perfect woman: a Hungarian who'd come to Italy after the war, not long after her first husband had died. A very wealthy *grófnő*—equivalent of a countess— who'd inherited vast estates in Romania and Austria. She was in his precise target range: fifty-one years old, two adult children who had their own individual bequests from her late husband, very glamorous and until recently living in a relationship with her lady companion, who'd also passed away not more than six months ago. I hadn't felt one twitch of jealousy when he'd told me that, after a night out with her, she'd invited him in. He'd kissed her hand and had confessed that he didn't like penetrative sex—with women, but he didn't say that—but offered to lead her to bliss by other means. She'd asked him to poke out his tongue—he could touch his chin with it, something that had given me a great deal of pleasure over the time we'd been having sex together—then grabbed his tie and dragged him into her apartment with, "You'll do!"

Although obviously I admired him as a man, loving his mind, his ability to take command and appear unruffled no matter what the situation, what I felt for Kendall was far more visceral, a sexual need that, once ignited, threatened to blow apart my everyday life. One thing I did know however, was that I'd never leave Giancarlo for him. No matter how great and overpowering my physical attraction was, my heart and soul belonged to another man. And that other man was missing in action, as I liked to say when he was away on one of his jaunts.

I hadn't meant to spend so much time inspecting my navel, as my brother always called it when I began one of my internal ruminations, but then realised when I checked my watch that I'd been standing at the window for over an hour and had smoked half a dozen cigarettes. I smelled like an ashtray, so tiptoed through the bedroom, closed the bathroom door and got under the shower. I soaped all over, shampooed my hair, towelled dry and brushed my teeth.

Kendall was lying face-down on the bed, the sheet thrown off him, his head nestled in the crook of one arm. I sat on the edge of the bed, allowing my gaze to wander over his body. The thick patch of blond hair in the small of his back had always made my engine purr. I wanted to bury my face between his arse cheeks then run my tongue up and over, through those golden strands and pull them between my teeth.

"Can I fuck you?" I whispered, half-hoping he didn't hear me. I was voicing my thoughts out loud.

He smacked his lips softly and raised his hips a little. "You never have to ask, Damson. You know you're the only one."

He reached up and pulled my head down to his. My half-wish dissolved the moment we kissed. He is, was, and probably would always be, the best kisser I'd ever known.

*****

I woke early. The clock on the chiffonier in the bedroom showed it was a few minutes to five. The interception of the ferry was due to take place in half an hour. Kendall didn't stir when I got out of bed. I pulled on a dressing gown and crossed the corridor to Benjamin's room, the guard outside opening the door for me.

He was on the telephone, naked except for his singlet, and was talking very rapidly in what sounded like Spanish. I sat down in a chair on the other side of the room, but he beckoned me over and slapped his knee. It made me smile so I sat on it. He held a finger to his lips. I understood.

Eventually, he hung up the phone.

"You told me you spoke Spanish … any other languages I should know about?"

"I speak fluent cocksucker, but you already know that," he said with a laugh.

"You never spend enough time for me to really appreciate that before you've got your arse in the air, Ben."

"A man's gotta do what a man's gotta do, my friend."

"Trouble?" I asked.

"The intercept is due shortly. James arrived and his team have been liaising with Pellegrini's men and our team. Because the interception will take place in international waters, there's no clear jurisdiction. However, the Brits had been keeping a close eye on Scavola in Greece, so they made a strong case for leading the operation. Probably better, because our guys can be quite trigger-happy."

"How long have they been surveilling Scavola? Why didn't they apprehend him in over there?"

Benjamin rubbed his fingers together. "The Greeks are more corrupt than the Italians… or our Republican party, if you can believe that. Where's Apollo?"

"Still asleep."

"I rather hoped you might come a-knocking last night, both of you."

"Didn't you end up going to the Colosseum with Wesley?"

"Nah, decided against it. His ass is rounder and younger than mine and I'm sure I'd end up fingering my own hole while I watched him take on all the talent."

I chuckled, despite my sombre mood. "You have a way with words, Mr Smollet."

"You know, Damson, it's been great to meet you. You're probably only one of two people in the world I could say such things to and not feel embarrassed over the words that come out of my mouth."

"Well, I'm honoured, and, as you know, no stranger to sexy talk. I'm sorry you missed out last night, but my mind was elsewhere, sorry … well, mostly elsewhere. I did succumb to Kendall's charms in the wee hours of the morning."

"Takes your mind off things; works for me anyway."

"Yes, it mostly does for me too, but, great as it was for half an hour, Giancarlo's disappearance is more troubling this time than his previous absences."

"I know it won't help much, but we're still helping to look for him. As he's so intrinsic to the case against Scavola, I had little problem convincing our people to fly in some specialists. They should arrive around midday and will head straight to Tuscany from Aviano."

"Talking of Aviano, any news of Luca?"

"We decided to take Gregorio, the carpenter from Rome, and his wife to join him; just as a precaution, you understand."

I was very pleased to hear that Gregorio was safe with Luca. I didn't think he was in any immediate danger, but one never knew. Surely Scavola would have remembered him from the war, especially in view of the fact that he'd been Mario Celestino's twin brother's lover.

"One thing puzzles me," I said, rising from his lap. He pulled open my dressing gown and kissed my dick. I ruffled his hair then moved away. I really wasn't in the mood.

"What puzzles you, Damson?"

"Why would Scavola want to leave Greece and come back to Italy? It doesn't make sense. From what I understand of the relationship between the two countries, he'd be safer in Greece, and, if he wanted to, it's an easy escape through Macedonia to Bulgaria and then Turkey. Why come back to Italy? Are you one hundred per cent sure that he's on the ferry? Are you sure it's not some sort of plan to divert attention so he can go elsewhere?"

"At the same time as we intercept the ferry from Patras, a crack team is due to invade the villa in which he's been hiding outside Chalkis. We know several of his senior cronies were with him there and … well, we have insurance to make them talk if he's in neither place."

"Insurance?"

"Their family members are in custody, Damson."

Someone knocked heavily at the door, making us both turn to look. A moment later, one of the guards opened the door. "You'd better put that phone back on the hook, sir," he said, nodding at the receiver, which the American had apparently forgotten to replace in its cradle.

"What's the problem?"

Before the man could speak, the lawyer who was supposed to have been representing me in court pushed the guard aside and burst into the room. His double-take at seeing me standing with my dressing gown agape and his boss naked except for the singlet he was wearing was memorable.

"Sir, there's been an incident. You need to get on the blower to the ambassador."

"An incident?"

"The ferry terminal at Brindisi has been blown to bits by a bomb. There are dozens dead, including some of our own."

"Oh, for fuck's sake!" I almost shouted, then it hit me. "Where's James?"

"Viscount Langley? He's on one of the boarding vessels," Benjamin said.

"You have to stop them. Scavola's not on the ferry." I yelled. "The bomb at the terminal is a diversion!"

★★★★★

"Where's Alessandro? Can you get him on the line?"

"Hold your horses, Damson," Benjamin said, then nodded at the telephone, indicating to the lieutenant that he should answer it. It had started ringing almost as soon as he'd replaced the receiver in its cradle. "Slow down; you're gabbling in your Australian accent. I can't follow what you're trying to say."

"He must have known you'd been following him and were going to intercept the ferry. The bomb is a diversion to create chaos and direct attention away from the ship."

"But our sources are reliable, as were those of the Brits. He was seen boarding the ferry."

"Someone needs to radio the captain. Find out if there were any emergencies, whether the ferry had to stop at sea or any irregularity."

He suddenly became very solemn, almost hard-faced; I supposed this was what he looked like at work, carrying out his normal intelligence tasks. I was about to move closer to listen in and to hear anything I could from the conversation but the lieutenant/lawyer moved to stand in my way.

"I suggest you cover up … sir," he said.

I poked him in the chest. "Or what, dickhead? Now get your nose out of my face!"

Our almost toe-to-toe confrontation was interrupted by Kendall bursting into the room. "Oh God, Damson," he said.

"You've heard?"

"Heard what?"

"About the bomb," I explained.

"What bomb? I've just been on the phone. My mother called. Father's had a heart attack and I have to go home. I'm sorry; I've chartered a DC-8 to take me. Wesley will take charge of things while I'm away."

At that same time, Benjamin started yelling down the phone. I caught the odd word, among them "Corfu". To the lawyer's absolute amazement, I grabbed Kendall by the lapels of his dressing gown and kissed him. "Just give me one very quick moment. Ask this bozo to tell you what's happened. I'm sorry, but this is extremely urgent."

I pulled at Benjamin's arm, speaking in French, telling him I needed to say something very important. He put his hand over the receiver. "What is it, Damson?"

"I don't need to know what you said and to whom, but I did overhear a mention of Corfu. Did you know there's a direct ferry service from there to Venice?" His eyes widened. "You need to speak to Alessandro Pellegrini urgently. The local police in Venice need to intercept any incoming connecting ferry out of Corfu that Scavola could have switched to."

For the next hour, chaos ruled in the room. I grabbed a pair of jockey shorts for Benjamin from his bedroom and threw them to him, did up my dressing gown and told the lieutenant/lawyer to forget everything he'd seen.

However, Kendall had been the most level-headed of us all. So many American resources had been funnelled into the interception of the ferry, and, with the number of dead, their focus was on Brindisi. Benjamin told us that his office would make an aircraft available, but not for four hours—far too late to get to Venice before the arrival of the ferry from Corfu. Kendall offered his private plane, which was hangared at Fiumicino. However, since he was flying to Sydney immediately, he told Benjamin that he'd have to find someone else to pilot it. He, two of his men and I could fly to the airfield that Kendall had landed at before, near Venice, and meet up with James, whom Benjamin had spoken with over ship-to-shore radio. James had offered to take Pellegrini with him in the plane he'd flown in to Brindisi and rendezvous with us in Venice.

*****

It was a forty-five-minute drive to Fiumicino. I drove Kendall's car, which had been delivered from Mestre. I was anxious for him; he was desperate to get home in case his father died. All going well, it would take two days to fly to Sydney. On his shoulders was the weight of the international Travert organisation: he was his father's successor.

"I don't know when I'll be back, Damson," he said, his hand resting on my knee, two black limousines following closely behind us. "But I will be back. I promise you."

I nearly told him not to make promises that he couldn't keep. I'd seen his father in operation in Sydney, running the vast media empire. There was no way Kendall could dump that on anyone else if his father died. It would take months, if not years, for him to not only learn the high end of the business. My heart sank a little more, but I took his hand in mine and squeezed it.

"I'm not going anywhere soon," I said. "You'll be back when you're back."

"The plane will have to refuel many times on the way. Alitalia hasn't been given permission to make commercial flights to Australia yet. It won't be until 1963; that's what the ambassador told me. I'll phone home every time we stop on the way to check on father's condition and I'll also call Randy to keep him up to date. He's the only one who won't be running around like you."

"I'll arrange it with him—"

"No need. I've already spoken with him."

Benjamin had found a pilot among his staff, a relatively young Korean War fighter pilot who hadn't been in a cockpit for a few years but, after five minutes at the controls with Kendall, told us to buckle up. I grabbed Kendall in a bear hug, told him to travel safely, then watched as he drove to the other side of the airfield, where I could see the large jet waiting for him, gleaming in the morning sunlight.

"I'm sorry about the way I treated your lieutenant this morning," I said to Benjamin in French as we taxied to the edge of the runway.

"He's so stuck-up. I hate his type."

"What type is that?"

"Men who protest too much, but don't protest when you stick your dick in them."

"What, him? No way," I said.

"Maybe you didn't notice that he couldn't take his eye off your cock all morning while we were sorting things out? He looked quite disappointed when you finally tied up your dressing gown."

"You talking about him or yourself?" I said, forcing a grin.

He chuckled. "This brings back memories."

"Of what?"

"Before battles during the war, the nonsensical humour. Surely you guys were the same?"

"Yes. Anything to keep your mind off what might happen."

Was there going to be trouble? Of course there would be; I should have thought of it beforehand. We'd been focused on the wrong place. After all, why would Scavola have been heading for Brindisi? No doubt he'd have put contingency plans in place; he'd have stashed passports, gold bars, traveller's cheques, but not in Brindisi. Far more likely in Venice, which was the centre of his operations. He was bound to have planned somewhere to go to start a new life, like the hundreds of Nazis who'd fled to Argentina and Brazil after the war. He was no one's fool. He'd have had protection planned in advance when he staged the explosion at the ferry terminal—I had absolutely no doubt he was behind it. Therefore, he'd obviously know that the police would eventually follow him home to Venice. When I voiced my fears, saying we needed to be extra careful, Benjamin agreed with me.

*****

The airfield, as Kendall had said, was indeed tiny. We watched as James's aircraft landed, twenty minutes after we'd arrived, coming to a halt at the end of the runway just a few metres from the overgrown field at its end.

Alessandro was met by half a dozen police in uniform and a handful of Italian soldiers, all armed. I listened to the conversation, barely under-standing most of it because of the thick Venetian dialect. However, the gist of it was that they would allow the ferry to dock, then, for passport inspection, funnel the passengers one by one through a narrow gateway. Scavola's henchman, the weasel-like man who'd delivered Alvise's pay, was there as a back-up to identify Scavola in case he was in disguise, his wife and five children in "protective custody" to make sure the weasel didn't try anything stupid. The man was a coward, Alessandro explained to me on the *motoscafo* during our crossing of the lagoon, a dozen similar vessels following us.

The San Basilio ferry terminal was empty when we arrived. Quite unusual; twenty minutes before a ferry arrival, the area was usually packed with family members and representatives of the various hotels around the city waiting to conduct guests to the places they'd booked to stay in.

The plan was to augment the terminal staff with police and soldiers in plain clothes, armed soldiers and *carabinieri* hidden in the surrounding area in case there were problems. Instead of the usual two gangplanks used for disembarkation, it would be explained aboard the ferry that due to technical difficulties, only the forward exit would be available and that, because of staffing issues, disembarkation might take longer than usual.

Alessandro was worried that Scavola would be accompanied by some of his henchmen, who could also be armed.

It was close to midday when the arrival bell sounded. That meant that the ferry had been seen rounding the Punta Sabbioni and would be docking in about thirty minutes. The terminal was on the Zattere, the promenade that stretched along the Grand Canal waterfront, and was perhaps a fifteen-minute stroll to the city centre. Not being a separate building but part of a stretch of structures along the promenade, it was impossible to isolate completely without evacuating the area, which would immediately become obvious to anyone on the ferry watching the ship come into dock.

The *Appia* was a larger ship than I'd imagined. In all the times I'd been to Venice, I'd somehow missed seeing it. When it hove into view, its grey-painted hull reminded me of a chunky wartime destroyer rather than the wooden steam-powered vessel I'd imagined. A large Italian flag flew at its stern, a single tug helping it into berth.

About two hundred metres from the dock, there seemed to be a commotion on deck: passengers running about, the sounds of whistle blasts reaching our ears. Something was definitely wrong. One of Benjamin's agents was standing next to James and me—we'd taken a vantage point in a window on the first floor of one of the buildings behind the dock. I grabbed his binoculars.

"Oh, fuck!" I said, then handed them to James.

"What am I looking for?"

"There on the starboard side of the bow, about ten degrees to the right, coming across the lagoon."

"What the hell are they?"

"I've heard about them but never seen them: gondolas with outboard motors attached."

I grabbed his arm and, followed by the man from whom I'd taken the binoculars, we thudded down the stairs to the dock. Alessandro had seen what I had too and had dispatched a police motorboat to the port side of the *Appia*, which was hidden from our view. Despite calls from the dockside and a whistle blast from the ferry, the police motorboat collided with the tug, which had let go its towline and had started to move away from the ship.

Alessandro swore, then ran down the dockside, calling to a few of his men to follow him. I suspected he was heading to the *motoscafo* in which we'd arrived.

"Come on." James started running in the opposite direction. I knew there was a small dock about fifty metres away where *motoscafo* drivers waited in their boats, ready to take passengers from arriving ferries to their waterside destinations around the city. Binocular man followed after us, and immediately after him, running faster than I thought possible, was Benjamin.

James thrust a handful of lire into the hands of the owner of the largest, most powerful-looking craft, yelling to him to "Follow that boat!"

"Which one?" the man asked, as the flotilla of outboard motor-equipped gondolas dispersed, setting off at high speed and in different directions across the lagoon away from the *Appia*. If Scavola had indeed been on board and had been picked up by one of the small craft, discovering which one was going to be a nightmare.

Benjamin landed in the boat just as we started to speed away from the dock, making a flying leap from the jetty and landing next to me just as I heard James yell at the driver, "That one, to the north. Go after it."

"Why that one?" Benjamin asked.

"Because there's a very tall woman standing in the prow holding a machine gun." He handed the binoculars to him, and Benjamin then passed them to me.

There was a stiff breeze and the water was choppy. Despite the speed of our craft, it plunged up and down as it ploughed over the peaks and shallows of the lagoon's surface, making it quite difficult to keep the binoculars trained steadily on the gondola. I grabbed Benjamin's shoulder for support. It had to be Scavola; the figure was tall, dressed Greek-widow style, all in black with a black scarf covering the head and wearing dark glasses.

The blasted gondola must have had an exceptional outboard motor. I watched as other gondolas peeled off in different directions, some carrying more than just the driver, others empty apart from the person at the helm. They were obviously diversions. Our speedboat driver was overprotective of his engine and we started to lose ground, the distance increasing between us and the gondola on which I was sure Scavola was making his escape.

James pulled off his Rolex and gave it to the man, yelling at him over the roar of the engine. All of a sudden the boat pulled out an extra few knots and I almost fell back with the acceleration.

"What are you thinking?" I asked Benjamin, who'd started to look very angry.

"Just fucking furious that we have no way of telling the Italians where we are."

"I think Alessandro is far more astute than you're giving him credit for. Either he or one of his people will have seen what we did and where we're headed."

He scanned behind us with the binoculars, holding on to my shoulder to steady himself. "Well, I can't see anyone following us, so he'd better fucking hurry up. Where's the gondola heading anyway?" We'd passed the Sacca di San Biagio on our port side a few minutes ago and were speeding across the bay that separated Venice from the mainland.

"Fusina," the driver of the boat yelled over his shoulder after James asked him.

"It's a small, rather commercial industrial town. Used to be full of historical buildings, but long since turned into factories and shipping docks," I said.

"And the main depot for the distribution of products made by Zaini industries," James explained with a scowl.

"Don't tell me Scavola owns that company …" I said.

"Got it in one, Damson," my English friend replied, withdrawing his pistol from its holster. He checked the magazine. The *motoscafo* driver glanced at it nervously, then inched up the speed. The boat sat back in the water, its outboard motor churning up the sea behind us. However, the gondola we were following, being very narrow and with next to no draught, sped across the water faster than our motorboat. Scavola and a person who was waiting for him dockside had disappeared into a narrow *calle*. They had a lead of perhaps thirty seconds before we docked, a tiny amount of time, but which seemed to stretch on forever while I watched them scamper into the alleyway through the binoculars.

With a cry of frustration, Benjamin and binocular man leapt from our boat the moment it reached the dockside at Fusina, the driver of the gondola staring in amazement as they gave chase.

"Take this, Damson," James said, offering me his sidearm.

"No, keep it," I said. "I have the gun you gave me."

I jumped out of the speedboat after him, but he turned and grabbed my arm. "Stay here. Someone needs to keep an eye on the—"

With a roar of the engine, the gondola in which Scavola had arrived zoomed away from the dock. The owner of the speedboat we'd come in prevaricated, his hands hovering over the ignition button.

"Don't even think of leaving before we're ready to go back to the city," I said. I opened my wallet and emptied it, handing him ten thousand lire, probably more money than he'd earned in the past three months. He fell back heavily into the driver's seat, staring at me in amazement. I could understand his confusion. Why were we chasing after a Greek woman and her companion? Of course, without the binoculars he wouldn't have been able to see the machine gun "she" had been cradling in her arms; but he had seen Benjamin and binocular man draw their weapons before running off, and then the pistol in James's hand when he'd offered it to me.

I'd lied to James; I thought he needed his weapon more than I would. I'd left my gun with the officer on duty outside Alfonso's hospital room. I'd been frisked before being allowed to visit him and in the confusion of being hustled away when the limousines had arrived to take me to Rome had simply forgotten to retrieve it. But, if there was to be some sort of confrontation in the maze of small alleys and laneways that led off from the dockside, James would need his gun.

I squatted at the edge of the dock, chatting to our speedboat driver, testing out what little Venetian dialect I had, occasionally checking my watch to see how much time had gone by since my friends had disappeared down the narrow alleyway, all the time my ears primed for the sound of a gunshot or voices yelling. Five, ten, then fifteen minutes went by. The driver was sitting with his head down, having taken off his shoe, and was trying to pick skin off a bunion on his big toe when a sound behind us made him look up. He froze.

"Don't do anything stupid," a voice said. I heard the click of a pistol being cocked; the sound made me aware it wasn't a modern weapon.

"I've already done something stupid, Scavola," I said. I hadn't thought for a moment he'd come back to the dockside and I'd left myself vulnerable, my back turned to the alleyway down which he'd disappeared, and without a weapon. "What brings you back here? Bra strap broken?"

"Bra? What is that word?" he asked rather angrily, so I switched to Italian and asked him whether he'd dropped a tampon from his purse when he'd jumped out of the gondola. Glancing over my shoulder at him, I tried to smother a smile; not a pleasant smile either. The scarf he'd been wearing over his head had slipped down around his neck and despite wearing sunglasses—which had now disappeared, as had his machine gun—he'd plastered on thick, aquamarine-coloured eye shadow and far too much make-up in an effort to hide his dark five o'clock shadow.

"Rip your stockings too?" I said, trying to goad him to hit me so I could attempt to disarm him. I knew I was poking a bear with a stick, but sometimes provocation in difficult circumstances could open an opportunity … for both players, unfortunately. Instead, he clobbered me hard over the head with his gun. Christ, it was a wallop and a half! I felt the sting right through to the bridge of my nose.

"Eyes front. Get in the boat, O'Reilly," he ordered.

He prodded me again with the barrel of his pistol so I did what he asked, stepping gingerly into the speedboat and wondering how I could place my weight and somehow tip the boat when Scavola got in after me. However, it was constructed of heavy marine plywood, built to cruise the coastal area on the ocean side of the Lido. It rocked a little, but not much.

"You," he said to the petrified owner of the motorboat. "San Giorgio in Alga, and full throttle. If I think you're not doing as I ask, I'll shoot you in the head."

He'd taken a step back from me, so I glanced at the dockside as we sped off. There was no sign of James, Benjamin or binocular man. San

Giorgio in Alga? Why the hell did he want to go to an unoccupied, barren island in the lagoon? As far as I knew, the last time it had been used was at the end of the war by the Germans to train underwater divers. Maybe he had another getaway boat stored there. I resigned myself to the fact that I'd have to wait until we arrived to find out.

"What do you want with me?" I asked.

"Hostage," he replied, in English. "Him too," he added. I guessed he meant the owner of the boat. "You're both expendable. He's only useful until I get where I need to go."

"And me?"

"Ah, they all love you. You're my bargaining chip."

"Where's Giancarlo?" I asked.

He snorted. "I've read *Living with Monsters* three times now."

I tried to turn to look at him, but he nudged me between the shoulder blades with his pistol. "Eyes straight ahead," he ordered.

"They'll get you, you know," I said. "There's nowhere in the world you'll be safe."

The driver of the speedboat, unable to understand what we were talking about, was looking more anxious by the minute, constantly wiping his brow on his shirt sleeve.

"You've no idea of the places I could go, O'Reilly, the countries that'd be happy to have someone with my millions of American dollars, the national leaders I could sway—"

Without warning, the driver of the speedboat threw himself over the side of the boat. It was all I needed. I bent forward quickly, thrust my hands between my legs, grabbed Scavola's ankles and pulled with all my might. He fell backwards, discharging a shot into the air. I'd noticed the speedboat's grappling pole near my left foot, so snatched it up and whacked the side of his face so hard I wondered whether I'd fractured his skull. The struggle for the gun was brief; I had it out of his hand before he knew what happened.

Stepping backwards, I took the helm of the boat and steered it out into the bay, the gun pointed at his face.

"Where's Giancarlo?" I asked again.

"Fuck you, you cunt!" he mumbled.

I shot him on the crest of the hip. He roared with pain. I turned off the engine and crouched down beside him, the pistol under his chin. He looked frightened, clutching the wound with both hands, blood oozing between his fingers.

"*Porco Dio! Mi hai sparato!*" he said in a quiet voice, his hand over the wound and his eyes wide in amazement.

"Yes, I fucking shot you. That was for calling me a cunt. There's another bullet for the other hip if you don't tell me where Giancarlo is." My voice was calm and cold, despite the rage in my belly.

"I told you I read your fucking book three times," he said, his eyelids fluttering.

"No! Don't you pass out on me!" I slapped his face with my other hand, the gun pushed into the soft triangle under his jaw.

He tried to spit in my face but started to lose consciousness. I shook him.

"Where's Giancarlo?" I shouted, thrusting the gun down the front of my trousers while I slapped his cheeks harder and harder with both hands. "Where the fuck is Giancarlo?" I yelled.

He came to briefly. "I'm going to die, aren't I?"

"You will if I let you bleed out, and even more quickly if I shoot you in the other hip," I said, retrieving the gun from my pants. "You have a choice. My friends will come looking for me very soon once they notice the boat has gone, and the police are probably scouring the area right now."

"Choice?" His voice was becoming weak. I knew he wasn't going to die; it was the shock of being shot. I remembered how to disable people, how taking a bullet in the iliac crest could mean it taking months if not years for relative full mobility to return. But Scavola wasn't to know that. Mental rather than physical torture right now was the aim of my game.

"Yes. I can tie my belt to the steering wheel and set the course for the open ocean. I'll tie you up so you can't move, then jump into the water, just as the driver did. I'll be picked up eventually, especially if I choose a spot close to one of those enormous buoys, like the one we're just passing. This *motoscafo* will head out eventually into the Adriatic

Sea and you'll die alone, your millions of American dollars useless to help you."

"The choice?" His voice came out hoarsely, through gritted teeth. I knew the pain was great, but he was trying to put on a brave face despite the fear in his eyes.

"Either I let you die, or I turn the boat around and take you back to the mainland for medical treatment. Oh, I'll call the police, don't worry; you're not going to get away."

The fury in his eyes changed to something unlike anything I'd seen before, animal-like in its intensity. I cocked the pistol.

"Now, I'll ask you one last time, where's Giancarlo?"

He fainted on me. It wasn't pretend; I saw his eyes start to glaze. I stood, running a hand through my hair, wondering how long he'd be out. Then I noticed a speedboat approaching—a speedboat with a flashing blue light on its prow. I'd told Scavola the police would be scouring the bay and it seemed I'd been spotted.

As the boat got closer, I saw Alessandro standing on the bow waving his arms. I signalled back, then dropped to my knees, pressing my thumb into the bullet wound on Scavola's hip. He woke screaming with pain.

I pushed the gun between his eyes and shouted, "Where the fuck is Giancarlo?"

He laughed, grabbed my hand weakly and managed to hoick up some sputum, which he spat out; it landed on my chin. "Feel familiar? My men told me he said you liked it when he squirted on your face."

Alessandro pulled me off him as I was in the process of turning his face into mincemeat. "What the hell have you done, Damson?" he yelled over his shoulder while kneeling over Scavola.

"Nothing I could help," I said, furious with myself. The Irish in me had taken over and it had suddenly dawned on me that perhaps I'd killed the only person who knew where I could find the man I loved.

EPILOGUE

Sunday 13 October, 1985

"How long will you be?"

"Give me half an hour," I yelled back.

He repeated the same question and I replied once more. He obviously didn't hear my response because the question came for a third time.

So, I sighed, got up from my desk—which was covered in documents and a pile of my diaries—and walked to the top of the stairs. I repeated my reply with my hands funnelled at the sides of my mouth like a megaphone.

I frequently regretted buying his latest gadget, a top-of-the-range vacuum cleaner. He used it far too frequently and, of late, this sort of exchange had become nothing out of the ordinary. Shouted conversations over the sound of the vacuum cleaner had become a regular part of our daily life since I'd bought the damned thing in a sale two months ago.

We had a long drive ahead of us, one which by now we were quite used to. However, this time our trip was for a few special reasons. We'd been invited as guests to the Vatican to be part of the mass to celebrate the elevation of Sister Ursula to "Blessed" status, something that had been twenty-five years in the making. Initially there'd been some pushback by members of the Curia who'd actively supported Pope Pius XII during the war. However, after the revelation during Scavola's trial that the Vatican had sanctioned her assassination, wheels had begun to move very quickly and, although no apology had been issued, a strong movement among younger members of the clergy had led to her veneration across the Catholic world. As she had performed no verified miracles, she'd never be beatified, but shrines dedicated to her had popped up all over the country since details of what had happened at the Vatican train station had become known.

Scavola had sat poker-faced during his trial, brazenly trying to state that everything he'd done had been on orders of the then fascist regime. However, his weasel-faced accomplice had been only too happy to reveal transgressions that had occurred after Badoglio had taken power, when Scavola could not argue that what he'd done was legal—yes, he did actually say that, and it had sickened me to the pit of my stomach.

It was the accomplice who'd revealed that the exposed, slaughtered Americans had not been killed for any racial reasons. It was simpler than that: one of the group who had always hung out together had whistled at a local Italian girl, the unrequited love object of one of Scavola's team. The black ribbons tied around the bases of the Americans' penises were in fact the armbands worn by the group, who, on the same day, had just attended a funeral mass for a local woman caught in crossfire in a street fight. Although there was no proof, they had believed that she was shot by the Allies, and the soldiers had been slaughtered as some sort of misguided retribution. The Nazis had been doing similar things, he'd argued, then shrugged when confronted with the barbarity of his team's actions.

However, the biggest eruption in the court, requiring the intervention of the attending *carabinieri*, had been when Scavola's weasel-faced accomplice had explained why the children's bodies had been dumped at the door of the convent. They'd simply been left tied up in their bags in the boot of Scavola's car for twenty-four hours, no one checking to see if they were all right, and they'd suffocated. Weasel face said he had just followed Scavola's orders and dumped them outside the convent.

Luca had had to be restrained. He'd tried to jump over the railing to get at the man but had been held back by Salvatore's assistants. He'd howled loudly at the description of the shooting of the nuns; Sister Ursula had treated him like the child he'd presumed she'd had to give up before she became a nun.

I closed the notebook I'd been going through that focused on the trial, rubbing the bridge of my nose between my thumb and forefinger. It was such a long time ago now, but, every time we returned to Rome, memories of that *processo* flooded my mind. However, I hoped this trip would be different and prove to be a joyous occasion. There'd been negotiations for weeks to catch up with all the actors involved around the time of Mario Celestino's death and our involvement in the Scavola case … those still alive, that was. Many of the people involved had passed away, including my dear Francophile friend Salvatore Venturi; the greatest personal loss of all was the death of my beloved friend Randy McCall, who two years ago, at the age of seventy-five, had dropped dead suddenly while having lunch with Arnie and his sister, Carla.

Alessandro Pellegrini had promised to be there, as had Cosmo, Luca and Gregorio. Whether Benjamin or James would turn up was anyone's guess. We'd seen them over the years and they'd both come to stay many, many times, although their visits had never coincided— whether that was planned or not, I never got a straight answer from either of them. James's "pater", as he'd always called him, had also passed away, and James, as the new earl, had a great deal on his plate. Benjamin had left the intelligence service not long after Scavola was locked up. He'd accepted a job as Kendall's chief of security in Europe, based in Rome but working mostly in the UK—possibly so he could be closer to James; that was my wicked thought, anyway.

As for Kendall, it had taken him more than three years to return to Italy and by then much had changed. Twenty years ago, he'd married his Hungarian countess, who these days, at the age of seventy-plus, demanded little of him other than a squeaky-clean public profile and his arm on the occasions he was in Europe and she needed an escort. When he wasn't around, her son filled that spot at her side, the son Kendall had soon discovered was happy to warm his stepfather's bed. I suspected that she knew, but he'd told me often enough that it was all very hush-hush.

I rarely thought of Scavola these days; far too much of what had surrounded him was still too painful to revisit. He'd died in prison quite gruesomely: a copycat of the murder of the British king, Edward II. He'd been found in the prison workshop wearing just his shirt, his legs tied up over his head, impaled by the long metal handle of a workbench vice. The coroner's report stated that it had probably been heated in the metal-working furnace to red-hot before insertion.

It was only recently, two years ago, that Luca had confessed to me that he'd paid prison guards to kill Scavola just a few months after he'd been locked up in Rome's Regina Coeli prison. The young man suffered no remorse for what he'd done; Scavola had been responsible for the murder of not only the nuns and his childhood friends during the war but also his mentor and benefactor, Mario Celestino. He'd inherited so much money from the dead film star that the eye-watering sum he'd reported to me that he'd handed over to a middleman to pay twenty-two guards—some to perform the assassination and others to keep schtum—was a mere drop in the ocean of his fortune. News of the success of Scavola's violent and painful death had allowed him the first restful night in decades, and there'd been scenes of jubilation in the streets and outside many churches across the land.

The sound of hoovering stopped. I could imagine him downstairs, running his finger over pieces of furniture, checking for dust, before winding the vacuum cleaner cord between the thumb and finger of his left hand and around his elbow before placing it on its hook on the machine. It was an action I'd seen more than enough times and it always made me smile; he'd invariably catch me with a grin on my face and say, "What?"—semi-puzzled but somehow pleased at our little exchange.

"Are you okay?" he asked a minute or two later, poking his head into the study.

"Yes, I'm fine; just cracking on. Do you think I need to take most of this stuff for reference?"

"It's an interview with Wesley, Damson. He was around at the time and he's a researcher. Besides, he knows more about you than anyone else in the world, apart from me."

I beckoned him over; he gave a pretend sigh of exasperation but sat on my lap facing me, his arms around my neck. I kissed him.

"Did you pack your tuxedo?" I asked. It was a rather pointless question because he never missed a trick.

"Yes, and I checked your suitcases too."

"Did I forget anything?"

"Nope," he said. "Let me go, Damson. I need to water the garden before we leave."

"There's nothing stopping you… it's me in your arms, not the other way around. Go! I'll be ready shortly." I slapped his arse as he left me.

While we were away, we were to attend the Rome première of the film version of my book, *Living with Monsters*, which had been a long time in the making, mainly because of arguments that had dragged on for years over the proviso I'd had written into the contract for the book rights. Casting had been foremost. I'd "allowed"—a word that had almost led to fisticuffs—the director to cast the French/Italian actor who played me. The casting of Lorenzo, Giancarlo and the other locals portrayed in the movie had been problematic until I'd yelled that all Italian films were dubbed even when the actors were Italian themselves. The movie was filmed in three languages, English, Italian and French, which turned out to be a production headache. However, the rushes I'd seen were marvellous. Had I really engaged in such derring-do? The scene in the olive grove at night with Frank White, Baldi, Alfonso and me was truly edge-of-the-seat stuff.

Over the past twenty-five years, I'd written two more books in the same genre as my earlier stories: *Living with the Enemy*—a book I'd been in the middle of writing at the time of the Scavola case—and *Living with Evil*, an historical record of the war in Italy, the Blackshirts, Scavola, Mario and the repercussions of that night in 1944. Like all my other books based on true events, I left out references to the characters' sexuality, even though we were now living in more modern, more accepting times. There'd also been a long series of *The Mouse in the House*, the children's stories I'd written with Stefano and illustrated myself. Not only had we published sixteen books about our mouse, but it had also become a very well-known cartoon series on Italian television.

However, despite looking forward to the ceremony at the Vatican and the première of the movie, I was not looking forward to a week of filmed interviews with Wesley Arnott, whom I'd first met in 1960 when he'd arrived to cover the Olympic Games in Rome. Now one of the world's most renowned documentary-makers and interviewers, he was piecing together a biography of Damson O'Reilly for a series of five episodes to be shown on the BBC's flagship programme *Spotlight*. Even though we hadn't started, I'd been told by Kendall that the series had already been sold to most English-speaking countries. There'd also be a local Italian version, which required re-filming with an Italian dubbing Wesley's voice and me answering the same questions in Italian. It was going to be a major pain in the arse; I could feel it already.

The phone rang.

"Hello, Damson, it's me, James."

"Well fuck me sideways, Your Grace." I laughed down the phone. "Don't tell me you're finally going to show your skinny arse in Rome."

He chuckled back. We'd become very close over the years. "Listen, old bean," he said—he knew I loved it when he pretended to be all "horse and hounds Pommy"—"I have a favour to ask."

"Go ahead."

"When are you leaving?"

I glanced at the wall clock in my study. "Half an hour, give or take."

"Any chance you have room for another person in your car? I mean me, not just some random person."

"Of course—where are you?"

"Walking up Chemin Saint-Pierre."

"What the fuck are you doing in Vence?" I asked.

"Wanted to see you … see you both. It's been too long. Where's his lordship?"

"Well, he's finished hoovering, we've packed, and he said he was going out to water the garden while he waited for me to get myself in order."

"Lovely! Don't tell him I called. I want to surprise him."

"Of course not. He'll be delighted to see you. But you were taking a bit of a risk … we could have left at any time and then you'd have been stranded." He still didn't drive after all these years.

"Sweetheart, it's me you're talking to. Do you think I don't know exactly where you are at any moment of the day? Besides, I need to call in at Pienza on the way and I know you were intending to make a pit stop there anyway."

"What do you need in Pienza?" I asked, rather puzzled that he knew I'd be stopping there to spend a few minutes at Lorenzo's grave, something I did every time I returned to Italy.

"We have a meeting with a certain American at the Bar Azzurro,"

"Oh, really? *We* have a meeting?"

"Yes, he's expecting both of you too. Besides, you're not the only one with ties there. I have a wedding present for Cosmo's daughter."

"I hope it's not a gun."

He laughed. So easy to forget that I'd lived in France for so long now, and only visited Italy when I needed to. James spent a lot of time in his parents' flat in Florence, so I heard from Carla, who these days lived downstairs in our apartment.

I smiled after hanging up the phone. James, here in Vence? I loved it when he visited.

There had been so much sadness, public scrutiny and turmoil during and after the Scavola case that I'd become unhappy living at La Mensola. Years ago, I'd promised to take Giancarlo to France to see the area I'd lived in for a year and a half before I'd moved to Italy. My heart had sunk when I'd pulled up outside Madame Tremeau's house; it was very neglected, falling to pieces, its roof half gone—but it had had a *For Sale* sign on the front gate. Impulsively, I'd decided to buy it, and that was where my man and I lived now, and had done so for the past twenty years. A test-drive of life in France for twelve months had turned into permanent residence.

I still owned La Mensola, of course, and we went back several times a year to meet guests at Il Fornaio and to liaise with Stefano and his two eldest sons, men now in their mid-twenties, who managed the whole shebang for me. The older of the boys, newly married and with his own children, lived in La Mensola these days and kept the sticky-beaks at bay.

I heard shouting from the garden, so walked out into the hallway to the window that overlooked it. There was James, his arms around the man I loved; they were twirling each other in the air.

And God, how I loved him. More than anything in the world. Not the passion I'd had for Lorenzo, the lust I'd felt for Kendall or the intellectual bonding I'd had with Giancarlo: Alfonso had been my world for twenty-plus years now.

I should have listened more carefully to Scavola on the motorboat that day back in 1960 when he told me that he'd read *Living with Monsters* three times. It had been Cosmo who'd suggested that, after three months of searching for Giancarlo, we should check all the locations where the bodies in that book had been found. And that was how we'd discovered him, in the charcoal burner's hut, a few miles from the Mori brothers' farm, lured from Pienza by a man Scavola's men had paid to seduce him and then had killed after kidnapping Giancarlo. The mystery of the rock-and-roller solved, a puzzle that had led to too many dead ends.

It had broken me, literally. I'd barely kept it together during Scavola's trial, sitting there every day listening to him waffle on, watching the smug look on his face as he tried to outsmart my friend Venturi, who'd come out of self-imposed hibernation to testify at the case. Scavola's lawyers had tried to have my evidence dismissed, saying I was too involved, too passionate, out for revenge—all those things were true because during every moment of that trial, all I could see in my mind's eye were the photographs of Giancarlo's body where the police had found him. I wanted to kill him; they'd got that right when it came to describing the day he'd abducted me from Fusina and Alessandro had pulled me off him while I'd been rearranging his facial features on the motorboat.

My world had fallen to pieces. I'd spent the year following the trial abusing alcohol, smoking reefer almost non-stop and allowing my body to be used, and abused, by any man who wanted it. It was totally unlike me. Two things, or should I say two people, saved me.

One night, two years after Giancarlo's murder, and pissed as a maggot, I had stumbled out of a hedgerow where I'd been swaying, spraying my shoes while trying to have a piss, right in front of the local bus. Had I not been so incredibly drunk I would have been much more severely injured than I had been. With broken bones all over, and internal injuries, I looked much like Alfonso had been after the beating by Scavola's men, so the doctor told me. Yes, the same French-speaking doctor in the hospital in Siena.

The first person to put me right was my brother, who'd flown from Australia the moment Randy phoned him. These days the flights to Rome were only about twenty-two hours, but back then flights took far longer, with a multitude of stops, so David had arrived not long after my fifth day in hospital, accompanied by the second person who'd saved me, who'd met him at the airport with his minimal English: Alfonso, who by then had returned to the priesthood. He'd wept at my bedside in his surplice while praying for me with my brother at his side.

A month later, he and David had taken me home to La Mensola and looked after me for over three months, until I was fit enough to look after myself and it was time for my brother to return to Australia. That was the day of the miracle that had changed my life.

Returning from the airport, I'd found Alfonso, once more Father Ignazio, on his knees, praying at the shrine in the stable with tears running down his face. When I asked him why he was so upset, he'd pulled me down beside him.

"God has told me what I should do," he'd said.

"And what's that?" I'd asked.

"That I should love you for the rest of my life."

It had taken a week at Randy's lakeside villa to sort things out between us. He'd been my closest friend since I'd arrived in Italy; we'd shared so very much together and, although I'd felt a very strong sexual attraction to him in the early days, I'd buried it. He confessed that he'd given in to Gaspard because of the unrequited physical feelings he'd had for me.

How hard it must have been for him. We'd shared a bed more times than I could count, swum naked together in both the ocean and my pool; I'd washed his body in the shower and I'd kissed him on the lips all the time I'd known him. It took me another four weeks alone in Venice to allow myself to believe that I loved him in a far deeper way than I'd allowed myself to believe. After that followed a year dealing with the guilt I felt at feeling so deeply for someone else so soon after

Giancarlo's death. Two and a half years seemed socially unacceptable: mourning was supposed to be forever.

The turning point had come on a day together during a pilgrimage to La Verna, the small hilltop retreat that was the centre of worship of St Francis of Assisi and where the saint was supposed to have received the stigmata. I'd always wanted to go there, having been told that there was a special, almost tangible spiritual feeling in the place, something more than religion or veneration of the saint. I felt it immediately we entered the Chapel of the Stigmata. We were alone; for some reason, the other visitors hadn't followed us down into the underground chapel. I kneeled beside Alfonso and took his hand in mine.

I wasn't entirely sure whether it was God who spoke to me at the moment that our fingers intertwined, but Alfonso's words on the day he'd confessed to me in the shrine at La Mensola had flooded into my mind. God had told him that he should love me for the rest of his life. I decided that, although the road ahead might be difficult, that was what I should also do.

We had shared a bed that night for the first time when sleeping wasn't the aim of the exercise. I'd surprised myself at how vulnerable I felt. Me, the sexually experienced man who'd done everything under the sun, tentative and almost afraid, despite the burning desire I had for him. However, it had taken me years after he'd left the priesthood—this time permanently—before I'd started to really "fall in love" with him—six years after Giancarlo had died and Kendall had left me to be at his father's bedside.

How had it happened that I'd fallen so deeply for Alfonso? I still had no idea. But I felt joined at the hip with him in a way that I hadn't with the other men I'd had strong feelings for. It said something that I'd committed to a monogamous relationship with an ex-priest, a man with a soul as deep as the ocean and a heart as big as the universe. Did I love him back with the same magnitude as he did me? That was a perpetual question that I had no answer for.

"Are you ready yet?" he said from the doorway, James standing behind him with his arms round him.

"I've been ready since the day I met you," I said.

James gave one of those little pretend "I'm going to be sick" sounds and screwed up his face, but Alfonso knew exactly what I meant.

"Then let's get going," he said. "The road to Pienza beckons."

I gathered up my notebooks and packed them carefully in my satchel.

AUTHOR BIO

From the outback to the opera.

After a thirty year career as a professional opera singer, performing as a soloist in opera houses and in concert halls all over the world, I took up a position as lecturer in music in Australia in 1999, at the Central Queensland Conservatorium of Music, which is now part of CQ University.

Brought up in Australia, between the bush and the beaches of the Eastern suburbs, I retired in 2015 and now live in the tropics, writing, gardening, and finally finding time to enjoy life and to re–establish a connection with who I am after a very busy career on the stage and as an academic.

I write mostly historical gay fiction. The stories are always about relationships and the inner workings of men; sometimes my fellas get down to the nitty–gritty, sometimes it's up to you, the reader, to fill in the blanks.

Every book is story driven; spies, detectives, murders, epic dramas, there's something for everyone. I also love to write about my country and the things that make us Aussies and our history different from the rest of the world.

I'm research driven. I always try to do my best to give the reader a sense of what life was like for my main characters in the world they live in.

Website – https://garrickjones.com.au
Facebook – https://www.facebook.com/GarrickJonesAuthor

ALSO BY GARRICK JONES

The Cricketer's Arms: A Clyde Smith Mystery
Book 1 of the Clyde Smith Mysteries Series
(July 2019) MoshPit Publishing, Australia

Clyde Smith is brought into the investigation of the ritualised death of pin-up boy cricketer, Daley Morrison, by his former colleague, Sam Telford, after a note is found in the evidence bags with Clyde's initials on it. Someone wants ex-Detective Sergeant Smith to investigate the crime from outside the police force. It can only mean one thing—corruption at the highest levels.

The Cricketer's Arms is an old-fashioned, pulp fiction detective novel, set in beachside Sydney in 1956. It follows the intricacies of a complex murder case, involving a tight-knit group of queer men, sports match-fixing, and a criminal drug cartel.

Was Daley Morrison killed because of his sexual proclivities, or was his death a signal to others to tread carefully? Has Clyde Smith been fingered as the man for the case, or will the case be the end of the road for the war veteran detective?

The Gilded Madonna: A Clyde Smith Mystery
Book 2 of the Clyde Smith Mysteries Series
(April 2021) MoshPit Publishing, Australia

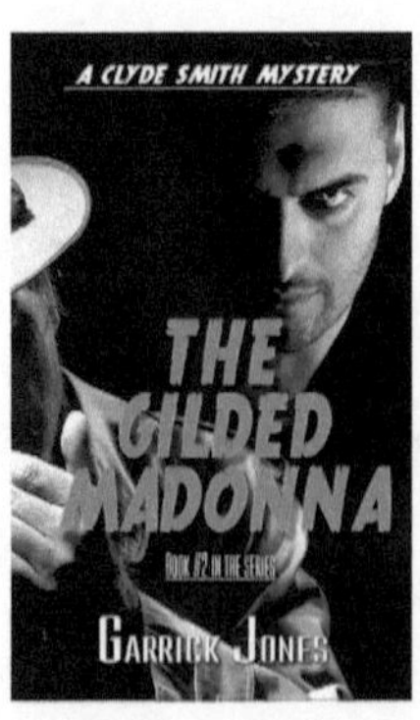

Clyde Smith's quiet, happy life, in love for the first time, working as a private detective and journalist, is suddenly thrown into disarray by the appearance, after a three year hiatus, of a body bearing the distinctive hallmarks of a string of murders he hadn't been able to solve when working in homicide.

Forced to cooperate with the new detective sergeant who'd taken his place in the local cop shop, Clyde has to not only deal with the enormous chip on the young man's shoulder, but also with a complex case that involves kidnapping, the re-emergence of the Silent Cop Killer, the historical abuse of young men and boys in orphanages across the State, and a ghost from the past who is out for revenge.

Will Clyde and the new DS be able to find the killer before he finds them? Or will they be his final prize, the last victims in his string of grisly murders? Perhaps only the local psychic, owner of a Romany religious statue, the Gilded Madonna, can provide the clue that might ultimately solve the puzzle, but which will also lead Clyde and DS Dioli into mortal danger.

The Grocers' Son: A Clyde Smith Mystery
Book 3 of the Clyde Smith Mysteries Series
(September 2022) MoshPit Publishing, Australia

An apparition in Sydney's fruit and vegetable market leaves the mother of one of Clyde's best friends believing that her brother, hanged for murder twenty-four years beforehand, has somehow risen from the grave and confronted her.

She is adamant that the visitation was real and visits Clyde asking him to investigate the mass murder her brother was supposed to have committed. She believes he was either set up or was covering for someone else's crime.

Could this vision have been a folie à deux, a delusional vision shared by both mother or son? As Clyde investigates, clues lead him to one of Australia's most famous silent screen actors, a man who, together with his murdered father, becomes intrinsically linked to the mass murder, known as The Killing at Candal Creek.

Wheels within wheels, lies, extortion, and coverups lead Clyde to a bloody confrontation on a deserted beach in the tropics. This time, it's not only his own life at risk but also that of one of his most valued and closest friends.

Bridge at the Beach: A Clyde Smith Mystery
Book 4 of the Clyde Smith Mysteries Series
(March 2024) Tellwell Talent

Clyde's idyllic afternoon in the surf with his mates is interrupted by the news that there's been a quadruple suicide in an apartment overlooking the beach.

Two of the deceased are the parents of Barry Wilkinson, one of Clyde's childhood friends, a man he hasn't seen since Clyde donned the khaki and left for war. Wilkinson engages Clyde to discover the identity of a mysterious woman who has been left a huge sum of money in his father's will.

On the surface, what appears to be a straightforward case evolves into a complex story of deception, lies, violence and murder. Relationships are tested, new ones formed and Clyde discovers that those connections that seem unrelated are closely linked behind a veil of secrecy.

The early summer of 1957 is a time in which Clyde nearly loses everything he holds dear—his own life included—all because of two couples who died while playing bridge at the beach.

The Seventh of December: The Czarina's Necklace
Book 1 of the Seventh of December Series
(December 2020) MoshPit Publishing, Australia

As bombs rain down over London during the Blitz, Major Tommy Haupner negotiates the rubble-filled streets of Bloomsbury on his way to perform at a socialite party. The explosive event of the evening is not his virtuosic violin playing, but the 'almost-blond' American who not only insults him, but then steals his heart.

The Seventh of December follows a few months in the lives of two Intelligence agents in the early part of World War Two. Set against the backdrop of war-torn occupied Europe, Tommy and his American lover, Henry Reiter, forge a committed relationship that is intertwined with intrigues that threaten the integrity of the British Royal Family and the stability of a Nation at war.

Neither bombs nor bullets manage to break the bond that these men form in their struggle against Nazism and the powers of evil.

X for Extortion: 14 Manchester Square
Book 2 of the Seventh of December Series
(September 2021) MoshPit Publishing, Australia

After returning from a secret mission in occupied France for His Royal Highness, George, the Duke of Kent, Lieutenant-Colonel Thomas Haupner is looking forward to a cup of tea, a hot bath, and the sleepy head of his American lover, Major Henry Reiter on his shoulder when he wakes up the next morning.

However, along with items Tommy has recovered for the duke, he has also discovered a secret stash of documents, which, when opened, prove to be a poisoned chalice. Tommy and Shorty find themselves caught up in a dangerous web of lies, enemy agents, assassins, and traitors. In an effort to save the reputations of not only their friends, but men and women high in both society and in the government, they themselves become victims of I.K.S., a former World War One international extortion ring, which has risen, phoenix-like, from the ashes of bomb-devastated London.

Farewell, My Boy
Book 3 of the Seventh of December Series
(March 2023) MoshPit Publishing, Australia

From the deserts of North Africa to the dark forests in the Third Reich, Tommy Haupner, together with his American lover, Henry "Shorty" Reiter, lead their team in a daring mission to rescue a gifted young savant from Nazi Germany's T4 euthanasia program.

They are forced to flee in a stolen bus in the dead of night across enemy territory with a precious cargo of 24 handicapped children destined for extermination. In a supreme effort to save their charges and to avoid capture and execution themselves, they mount the most daring and dangerous rescue mission possible, the results of which almost end in disaster.

This third book in *The Seventh of December* series is an action packed wartime adventure set in the early months of 1942. Stolen aircraft, kidnapped senior Nazi officials, doctors of death and bloody revenge massacres, all of which are intertwined with the love of a helpless, rescued child. *Farewell, My Boy*, deals with not only the frailty of men's hearts, but the truth that even the bravest are not exempt from the pain of loss, even when it is for a greater good.

The Perfume of War
Book 4 of the Seventh of December Series
(November 2024) Tellwell Talent

"Please donate generously to Mrs. Roosevelt's charity. Every penny raised from this series of concerts along the eastern coast of the United States will help with the resettlement and care of child refugees from war-torn continental Europe."

Over dinner with J Edgar Hoover in Washington, Tommy Haupner is shocked to learn that his forgotten and empty Swiss bank account has been topped up regularly with staggering sums of money … deposits that originate in Nazi Germany. Could this bank account have something to do with anonymous letters posted to him at home in London, their contents a single blank slip of paper on which are written two words: NAZI GOLD?

When he returns to Britain, he soon discovers that not only is his own life in danger but also those of his nearest and dearest who become pawns in a savage game of revenge.

My Name is Jimmy
(June 2022) MoshPit Publishing, Australia – Ebook only

In 1947, James "Jimmy" Bacon becomes involved in a violent workplace altercation fuelled by a PTSD-induced rage. His boss, a fellow war-veteran, tells him to take a few months off work, have a holiday, go somewhere warm, and get his head together.

Jimmy decides to take a coastal steamer to the northernmost outpost of Australia, Darwin, the capital of the Northern Territory, to visit the grave of his oldest friend, Sandy, killed during the

Japanese bombing of the city in 1942. Upon arriving, he discovers that Sandy's death is not as simple as military records seemed to indicate. After learning that Sandy's grave contains only an arm with no distinguishing features, he starts asking questions around town in order to find out what really happened to his mate.

The more he asks, the more he discovers that Darwin is less about post-war reconstruction and more about drugs, gambling, and the excessive consumption of alcohol. It's a lawless city where 95% of the population is male and prostitution is banned, creating a thriving underworld where rough frontier-town blokes and men from the armed forces are doing more with each other than having a beer and passing the time of day.

While digging deeper, Jimmy discovers a terrible truth, arousing the interest of men who would do anything to keep the past a secret—men who consider his life of little value. Jimmy is forced to rely on quick thinking and his army training when death comes looking for him in the dead of night.

Servants of the Crown: The Turkish Pretender
(March 2022) MoshPit Publishing, Australia

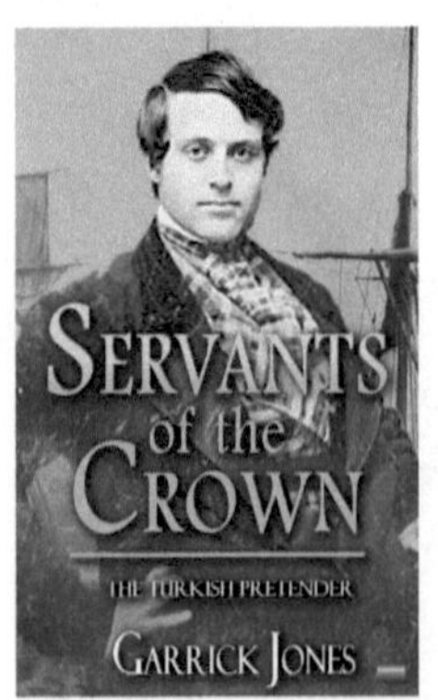

Intelligencers: men and women from all walks of life and from all sections of society, servants of the Crown who work for the Home Office gathering information vital to the security of the nation.

London, 1855. While Great Britain is at war with the Russians in the Crimea, a cadre of disaffected seditionists and insurrectionists, made up of members of the aristocracy and wealthy industrialists, have set a plan into action that's been decades in the making—a plan that aims to overthrow the Queen and to install a puppet king on the throne in her place. With the war raging and disquiet in the industrial north and in Ireland, their perfidious plot, unless stopped, threatens to bring about anarchy and revolution.

Aware of the imminent danger, Sir George Grey, the Home

Secretary, has tasked The Brothers, a band of four men, friends of over twenty years, to root out the source of the infection, destroy the clique, and track down and eradicate its foreign pretender by any means necessary. From molly houses to state banquets, from hospitals to steam baths, from aristocratic households to the meanest of slums, the friends find themselves in a succession of increasingly perilous situations.

Like the mighty Thames, undercurrents flow swift and deep as they uncover plot after plot and treachery and treason in abundance.

Wheelchair: Antarctica. Snow and Ice
(September 2020) MoshPit Publishing, Australia

You can never judge an academic book by its cover. Simon Dyson, a quiet assistant professor, is a man of hidden depths. To the world he presents as a harmless, innocuous, shy and retiring intellectual. However, the man who lurks behind that public persona is far more interesting … and dangerous … and driven.

Wheelchair is a slow-burn contemporary psychological crime thriller about a man who suffers from both OCD and PTSD, a man who is unwittingly caught up in a cross-border war between rival crime gangs—a conflict that almost leads to his death, and more than once.

It's a study of compulsion and of disability, and of the many faces of emotional dependence and sexual compulsion. It's about how some men cannot just love or make love because their hearts or their bodies lead them to it, but who can only connect emotionally and physically through self-imposed rituals which involve struggle or self-abasement.

The House of a Thousand Stairs
(March 2020) MoshPit Publishing, Australia

Warrambool

In Gamilaraay, the language of the Kamilaroi peoples of north-western New South Wales, it's the word for The Milky Way. It's also the name of Peter Dixon's homestead and sheep station, situated in the lee of the Liverpool Ranges.

In 1947, Peter returns from war, his parents and younger brother dead, the property de-stocked and his older brother, Ron, having emptied out the family bank account and nowhere to be found.

The House With a Thousand Stairs is the story of a young man, scarred both on the inside and the outside, trying to re-establish what once was a prosperous and thriving sheep station with the help of his neighbours and his childhood friend, Frank Hunter, the local Indigenous policeman.

Enveloped by the world of Indigenous spirituality, the Kamilaroi system of animal guides and totems, Peter and Frank discover the true nature of their predestined friendship, one defined by the stars, the ancestral spirits, and Baiame, the Creator God and Sky Father of The Dreaming.

Maliyan bandaarr, maliyan biliirr.

Australia's Son
(November 2019) MoshPit Publishing, Australia

A wrongly delivered letter sparks a chain of events that threaten the life of Edward Murray, "Australia's Son", the most renowned operatic baritone of his day.

It is 1902, and Edward has just returned to the Metropole Hotel after a performance of La Bohème at the Theatre Royal in Sydney, when the manager phones his apartment to tell him the police have arrived with bad news.

Edward, and his vaudeville performer brother, Theodore, are shocked to hear that Edward's dresser, the brothers' oldest friend from childhood, has been found dead, stabbed in the back, in Edward's recently vacated dressing room. Following a sequence of gruesome killings, Edward and the detective assigned to protect him, Chief Constable Andrew Bolton, are lured into a trap by a man whose agenda is not only personal, but driven by a deranged mind.

Set around the theatre world of early Edwardian Sydney, the story is steeped in the world of class divides, of music and the theatre. Its themes of murder, treachery and foul play, are ofttimes confronting, but the story is linked throughout by Edward Murray, the man with the golden voice, whose overarching belief is that even in the darkest of times, a sliver of light can mean that hope is at hand.

The Boys of Bullaroo: Tales of War, Aussie Mateship and More (Nov 2018), MoshPit Publishing, Australia

Six tales of men and war, spanning sixty years, and linked by a fictional outback town called Bullaroo. From the deserts of Egypt in 1919 to the American R&R in 1966, the stories follow the loves, losses and sexual awakenings of Australians both on the battlefield and in the bush.

All available from your favourite on-line retailer

www.ingramcontent.com/pod-product-compliance
Lightning Source LLC
Chambersburg PA
CBHW051237210726

48287CB00002B/284